Praise for the NOVELS OF SYDNEY CROFT

Taming the Fire

"Sydney Croft creates a thrilling paranormal read with action and scorching romance at every turn." —Darque Reviews

"Totally outstanding... [a] sizzling hot series that has never failed to keep my undivided attention. The collaboration of Sydney Croft is nothing short of brilliant." —Fresh Fiction

Seduced by the Storm

"If you like intrigue, espionage, danger and sexy secret agents with psychic abilities, you will love this book—especially when one agent has to disperse a hurricane with sexual energy! Croft's realistic characters have real, flawed motives that keep the action suspenseful and the sex extra hot." —*Romantic Times*

"Ms. Croft pens a tale where she manages to combine action along with sizzling hot passion. You will not be disappointed in this book, it is a keeper." —Night Owl Romance Reviews

Unleashing the Storm

"Red-hot romance and paranormal thrills from the first page to the last! Sydney Croft writes the kinds of books I love to read!"

—LARA ADRIAN, *New York Times* bestselling author

"The tension, both romantic and plot-driven, was well created and upheld. . . . This is an author to watch."

—All About Romance

"This second book in the ACRO series is fabulously sexy and intriguingly hot. I have become addicted to the collaboration of the two authors known as Sydney Croft, and I'm ready to find out what happens next. Definitely a must-read."

—Fresh Fiction

"*Unleashing the Storm* is one of those rare reads where the characters linger long after the story ends. Intense intrigue, action, eroticism and a fascinating world combine to create an enthralling winner. Sydney Croft is a fabulous new talent."

—CHEYENNE MCCRAY, *USA Today* bestselling author

Riding the Storm

"In this action-packed, inventive tale, each character's strengths and weaknesses are more fantastic than the next. The various plots and characters ebb and flow together seamlessly. . . . Croft redefines sizzle and spark with weather-driven passion."

—*Romantic Times*

"Absolutely fabulous!! *Riding the Storm* has the perfect balance of action/adventure and hot, steamy sex." —Fresh Fiction

"*Riding the Storm* will ride your every fantasy . . . a power punch of erotic heat, emotion and adventure. Remy takes you on an adventure you won't soon forget."

—Lora Leigh, *USA Today* bestselling author

Also by Sydney Croft

RIDING THE STORM

UNLEASHING THE STORM

SEDUCED BY THE STORM

TAMING THE FIRE

HOT NIGHTS, DARK DESIRES
(with Eden Bradley and
Stephanie Tyler)

TEMPTING
the
FIRE

Tempting *the* Fire

Sydney Croft

BANTAM BOOKS TRADE PAPERBACKS
NEW YORK

Tempting the Fire is a work of fiction. Names, characters, places, and incidents are the products of the authors' imagination or are used fictitiously. Any resemblance to actual events, locales, or persons, living or dead, is entirely coincidental.

A Bantam Books Trade Paperback Original

Published in the United States by Bantam Books,
an imprint of The Random House Publishing Group,
a division of Random House, Inc., New York.

BANTAM BOOKS and the rooster colophon are registered trademarks
of Random House, Inc.

Library of Congress Cataloging-in-Publication Data
Croft, Sydney.
Tempting the fire / Sydney Croft.
p. cm.
ISBN 978-0-385-34228-5
eBook ISBN 978-0-553-90759-9
1. United States. Navy. SEALs—Fiction. 2. Animal communicators—Fiction.
3. Rain forests—Fiction. 4. Brazil—Fiction. I. Title.
PS3603.R6356T46 2010
813'.6—dc22
2010006267

Printed in the United States of America

www.bantamdell.com

2 4 6 8 9 7 5 3 1

To all the members of LIST and the Writeminded Reader Loop:
You have been enthusiastic, supportive—and, basically,
you all rock!

And with thanks to M. Sgt. Richard Walker, who is always there
to provide technical support. Our plane crashed nicely
with your help!

Big thanks to Gina Scalera, Rosemary Potter and every
bookseller who has supported authors everywhere. We
appreciate all you do!

TEMPTING
the
FIRE

PROLOGUE

Chance McCormack had been given his name about three minutes after being born on the floor of a Las Vegas casino, his mom too busy playing craps to care about something as unimportant as labor pains.

"We're from strong stock—farm stock," she used to tell Chance, who wouldn't bring up the fact that she'd never lived remotely close to a farm in her life and that her entire family had been born in Manhattan. But she seemed to enjoy having that make-believe become a part of her life and Chance never had the heart to break her out of fairy-tale mode.

She had a pretty shitty life and if telling stories like that made her happy, he was all for it.

And so Chance had grown up on the edge, skating the thin line between right and wrong and counting on luck of the draw to carry him through.

Today, though, he had a sickening feeling that his luck might've run out, had known something was wrong the second he stepped into the goddamned jungle, and it had nothing to do with the tangos waiting in ambush. His SEAL team had taken care of most of them, cleanly, efficiently and, most important, silently.

So yeah, a typical mission with the typical shit going down, and still, unease sat in his gut like a fucking boulder.

Sweat trickled down his back, when suddenly, inex-fucking-plicably, he shivered.

He heard breathing and it wasn't his, wasn't Billy's or Campbell's or Joe's. No, it was a harsh sound. Inhuman.

He gripped the butt of the rifle so hard his fingers were nearly blue, kept his eyes level to the horizon and tripped before he took three steps.

Billy. The only way he could identify the SEAL was the patch on the uniform.

All that was left of the man beyond the bones was the skin on his face, his mouth stretched into a mask of horror. His eyes were wide open, as if looking over Chance's shoulder.

As if warning him.

Chance stiffened, held tight to his M14 and turned to face a wall of fetid breath. He readied for the fight of his life, knowing that, for as long as he lived, he would remember the red eyes of the beast staring back at him.

He knew there wasn't time to scream if he was going to make it out of this alive.

CHAPTER *One*

Sela Kahne sat at her desk, staring at the computer screen and wondering why she hadn't taken one more day of vacation time. An extra day would have meant another layer of tan on her normally pale skin, another couple of chapters of the latest James Patterson novel read and a few more hours' reprieve from typing up reports that all said the same thing in conclusion: *HOAX*.

She sighed heavily and reached for the bag of Skittles she kept on her desk. She popped two into her mouth and cringed. She'd lost a filling during her vacation and desperately needed to see a dentist.

"ACRO's dentists are the best in the area," Torrence Olivia, the only other psychic besides Sela who worked in the agency's Covert Rare Operatives' Cryptozoology department, said as she walked by.

"I hate it when you do that," Sela grumbled, mainly because her own psychic ability was restricted to reading people only during orgasm.

"Hon, I didn't do anything. You have *dentist* written on your to-do list." Torr tapped the notepad next to the computer with a crimson-painted nail.

"Oh."

"What's wrong?" Torrence crossed her arms over her chest, her dark skin contrasting beautifully with her cream blouse. "You just got back from vacation. You should be vibrant. Unless... was Puerto Rico not as relaxing as it should have been?"

Sela stiffened. "How did you know I was in Puerto Rico?"

"Hello?" Torr tapped her temple. "Psychic."

She never knew whether or not Torr was kidding when she said things like that, but given that Sela had told everyone, including her immediate boss, Mitch, she was going to the Bahamas, she could only assume that Torrence had gone psychic on her.

"You didn't tell anyone, did you?" Not that her change of plans had been a huge secret, but she was supposed to have been drinking fruity cocktails on a beach instead of investigating the origins of el chupacabra.

She couldn't wait to debunk the myth of the "goat sucker" once and for all. Confirming that the crazy things people believed in were false was a passion of hers, and it made her one of the few cryptozoologists in the field who was in it to *dis*prove mythical creatures' existence.

And the cryptid she wanted the most to prove didn't exist was the one highlighted in the book in front of her, *Chupacabra: Myth No More*. The author, an eccentric, egomaniac billionaire she'd met half a dozen times at cryptozoological society gatherings, claimed to have spent years in the jungles of Central America observing chupacabra behavior like one of those nuts who infiltrated a pack of wolves.

The chupacabra is a solitary creature that will kill others of its kind, though they do appear to mate for life. They give birth to a single offspring, which is capable of living on its own within six months. Males are larger than females, and they mark their territory by spraying scent and clawing trees and fences. Their ability to heal from wounds is nothing short of amazing, something I witnessed after a young female was attacked and nearly killed by a jaguar . . .

What a freaking blowhard con artist. The book had made Parker Grady a celebrity in the cryptozoological circles, but Sela thought it only made him look like an idiot.

"Earth to Sela . . . " Torr waved her hand in front of Sela's face. "I just said I won't tell anyone about Puerto Rico. It's not my place." She shoved her glasses up on her nose. "I'm going down to the lab. Oh, I almost forgot—a messenger delivered that package on your desk. He said after you watch it, you're supposed to call Dev."

Dev. The big boss. Head of ACRO, whom she rarely saw . . . and she preferred it that way. He hadn't exactly hired her under normal circumstances five years ago, and while she didn't regret how she'd come to ACRO, she did feel a little sleazy about it.

Twenty-one, cocky and just sure she was smarter than ninety-five percent of the planet's population, she'd pretty much forced her way into the agency. Only later had she realized that Dev could have taken her apart and made her disappear so completely there wouldn't have been a trace that she'd ever existed.

For some reason, he hadn't. He'd played her game, let her believe she had the upper hand . . . and even after she figured out Dev had been one move ahead of her from the beginning, he never rubbed it in. But he knew she knew. It was in his gorgeous brown eyes every time he saw her.

Stop thinking about it.

She shook out of her past, out of the things she'd done before she'd come to the Crypto department, and opened the padded envelope. Inside was a DVD. She slipped the disk into her computer, entered her individual access code and palmed a handful of Skittles.

The screen filled with trees. Thick brush, vines . . . a jungle. The camera shooting the scene was in motion—a helmet-cam? Yes, definitely. The person wearing the camera turned to the side, and she made out two men in camouflage, their faces painted, their rifles aimed and braced against their shoulders.

She popped a piece of candy into her mouth, remembering too late to chew on the left side. Pain shot from her molar into her skull.

On the screen, one of the men made a hand signal, and the camera panned to the right. Slowly, it moved forward. The camera jolted and then focused on the ground.

Sela slapped a hand over her mouth to hold in a gasp of horror. What was left of a man lay strewn about on the forest floor, his bloody mouth frozen in a terrified grimace.

And all hell broke loose. The sound of guns firing, men shouting and *something* screeching had Sela reaching for the volume.

The camera jerked around wildly, giving her only glimpses of the action, but what she saw sent chills up her spine. The men seemed to be fighting off some sort of creature. It moved fast, and if the film could be trusted, it had red eyes and huge fangs.

What the *hell* was it?

Suddenly, the camera stopped moving, its angle skewed, apparently lying on the ground. Sela saw clawed, scaly feet approaching. Her heart shot into her throat, blocking the candy as she tried to swallow. Between the thing's legs she could see the men. Well, parts of them, lying in a growing pool of blood.

A snarl vibrated the camera, and then there was a gaping mouth, a splatter of blood on the lens . . . and all went black.

Sela choked on her own breath. Dear God, those men had been . . . slaughtered. Dismembered, disemboweled.

Her phone rang, and she nearly bit her tongue. She'd seen some gruesome things during her career as a cryptozoologist, but nothing could have prepared her for seeing humans torn apart before her eyes.

She picked up the phone with a shaky hand. "Sela."

"It's Dev. You watched the video?"

"Yes."

"Meet me at my office in ten minutes." He hung up, and she slumped back in her chair. Something told her it was a good thing she hadn't unpacked yet.

ANNIKA SVENSON WASN'T READY FOR ANOTHER ROUND OF your-lover-is-an-ass with Dev, but Gabe was fucking impossible to deal with. The guy had learned to go invisible with more control, which was great, but he was relying on his invisibility to get him out of trouble. Which meant that he was slacking off on learning the basics of self-defense, combat and intelligence work. He had yet to figure out that no matter how great your gift was, something could always circumvent it.

Everyone had a kryptonite.

Creed was hers, and speak of the sexy devil, he was just leaving Dev's office, so things were looking up. Grinning, she waved as he started down the old military building's steps, but he didn't see her because he'd been accosted by Sela Kahne.

Sela's black hair fell in a severe angle, shorter in the back to longer in front, coming down just below her jawline, but as she looked up at Creed, she tucked one side behind her ear, which was pierced all the way around. Creed, being pierced *everywhere*, probably loved that.

Not that Annika was jealous. Creed wasn't going anywhere, and if he tried, Annika would kill him.

Simple as that.

Still, she really wanted to slap the smile off Sela's face. Annika had never been overly fond of the woman, whom she mostly saw only in passing, but the way she was looking at Creed, with a little too much familiarity, made Annika's electrical battery charge up. Lightning tingled on the surface of her skin, and she had to take a deep breath to calm herself. Anyone who touched her right now—anyone but Creed—would get a nasty shock.

"Hey, baby," Creed said, when he saw her approach.

She mounted the steps until she reached him, smiling when he hooked an arm around her neck and tucked her next to his big body. He always knew how to handle her, knew when she needed a little extra attention or needed to be left alone.

Sela nodded in greeting. "Annika." She looked at Creed again, all smiles and exotic green eyes. "Nice seeing you."

"You too."

Sela headed up the steps, and once she'd disappeared into the two-story building, Annika peeled away from Creed. "I don't like how she looks at you."

Creed cocked a dark eyebrow, making the piercing there climb up. "How does she look at me?"

"Like she wants to lick your tattoos." Which weren't truly tattoos, since he had been born with every single one of the Native American symbols that covered his entire right side from head to toe.

Creed just laughed. "She didn't lick them."

"I know that." Annika rolled her eyes. "I don't think she'd just walk up to you in public and—" Wait. Something about the way he'd said Sela *didn't* lick them... and the familiarity in her eyes...

"Oh, my God," Annika breathed, which was difficult, because a band of jealousy had just wrapped around her chest. "You slept with her."

Creed's big brown eyes got a whole lot bigger. "Ah... I thought you knew."

"Why the hell would I know?"

"Because that's how she came to ACRO."

This time when her body flooded with electricity, she didn't bother tamping it down. Maybe Sela would come back out and "accidentally" touch her. "What the fuck are you talking about?"

"I just figured Dev would have told you back when it happened." Creed tugged on his jacket a little uncomfortably, and yeah, Annika would just bet he was sweating despite the cool spring breeze. "Sela and I, uh . . . we got together for a night. Years ago. She didn't know about ACRO, but she's—"

"Sexually psychic," Annika ground out. "I know. She was assigned as a Seducer when she first came here."

"Yeah. She read me during sex. Found out about ACRO."

"So . . . what? She blackmailed you? Said she'd spill the beans about ACRO if she didn't get a job?" Actually, Annika didn't see that happening; Dev would've had Sela shut up if he'd believed she was a true danger to the agency.

Creed sighed. "After she left my place—"

"She was at *your place*? In the bed *we* share now?" Annika's voice had gone shrill enough to make Creed wince, but she didn't care. Didn't care that she was acting like some sort of jealous fishwife either. She'd never really gotten too worked up over the scores of skanky women she'd run into who had bedded Creed, because they had been disposables who didn't work at ACRO.

But Sela . . . she wasn't one of the bar whores Creed had fucked before he'd gotten together with Annika. She was beautiful, intelligent and . . . right here in the same organization.

Now Annika knew how Creed had felt when he discovered her lessons with one of the male Seducers years earlier.

"Annika, it was a long time ago. And it was just the once." Of course it was. His ghostly guardian, Kat, had never let him sleep with any woman besides Annika more than once or twice. He ran his hand through his shoulder-length hair. "She spent a couple of days afterward investigating ACRO. I think she must have seduced a gate guard or something. She came back to my house and laid out what she knew . . . and insisted on meeting Dev. I arranged it, and Dev hired her. Simple as that. I hardly ever see her anymore."

"I hate her." It was a childish, stupid thing to say, but whatever. Annika had never been in a relationship before, thanks to her tendency to shock men to death during orgasm, and even though she'd come a long way, maturity-wise, she still had relapses. Like now.

Creed smiled, the one that made her stomach flutter, and then he cupped the back of her head and brought her in for a gentle kiss. "You have nothing to worry about, you know."

That fast, she calmed down. "I know," she sighed. "I don't doubt you at all."

"Something's wrong, isn't it? You've been restless lately."

She had. She'd been a mix of extra-clingy and extra-distant. Their relationship had been going well, though Creed had been increasingly anxious when she went off on missions.

"No idea. I've just been tired, I think."

Creed frowned. "You're never tired."

"I know. It's weird. Maybe I'm getting old."

His hand came down on her shoulder, and he bent to look her straight in the eyes. "You got your birth control shot, right? *Right?*"

Well, if that didn't just chill her blood. And piss her off at the same time. No way in hell did she want a kid, but for some reason, the way he said it, like having one with her would be a horrible tragedy, set her the fuck off.

"Well, duh," she snapped. "How stupid do you think I am?"

The immunization ACRO had developed to prevent pregnancy in females, and disease in both sexes, was required for all operatives who worked the kinds of missions that might require them to screw someone. Annika had never needed it, but now that she was with Creed and sleeping with him, she'd been anal about getting the quarterly boosters.

"Whoa." He held up his hands and took a step back. "Just checking. You've been moody and tired."

"Moody?"

"Ah . . . well . . . "

"Moody?" Oh, she'd show him moody. She spun around and took the steps two at a time. The thud of heavy boots followed her, and she wheeled back to him with a snarl. Creed drew up like he'd hit a wall. "Don't. You wouldn't want to touch me and get me pregnant or something."

He blinked. "Are you upset because you *want* kids?"

"Hell, no, I don't want any little drooling rug rats!" A couple of guys dressed in the standard ACRO uniform—black BDUs—stared as they walked past, and she flipped them off. But she also lowered her voice. "But you know, you could at least pretend that it wouldn't be the end of the world if I did get pregnant."

Except, it would be, because she'd been raised by CIA monsters to be a robotic killing machine with no morals or feelings, and she wouldn't even know where to start raising a kid. She wasn't mother material and never would be. Apparently, Creed agreed, because his face markings stood out starkly as his tan skin paled.

"It wouldn't be the end of the world, but—"

"But what?" Fuck. She had no idea what she was upset about. At all. But she kept getting angrier and more irrational by the second.

"It's just . . . it's something we should talk about," he said quietly.

A weight settled in her gut, which had started churning. She knew he wanted kids. He knew she didn't. It was a reality they'd have to face eventually, but she didn't want it to be now.

"I have to go."

"Annika—"

"Later."

She took off as if she had a fire lapping at her combat boots' heels. God, how long had it been since she'd walked away from Creed in a moment of anger? A year, at least. And here she was, reverting back to her old self, and why?

Because he'd asked her if she was current on her birth control?

Of course she was . . . wasn't she?

As she jogged through the little park in the middle of the base, she recalled her last visit to medical. She'd had a question for Kira, ACRO's most talented animal whisperer, but the woman hadn't been at the kennels or stables where she usually was. Annika had had to track her down at ACRO's day care facility, where Kira's triplets stayed while she and Ender were working.

Annika hadn't been breathing in the scent of baby powder and diapers for even two minutes before she'd practically run out of there and had gone straight to the medical facility, where she'd demanded a shot—four weeks early.

That had been three months ago. Three months and three and a half weeks ago, actually.

Oh, God.

Annika clutched her belly as a wave of nausea rolled through her. She was overdue.

Over. Due.

Fuck.

She glanced at her watch. She had to teach a class in half an hour. That gave her enough time to jump in the Jeep and head to a drugstore.

Five minutes after that, she should know if her world was still safe and sound.

Or if it had just ended.

SELA COULD STILL FEEL THE BURN OF ANNIKA'S EYES IN THE middle of her back as she entered Dev's office. He was sitting at his desk, grumbling at a PDA, which he put aside when Sela sank into a chair.

"Things were so much easier when I was blind," he sighed,

and she had to admit, he'd been scary-efficient as a blind man. Now he seemed more harried. He didn't miss a beat, though, and pushed a file at her. "You're going to South America. Brazil, near the Colombia border."

"To investigate what I saw on the video?"

He nodded and ran his fingers through his spiky brown hair. "Any idea what might have attacked those men?"

"I can't say. It looked like some sort of animal, but I'd rather not speculate until I learn more." And animal, her ass. It looked like a monster.

His smile was slow and all-knowing in that freaky way of his. "How was Puerto Rico?"

Christ, did everyone know about her trip? "It was as enlightening as I expected it to be," she said. "Which means I found no new evidence that suggests chupacabras are real." She tapped the folder. "And if you're thinking that a chupacabra attacked those men, well, that's not likely."

"Because they don't exist?"

"That, and even if they did—which I don't believe they do—the Amazon isn't a hotbed of reported chupacabra activity." Except, she'd checked the logs before she left her office, and recently there *had* been a number of sightings in the region, as well as an increase in bizarre livestock deaths.

"This is why you're perfect for the job. You're a skeptic, so you'll be going in without any preconceived ideas."

Sela grumbled. She hated the jungle. "I do have a preconceived idea. I think it's probably a jaguar or gorilla." A deformed, superfast, superstrong jaguar or gorilla. Which was almost as unlikely as the chupacabra. "Who were the men?"

Dev sat back in his chair and steepled his fingers. "Well, this is where it gets interesting," he said, as if the mysterious cryptid wasn't the most fascinating part. "They were SEALs on a mission. Obviously, not easy to kill, but whatever attacked them took out the entire team. One is MIA, presumed dead."

"Maybe the MIA is responsible."

"Could be. Can't rule out anything yet."

"And the Navy wanted our help on this?" Seemed a little extreme for them to call in ACRO, but then, as a secret paramilitary organization, ACRO had covertly worked side by side with all of the branches of the military for years.

"The Navy didn't contact us." He gestured to the thick file. "It's all in there. You can catch up on the plane. Can you leave in an hour?"

"I'm already packed." She flipped through the folder's contents but didn't stop on any particular page or photo. "Am I going alone?" Usually she went with another cryptozoologist and a small contingent of specialists to assist in photography, research, electronics, etc., if the mission wasn't deemed to be dangerous. If it was, ACRO sent her with all of that plus a security team.

Dev's long pause sent a chill up her spine. "You're going with Marlena."

"Marlena?" Sela frowned. "Your secretary?"

"She's no longer my assistant. She's a Seducer now. She's fully trained, but this will be her first real mission."

"Ah . . . forgive me, sir, but why in the world would I be taking a Seducer on a crypto assignment?"

"Because this is more than a mission to find a mysterious species. Two weeks before the attack, a company called Global Weapons Corporation set up camp near where the SEALs were killed. Satellite photos showed that the camp was still there as of three days ago, but now it's gone and can't be located. However, I have intel that indicates they're in the area. It's possible that GWC was either hired to take out those SEALs, or they used the team as a test for their creation."

"The creation being the creature."

"Yes."

"This sounds very Itor."

"We know that GWC has supplied Itor with weapons in the past. It's likely that Itor contracted GWC after they failed to turn Rik into their ultimate animal weapon."

Ulrika was a recent acquisition, a powerful shape-shifter who now worked in the Cryptozoology department. As the first truly mythological creature proven to exist, Ulrika had been a shock to Sela's system. Then again, Ulrika had been, in part, an Itor lab creation, and since her entire family had been destroyed, there was still no proof that shape-shifters existed as natural creatures in the wild.

"So why not send a combat agent into this? Why me?"

"Once you get the intel, proof that GWC is working with Itor, or proof that the creature exists, I'll send in combat agents. But to start, we need you. The guy GWC sent to join the camp at around the time of the attacks, the owner's son, Logan Mills, isn't stupid. He's not going to fall for a story that some lone person just happened to stumble onto his camp in the jungle. We need to be convincing. I need a cryptozoologist and her assistant to be investigating reports of a . . . what's it called, a goat fucker?"

"Goat sucker. Chupacabra."

"Fine. Chupacabra. You'll need to get captured, and when you do, they'll realize you're the real thing. A cryptozoologist investigating sightings by the locals."

"And then?"

"You find out the truth."

A feeling of dread crept up from the depths of her bowels, and she slowly placed the folder on her lap, open to a photo of Logan, apparently taken at some sort of backyard party. He had a beer in one hand, and his other was slung around some chick who resembled Marlena. Tall, dark-haired and muscular, he was hotter than hot, which, combined with Dev's "truth" statement, set off all kinds of warning klaxons.

"Since we're talking about the truth," she said, "maybe you could be straight with me. The reason you picked me for this assignment has nothing to do with my outstanding record in my field, does it?"

"You *are* our best cryptozoologist," he hedged.

"No shit." Probably not the best way to talk to the boss, but she had a bad feeling about this. "And?"

"And . . . in addition to your cryptozoology experience, you may need to employ your . . . other skills."

Fuck. Just . . . fuck.

"Exactly," Dev said, and she knew he'd read her mind. "If Marlena can't seduce information out of someone, you'll have to."

"Dev—"

"I know I'm asking a lot," he said gently. "But you really are the only person we can send in with Marlena. No one else in your office has undercover training."

No, they didn't. Everyone at ACRO was sent through exhaustive physical instruction so they could defend themselves in pretty much any situation, but as an undercover field operative, her training had gone well beyond that. She'd been trained in covert operations, weapons handling, combat techniques—and as a Seducer, she'd been given specialized instruction in sex. And, like all operatives, she was immunized against pregnancy and sexually transmitted diseases, thanks to ACRO's advanced science.

But none of that had protected her on her final mission as a Seducer, and her bones began to ache in all the places where they'd been broken three years ago.

"Marlena is good," he said. "Really good. And she fits the profile for the type of woman Logan likes. You shouldn't have to do anything beyond nose around and look for whatever it is GWC is playing with."

God, she hoped so. Because Sela hadn't touched a man since the day one had nearly beaten her to death.

She was glad her hand didn't shake as she closed the file, shutting out Logan's face. Because she wasn't afraid as much as she was angry. There was a reason that Seducer mission was her last, and it had nothing to do with nearly being killed.

She'd hated seducing men for information, hated getting a head full of their deepest, darkest secrets, which often left her feeling ill for days. The men she'd been assigned to seduce weren't pillars of the community, and the things they'd done still sat in her memory like cyanide pills, leaking poison into her system and making her sick at the most inconvenient times.

One more horrible memory might put her over the edge, and that Logan guy looked like just the kind of man to do it.

EVEN THOUGH THE ANSWERS WERE ALWAYS THE SAME, MARLENA West had woken early and headed to ACRO's science labs anyway for her monthly check-in with the team that had been following her case for ten years.

Dr. Petra James was in charge of the case very few people knew about. A small woman with serious brown eyes, she had taken up the charge to find answers for Marlena at Devlin O'Malley's request. Although, knowing Devlin, it most likely was more of a demand.

And even though Marlena never got her hopes up, the small shake of Dr. James's head still hurt. *Unable to find a cure. We'll keep looking. Don't ever give up.*

Now, back at the Seducers' housing where she lived, she stared between the orders placed on her bed, indicating her next mission, and the picture of her sister that had fallen from the book she'd pulled off the shelf.

Stepsister, to be accurate. Kelly had been killed in a car accident years ago, taking with her any chance of true happiness Marlena could hope for.

Kelly had been strangled by hatred and jealousy toward Marlena from the day Marlena was born. A practicing witch, Kelly came up with a curse that wouldn't allow Marlena to find love or happiness with any man. The curse doomed Marlena to fall insanely in love with any man she slept with—and ensured that no man would ever love her back once that happened. And the curse was so complete and malicious, it promised that Marlena couldn't fall in love with a man *until* she slept with him. Indeed, couldn't have any feelings at all in that regard, would never feel that excitement of falling for someone, the way she did when she was a teenager, before the curse was cast.

Thus, for Marlena, sex had always been something completely out of her control—the thing that would cause her emotions to plummet wildly. She'd been lucky enough to find ACRO years earlier—or, more accurately, they'd found her after some of her modeling photos caught their attention. She'd immediately felt at ease with Dev, and after she'd confessed the truth about her curse, he'd assured her that they wouldn't stop searching for a way to break it.

And he'd promised that no matter what, she would always be safe at ACRO.

She'd agreed to join then, because she'd been scared and alone and because she'd instantly trusted Devlin.

In all the years since, he'd never let her down. He'd been a safe man for her—he'd given her a job as his executive assistant and he also let her satisfy him, and him her. Falling in love with him had been inevitable and painful, but Devlin had been gentle with her heart.

But now, with her new job as an ACRO Seducer, she defined sex on her terms. No intercourse, if possible. Controlling the man's orgasms. She was the one who made all the rules, and thus she was able to keep men at a distance.

Though she hadn't been at it long, becoming an ACRO Seducer could've been akin to a form of self-torture. Forced to use her sexuality in a way that could actually help people, Marlena took a chance on becoming a victim of the curse every time she went on a mission.

Of course, she made every effort to ensure that did not happen. Unlike most Seducers, whose specialized psychic talents required them to have sex with their targets in order to gather intel, Marlena could rely on her beauty and flirting skills to pry the information out of her mark, so sexual relations were unnecessary. She knew how to make a man go ga-ga over her, and for some ops, it was—and would be—enough. On other missions, she'd use her other talents, because a lot of men would give up their mothers for an amazing blow job.

Up until this point, she'd been on four small jobs—training missions that required sexual skills but had put her in no real physical danger. The goal had been to see if she could finally resist falling in love with any man she slept with. She'd been hypnotized by ACRO's best, prodded by their scientists and sent out with high hopes for all her missions.

She'd gotten through the first three without having to resort to intercourse—each of those missions a complete success.

The fourth required sex. She'd fallen in love and the man had been repulsed by her as soon as the deed was done. But then, she'd already gotten the information she needed, and she accomplished what she'd wanted—she'd fallen out of love with Devlin O'Malley.

That had been a relief in and of itself. Now she was in love with some horrid ACRO enemy she might never see again, certainly not on a daily basis.

Compared to the hell some ACRO agents went through because of their powers, Marlena felt, in comparison, she had no right to complain. And she didn't. But she knew she was getting colder, keeping everyone at arm's length.

And she knew that would only get worse if she continued in this job.

CHAPTER *two*

Logan Mills smelled the hot, fetid breath of the beast hanging heavily in the humid air of the Amazonian jungle. They were close but somehow no closer than they'd been since they'd begun this mission.

The animal was smart—and Logan had a sickening feeling that he and his team were actually the ones being hunted.

He took a swig of water from the canteen that hung from a line on his pack and then capped it and checked his weapons again—an M14, a Sig and two tranqs with enough juice to put down a hippo.

His body had finally adjusted to the heat after thirty-plus days in this place—he'd gotten used to sweating as his body tried to keep up with the constant water loss, and all of this reminded him of his days in Special Ops.

"Hey, Lo, we gonna call it a day soon?" Dax, one of his men, muttered. Logan glanced at his watch—1600. Thanks to the overlay, they'd find themselves in total darkness sooner than later.

They'd been on the move since 0600—nonstop except for water breaks—and while they'd found evidence of the escaped beast, they still hadn't been able to track it down.

His men were tired—of the jungle, of this mission, of Logan's nonstop barking and near obsession with recovering the creature he didn't know anything about beyond the fact that it was lethal.

His men didn't understand the full consequences; and if he had his way, they never would. No one else would either, and that's why Logan planned on continuing his search for a few more hours.

"I'm not paying you to sleep," he answered Dax evenly.

The man shook his head and held up his arms in silent surrender, and Logan sighed. He got it—they were exhausted. It was a feeling he could barely remember, and so garnering sympathy for it was hard.

He wasn't tired, never got tired anymore. In fact, he often had to force himself to sleep so the still-human part of his mind could rest.

He was a product of his father's company, a company he now oversaw—one he had controlling shares in, due to his father's continually bad decision-making. Global Weapons Corporation had been his father's brainchild and was now Logan's baby, since he had turned the company from nearly complete financial ruin to a growing enterprise in a little over three years.

It had been severely mismanaged, thanks to his father's ego; the old man could never see past the get-rich-quick aspect of weapons development to realize that GWC could be a huge asset to the American government in the fight against terrorism.

Unfortunately, his father still insisted on making decisions behind Logan's back. Like this most recent one—the reacquisition of some kind of species, labeled Unclass 8, that killed an entire SEAL team last month, when GWC had accidentally released it after nearly three years of modifications.

Logan's gut twisted as he thought back to his own injury four years earlier—when he'd been shot to hell and left for dead at the bottom of a ravine for three days.

After he was found by the Marines, his father had him airlifted from the military hospital in Germany to a private facility in London, where a team of scientists and surgeons waited to save Logan's life.

He'd been rebuilt with special bioware—his right arm, his legs, part of his brain. He functioned with an efficiency that scared even him, and he wondered if maybe the company had taken things too far.

But how could he tell his father he'd done the wrong thing by not letting his son die?

"We'll work for another hour and then head back to camp," he told Dax, who nodded and let the other four men know there was an end in sight to today's mission.

Logan turned back toward the twisted path and studied the broken branches tipped with the blood of the animal's most recent kill—a deer they'd found fifty yards away. He'd told his men they were hunting something that looked like a Komodo dragon, when in all honesty he didn't know what the hell this thing was, never mind what it looked like.

He and his team had been in the jungle only two days searching for it when they'd stumbled on the massacre—what he now knew were four Navy SEALs, torn to pieces.

He'd just ordered his men to continue their search for more bodies or survivors when he tripped over something, then cursed and turned back to kick the branch out of the way.

But it hadn't been a branch. It was a human, or what was left of one. Immediately, he'd motioned to Dax, and the two of them brushed the leaves off the body and uncovered what Logan believed to be another dead SEAL.

Tentatively, he'd felt for a pulse and nearly jumped out of his skin when the man, later identified as Chance McCormack, grabbed his wrist and whispered, "Watch out . . . it's coming for you."

They'd gotten him to their base camp, and because of that decision Logan was forced to leave the massacred SEALs behind for the Navy search-and-rescue to find. Which they had; they'd also had evidence of the slaughter, thanks to a helmet-cam one of the SEALs had worn, but no clear shot of the animal that was responsible for the rampage.

And so Logan had been hiding Chance for the better part of the month, even after the Navy had called off their search. Hiding him, healing him . . . and figuring out what the hell to do next.

Watch out . . . it's coming for you.

Now, as he moved forward through the ever-darkening jungle, those words continued to echo in his ears.

CHANCE OPENED HIS EYES AND REALIZED IMMEDIATELY THAT he was alive. Because of the pain.

In this case, the lingering yet somehow transient pain was a damned good thing.

"He's awake." A white-haired man peered down at him, a worried frown on his face. "You're okay, son. You're going to be just fine."

He wanted to ask the man if he was supposed to know him, if he was back on a military base. Wanted to know what the hell happened. "My team . . ."

The man's frown got deeper. "What's your name?"

"Chance."

"And you're a soldier . . ."

"A SEAL. Navy."

"Good. Do you remember what happened?"

He closed his eyes for a second and then opened them when he realized he did indeed remember what happened out in the jungle—and didn't want to.

"I remember everything," he whispered finally.

He also recalled thrashing around during his narcotic-induced sleep, remembered hearing screams, smelled the beast in the air—and fuck, he wondered how long he'd been out, how long he'd been having nightmares about the monster that had nearly killed him.

His arms still bore the bruises of mortal combat he'd been locked in. He wondered how he'd survived—or if he'd taken down that animal, whatever the hell it was. And he wanted to ask all those questions but his brain was fogged and the old man said, "When Logan gets back, he'll talk to you. He'll explain everything."

Logan? Who was Logan, and who the hell was this *guy?*

"How long . . . ?" he started, but was unable to finish.

"You've been with us for about four weeks."

Chance nodded. His skin felt tight, his body different, as if he didn't fit into it any longer. And when he tried to sit up, he realized he'd been tied down to the bed.

"It was for your own good," the man said gently. "You were moving a lot—we were afraid you were going to hurt yourself."

Chance saw the hesitation in the old man's eyes before he leaned forward and unlocked chains that wound around Chance's ankles and the cuffs around his wrists. Even though he was covered in blankets and bandages, he knew he was naked on the bunk.

And as the man walked away, Chance noticed that one ankle was still chained.

Being held prisoner was never for anyone's own good, not in his world. As he stared down at the cuff, his Special Forces training kicked in, overriding the fear and sadness and pain, and his need to escape raged through him like a fire.

No matter if these people were friend or foe, he was getting out, getting back to his base and reporting what he'd seen. There were too many families who wouldn't have closure if he didn't.

Of course, his wasn't one of them. His momma had died eight years earlier. Sure, he might have relatives somewhere he could dig up, but what the heck would they want with a twenty-five-year-old grown-ass man?

Maybe one day, he'd have his own family. Or at least that's what he always figured, that he'd have nothing but time on his hands.

Born lucky, always lucky, Momma used to say, and for a long time he'd believed her, until common sense reared its ugly head to remind him that being born near the craps table didn't mean . . . well, crap.

Especially when his mother had been unwilling to leave because she'd been losing at the time. Too busy for labor.

Too busy for him, most of the time, except when she needed him.

When he was still just a kid, he'd been forced to become a chameleon, pretending to be whoever his mom wanted him to be at the time. A petty thief and con artist, she'd dragged Chance into her schemes until his twelfth birthday, when he'd been thrown off a fourth-floor balcony as a result of her ways—a deal gone wrong. He'd tried to protect his mom from her enraged victim by jumping in front of her and found himself plummeting to the ground below.

By some miracle, he'd ended up with only a broken arm, which had healed so quickly he hadn't needed a plaster cast.

The thing was, he remembered being far more hurt than that, even if only for an instant. He hadn't been able to move his arms or legs . . . saw himself floating above his body. And then he'd woken to his mother and the police and walked to the ambulance . . . and he'd never told anyone.

Nothing like that had ever happened again. Sure, he'd always healed faster than others, but this—what that monster did to him—he should've died.

Born lucky, always lucky.

He'd graduated to becoming a hell of a pickpocket and semi–juvenile delinquent. He'd always stayed far away from gambling and casinos, but looking back, he realized he gambled with something much more important in the military—his life.

And the expression *shit out of luck* never seemed to fit more perfectly than right now.

SELA HAD TO HAND IT TO MARLENA—FOR BEING COVER-MODEL gorgeous, she was tough.

They'd been tramping through the jungle for eight hours now, and not once had the blond woman whined about the insects, the thick brush or the weight of their fully loaded backpacks. Not even the sweltering heat seemed to bother her, even though their BDUs stuck to their skin like damp sheets.

Both had long ago stripped off their long-sleeved outer shirts and were down to their brown tees, but it hadn't helped a whole lot.

They'd finally found the area where Sela believed the SEALs had been attacked, and for the past hour, they'd been collecting evidence. Back at ACRO, while Sela was having her cavity filled, Marlena had studied investigative techniques, as well as the history behind el chupacabra, and on the plane, Sela had given her a crash course in cryptozoology.

Marlena was a quick study, but truthfully, Sela wasn't too worried. The cover story would be that Marlena was new to the work, which would explain any uncertainties, holes or mistakes. Sela had enough experience and knowledge for them both.

Now she just had to hope that Marlena could do what she'd been sent to do: seduce Logan while Sela determined what had killed the SEALs. Apparently, Marlena was one of the few Seducers who lacked the sexual psychic ability that made Seducers good at their jobs. She must be *really* skilled in bed.

"I think I found something." Marlena was crouched near a fallen log, her long hair pulled up into a ponytail and somehow looking perfect.

Apparently, Marlena's superpornpower was being beautiful at all times, in any circumstance.

Sela joined her at the log. Claw marks scored the dead tree, but it was the piece of gray material wedged into the bark that drew her interest.

"Looks like a scale. Reptile, maybe, but it's huge." Sela dug a vial and tweezers out of her backpack and carefully extracted the scale from the log. She dropped it into the vial and stood. "Okay, let's follow the path—"

The chilling and unmistakable sound of weapons being brought to bear froze her tongue to the roof of her mouth. Unbelievable—she'd been so into the investigation, she'd actually forgotten the real reason they were there... and been caught with her pants down.

"Hands over your head." The deep male voice rumbled through her. Though it chafed, she turned to the dark-haired man who stood at the edge of the clearing holding an M14 aimed at her chest.

At least half a dozen men in jungle fatigues surrounded them, all pointing weapons and all looking like they'd have no problem killing two unarmed women.

Not that Sela and Marlena were completely helpless. Both had been through extensive ACRO self-defense and survival training, and in their packs they had knives, pistols and tranquilizer guns.

"Look," Sela began, speaking to the man she recognized from file photos as Logan Mills, "we're just tourists—"

"Because the Amazon jungle is such a popular vacation spot," Logan interrupted in a slow, sarcastic drawl. He gestured to one of his men. "Get their packs."

"No!" Sela feigned alarm. "I have medications I need."

"Don't worry," Logan said. "We won't let you die until we're good and ready."

Marlena edged closer to Sela, doing a damned fine impression of being terrified. Of course, if she wasn't a little nervous, she'd be an idiot. Sela's adrenaline was dumping into her system by the bucketload, turning her into a shaking, panting mess.

Logan moved in as his goon stripped her of her pack. "What's in the vial?"

Sela hid it behind her back. "Nothing. I mean, I'm an amateur entomologist. It's an insect wing."

"Really." He signaled to the goon, who tore the vial from her hand.

"You asshole," she snapped, because although he'd done exactly what she'd expected and wanted him to do, it still pissed her off.

Logan smiled, a cold lift of one corner of his mouth. "Haven't heard *that* before."

"Please," Marlena said, playing her role of innocent female in need of protection to the max, "don't hurt us."

Logan turned to her, his eyes sliding slowly down her curvy body and back up. Good. Marlena was great bait. "So," he said softly—and really, did he have to sound like he was getting ready to invite both of them to bed? "You're here for a vacation."

"Yes." Sela stepped forward as if to shield her friend from Logan. "So if you'll just let us go, we'll forget we ever saw you."

Before she could blink, he had her by the shoulders and had backed her into a tree. "You," he said against her ear, "aren't calling the shots. And you sure as hell aren't telling me the truth."

"Lo!"

For a long moment, he remained where he was, his body pressed against hers, not hurting, but the message was clear. He was big, he was strong and he was in charge. Once he felt the message had been delivered, he pushed away and swung around to the man who had taken her pack.

On the ground, spread out in a display, was her pistol, dart gun, specimen kit, hunting knife, maps, cryptozoology book and handwritten notes about chupacabras.

"Well, now," Logan murmured. "I think someone has some explaining to do."

Marlena cleared her throat delicately. "We don't mean any harm. If this is your spot, we'll move on." She made her voice shake, and her big blue eyes even filled with tears.

God, she was good.

Sela held her breath as Logan moved toward Marlena, slowly, his shoulders rolling like a jaguar on the prowl.

Get him, girl, Sela thought, but he stopped a few feet from the other woman, squatted on the ground and opened her pack. He pawed around in it and then froze, and Sela bit back a smile, knowing exactly what he'd found. Marlena feigned horror as he drew a small pink vibrator from her pack. Somehow, she even managed to turn about ten shades of red. The woman belonged in Hollywood, not at ACRO.

The men made lewd noises and comments, but Logan cocked an eyebrow, looked from Marlena to Sela. "Are you two . . . involved?"

"Wouldn't you like to know?" Sela snapped.

He shrugged. "I'd like to watch."

"You're a pig."

"I'm a guy who's been in the fucking jungle for a month without a woman."

Marlena was still looking mortified. Almost as though Logan felt sorry for her, he shoved the vibrator back in the pack and stood. "Cuff them. We're taking them back to base."

The man closest to Sela whipped flex-cuffs out of his pocket. Sela waited until he jerked her arms behind her back, and then she spun, took him down with a knee to the groin. Before anyone could move, she shot into the brush, running as fast as she could. She knew she was going to get caught—this wasn't about escape, it was about making sure Marlena was the good girl, the one everyone would want to be nice to, protect, fall for.

Sela was going to be the hard-ass, uncontrollable bitch. Which really wasn't a big stretch of her acting abilities.

Branches slapped at her face, snagged her hair, and twice she nearly went down when her boot caught on tree roots. She leaped a small stream, but when she landed on the other side, her foot slipped, and she tumbled down an incline. She rolled to a stop, pain shooting through her shoulder. Shit. The sounds of pursuit grew closer. Wincing, she shoved to her feet and started toward a dense copse of trees—

Something hit her like a train, and she went down. Hard. Agony screamed through her shoulder, and she cried out before she could stop herself. She lay on her belly, a heavy body on top of her. Strong legs pinned hers together, and a thick arm pressed into the back of her neck.

"That was a stupid move," Logan growled into her hair.

"Bite me."

Teeth caught her lobe. The son of a bitch actually *bit her.*

"Lesson number one," he said. "Don't ever say anything to me you don't mean."

"Fuck you," she spat into the dirt. "And I do mean that."

"As an offer?" He ground his pelvis against her—and did he . . . ? Yes, he did. He had an erection. Maybe the vibrator had put some ideas in his head.

That, or the month in a jungle with no woman.

"As in, go to hell."

He laughed, but there was no humor in it. "Sweetheart, I'm on my way." He shifted his weight, taking pressure off her shoulder, which was throbbing. "Now, do you promise to be good?"

"Oh, yes," she said sweetly. "Absolutely. You've totally cowed me."

"You're a real piece of shit, you know that?" He yanked her arms behind her back, and she gritted her teeth against the pain in her joint. "You left your lover alone with a bunch of armed, horny guys."

"I panicked." She winced as he secured her wrists with flex-cuffs. "Is she okay?"

"Dunno. Maybe if you'd shut your trap, you could hear her scream."

She roared with anger, which wasn't entirely feigned. "You fuck! If you hurt her—"

"You'll what?" He rolled her over so she could look into his deceptively handsome face. Deceptive, because behind his mossy eyes and beneath his tan skin, he was a monster who was in bed with Itor. "Seems to me you don't have a lot of room to make threats."

Distant memories ran through her head, sad ones, of her puppy, Max, being hit by a car, of her best childhood friend, Misty, moving away. Of her mom, in the hospital, dying. Tears sprang to her eyes, just the way she needed them to.

"You're right," she rasped. "I'm sorry. Don't hurt Marlena. Please."

Something in Logan's face softened, just for a moment. Maybe he was human in there somewhere. With the backs of his fingers, he brushed away the dirt clinging to her cheeks.

"What's your name?" When she said nothing, he sighed. "You'll find that cooperating will go a long way with me."

"Fine," she bit out. "It's Sela."

"See? That didn't hurt, did it?" He pushed to his feet, giving her the opportunity she needed.

Rolling, she swung her legs out, caught him in the knees... and he went down like a log. Granted, he was up again in a heartbeat, snarling with fury, but still, it felt good to give him a good whack.

"You can't help it, can you?" he snapped. "You keep doing stupid things."

"You keep pissing me off!"

He blinked. And then he laughed, and good Lord, the man was drop-dead, fucking gorgeous when he did that.

"Come on." He grasped her by the forearms—keeping out of the way of her legs—and yanked her to her feet.

The pain in her shoulder was like an arrow of fire, and she sucked in air.

"What's wrong?" he asked, his brows drawn, almost as if he was truly concerned.

"Nothing," she said through clenched teeth.

He narrowed his eyes at her, but after a moment, he shrugged. "If you're too stubborn to ask for help, you'll suffer."

"Asshole," she muttered.

He smiled and pushed her into motion ahead of him, but this time, he wasn't rough with her, was actually careful not to touch her injured shoulder. He probably wanted it to start feeling better so he could poke her there later.

She started walking back the way she came, which wasn't easy, given that her arms were wrenched behind her back. "We're not lovers."

"What?"

"Marlena. Me. We're not sleeping together. I mean, we'd planned to be out in the jungle for a while, so, you know . . . big deal if she wanted to bring a toy with her." She stepped awkwardly over a log, jerked away from Logan when his hand shot out to help her.

"Hey, I'm all for a woman enjoying toys."

Hopefully he was picturing Marlena with the vibrator right now. "Well," she said, "my point is that we're not together. We like men."

"Is that right?"

Sela shot him a glare over her shoulder. "*Some* men. The kind who don't hold us at gunpoint."

"Huh." Suddenly, he was against her, his chest to her back, his arm around her waist. "Good to know." His hot breath fanned her ear, and a shiver of feminine appreciation, which was utterly inappropriate given who he was and the situation she was in, skated over her skin. "That's very good to know."

She broke away from him, her heart pounding, her breath coming in gasps. She'd gone into this mission knowing it would be dangerous. Terrifying.

But this man was going to chew Marlena up and spit her out.

God, she hoped Dev knew what he was doing, because she was starting to think they were in way over their heads.

CHAPTER *three*

Every man's eyes were on her as Dax walked her through the camp. When Marlena was a teen, the attention had made her cringe, but now, at twenty-nine, she'd long ago grown to accept it and use it to her advantage.

Except this one would be tricky. She'd have to play good little prisoner and try to wind every man in the camp around her finger, since Logan wasn't playing along. And then she needed to *make* Logan play along, since Sela hadn't looked at all happy to be left alone with him back at the big tent near the camp entrance.

Marlena would have to find a way to bond with him, and fast. Many of the men she worked with at ACRO were former military—the one thing they had in common was an inherent need to keep the women who surrounded them safe; she could only hope Logan and the rest of his men reacted the same.

But despite the fact that Dax couldn't stop his eyes from traveling over her body, he easily handed her off to a man he referred to as Shep. "Cuff her to a cot in the medical tent. Lo's orders."

Shep nodded and took her firmly in hand. Sheesh, you'd think that men who'd been in the jungle this long would want to do nothing but rip her clothes off. But no, these men were all far too focused on the chupacabra—she could almost smell their focus, and had to admire them. Would admire them more if it didn't interfere with her job, of course.

Shep was walking fast—too fast for her to put the extra sway in her step or to maintain any kind of effective conversation. But the lack of talk gave her a chance to study her surroundings.

The camp was compact, a tent city comprising a couple dozen small tents—personal tents for the guys, she guessed—and three larger, sturdier ones, identified by ACRO intelligence experts who studied satellite photos to probably be central command, a medical tent and a supply/research tent. Vehicles were parked along the perimeter of the camp.

She turned to Shep as they reached the door of the medical tent, made her voice sound breathy, as if she wasn't used to these conditions. "Shep, listen . . . will you stay with me? I'm a little scared to be here all alone."

It was her helpless act—and she knew it was damned good.

As Devlin's assistant, she'd been in shape, but now, as a Seducer, she was transformed. She was completely, utterly lethal, her body a mix of fine muscle and curved perfection. The job required her to be pampered on her off time. Massages. Body wraps. The highest-quality sheets, towels and loungewear. Exercise and the best food known to man, cooked to her personal specifications.

Shep cocked a brow. "Sweetheart, I'm a busy guy. Don't have time to babysit. Besides, you won't be alone." He pushed her roughly.

She stumbled into the tent and noted that, as Shep promised, she wasn't alone. But she'd never expected to find a man so . . . beautiful sitting there. Even bruised and battered, she could see the lean chisel of his cheekbone, the full mouth, the square jaw.

He was utterly and completely naked—tall and tanned, and there, along his side, she saw them. Bite marks. Well on their way to being healed, but there was no mistaking them.

She scanned the floor and the small table and saw what she was looking for—dog tags. She couldn't read them, but she'd bet anything this man was part of the SEAL team that had been attacked. The search-and-rescue teams had been unable to locate one man, and she had a feeling she just had.

The bites were large, surrounded by deep bruises, but they appeared to be healing and not infected. He must've been here a while, receiving medical attention.

She wondered if he could describe what had nearly killed him.

Shep pushed her forward again, and she moved toward the double bunk, across the room from where the man was chained to the floor by one ankle. Roughly, Shep took her wrists and with a three-foot length of chain cuffed them to a bunk so she could sit, lie down or stand.

She drew a breath, realized the air felt . . . heavy. As if she was moving through a thick fog, and yet somehow her blood ran hot, the sudden arousal startling her.

Shep completely ignored the man. In turn, the wounded man ignored her and instead watched Shep intensely. Studying him. Looking for weaknesses. Assessing his prey.

An involuntary shiver ran through her, because she felt the danger radiating from the naked man. And because it wasn't an altogether unpleasant feeling.

"Have fun. Don't do anything I wouldn't," Shep told her, before laughing at his own stupid joke on his way out of the tent.

As soon as Shep was gone, the man started tugging on his chain.

This man—whoever he was—was as much a prisoner as she was.

She spoke first, when it became obvious he was just as happy to pretend she didn't exist. "I'm Marlena."

"Good for you," he muttered without so much as looking at her. "I'm Chance."

His voice vibrated through her like a rough touch. She wondered what his hands would feel like on her body.

What was happening to her? "They're keeping me prisoner too. Why are they keeping you here? Maybe if we work together—"

"You're not going to try that scared shit on me, are you? Because if it didn't work on a half-wit like Shep, no way in hell it's working on me."

The problem was, it was working on *her*.

Most times, it was all an act. This was not one of them. No, she wanted to rip off all her clothes, and it had nothing to do with the jungle heat. She wanted to give herself to him.

He wanted her too—as detached as he tried to act, there was no hiding the arousal that grew, jutting up impressively toward his abs.

There was nothing he could do to hide it.

She dragged her eyes up to his face. "You don't believe I'm here against my will?"

Finally, Chance glanced at her, raking her over with a gaze so hot she felt blood rush to her cheeks. "I've got problems of my own. I'm not really in rescue-the-damsel-in-distress mode. I'm calling bullshit on your being helpless anyway." He seemed not to care that he was completely naked and exposed as he yanked on his chain, unaware that his body, despite the bruising, looked impossibly perfect. A body made so by hard work—real work, not simply hours spent in a gym.

But who was he?

She'd never wanted someone so much in her life. It was like pheromones gone wild. "Maybe I can help?"

He shook his head. "Unless you've got a blowtorch on you, forget it."

Her body felt like it radiated that kind of heat, especially as she watched his hands continue to work. Large, strong hands. Capable.

The things those hands could do to her . . .

Dammit. She forced herself to look away from him. She was supposed to make men feel like this—wild and out of control.

Focus, Marlena. Ask questions. Get intel. Do your goddamned job.

She shifted, the wet heat between her legs suddenly unbearable.

She was swiftly losing any semblance of control. What was worse, she didn't care.

CHANCE WAS CHANGING. GROWING STRONGER. AND WHILE he'd always been in damned good shape, what was happening to him was something altogether different and well beyond the quick healing he was used to.

He couldn't worry about it now, would simply use it to his advantage. Had to get the hell out of this camp and back to civilization and so he'd played along with the doctors, pretending he was down and out, all the while his senses of smell and hearing surprising the shit out of him.

If he concentrated, he could hear people talking anywhere in the camp—and although conversations jumbled together, he could still make out a few things. Like who Logan was. About Global Weapons Corporation.

The fact that these men were out looking for the monster that had killed his team.

And while that alone should've made Chance feel like he'd been saved by the good guys, a large part of him was really uneasy with the entire situation.

The chains didn't help make him any more comfortable.

"Hey, maybe we could put our heads together and come up with a plan." Marlena was still talking. Jesus, the gorgeous talking woman was a huge freakin' distraction.

He'd known they were bringing her in too—he'd caught the scent of her.

Caught the scent. What the hell? Was he part fucking bloodhound now? It hadn't been that long since he'd had sex...

Or had it?

Forcing himself to ignore the beautiful woman chained fifteen feet from him for a few seconds, he stared at the metal cuff and the bunk and he tugged... and felt the chain give. He put a little more muscle into it, and the metal began to separate along the chain links until one finally snapped.

"What the hell—are you like Superman?" Marlena stared between the chain and him, and really, he wasn't sure how to answer that.

Right now, he sure felt like Superman.

Swiftly, he was on her, pinning her to the cot. "Who are you and why did they put you in this tent with me?"

"Get your hands off me or—"

"Or what? You'll call that asshole Shep, whose dick you just tried to wrap around your finger?" He snorted even as she struggled with both her chain and him. "You're not fooling me. You're in the jungle with another woman. Two women, alone in the Amazon. Random scientists don't do shit like that. They have teams."

She stared at him. "How do you know I'm a scientist?"

"I heard..." He'd *heard*. What the fuck? "I heard Shep talking before he went to get you. Goddamned guy can't stop running his mouth."

She nodded, but didn't look convinced. "My friend and I, we were lost. We went too far and got separated from our camp."

"So these guys rescued you."

"I guess so." She yanked at the handcuff attached to the cot and looked miserable.

And hot. Like, the good kind of hot. And he was getting hot

too, and what the hell? Maybe she was wrapping *his* dick around her finger . . . and maybe he was way more dim-witted than Shep.

Or maybe . . . maybe it was all the changes he was going through. Because there was no way he'd ever healed this fast before. He'd been on the goddamned brink of death.

He inhaled. Damn, the woman smelled good.

"Chance . . ." The word came out a whisper, because she had no recourse against his approach.

"Your scent . . . it's killing me," he growled against her ear, then buried his face in her neck, her hair, his hands traveling along her body while she remained trapped on the thin mattress.

"Why don't you even the playing field?" she asked, rattling the chain, but he was far too intent on getting into her pants.

His hand slid under her shirt, along her bare belly. He needed to touch her. Taste her.

He simply needed. She didn't resist, parted her thighs for his touch. Wanted him too. And when his fingers found her, rubbed her hot, wet sex, he captured her groan against his mouth. His erection jutted against her side as he attempted to shift her so they could press together.

Her handcuffs were in the way, but he continued kissing her, and even in his sex haze, he knew she was voluntarily kissing him back, her tongue teasing the roof of his mouth as she rocked against his hand.

He wanted to drop to his knees, tongue her, taste her . . . but his need to mark her, to fill her was stronger. That was a keen, unbearable longing he would not be able to stop.

With a sharp tug, her pants and thong were pulled down, but they wouldn't fit over the heavy boots she wore. Frustrated, he managed to free one leg enough for him to hook it around his waist. To open her to him.

Her wet sex welcomed the head of his cock easily. Teased it, and for a second he wondered what the hell was going on here, why he couldn't stop. Why she didn't want him to.

Why all of this felt so goddamned right.

With a harsh cry he didn't recognize as his own, he thrust inside her. Felt strange at the lack of guilt, because he hadn't asked her if any of this was okay.

But even though Marlena was bound, she was consenting. Opening for him. Wrapping her legs around his waist as he balanced them both, her head thrown back in pure ecstasy.

From there, it was all happening in slow-motion flashes. He was vaguely aware of her cries of pleasure. The room seemed to spin and he was seeing Marlena's face . . . and then jungle . . . and then just a white light that burned hotly through him as he came, harder than he'd ever come in his life.

He thought he was dying. Having a heart attack at the very least. But then the tightening in his chest subsided and gradually he floated back to consciousness, and to the woman he'd collapsed onto.

He lifted his head and they stared at each other, half in shock in their post-orgasmic haze. He eased Marlena's legs from around his waist and steadied her when her feet hit the floor.

Her BDUs remained on one leg and he bent quickly and got them back on her. Because they were coming for her—for them—and no one would see his woman naked but him.

His woman. Shit.

Before he could say anything, explain—and what the hell kind of explanation could he give anyway?—Shep burst into the room.

"What are you doing?"

Chance wheeled away from Marlena and faced Shep, who had a pistol pointed directly at him.

"Back the fuck away from her now," Shep ordered.

Chance heard a low growl . . . and spun, searching for the source. Until he realized it had come from him.

What happened next was both completely unexpected and

strangely natural, and like most things he'd done in his life, he simply went for it.

BITING THAT WOMAN ON THE EARLOBE HAD BEEN ONE OF THE stupidest things Logan had ever done in his life, because it had made the whole I've-been-in-the-jungle-for-a-month-without-a-woman thing start screaming inside his pants.

God, she was pretty. Pretty and sweaty and pissed as hell, which, yeah, was another one of his turn-ons, right up there with the whole earlobe thing. She'd tasted a little salty, smelled like vanilla, and fuck it all, why, today of all days, was there actually hot water in this godforsaken shower when he most definitely needed cold.

He was horny as hell, and it was at times like these that he thanked God he wasn't fully a machine, that he could still feel all the normal male urges. That he wasn't a complete monster like the one Frankenstein built, full of wires and steel and mechanisms.

Since the accident and subsequent rehab, his emotions felt flat—he'd been unable to feel truly passionate about anything he did work-wise. Or anything-wise. Sex was the only way he could convince himself that he was still capable of feeling, and hell, that was something.

Now he leaned his forehead against his arm, which was propped up against the wooden wall of the outdoor shower, his body still soapy, the dirt running down the small hole that acted as a drain.

He was rock hard, uncomfortably so, and Sela was waiting a few feet away, handcuffed to a pole with no choice but to wait for him.

"What's taking you so long?" she snapped—and oh, yeah, if he could keep her talking . . .

"You miss me, darling?" he called, the hoarseness in his voice apparent to his own ears as he palmed his shaft and closed his eyes and pretended she was touching him. Stroking him. Maybe even getting on her knees to take him in her mouth. She'd be hot and wet and would put that sharp tongue to use in much more pleasant ways. He could already feel it swirling around his glans and flicking over the tip while her lips created a groan-inducing suction.

"I want to take a shower too," she said, and *Christ*, the thought of her in here, with him, almost made him lose it.

Too soon—he needed to enjoy this. Deserved to, since he'd been pulled out of the office and into the fucking jungle to clean up another mess. And yeah, he was about sixty seconds from making a fucking mess of his own, considering he hadn't been able to keep his eyes off Sela's ass instead of on the tracks leading to the escaped animal.

She'd been huffing a little as they'd gotten farther into the brush, each sound, each breath sounding like . . . like fucking sex noises. He needed to get this job over and done with and get this woman out of this country and away from Chance and the beast running free in the wilds of the Amazon.

"You can join me, in the name of water conservation," he called back, imagined her slick, soapy body rubbing his. He'd bet anything she was wild in bed; she was the type—all buttoned-up and serious on the outside, but once she got turned on . . . she'd probably rake her nails down his back when she came.

Oh. Fucking. Yeah.

He stroked himself harder, the buildup nearly too much, and he forced himself not to bite down on his own arm. She'd probably bite. And scratch. She'd lock those long legs around his waist and tease him by rocking her slick sex, her swollen clit, along the length of his shaft, working her honey all the way to his balls.

Which were drawing up, boiling with come. He imagined her palm cupping them, rolling them between her long fingers as she arched up, finally taking him deep. They'd both shout at the joining, and she might even reach her first orgasm when his cock raked a sensitive place inside.

"Do you think you'll be ready soon?" she persisted.

"Yeah," he panted. "Really ready."

God, she'd be hot and tight—his hips rocked a little as he thrust into his fist.

"Because then we need to discuss the fact that you're keeping me prisoner . . ."

Sela in handcuffs in the shower naked with him. "Yeah. Prisoner." At his mercy, spread-eagle and calling his name . . .

"Logan, do you hear me?"

"Mmmmmhmmm."

"Because that's against the law."

"Oh, yeah. Against." Pressed against, her nipples rubbing his chest, her core contracting around him, and fuck, he was at the edge and he was going over fast.

"Why are you suddenly being so agreeable?" Her voice had turned suspicious and he was seeing the white light behind his eyes. He pumped his hand faster, long strokes from base to tip, adding a twisting motion at the head that made the white light turn blinding.

"Because . . . it feels . . . so damned good," he ground out. Sensation sizzled like a lit fuse down his spine to groin, where the pressure that had been building combusted. His balls tightened and his dick pulsed in his hand and he came, hard and fast, shooting on the floor while the water ran down his back like a soft caress.

There was dead silence on her end, and then, "I hope you enjoyed yourself in there, as that's the closest you're ever getting to being with me."

He finished rinsing off and opened the door without bothering with the towel. In this weather, he'd never dry fully anyway. Fucking humidity. "Who said I was thinking about you?"

"You said my name when you came," she said dryly before she turned away, as if she didn't see anything that impressed her.

Chuckling, he pulled on a fresh pair of jungle camo BDUs. She had sass, and dammit, he liked sass.

He uncuffed her, watched her rub her wrists. They were a little red, but that would fade quickly. His little shower fantasy, however, would not.

CHAPTER *Four*

Sela rubbed her wrists, mentally cursing Logan and praying that Marlena could start work on seducing him. "Where is Marlena?" she asked, and he smirked at her.

"My boys took her to the medical tent. It's reinforced, doubles as our holding tank."

"Will she be okay? I saw the way your *boys* leered at her."

He scowled. "Yeah, you'd think they'd never seen a fucking woman before."

Oh, *he* was one to talk, given what he'd done in the shower while she was right outside the door. And what the hell was up with that? Sure, she'd discussed sex toys in the jungle to get him worked up and his mind in the gutter, but it was supposed to be there with Marlena and her vibrator, not Sela.

And now she was the one with her mind stuck in the gutter, because when he'd stepped out of the shower, water running in crystal rivulets along the valleys of his sharply cut muscles, she'd had to turn away to keep from staring as though *she'd* been in the jungle for a month.

"Logan!" Dax's shout rang out at the same time as the sound of a scream and an inhuman snarl. "It's Chance . . . Quick! He's attacking Shep!"

Logan sped toward the medical tent, and Sela's heart nearly busted through her rib cage. That was where he said they'd taken Marlena. Sela ran after him, the sounds coming from the tent scaring the daylights out of her.

Logan tore open the door and drew up so fast Sela ran into him. "What the fuck is that?" he barked, and Sela wished to God she knew the answer.

Shep was on the ground, moaning, blood streaming from his mouth, scalp and nose. A naked man stood over him . . . at least, she thought it was a man. His skin was grayish, textured like a reptile's, and his teeth . . . God, they were sharp, fanged.

Marlena was huddled on a cot, cuffed, her clothes askew, and Sela wondered if this man-creature had attacked her. He watched them with slitted eyes, his entire body coiled inside and ready to strike. An injured animal preparing to defend itself from predators.

And judging by the way he seized Marlena's forearm, he was prepared to defend her too.

Or maybe eat her.

"Someone get a goddamned tranq!" Logan shouted, and the man-thing snarled. Logan held up his hands and lowered his voice. "Chance. It's okay. Let the woman go."

"Fuck off."

Alarm skittered up Sela's spine at the man's deadly tone, but Marlena, to her credit, remained calm despite the fact that she was in the grip of something that wasn't entirely human.

A man in BDUs and with a stethoscope around his neck eased into the tent, a tranquilizer gun in his hand. Two men behind him carried pistols.

"Doc," Logan said quietly, "flank me."

Logan gestured to Dax, and in the next instant, Dax grabbed Marlena, and the doctor and Logan shoved Chance onto the cot.

"Get Shep and the women out of here!" Logan shouted. Chance roared, his struggles knocking Logan and the doctor, whom Dax called Wes, off balance.

A set of arms circled Sela's waist as Dax dragged Marlena out of the tent. Sela elbowed her attacker in the ribs. He grunted, but his hold tightened, and she felt herself being tugged backward. As hard as she could, she brought her booted foot down on his, and at the same time, she rocked her head and cracked the back of her skull against his mouth and nose.

"Ow! *Fuck!*" His agonized curse accompanied a rough slam to the ground and a knee in the back of her neck, another jammed into the small of her back.

Sela's breath was ripped from her lungs by the impact, and she gasped like a fish on the bank of a river. Memories of the beating she'd suffered flashed through her head like a movie on fast-forward, but mercifully, the man holding her down made no move to hurt her, and awkwardly, she cranked her head so she could see, past Dax, the struggle between the three men.

An ungodly, high-pitched screech pierced the air.

"Oh, Jesus."

Sela didn't know who spoke, but suddenly, Logan flew backward, landing in a heap next to her.

Wes hit one of the tent poles, cracking it in half. One side of the tent collapsed, and then, standing near the bed where Chance had been, its eyes glowing red and drool dripping from its tiger-long fangs, was a fucking chupacabra.

They were real. Dear God, they were *real.*

THERE WAS A MOMENT OF SILENCE, AND THEN CAME A CLICK OF a weapon and the huff of a dart gun. The chupacabra roared, clutching at the dart in its belly.

The man holding Sela down leaped to his feet, giving her the opportunity to come to hers.

"Oh, my God," she breathed. "You've got a chupacabra. But how? It was a human. How did it turn—"

"Fuck if I know," Logan said, as he eased toward the creature, which had slid to the floor. If he was surprised that she recognized a chupacabra, it didn't show.

It began to writhe, and slowly, its form changed to human again. "What . . . happened . . . ?" Chance panted, clutching at his belly.

Logan crouched next to him. "Hey, man. It's okay. It's me, Logan."

"I . . . remember. What happened in the jungle." Chance swallowed, panted. "Attacked . . . attacked by some creature. My team . . . dead."

"I know." Logan looked at Wes. "Did you see any signs that this could happen?"

"No. Nothing."

Okay, so these guys were clueless. And clearly, they hadn't known the injured guy was going to turn into a monster.

"Who is this man?" Sela asked, though given what he'd said, she suspected he was a member of the SEAL team that had been slaughtered in the jungle.

Instead of answering, Logan signaled to the guy who had grabbed her earlier. The one whose nose was bleeding from her head-butt.

"Get her out of here."

The jerk came at her, but she ducked and darted to Chance. "Chance. Hey. Did the thing that attacked you have spines on its back? Red eyes? Claws?" *Like you had.*

"Yeah," he rasped. "Yeah." He closed his eyes, his breathing settling into a steady, shallow rhythm.

"He's out," Logan said. "Anyone want to share a theory on what the fuck just happened?"

Sela frowned. "Was he normal before this?"

"Before he was attacked, you mean?"

"Yes."

Logan and Wes exchanged glances, and Logan shook his head, as if telling the other man to keep his mouth shut. He turned to her. "Go with Eric. Now."

"I can help," she snapped. "I'm a cryptozoologist, and chupacabras are my specialty."

Logan cocked an eyebrow. "Really? I thought you collected bugs." Sarcasm dripped from every word.

Clearly, he hadn't bought her lie, but then, she hadn't wanted him to. "I didn't think you'd believe me. But obviously, you're running some sort of scientific operation here, and you have your own pet chupacabra. So yeah, I'm thinking you'll believe the truth now."

He crossed his arms over his broad chest. "Fine. Tell me what you know, O great chupacabra expert."

"You're an ass."

He stared at her. The ass.

"Maybe you could start with what's going on with this man." She crossed her arms over her chest in a blatant imitation of Logan's arrogant stance.

"We don't know. We found him injured in the jungle."

"And what are you doing here in the first place?"

He didn't miss a beat. "We're researchers. Studying the local fauna. It's our job to know what kind of dangerous wildlife we could run into."

"Really? Do all botanists carry semi-automatic weapons and set up military base camps?"

"We hired mercs as guards. This area is a hotbed for drug cartels."

He made it all sound so legit. Too bad she knew his company made even the worst drug cartel seem like a bunch of kittens. Anyone who dealt with Itor needed to be taken down.

She glanced at the men standing around her, all armed except for the doctor, who was listening to Chance's chest with a stethoscope. "Look, maybe we could talk in private? Call me a wuss, but I'm a little unnerved by all this."

Besides, rule number 246 in spywork was to get your target separated from others. A man alone was less likely to censor his words.

Logan narrowed his eyes at her, but after a moment, he nodded. "Let's go."

She followed him to a tent near the shower. It was smaller than the medical tent but still sizable, with a cot, two folding chairs, a small table scattered with papers, a laptop computer and an open satellite phone case. A duffel large enough for her to climb inside took up one corner.

"Have a seat," he said, gesturing to one of the chairs. She sat on the end of his cot. One corner of his mouth tipped up, and he reached for a bottle of Glenlivet. "Drink?"

"Make it a big one."

He poured two fingers of Scotch into a clear plastic cup and handed it to her. "Sorry about the plastic, but we're not running a country club."

She clutched hers to hide her fingers' trembling. Her adrenaline still raced from coming face-to-face with a creature she hadn't believed existed, and now she was alone with another creature, who was better-looking but no less dangerous.

"So tell me about chupacabras."

"Have your boys bring Marlena first," she countered.

He cocked a dark eyebrow. "Why?"

"Maybe you didn't notice that she was cuffed inside a tent with a dangerous creature? She's got to be terrified. Maybe hurt."

"I'd have been informed by now if she'd been injured." Still, he went to the tent flap and shouted for Marlena to be brought to him.

A minute later, Marlena arrived, somehow looking like she'd stepped out of the pages of *Playboy*. She'd taken her hair out of the ponytail, and now it fell in soft waves around her shoulders. Her tight tee outlined braless breasts, and she'd tied the hem in a knot that exposed her flat stomach. Her BDU bottoms, specially made by ACRO for her build, rode low at the hips, giving her a dangerously wanton appearance.

"See?" Logan said, giving her a lingering once-over before gesturing to a chair. "She's fine."

Maybe Marlena wasn't injured, but she was far from fine. She was too pale, her posture too stiff. What had happened in the medical tent had shaken her. Marlena sat, but before Logan could do the same, Sela stood.

"Logan? Could I get a minute alone with Marlena? Please?"

He narrowed his eyes at her, but nodded. "You have one minute." He slipped out of the tent, and Sela knelt beside the other woman.

"Are you okay?"

Marlena smiled so brightly that Sela could almost believe that nothing had happened. "I was scared for a few moments, but really, I'm fine. We see weird things all the time."

At ACRO, yes, weirdness was the order of the day. But it wasn't often you got chained next to a man who turned into a mythological creature. "Look, we'll forget the plan. You just take it easy—"

"Sela." Marlena's voice cracked like a whip. "I'm fine. I can handle this."

"But—"

Marlena grabbed Sela's wrist, her nails digging in as she put her lips to Sela's ear. "Don't treat me like I'm a fucking China doll," she whispered harshly. "I will do my job, and don't you dare tell Dev otherwise."

Okaaaay.

"Now, this is the kind of thing I like to see," Logan drawled, and Sela leaped to her feet. He was smiling, that cocky, sexy one she hated. "I knew you two were a thing."

"Oh, go screw yourself," Sela snapped, and he laughed as he planted himself behind his makeshift desk.

Marlena, as if she hadn't just dressed Sela down, shifted her hips far forward in the chair, so that her back arched, allowing her breasts to subtly push up and out.

Damn, she was good. When Sela had worked as a Seducer, her methods had been more aggressive, but then, she'd had less to work with than Marlena, who needed only to sit there in order to draw men.

Logan handed Marlena a drink, which she downed in a single shot before holding out her cup for more. He poured, and then turned to Sela.

"So. The chupacabra."

"They're mythical creatures whose origins—at least, the legend of their origins—are rooted in Puerto Rico. There have been numerous sightings, mainly in the American Southwest, Mexico and parts of Central and South America. Recently, sightings here in the Amazon have been reported, which is why we're here."

Logan ran his long fingers up and down his cup. "Is anything known about their behavior in the wild?"

In the wild? As opposed to what? Zoos? Sela shook her head. "Everything is theory. Based on kills and sightings, some cryptozoologists think they might be territorial. They're not pack animals, probably loners, but there have been sightings of pairs, so they may take mates rather than breeding nonselectively. But like I said, there's little fact here, and a lot of speculation." *Unless Grady's book was truly an account of chupacabra life.*

"Has anyone ever captured one?" Logan asked, and Sela shook her head. "A few strange creatures have been killed or caught, in places like Texas, but scientists determined that those animals were diseased coyotes, and they never did fit the profile of the infamous goat sucker."

"Which apparently looks like that thing in the tent," Logan muttered.

Marlena's hand shook as she poured herself another shot of liquor, but she covered quickly by bracing her forearm on the table. "That was . . . weird."

"You think?" Logan snorted. "So, what exactly are chupacabras?"

Marlena downed the shot. "Some theories floating around out there suggest that chupacabras are actually escaped alien pets."

"Which is ridiculous," Sela scoffed.

Logan took a gulp of his Scotch. "You just found out the thing is real. So why is the idea that it's an alien so out of the realm of possibility?"

"Because aliens don't exist."

Marlena shrugged, regaining her Seducer persona with a slow roll of one sexy shoulder. "Until ten minutes ago, you didn't think chupacabras existed."

Sela shot her a scowl. "In any case, not once has the chupacabra legend been associated with humans turning into them." She turned her gaze on Logan. "I need to know who the man in your medical tent is."

Logan looked up at the roof. "We found him nearly dead. He's American military. The only survivor of an animal attack. We expected him to die, but he healed so quickly it's miraculous."

"So you don't know anything about him."

"I know the military doesn't make a habit of enlisting people who change into man-eating beasts, so I'm going to throw out a wild guess that whatever attacked him also infected him."

"We need to talk to him," Marlena said, coming to her feet. She swayed drunkenly, and Logan caught her. She smiled apologetically, but when he tried to release her, she clung to him. "Sorry. I'm just . . . a little tipsy."

"Jungle heat will do that to you." He guided her back to her chair, but still, she clung to him, running one hand up his arm, the motion causing her breasts to rub against his chest.

Sela watched curiously, wondering if he'd take advantage of Marlena's "drunken" state.

"I want my backpack," she purred.

"Why?" Logan's voice was rough, but with irritation or arousal, Sela couldn't tell. "Want your little vibrating buddy?"

"I've never been one to deny myself pleasure whenever I can find it. And in a hellhole like this . . ." Marlena shrugged.

"Really . . ." Logan tugged her close, and for some reason, Sela felt a twinge of jealousy. "So if I wanted to get down to it with you, right now, you wouldn't have a problem with that?"

"Why should I?" The words were casual, but there was a slight tremor in Marlena's voice. She was definitely not okay, but she was soldiering on, determined to do her job.

He turned to Sela. "What about you?"

She nearly choked on her own tongue. "What about me? I'm not into threesomes." She ground her teeth and added, "Not with women anyway." God, she hoped things didn't come down to that. To a threesome of any sort.

"I wasn't talking about a threesome. Mainly because I don't share well." He plunked Marlena in the chair and left her to sink down beside Sela, so close his heat rolled over her like a caress. "I'm wondering about *you*. Do you look at sex the same way? A moment of pleasure to be had in any situation, no matter how extreme?"

She smiled sweetly. "You mean, like jerking off in a shower while your prisoner is cuffed to a pole right outside? That's a pretty extreme situation. Seems to me that given your little shower adventure, you have a lot in common with Marlena."

"You're mouthy."

"You like it."

His gaze dropped to her mouth. "I know *where* I'd like it."

An image of her with her lips wrapped around his cock swamped her brain, which was insane, because no way was she having sex with him. Then again, he was showing no interest in Marlena, and even if he were, Sela couldn't let Marlena continue this charade. The woman had been through enough.

"Logan," Marlena began, but he cut her off with a wave of his hand and called for one of his men, who must have been right outside, and told him to take Marlena away.

Sela couldn't decide if she was relieved or not, but as Marlena exited the tent, she flashed Sela an apologetic look, and Sela knew without a doubt that Logan's balls were now in her court.

CHAPTER *Five*

Sela waited until the flap closed, and then she came to her feet with an indignant huff. "Where are you taking her?"

"Supply tent for now. There's a cot in there. She'll be comfortable until we find a more permanent solution."

Well, it was better than putting Marlena back in with Chance. "And where will I stay?"

Logan poured more Scotch into his cup. "You stay with me."

Sela managed an outraged gasp that wasn't entirely feigned. "Why?"

"Because you're a troublemaker. I want to keep an eye on you."

She jabbed him in the chest so hard the last of his liquor sloshed out of the cup. "You have no right to hold us like this."

He dropped the cup and seized her wrist. "You'd rather be out in the jungle with that creature? It tore apart an entire SEAL team. What do you think it'll do to two helpless women? And if it doesn't get you, there are plenty of drug thugs who will."

The helpless thing really pissed her off. She'd show him helpless soon enough. "So I'm supposed to believe you're keeping us prisoner out of the goodness of your heart?"

His laughter cut through the air. "I don't do anything out of the goodness of my heart, babe." He hauled her close, so her breasts mashed against his chest... and his erection pressed into the softness of her belly. "I have some seriously selfish motives."

"You going to rape me? Because you'll have to," she spat.

"Rape?" He leaned in, so his lips brushed her ear. "I *so* wouldn't have to."

Had she been in any other situation, she'd have kneed the arrogant bastard in the balls and jammed the heel of her palm into his nose. But she really did have to get into bed with him, so she stayed where she was and whispered, "You're so full of yourself."

"Soon," he whispered back, "you'll be full of me too."

Fury shot through her, and job or no, she slapped him. He grabbed her other arm and held her immobile with an incredible amount of strength.

"That," he snarled, "was a huge mistake."

A thread of terror wove its way into her soul as a scene from her beating slammed into her head. The man who'd nearly killed her had said the same thing, right before he knocked her across the room so hard her shoulder had dislocated on impact with the wall. Worse had followed.

But instead of striking her, Logan fisted her hair and held her for his sudden, punishing kiss. Sela wanted to fight, but at the same time, she wanted to kiss him. His lips were hard but not cruel, and when his tongue stroked at the seam of her mouth, she opened up to him.

Instantly, the air seemed to arc with electricity, thickening around them. He deepened the kiss, turning it into something so hot that she clung to his shirt, preventing him from breaking away.

Desire speared her, went straight to her sex and radiated out. As if he knew, he dropped his hand to her thigh and lifted her leg to his waist, putting her core in contact with the hard ridge of his erection. His warmth put the jungle heat to shame, and yet she shivered as his mouth blazed a trail along her jaw and down her throat. He bent her back on his arm, exposing her neck to him, and one hand came up to jerk her tee out of her pants.

He sucked lightly on her neck as he slid his hand up her shirt, leaving a trail of tingles behind it. Her nipples tightened against the silk fabric of her bra, becoming instantly sensitive, feeling almost abraded as his palm cupped one breast.

Tension made her belly taut and her lungs tight, and when his thumb began to rub slow circles around her nipple her muscles locked up hard, as if her body was trying to fight the pleasure. But it wasn't her body doing the fighting; it was her brain.

Sela hadn't had sex since the attack, and before that, it had been about the job. Oh, she'd sometimes taken pleasure from it, if her partner was skilled or considerate, but usually, the sex was all about measuring his response. Getting him worked up for the most intense orgasm of his life so he'd spill more secrets into her brain as he spilled his semen into her body. Usually she was so occupied with making him feel good that she would fake her responses, putting on a show worthy of an Oscar.

Sex on the job had never been about her orgasms. It had been about theirs.

But something about Logan made her curious about his skills and made her want what her feminine instincts said he could give her.

And that scared the crap out of her, because out of all the men she'd screwed for the good of ACRO and the country, this one, with his weapons company and connections to Itor, had the potential to be the baddest of the bad, with a generous topping of evil.

Evil, for sure, because even now, his wicked fingers were sliding beneath the fabric of her bra to her bare breasts, and she couldn't stifle a moan.

"You like that," he murmured against her neck.

"No shit." She spoke softly, mindful of the tent's thin walls.

His chuckle sent an erotic tremor down her body. Slowly, his hand followed, skimming over her ribs to her stomach, until his fingertips were working the buttons on her BDUs. Panic reared up, and she squirmed, but he tugged her close and wedged his thigh between her legs, trapping her, but creating a delicious pressure against her core that settled her down no matter how badly she wanted to get away.

It's just a job. It's just a job. She repeated the mantra in her head and tried to concentrate on giving instead of taking. Boldly, she palmed his neck and pushed his face to her breasts as she dropped her other hand to his ass and squeezed. That fast, it was his turn to groan. He arched into her, grinding that massive erection against her sex.

His mouth did sinful things to her breasts, even through her T-shirt and bra, and she pictured them together with no clothes between them. If he could affect her like this fully dressed and standing up, in a tent, she could only imagine his talents in a real bed, with no clothes and no worries about who might hear them.

His fingers no longer played with her pants' buttons. He tore the fly open and dipped his hand inside. "We don't have time for what I want to do to you," he breathed into her shirt, "but fuck if I'm going to wait another second to touch you."

She didn't have time to say anything. His fingers slipped beneath the lace edge of her panties and found her clit. Sela damn near shouted at the sudden pleasure that crashed into her. The unaccustomed sensation sent her into a fresh panic, and she shoved against Logan's chest, but again, he brought her down with pressure right where she needed it.

"Shh," he whispered, rolling her swollen nub between two fingers. "Just let yourself go."

Oh, God, she wanted to. Wanted him to squeeze harder and rub faster, and *yes,* that was what he was doing now. Once again she remembered that she was supposed to be rubbing and squeezing him, not the other way around. But she ached so badly, and really, what would it hurt to get a little something out of this godforsaken assignment?

She let her head loll back in surrender, and in that instant, Logan growled low in his chest, a male animal taking possession now that the female had given in. Oh, but she hadn't completely rolled over, and even as he pushed two fingers inside her weeping core, she tore open his pants and took his hard cock in her fist.

She'd seen it when he'd come out of the shower, and only just semi-erect, his penis had been impressive. But fully engorged, she couldn't even close her hand around it. A silky drop formed at the tip, and as Logan found a rhythm with his thumb against her clit, she matched it, spreading the moisture over the head of his cock.

"Oh, yeah." His voice was gruff, breathless, and it turned her on like nothing before.

Slow, skilled strokes in and out with his fingers built pressure inside her that threatened to blow out her ears. She cried out when he found her G-spot, and he smiled impishly, went to work with unmerciful flicks of his fingertips over the swollen pillow of nerves.

"Bastard," she moaned. "You're such a . . . ah, yes . . . bastard."

"And don't you forget it." His words came out slurred; he was panting as hard as she was now, his hips thrusting into her grip.

His strokes turned into luscious twists of his thick fingers. Each rotation raked her inner walls, the friction charging her up until her release hovered just out of reach . . . and he knew it. He fucked her with his talented fingers, letting his thumb just barely brush her hypersensitive knot.

Panting and grinding, she arched into him, riding his hand until her orgasm came at her as if it had been fired out of a cannon, hit her hard and knocked her breathless and was so fierce it almost hurt. Her pussy clenched around his fingers, pulling them deep, and damn, she wished his cock was filling her instead. Her chest heaved and her breath snagged in her throat, and she had to sink her teeth into his shoulder to keep from screaming.

His snarled "Yes!" told her he didn't mind the bite.

Though she scarcely had the energy, she locked her knees to keep from sliding into a boneless puddle and increased the speed of her strokes on his shaft. His hand, wet with her juices, joined hers, creating a silky lubricant. Together, they caressed him, up and down his erection, faster, faster . . . until the only sounds in the tent were of his harsh breaths and the soft slide of their hands rubbing his hard flesh.

Logan's head fell back, his teeth bared in ecstasy, the tendons in his neck standing out in stark agony, and wow, he was handsome like that, a perfect male specimen on the verge of pleasure-pain. The sight sent flames licking through her again, but she concentrated on him, needing to get him there . . .

He grabbed her hand and forced her to concentrate her motion on the head of his cock, rubbing gentle circles as he used his fist to take himself the rest of the way—another sight that had her squeezing her thighs together as though she hadn't just had one of the most explosive orgasms of her life.

Another crystal drop formed at the dusky purple tip, and she smoothed her thumb through it, loving how his massive body jerked and how his breath caught. His hand pumped faster, the rim of his fingers meeting hers on every upstroke. Three heartbeats later, he came with a muffled shout, and instantly, his thoughts and memories shot into Sela's brain. Thoughts about . . . how sexy she was, how hot, how he wished his cock was inside her. At the same time, memories washed over the surface of her mind, memories from childhood.

She didn't have time to waste on things that weren't relevant to the present, so before the psychic airwaves shut off as his orgasm waned, she poked around in his brain, looking for recent memories . . . but she ran into what amounted to a virtual wall.

Odd. She'd been trained to detect a mental shield, but this wasn't one of them. Her probes kept pinging back at her, like sonar hitting the metal hull of a ship.

And then the connection was gone, and she was alone inside her head, sifting through images of a young Logan on a playground by himself, and then in a backyard throwing a ball for a mixed-breed mutt.

"That," he rasped, "was really . . ."

"Intense?"

He took in a ragged breath. "I was going to say embarrassing." He looked down at his cock, still in his hand. "We're like fucking teenagers."

"Without the fucking." God, she couldn't believe how fast the flames had built between them . . . they hadn't even made it to the cot, were still propping each other up. She pushed away from him and jerked up her pants, which had ridden down to her thighs. "I, uh, need a bathroom."

Logan didn't meet her gaze as he began to clean himself up with a napkin from his table. "Outside to the right."

"Not worried I'll run away?"

"There's someone outside my tent to keep an eye on you."

Great. That someone had probably heard everything that had gone on in here. She ducked out of the tent, and sure enough, Dax was standing there, a knowing smile on his roundish face. She flipped him off and headed for the portable toilet, but spun around when she was halfway there. She wanted her backpack and the micro-satellite phone inside. Her minute alone in the toilet would give her a chance to send Dev an update.

Quickly, she tore back the tent's flap, but drew up short as she entered. Logan was sitting on the cot. He jerked in surprise, his head whipping up to stare at her. In his hand he held a syringe, the needle poised to enter his shoulder.

"What?" he snapped. "Never seen a diabetic before?"

"I just... ah, I wanted my backpack." She snagged it and ducked out of the tent, heart pounding.

Because whatever Logan was doing in there had nothing to do with insulin.

The substance in the horse-sized syringe was black.

LOGAN DIDN'T GO AFTER SELA. THERE WAS NOWHERE FOR HER to run to anyway, and she was smart enough not to take off into the jungle at night on her own. Besides that, Dax had been waiting outside the tent the whole time, told to not let Sela out of his sight.

He stood and massaged the injection site—he didn't feel pain there but the liquid tended to bubble the skin. He felt the thick, viscous substance seep into the biomechanics in his legs, his right arm, half his brain.

And then the sting began; it always stung the parts of his body that were still human. He closed his eyes and tried to ignore it—and forget the look on Sela's face at the same time.

She knew damned well this wasn't insulin and now he had a third problem, one as big as the two chupacabras.

Sela might be a cryptozoologist, but for all he knew, she could be a spy for the government or a rival research or weapons company. She could even work for Itor, sent here to find out if he'd had success capturing the Unclass 8, which was apparently a chupacabra.

GWC hadn't known what it was—they knew they had something special, but they hadn't known it had a name. And now it was running around the fucking jungle infecting innocent people.

At times like this, he was very glad his father wasn't close enough for Logan to fucking strangle him. Because this was bad. Really fucking horrible.

Three years ago, under his father's orders, GWC captured the chupacabra while on an Amazonian search for undiscovered species. A few weeks ago, when it got loose, Logan's father informed him just how much money GWC would lose if they didn't recapture the beast. Apparently, his father had a contract with Itor Corp, a freelance paramilitary agency.

Logan had his own suspicions about what Itor wanted to do with the Unclass 8—after meeting it face-to-face, he was even more wary. And even though his father and Itor wanted the creature captured and brought back alive, after what happened to Chance, Logan had other plans.

He dialed his father, who answered on the first ring.

"Logan! Did you recapture the Unclass 8 yet?"

He bit back a sharp reply. "No. And the SEAL survivor? Apparently, he was infected by its bite, and now he's turning into that fucking creature."

When his father spoke again, he sounded shaken. "Let me call Itor and see what they want to do."

"I don't really care what they want," Logan said evenly. "I want to kill it. And we need to find a cure for the man who's been infected. We fucking owe him that."

"Don't be hasty. Let me make some calls. In the meantime, find that creature before it does any more harm."

Logan didn't agree to anything, hung the phone up and took a breath. He didn't like thinking about the experiments that had already been performed on the chupacabra, and why. Didn't like thinking about himself as an experiment either, but that's what he was. One giant mishmash of scientific parts that needed a daily injection simply to keep it alive.

None of his men knew what he was and why he was really here—neither would Sela, if he could help it.

It would help if you could keep out of her pants, dumbshit.

He'd have to do some fast talking about what she'd seen. He'd tell her it was a special kind of insulin, GWC's pet project since he was diagnosed as a child. He'd tell her he was their living, breathing, willing experiment.

He almost choked at the "willing" part, remembered waking up and trying to rip the bioware out of his body, forcing the scientists and surgeons to sedate him until he'd healed more fully.

He told himself to cut the shit and continue with his plan—there was too much at stake, too many lives potentially lost to this Unclass 8 for him to sit around feeling sorry for himself.

As he paced the tent, he formulated his next moves. Marlena would stay here, under guard. He'd invite Sela along on the trek to hunt the Unclass 8, where he could keep an eye on her and capture the chupacabra, perhaps with her help and knowledge of the creature. Two birds with one stone.

Now he only had to wait until dawn to burn off the nervous energy that coursed through his body. He could think of a few ways to do so, but all of them involved Sela, and for now he'd stay out of her pants and let her sleep.

Thanks to the bioware, he didn't need much sleep at all, was more machine than man, but still the desire he'd felt coming in Sela's hand earlier was so fucking real he'd almost cried.

There had been nothing mechanical about it.

CHAPTER *Six*

Chance was awake, but no one knew that. The drugs they'd given him had lasted for maybe half an hour before he'd begun to come to, and he'd remained silent. Thinking. Listening to their plans. Feeling their fear.

Trying to figure out what the hell had happened to him.

He wanted to ask the doctor questions, but he didn't want to risk being tranqed again. And so, when one of the docs leaned over him, closing his eyes while he listened to the steady beat of Chance's chest with his stethoscope, Chance stealthily stole a set of keys out of the man's pocket.

It was habit born from a need for survival, and it made him feel better that his mind was still functioning in that mode. He could—and would—escape from this place, get out of the jungle and figure shit out.

And when the doctor left, he planned on doing exactly that. But just then, his senses stirred—his body tensed as he smelled her . . . Marlena. When he turned, there was no one in the tent with him, but he was sure she was close. And even though he was more than slightly freaked by his newfound ability to track with his nose, he breathed in deeply and wondered if she was coming here, to him.

She shouldn't, but he wanted her to.

He wanted to get up. To go find her. He needed to find her—he knew that for sure, although he wasn't clear on the whys of it.

But he was . . . achy. Tired. For the first time in his recovery, he felt like he was falling backward, health-wise.

His body felt like it did when he'd been a teenager with growing pains—and images of Marlena in his arms interspersed with others of the monster flashed in front of his eyes as if he was watching a slide show gone out of control.

He was vaguely aware that he muttered her name, over and over.

Marlena.

Somehow, he was sure she was the only one who could possibly save him now.

SELA FINISHED UP IN THE BATHROOM, A TYPICAL FIELDWORK outhouse constructed of green plastic, complete with a small hand-washing station. She cleaned up with the baby wipes she'd brought, and then checked her backpack to make sure the important item was still safe and hidden. As expected, Logan's men had gone through her backpack and taken her satellite phone, but hidden in the base of the bag, beneath a flap of canvas, was a credit card–thin disposable texting device ACRO had developed. Good. The little item was how she'd contact Dev to let him know when to send in the troops. She definitely didn't want to have to use the backup method—the Triad.

She was connected with ACRO via the Triad, a constant connection to three psychics who took turns monitoring her. They didn't spy, they simply kept apprised of her location and her health, unless she made an active attempt to contact them.

But it was a rather unreliable way to communicate—an agent connected to a Triad could only transmit visuals. No actual speaking, as verbal messages could get garbled or misinterpreted. In addition, the process required no distractions and such intense concentration that it often resulted in a splitting headache.

That idiot Dax pounded on the side of the outhouse. "You drown?"

"Eat me," she snapped, and threw open the door.

"You promise?" He winked. "Because if Logan didn't satisfy you, I'd be glad to help out."

She shook her head and stalked toward Logan's tent. She whipped the flap open just as he was taking a seat at his makeshift desk. "You need better help."

He cocked an eyebrow. "You're awfully demanding for a prisoner."

"An *illegal* prisoner."

His casual shrug told her how he felt about that. Her situation was about as important to him as that of an insect that had been stuck to a fly strip.

Behind her, a man entered carrying a sleeping bag. He tossed it to the floor and ducked out.

Logan leaned back in his chair and kicked his feet onto the desk. "You up for a chupacabra hunt tomorrow?"

She clapped her hands together. "Oh, really? The big boys are going to let the little girl play?"

"You," he said in a husky, low voice that made her insides quiver, "are no little girl." His eyes slid down her body and back up, until he locked gazes with her. "You're all woman, as I think we've established." She didn't have time for a snappy comeback, because he shifted gears with the speed and efficiency of a race car driver. "We could use your expertise during our hunt. What do you say?"

"A *please* would be nice."

A smirk turned up one corner of his sexy mouth. *"Please."*

"Fine. You want my help, you tell me the truth about your *diabetes.* And while you're at it, I'd like the truth about why you're here. I don't buy for a second that you're just out here researching plants."

Logan folded his hands across his abs, drawing her gaze and making her remember how he'd looked when he'd stepped out of the shower, water running in rivulets down his muscular chest to his belly, where his six-pack rippled with every step. She tore her eyes away with a disgusted huff.

"My company does research plants. That's the truth," he said, and she knew he wasn't lying. GWC did have a botany division to study the way plants could be made into weapons, but this particular trip was not a mission to gather daisies.

"And?"

"And we ran into trouble when we found Chance. This creature is obviously dangerous, and we're going to have to capture or kill it before it hurts anyone else."

"Ah. So you're a bunch of humanitarians."

He snorted. "Hardly." He looked up at the roof of the tent for a moment and then dropped his gaze back to her. "Look, you'll probably notice a logo on some of our equipment. I work for a company called Global Weapons Corporation. Ever heard of it?"

"Nope."

"Well, the name says it all. We develop weapons."

"For who?"

"For whoever contracts us."

"So you could be selling weapons to terrorists, then."

He shrugged. "What one person calls terrorism, another calls legitimate offense or defense. It's all in the eye of the beholder."

"You're vile. You might as well be selling anthrax to Al-Qaeda."

She thought she saw a flash of disgust, maybe anger, in his eyes, before he settled down again, and it struck her that maybe he was trying to bait her. Maybe he didn't believe this crap he was spewing. Then again, he ran GWC. Of course he believed it.

"Come on," he drawled. "Even evil corporations like mine have to draw the line somewhere."

"So kidnapping is okay, but anthrax isn't."

"It's all a judgment call." He gestured to a box she hadn't noticed beneath his cot. "Hungry? It's full of MREs. Or you can go to the mess tent. You'll still get MREs, but there are also a few packaged snacks there, plus hot coffee."

She threw down her backpack, a little harder than necessary. This guy was just so . . . frustrating. And hot. And sexy. But mostly irritating as hell. She dug through the box until she found a decent menu—cheese tortellini.

"That's my favorite," he said, as she took a seat across from him at the table. "Of course, the best of crap is still crap."

A laugh burst from her before she could stop it. "That's true." She ripped open the plastic pouch and pulled out the biggest box inside. "Now, why don't you tell me all about your superspecial insulin."

"That's really none of your business."

She poured water from the pitcher on the table into the chemical heater and stuffed it into the box next to the tortellini pouch. "I suppose not, but if you don't tell me, I'm going to assume that you're some kind of drug addict. Or worse."

"Worse?"

"That maybe you're some kind of beast that has to dose every day to keep from turning." She was kidding, but the brief flare of his eyes told her she'd hit on something.

"You realize that sounds crazy."

She was too hungry to wait for her tortellini to heat up any more. Besides, in this heat, it didn't need extra time anyway. She pulled the pouch out of the box and ripped it open. "You have a man in your camp who can turn into a chupacabra," she pointed out, using a plastic spoon to gesture in the direction of the medical tent.

"Touché." He watched her wolf down the tortellini for a moment. "The substance is an experimental insulin. Developed by my company for a unique diabetic condition I developed as a child."

She cocked her head and studied him, unsure what to believe. She didn't know anything about diabetes, and she didn't know enough about experimental medicine to call bullshit on his explanation. He could very well be telling the truth.

"Do you have to watch what you eat?"

He shook his head. "That's the beauty of the whole thing. I take the shot once a day and I can eat whatever I want. The company has been working on a way to make it work for more common types of diabetes."

"Of course, only the wealthy would benefit from this drug, right? No doubt you'd make a fortune off it." His gaze skipped away. "What's the matter?" she taunted. "Prick your conscience?"

When he looked at her again, flames danced in his eyes. "Is that so hard to believe? Maybe, just maybe, I don't like everything that happens inside my company."

A little disoriented by his words, because in her opinion, ethics and big companies often didn't mix, she studied him. "No company is perfect. There are problems with payroll, employees, policies. You can't like everything, right?"

"That's not what I'm talking about, and you know it. And," he said, one dark eyebrow cocking up, "playing dense doesn't suit you."

Oh, she disliked this man—intensely—but she couldn't deny that he surprised her, and that beneath the *corporate slime-coat*, there was a hint of humanity in him, and that didn't sit well with her at all. She liked evil scumbags to be . . . well, evil, with no redeeming qualities. It was so much easier to take them down that way.

"Then why do you work there?" she asked, genuinely curious.

"So I can make sure that some things happen that I *do* like." He poured a cup of Scotch, held the mouth of the bottle over a second cup, but she shook her head. "You can't tell me you agree with everything your colleagues do."

"That's different. I don't own a company."

"I can't police everyone, and I do have others to answer to." Logan took a swig of his drink. "So you've picked my brain. How about you tell me the truth about you. The bug-collecting thing was just dumb."

She had the incredibly childish urge to call him dumb right back. "I work for a small cryptozoological agency in Wisconsin. We're self-funded, so we can't afford many foreign expeditions." This was all easy, because it had been true before she went to ACRO. "And it isn't like the United States isn't crawling with cryptids to study. There's Bigfoot, the Wallowa Lake Monster, the Jersey Devil—"

"Okay, okay, I got it." He'd cut her off, but there was amusement in his voice, as though he were humoring an excited child. And she supposed that was what she sounded like. She might be a skeptic, but she loved the field she worked in.

"Well, anyway, there had been new and urgent reports of sightings in this area. So Marlena and I got permission from Marc, the head of our group, to use up the last of our funding, and we came." She shrugged. "I suppose we should have been more prepared. You know, for people who might kidnap us."

"Guess you won't do that again, huh?" He knocked back the rest of his Scotch. "So how many people are in your group?"

"Eight. We're pretty small."

"Are there a lot of you? In the United States?"

"Cryptozoologists? A few. It's not exactly a respected—or,

some would say, legitimate—branch of science, so working in the field is mostly a labor of love."

"Not much money in it, then?"

She laughed. "None. Like I said, labor of love."

He appeared to consider that for a minute. "Tell you what. You help me catch this creature, and my company will compensate you."

"How much?"

"Say . . . a hundred thousand?"

She nearly choked. "Are you serious?"

"Why not? It's the least I can do for taking you prisoner." He grinned, that devastating one that made her want to jump over the table to get to him. "Besides, if you get paid, you won't do something stupid like try to run away. You'll be working with me. Not against me. And I won't have to hold you against your will."

He was a crafty one. And he would have been right, had she been who she said she was. Still, she'd take the money if she could get it. And she'd hand it right over to the very crypto foundation she'd been talking about. They'd be more than thrilled to get the money. Of course, the trick would be getting it—and the chupa—without tipping the ACRO hat. That's the way Dev wanted it—in and out without anyone ever knowing ACRO had been part of it.

It wouldn't be easy. Not to mention, an exchange of money might get her into a shitload of trouble with Dev. Oh, well. She had to try.

She reached her hand across the table, and Logan took it. "Deal."

They shook. "Deal."

He didn't let go of her. Instead, his thumb swept over her knuckles in long, smooth strokes. Her heart rate doubled, and she started to sweat.

"Logan!" The tent flap whipped open, and Dax burst inside. Logan dropped her hand. "It's Chance. Something's wrong."

Sela and Logan rushed to the medical tent and found Chance lying on the floor, eyes open, pained yet intense.

"What's wrong?" Sela asked, moving toward him. Logan grabbed her arm and yanked her back.

"Fever," the doctor said. Wes, if she remembered right. "He woke up like this."

"Have you been able to examine him?" Sela asked.

"Not much. He . . . growls."

"Let me try."

"No fucking way," Logan said.

Speaking of growling . . .

She shook off his hold and eased close to Chance. His fevered gaze took her in, and as she knelt next to him, his lips peeled back.

"Hey. It's okay. I'm not going to hurt you. We want to find out what's wrong."

His gaze skipped to the men in the room and then back to her. "Marlena . . . "

"She's okay. She's safe. Shep is—"

"No," he growled. "Mine."

She frowned. "What's yours?"

Lightning fast, his hand flew out to grip hers. Behind her, the unmistakable sound of weapons being brought to bear cracked in the air. Her heart went into overdrive as Chance squeezed her hand, his skin so hot it felt blistered.

"Marlena," he rasped. "She's mine. I . . . need her."

Now Sela's heart stopped as a chilling suspicion put a knot in her gut. Gently, she peeled his hand away and stood. She turned to Logan, who lowered his pistol, a silent signal for the other guys to do the same.

"I need to speak to Marlena," she said. "Now."

MARLENA PUSHED THE SCRATCHY BLANKET OFF HER AND STARED into the darkness of the supply tent, where Dax had housed her for the night.

He hadn't handcuffed her, which she was happy about, but there had to be a guard stationed outside the tent. They wouldn't want to risk finding her with Chance again, had no way of knowing that was the last thing she wanted right now.

Didn't matter that her blood ran hot when she thought about him. Her fear was more potent than her lust at the moment.

Sela was on her own with Logan. Truth be told, relief had coursed through Marlena when Logan had her escorted out of his tent.

She'd felt bad when she'd caught the look on Sela's face, knew that her fellow operative was no longer a Seducer for ACRO and had not wanted to have to work that particular angle for this mission. But there was no way Marlena would be able to seduce anyone right now.

Well, except for Chance—she could apparently do that with no problem. Or was it he who seduced her? She couldn't be sure now. It happened so fast, like some kind of steamy jungle porno, a prison theme complete with handcuffs.

She shook her head to clear it, realized she needed to steel herself for what lay ahead. The mission had changed, and she would change to accommodate it.

The rational, goal-based part of her brain told her that discovering Chance was a chupacabra was pretty damned big news.

And still, she couldn't wrap her mind around what had happened, and she'd seen some crazy things in her days with ACRO. But that handsome man changing into a beastly, uncontrollable killer...

Something the wild chupacabra had done to him must have been responsible for Chance's condition. Maybe its bite? Or a scratch? Panic made breathing difficult as she replayed every moment of contact with him. She didn't think he'd bitten her, or scratched her, or marked her in any way. At least, not physically. He'd definitely marked her mentally, and she couldn't say whether that was a good or bad thing.

Physically... God, she needed a full-length mirror so she could check. Maybe he could make her into one just through his saliva, in which case, she was most definitely screwed.

She stared down at her hands as though they were already clawed, and wished she could've gotten Sela alone to ask her about this.

She also wished she understood why she wasn't head-over-heels, crying-into-her-pillow, sure-her-life-was-over in love with Chance. She was sure the curse wasn't broken, and for a moment she considered sleeping with Shep to test that theory.

Maybe he had more intel than he knew, she attempted to justify to herself; it didn't work.

And she knew what a new part of her mission needed to be—bringing Chance safely into ACRO without hurting him or having him hurt anyone else.

As humanely as possible, Dev's voice echoed in her mind, something she'd heard a thousand times before when he spoke to ACRO's Convincers. She'd never actually been privy to the Convincing part, although she'd had some training in that area.

She'd definitely have to grab some more alone time with Chance. And try to keep him from turning into a chupacabra. And try to forget that maybe he could actually fall in love with her.

As strange butterflies flittered in her stomach at the possibility, she tried to push the thought of love out of her mind.

Love was not part of the mission.

Unless, of course, you were an ACRO agent, and then it seemed to be par for the course.

And you are an ACRO agent now.

She curled into a ball and tried to forget she'd had sex with a man who'd turned into a monster, even as she continued to think about why she wasn't head over heels in love with him. And she wasn't sure how much time passed before she heard "Marlena?"

It was Sela's voice floating through the darkness, and Marlena's stomach dropped, because maybe she wasn't ready to talk about it at all.

"Is everything okay?" Marlena managed to make her voice sound normal, watched as Sela made her way toward the cot with a small lantern.

She set it on a crate as she sat down on the end of the cot. "There's a problem. With Chance."

"Did he . . . change again?"

Sela chewed her lip. "No, nothing like that. He's running a fever. I don't know if the transition was just really hard on him. I mean, God, there's no data on what happens to someone when they're bitten by a chupacabra and become one, you know. But you might be able to help."

Marlena sat up. "What do you think I can do for him?"

"Can you tell me exactly what happened when you and Chance were together? Even if it seems insignificant, it might help. He tried to hurt Shep and Dax and anyone else who got too close, but he wouldn't let go of you. It was like he was protecting you."

"Shep handcuffed me to the bunk and Chance was trying to escape. We, ah, talked. And I felt . . . funny, in his presence."

"Funny? Like sick?" Sela looked concerned.

"No, not like that. I was . . . turned on."

Sela cocked her head to the side but didn't say anything and Marlena continued. "He was able to break the metal chain without much effort—he seemed as surprised as I was by that. And one minute we were talking and the next . . . he was on me. Telling me my scent was driving him crazy. And he . . . he wanted sex. I had no way of stopping him. And I didn't want to. It was like I had no control. My hormones went wild." She stopped, her face hot with embarrassment. "So I had sex with him, then Shep came in and yelled at Chance to move away from me. And that's when he turned."

Sela pressed her lips into a grim line. When she spoke next, her voice was deadly serious. "Marlena, we have a problem."

"I know. I'm probably a chupacabra now, just like Chance," she babbled miserably, but Sela put a hand on her arm.

"We'll test you for sure, but that's not the problem I'm talking about."

CHAPTER
Seven

Sela stood there like a dope, trying to figure out a gentle way to break her theory to Marlena.

"Marlena, you're sure you had sex with him? It wasn't a dream or hallucination or anything?"

The other woman swallowed. "I did."

God, the courage it must have taken for her to admit that she'd screwed a beast.

Then again, Sela had fucked her share of monsters in her time too. Sure, her monsters had been fully human, but that only made them more frightening. It was harder to see the claws coming at you when the owner wore clothes and a smile.

Sela took a deep breath. "How far did you get in the book I gave you to read?"

Marlena frowned. "*Chupacabra: Myth No More*? Not very far. I paid more attention to the files you told me to study, since you said the book was fiction."

Fiction. Sela still wanted to believe that Grady was full of shit, but given what she'd learned over the last few hours, she had to at least consider the possibility that his accounts were true.

"Yeah, I said it was fiction. But if it's not . . . " Sela swallowed dryly. "You're probably aware of the fact that some species of animals mate for life. When their mate is taken away or is killed, the survivors sometimes exhibit very pronounced physical reactions. They can become agitated, ill. They can even die."

"That's very sad," Marlena said, "but what does this have to do with anything?"

"Chance is sick." Sela's throat felt tight. This was seriously awkward. "He's asked for you, and he . . . Well, he's very possessive. We don't know this for sure, but in his book, Grady says that chupacabras appear to mate for life, so if he's bonded with you . . . " She trailed off as Marlena paled.

"Oh, God." She covered her mouth and turned away. For a moment, Sela thought the other woman would break down. But shockingly, a couple of heartbeats later, she turned back, chin set in a stubborn line. "You said he's sick."

Sela nodded. "Like I said, it's just a theory—"

"Take me to him."

"What? No. Marlena, if I'm wrong—hell, if I'm *right,* it's a risk I'm not willing to take."

"It's my risk, and I'm willing."

"This isn't necessary." Shooting Marlena a meaningful look, Sela put emphasis on the last word, wanting her to realize that what Marlena was asking her to do went beyond ACRO duties.

"We're here to study chupacabras, right?" Marlena said loudly, for the benefit of anyone listening outside the tent. "So let me do my job."

Damn her. She was using their cover to do something Dev would no way approve of. Why was she so adamant? Sela ran her hands through her hair and froze as a horrible thought popped into her mind. If Marlena was infected, she might very well feel the mate bond. "How are you feeling? Right now."

"Annoyed. If he's sick, and I can help, I want to do it."

"I mean, are you feeling a *need* to go to him? A primal pull? Or is this just concern?"

Marlena appeared to consider Sela's question. "Concern. Why?"

"You sure?"

"Yes."

Relief flooded her. Maybe Marlena wasn't infected. "We just need to get you tested."

"Not until I see Chance."

"That's not a good idea—"

"I don't care." Marlena lowered her voice and leaned toward Sela. "I need to get close to him. And we need to get him into ACRO. You know that."

True. And if they could enlist his help, they could get him away from GWC and Itor. Chance was now very valuable to almost anyone who knew about him. The healing abilities Logan mentioned would make him a gold mine for medical researchers; his ability to shift, aggressiveness and killing abilities would make him a major find for weapons developers—and pretty much every scientist on the planet would give a limb to study him.

"Okay. But be careful. I'm going to take saliva, blood, tissue and hair samples and get as much information logged as possible to take back to ACRO, just in case something goes wrong and we can't bring in Chance or the chupacabra."

Marlena moved back and said loudly, "I want to go to him. Now."

Sela cursed and threw open the tent flap. A few feet away, Logan waited, and when he turned, she saw in his expression that he'd heard everything they'd wanted him to hear.

"I don't like it," he said flatly.

"I don't either. But it can't hurt to just let them see each other and go from there." Sela glanced at the medical tent and back at Logan. "Would you rather have him die?"

"You really think it could come to that?"

"I don't know. But the thing is, Marlena has already been with Chance. If he was going to hurt her, he could have done it earlier."

Finally, Logan nodded, and Sela called for Marlena. They walked to the medical tent, and although Marlena's hand shook, she opened the wood-framed door and entered without hesitation. Almost instantly, Chance's entire body seemed to relax, and when he saw Marlena, he simply closed his eyes, as though now that she was here, they were both safe.

"Marlena," Sela whispered, catching her by the arm. "I need you to keep track of how he's feeling. We need to know if his fever breaks, or if anything else unusual happens, okay?"

Marlena nodded.

"Also," Sela added, "keep in mind that in most animal relationships, especially in bond-mate relationships, the female holds the power."

Marlena gave her a startled, confused look, but then shrugged and said, "You'll leave us alone?"

"No," Logan said. "There will be guards right outside, and I'm going to have Wes come in hourly to examine Chance."

Sela cleared her throat. "I want some tests run. I want to know if he can transmit any kind of virus through a bite while he's, ah, in human form."

Logan nodded. "You got it. Chance, will you let us do some tests?"

"Yeah," he croaked.

Sela and Logan headed back to his tent. "You sure she'll be okay?" Logan asked, and Sela wished she could say yes.

"I'm a little surprised at your concern," Sela said, as they ducked inside.

He rounded on her. "My order put her inside with him in the first place. He attacked her, forced himself on her and could have done much worse. Now I've left her in that situation again. So yeah, go figure, I'm a little concerned."

She held up her hands in surrender. "Okay, okay. Sorry. Didn't mean to offend you."

Cursing, he reached for his bottle of Scotch. "Ah, hell. Can't blame you for wondering. We did take you captive." He held up a cup. "Want one?"

"Damn straight."

He smiled, the one that took away her breath. He splashed a couple of fingers of Scotch into two cups, handed her one, and then held up his own in toast. "To you and Marlena, the most dedicated cryptozoologists I've ever met."

"The only ones you've ever met," she muttered wryly, and tapped her cup against his.

"Good point."

They downed their shots, and silence fell in the tent. "Well, what now?" she asked.

"I think," he murmured, "it's time for bed. We have to get an early start."

Her mouth went dry, and all she could do was nod.

"Good. It's settled." He climbed onto the cot and rolled toward the tent wall. "You get the floor."

CHANCE WAS LYING ON THE COT, HOOKED UP TO AN IV, AND HE looked . . . pale. Sick. But infinitely more relaxed the closer Marlena got to him.

She was vaguely aware of the door closing, of Sela and Logan and everyone else leaving her alone in the tent.

Suddenly, her heart beat faster. The air changed, her body warmed, her nipples hardened. She was completely and utterly turned on by Chance, despite the fact that he'd morphed into a chupacabra in front of her mere hours ago.

But now he was all man. A gorgeous, albeit tired-looking,

man—one she was both frightened of and drawn to, judging by the fact that she was now kneeling next to his cot, taking his hand. Staring down at the tanned fingers twined with hers.

But there was still none of the overwhelming, head-over-heels-in-love feeling she normally got after sleeping with a man. No, this was pure and simple lust.

Apparently, *this* was normal.

Listen to yourself, Marlena. There's nothing normal about any of this.

"You're afraid of me," Chance said, his voice gruff. She turned her gaze from their joined hands toward his face. His eyes were bright and he appeared to have suffered no ill effects from the massive doses of tranquilizers they'd pumped into him . . . or from changing into a chupacabra.

How much he knew—remembered—that was another story.

We don't know this for sure, but in his book, Grady says that chupacabras appear to mate for life, so if he's bonded with you . . .

If he'd bonded with her and she left him . . . My God.

She needed to focus on the mission. Keeping Chance calm. Let Sela figure out what the hell they would do next. "Are you in pain?" she asked, ignoring what he'd said about her being afraid.

He shook his head slowly. "Whatever was happening, it's better now. Since you walked in." He paused. "What the hell happened, Marlena?"

"You don't remember?"

"Bits and pieces. Like a dream." He made a noise in his chest, something like a purr, but as his expression hardened, it turned into a growl. "Or a nightmare." He shoved himself onto one elbow. "What did I do? And why do I want you so much?"

When she didn't answer, because how was she supposed to say that he'd jumped on her, screwed her and then shifted into a beast, he gripped her hand tighter.

"We were talking—"

"I remember that," he broke in. "Get to the part where . . . I think we fucked."

"We did. And then Shep came in, and you went crazy."

"Why?" he said quietly, his voice low and deadly. "What did they do to me? What did *you* do to me?"

"You think *I* did something to you?"

"Why else would I act like that? I'm not in the habit of fucking strange women or attacking people at random."

"Go to hell." She shoved away from him. "I'm not in the habit of fucking strangers either, and how conveniently you forget that I was chained to a damned bed, while you were loose." She was supposed to be keeping him calm, but fuck that. Since the moment she and Sela had been captured, she'd lost all control, and it was time to take some back.

THERE WAS SOMETHING MARLENA WASN'T TELLING HIM. HELL, there was something they were all keeping from him—Chance could see it in their eyes. The careful way they moved around him. The way they hustled Marlena in to him when he'd demanded her, even though he was a fucking prisoner.

He didn't know much, only that his aches and pains went away and all he wanted to do was be with her.

They had to have drugged him. This was a trick.

She wasn't acting like this was a trick, though, and what had she said about being chained to a bed?

His mind worked furiously, trying to scrape together memories that were way too fluid. It was like trying to ladle soup with a slotted spoon.

He remembered needing her like he needed air. He'd had to mate with her, make her his no matter what . . .

No matter what. Mate. *So . . . animalistic.*

His gut turned over as fresh memories slapped his brain. Even if these people had drugged him with some sort of crazy libido drug, Marlena hadn't been part of it. He remembered the terror on her face when he . . . Oh, Jesus.

His hands shook as he scrubbed them over his face as if that would scrub away the reality of what had happened. "Shit," he breathed. "God, Marlena, I'm sorry." Sorry? That was lame. And if her glare was any indication, she thought so too.

"You'd better be sorry for accusing me of drugging you or some shit," she snapped, and then softened her tone. "But don't be sorry about the rest."

He blinked at that. "I attacked you. I remember—"

"I didn't fight you, did I?"

His fists clenched, the way they had around her wrists as he held her for his thrusts. A wave of both heat and nausea rolled over him. "I didn't give you much choice."

"I could have screamed."

True. He hadn't gagged her or anything. *Excellent. Good to know some measure of civility had tempered the caveman instincts.* "Why did you let me do that to you?"

Marlena rolled her bottom lip between her teeth, drawing his attention to her mouth. If she'd just move closer . . . "I don't know."

"Maybe they drugged you too."

"We weren't drugged," she said, and as though she'd heard his stray thought about moving closer, she took a couple of steps, bringing with her the heady scent of aroused female.

"We had to have been."

Her gaze sharpened, and her scent turned bitter. "Why? Because you couldn't possibly want to have sex with me without the aid of chemicals?"

A low growl erupted in his chest, surprising him as much as what came out of his mouth. "You're mine. Trust me, I want to fuck you ten ways from Sunday." He cursed, punched his pillow so hard it popped and feathers exploded from the end. "Dammit! Goddammit! I don't know where that came from. I don't know what I'm feeling, I don't know why I'm feeling it. And why the *ever-loving fuck* can I smell every change in your moods?"

Suddenly, her hands were on his shoulders, and she was pushing him back down flat on the cot. For some reason, he calmed instantly, as though she were pulling all his strings and he liked it.

"Calm down, Chance," she whispered. "Please. You're going to attract the guards." Her fingers tightened, digging into his skin, and he nearly groaned from the sheer pleasure of being touched. "I know you're frustrated and confused."

"You need to get away from me," he said, even as he gripped her waist and pulled her down on top of him. "*Get. Away.*" The words were there, but he was holding her so tight she couldn't leave if she wanted to. His rational mind screamed at him to get rid of her, but his body and instincts beat the fuck out of his thoughts.

"Get away, or what?" she challenged, and he pressed his hips into her, his rock-hard cock showing her exactly what. "Oh, no." She shook her head. "You took all control from me earlier. I'm going to take it back on my terms. So let go. *Now.*"

For some crazy reason, he did. He obeyed like a fucking pussy-whipped loser. Oh, he still wanted her, wanted to claim her, mark her, fill her with his seed. But she was absolutely right—she had control here.

"Marlena, look, I don't understand it, but I need you. I don't want you to go. I just . . ."

"Shh." She slid her palm over his chest and down his abs. And then lower still as he held his breath and watched helplessly.

He could stop her now, tell her he wasn't sure this was the best idea.

He didn't trust his voice, but his body had already betrayed him. Badly. And when she ripped open his pants and put her hand around his hard cock—man, oh fucking man, he hoped she wouldn't stop.

She stroked him, up and down, and his hips began to rock to the rhythm she set.

"I don't understand any of this either," she said. "I was afraid of you when I first came in here. I admit it. I nearly ran out. But I'm not anymore."

"You should be, but holy shit, keep doing that."

A little smile tilted up the corner of her mouth, as she moved her other hand between his legs to caress his balls. When she rubbed a finger along his perineum, he swore he saw stars.

"Marlena . . . don't stop, okay?" he breathed, and Christ, no one had better interrupt them or he'd kill— "Fuck. Stop. I can't—"

She shut him up with a finger against his lips. "You can. We'll figure out what's going on afterward. But right now, we're doing this."

Well. Okay. Far be it from him to argue with his mate.

Mate?

His woman. Yeah. His woman.

Fuck. Whatever. She was his, and like she said, they'd figure out the rest later.

MARLENA BENT AND PRESSED HER LIPS TO CHANCE'S, DETERmined to prove that she was still in control . . . of her heart, at least, if not her body.

The kiss was electric, made her gasp into his mouth. Within seconds, she was crawling onto him. His hands slid along her back, holding her, pulling her closer to him, kissing her like he needed that to live. The kisses intensified, his tongue dueling with hers, and her body responded to his touch, despite hearing the chains clanking . . . and the fact that he was dangerous as hell in so many ways.

His hands drifted down to cup her ass through her BDUs, and he rocked her against him as his tongue teased hers. She felt the strength in his body surge as he locked a leg over hers as if to keep her from leaving.

There was no chance of that, not when his hand moved to caress her breast between their bodies, his fingers brushing her nipple. Her own hands traveled as well, caressing his shoulders, his biceps. She did a slow grind of her hips against his as he palmed the back of her neck, pulled her mouth to his and kissed her until she could barely breathe. When he finally let her up for air, his voice was thick as he murmured in her ear, "I want you so badly . . . but I don't want to hurt you."

She didn't bother telling him that he'd hurt her anyway. It was either a suicide mission or a leap of faith.

He shifted so they were on their sides. He pushed the low-slung BDUs off her hips impatiently and stroked a finger along her slick folds, making her cry out softly. The pad of his thumb found her clit as he slid a finger inside her, slowly driving her mad as he tongued her nipple through her already wet T-shirt, making the soft cotton hot against her skin.

"Chance . . . please . . . yes."

He pulled her T-shirt up with his teeth and she impatiently tugged it over her head.

The restraints weren't holding him back at all. His hands were working their magic as he spread her legs, told her, "Wanna make you come so hard, baby . . . make you feel so good you can't stand it."

With her job as a Seducer, it was never about her pleasure. Couldn't be. But this . . . this was completely different.

She wanted to know if lightning could really strike twice.

She wanted to climax in his arms, from his fingers, his tongue . . . his cock. And she told him so, whispered it in his ear and watched him still at her words and then give her a smile rife with desire.

"I'll do everything you want, honey. As many times as you can stand it," he promised as he took her pants down and let her kick them off, leaving her naked next to him. "Fuck, you're beautiful."

She blushed like it was the first time she'd been told that and looked up at him. The man was beautiful in his own right.

"Come on up here," he urged, tugging at her hips.

On the small cot, she straddled his face with her thighs on either side and let him pull her sex to his mouth. She swallowed a cry yet couldn't help but let the moans spill out as he licked and sucked her, holding her in place as she rubbed against his face wantonly. His tongue worked the swollen nub of nerves relentlessly until she couldn't hold back any longer.

She fell forward, clinging to the end of the cot because she had no balance left as the first orgasm rolled through her. He didn't stop, though, held her to him as he pleasured her through two more climaxes in quick succession.

When she climbed off him, her legs were trembling. Chance hooked his arm around her thigh and pulled her close. "I'm not done with you yet."

If she had any kind of self-control, she would quit while she was ahead and leave with beautiful memories of a man who'd actually still wanted her when she left him.

Since she found herself on top of him again, she guessed the self-control thing had gone out the window. Her sex cradled his arousal and Chance traced a nipple with his finger.

"Come on, Marlena, let me in," he growled, and she lowered herself onto him, slowly let his girth fill her, inch by inch.

She'd been taught to compliment men on their size, but she wouldn't have to pretend with Chance—he was big and thick, his cock heavy with need.

He was trapped by the chains and still he was somehow in charge, rocking his hips up hard, thrusting into her until she was biting back a scream. Her belly tightened and she forced herself to look him in the eyes, to see his lust-filled gaze for her as he started to orgasm—his pace sped up and her own climax tore through her, a rapid-fire, exquisite release she rode as long as she could.

SELA HAD GRUMBLED ABOUT THE FLOOR, BUT SHE'D FALLEN asleep nearly immediately. Once Logan saw she was dead to the world, he'd picked her up and placed her on his cot.

She'd immediately curled up, hugging his pillow tightly.

He liked that she seemed comfortable out here in the middle of nowhere. And he liked her in his bed.

Idiot.

He turned to his laptop to check his emails, scanned the unnecessary ones his assistant would deal with and opened the one from his sister instead.

Caroline was twenty years old, a product of Dad's second marriage. But Logan never thought of her as a half sister, because the two of them were so much alike. Even though fifteen years separated them, he'd always been extremely protective of her.

He'd always spoiled the shit out of her as well.

She was in college in the States—Virginia. She was beautiful and brilliant and kept telling him she wanted in on the family business.

He'd do anything in his power to keep her out of it.

Her email was full of talk of parties and classes and fun and he was smiling as he read. He made a mental note to wire her more money, just in case, and then he closed his laptop.

Leaning back in his chair, he thought about what Sela had accused him of earlier. Of selling weapons to terrorists.

Thought of how he hadn't taken an interest in what GWC did until they implanted their stamp inside his body and he became their personal Frankenstein's monster.

The more he thought about it, the more he knew killing the chupacabra was the right thing to do. Fuck the contracts and the money, fuck it all. GWC had to start being responsible for its actions. They couldn't continue selling weaponry to anyone with a big enough checkbook, not in today's world.

But what to do about Chance?

GWC could try to develop a drug to reverse the infection, but that could take years. For a minute, Logan wondered if the bioware could be of any help, if they replaced part of Chance's brain with the metal and steel and wires, if that would stop him from changing. Or if the infection was too widespread. If eventually Chance would no longer be Chance at all.

Logan realized he wasn't ready to go there yet.

Restless, he rose and left Sela sleeping to grab some coffee. Dax was waiting outside, watching Chance's tent. Close enough to get there fast if he heard screams, but far enough away that he could survey the entire camp for enemies. Or chupas.

"I have Shep on patrol. Marlena's okay," Dax said in a low voice when Logan got closer.

Translation: Chance had retained human form and Marlena was still alive.

Logan nodded. "Sela's sleeping. I'll stay here for a few—you take a break."

Dax nodded, ambled off toward the mess tent. Logan moved next to Chance's tent, closer than Dax had been. He needed to check for himself that everything was okay in there, because his conscience was killing him. If he hadn't ordered Marlena locked up with Chance in the first place . . .

It's not like you knew what Chance would turn into.

It was then he realized that Chance would no doubt have questions about what happened. Logan and Sela had worked so fast to get Marlena to him that neither of them prepped her for what to tell Chance about his . . . transformation.

Shit. He put his ear close to the flapped window, hoping to get some insight into what they were talking about.

And then he realized that Chance and Marlena weren't talking.

With the faint light from a lantern shining inside, he could make out two shadows moving on the other side of the canvas.

He stood frozen as a woman's shape moved up and down, pictured Chance beneath her, and his own cock hardened as he pictured Sela riding him like that.

"Fuck, Marlena . . . that's it . . . yeah, baby." Chance's hoarse voice leaked out of the tent, and Logan took a drink of coffee and scalded his tongue.

He spit it out and wiped a hand across his mouth, knowing he should leave. But he was transfixed by the sounds, by the way Marlena wasn't worrying about what Chance had become, that he could change into a monster at any moment.

No, she was treating him like a red-blooded man.

A rustle drew his attention to the other side of the tent and suddenly he realized he wasn't alone anymore. Hadn't been for a few minutes, based on the look in Sela's eyes.

She was as mesmerized as he was. Even in the moonlight, he could see the flush on her face, the way her lips parted slightly, and his gaze held hers even as Marlena's soft cries filled the air around them.

His cock strained his BDUs and he wished he could cross the distance between them, take her on the soft jungle ground . . . forget about everything else.

What would Sela do if she knew what was really inside Logan? Could she accept it as easily as she'd accepted the existence of the chupacabra? Would he become merely another object to study—or something more?

"Oh, God, Chance, yes!" Marlena's voice rose and then was followed by a long, low moan. Logan clenched his fist so hard the paper coffee cup crumpled and hot liquid spread over his hand and arm.

That brought him back to reality fast.

Sela rushed over to him, took his hand, wiped away the liquid with the bottom of her shirt. "Are you burned?"

He snatched his hand away, because no, he wasn't burned. That hand would need to be chopped off to not work, and even then he would barely feel pain beyond skin level. "It's fine."

He knew his cheeks were as red as hers—lust and embarrassment. He mentally berated himself for listening to something so private. For getting caught. For having feelings.

"I was . . . just checking." Sela motioned toward Chance's tent.

"If you leave the tent again, I'll handcuff you to the bed," he growled, although the image of Sela handcuffed anywhere for his pleasure made him grow even harder.

As if she knew, she looked pointedly between his legs. Smiled. Then turned and walked back to his tent, shooting her middle finger up in the air as she went.

He'd definitely wait outside with Dax until morning light. There was no way he'd trust himself alone with Sela right now.

CHAPTER *eight*

Sela woke to the sound of monkeys screeching and jungle birds squawking. The other noises, those of a camp gearing up for the day, pierced her sleepy fog. The smell of coffee jerked her right out of it.

Yawning, she sat up. And then felt her cheeks heat at the memory of last night. She'd awakened when Logan exited the tent. Curious, and wanting to check on Marlena anyway, she'd snuck out behind him, slipping into the shadows to follow.

She'd stopped breathing when she saw him behind the medical tent, his body taut, his broad shoulders rising and falling with each breath. Butterflies flitted in her belly at the memory, at the sounds of sex from within that had held him so rapt.

Then he'd turned, his eyes locking with hers. God, that had been embarrassing. Because truth be told, she'd been listening too. Listening, and picturing. Except the pictures that formed in her head had been of her and Logan, and what was up with that? She hated him. Who *wanted* to have sex with someone they hated?

My mother's daughter, that's who.

Swearing softly, she swung her legs over the edge of the cot. She'd come back to the tent and collapsed, and at some point someone had removed her boots, which sat in a neat row beside the bed. Still groggy, she shook them in case some poisonous creepy-crawly had taken up residence, shoved her feet into them, and laced them up with fingers that were swollen from the heat and humidity.

Man, she hated the jungle.

She stood. First, coffee. Next, she needed to talk to Marlena. Then a shower.

Dragging her hands through her hair, she exited the tent. GWC people bustled around the grounds, and heavily armed security guys patrolled the outskirts. There was no sign of Logan or his shadow, Dax, so she headed for the medical tent, where, as luck would have it, Marlena was standing outside. As always, she looked like she'd stepped out of a magazine. Sure, her hair was a little frizzy, and she wore no makeup, but that only gave her a casual beauty, like someone had dropped a model into a jungle.

"Hey," she said quietly. "You okay?"

Marlena nodded. "I was just going to get something to eat."

"Chance is all right with you being away from him?"

Marlena chewed on her lower lip for a second. "We haven't really talked much. He told me to get some breakfast, and I didn't argue. I guess he's okay."

Huh. So lots of hot sex, but no talk? Sela gestured for the other woman to follow, and they headed to the mess tent.

After loading trays with eggs, pancakes and coffee, they sat at one of the empty tables.

"So," Sela began in a hushed voice, "how is Chance? How are *you*? Really."

Marlena ran one manicured nail around the rim of her coffee cup. "Chance is better. Fever is gone."

"And?" Sela prompted when Marlena didn't continue.

"And I'm fine too."

Well, that was pretty evasive. Maybe she was embarrassed about having sex with Chance after learning what he was. If so, Sela wasn't going to mention last night. Marlena would be mortified to know that they'd been heard.

"Have you learned anything useful?" Sela paused as a GWC guy walked past. "Does Chance know what happened to him?"

"He doesn't remember much. I don't think he knows what he turns into."

Sela sipped her coffee. "Is he wondering why he's being kept chained?"

"He thinks he's a prisoner. But he doesn't know why or who these people are." Marlena cut a bite-sized chunk of pancake. "Do you believe that GWC didn't know what Chance was before last night?"

"I do. I think they were keeping him to get information about the creature that attacked him. But now he's turned into something more valuable."

Marlena chewed and swallowed. "Do you know what they plan to do to him?"

Sela wouldn't put it past a company like GWC to experiment on him until there wasn't much left. The ACRO shape-shifter, Ulrika, had been through exactly that with Itor; she still had post-traumatic issues now and then.

Chance was in a very precarious position right now. GWC wouldn't let him go—and even if they did, ACRO would snatch him up. He was too dangerous to be let loose upon the world. At least ACRO would give him a shot at a normal life. GWC would either take him to some lab and keep him for the rest of his life, or they'd kill him.

And where that left Marlena was a huge, and awful, question. If GWC kept Chance, and if he'd truly bonded to Marlena, they'd have to take her too. The thought sent a chill up Sela's spine. It was more important than ever to get into Logan's head and find out what they intended to do.

Sela gave Marlena a reassuring smile she didn't feel. "I don't think they've had time to make plans for him yet. Right now they're after the chupacabra, so as long as they're focused on that, Chance won't be a priority."

Marlena nodded, but she looked understandably troubled. "What about you? Did Logan reveal anything?"

Sela jabbed her fork into her eggs. "Not much." Sela sighed. "But he did admit that they are looking for the chupacabra. He said it's because of Chance, that they didn't know about it before then, but we know that's a lie." She took a bite of the eggs and grimaced. Powdered. Bleh.

"He's still sticking to the plant researcher story?"

"Well, he did cop to what his company does."

Marlena raised a delicate eyebrow. "Really?"

"Yep. He also said he'll pay us a hundred grand to help him catch the creature."

A second eyebrow joined the first. "Wow. That explains why no one is watching me like a hawk today."

Sela nodded. "He thinks that if we're partners, we won't take off or sabotage his efforts or something." No doubt they *were* being watched—just more covertly.

"Excellent." Marlena sipped her coffee, her expression thoughtful. "I guess we did a good job making him believe we wanted to escape."

"And now he'll buy our reasons for staying and cooperating."

Marlena casually looked around once more. "Did you get anything out of Logan's head?"

Basically, Marlena was asking if Sela had fucked him. "No." Which wasn't exactly a lie. Sela had neither fucked him nor gotten any useful information during his orgasm—a fact that still bothered her.

"So what's the plan for today?" Marlena asked.

Sela finished up her last bite of eggs. "We're going hunting. I think Logan will be okay with you staying behind." She stood. "You *are* okay with staying behind, aren't you? I don't want to put you in a bad situation with Chance if you aren't comfortable."

"I'll be fine."

"Okay, then see what else you can get out of Chance. Things he might have overheard, anything that might be important. And if you get the opportunity, poke around the camp."

Marlena nodded. "When will you be back?"

"By nightfall, I'm sure. Keep an eye on things. And don't tell Chance more than you have to. I'd rather be the one to tell him what's going on with him, and I don't want to do that until we get all the test results." She squeezed Marlena's shoulder, an inadequate gesture of comfort. "And be careful."

"You too."

Sela headed back outside, but on the way to Logan's tent, she caught sight of something large and square covered by a tarp. Curious, she moved toward it. No one was looking, so she lifted the corner—

A hand clamped down on her wrist. "Nosy, are we?" Logan's voice was a harsh growl in her ear.

"I didn't know being curious was a crime in the police state of Loganland."

When she didn't drop the tarp, he squeezed her wrist until she was forced to, but not before she caught a glimpse of what was beneath. A cage.

"It's just equipment. Nothing interesting." He released her, and she rubbed her wrist even though it didn't hurt. "We're leaving in half an hour, so you best get ready to go."

"I'd like to shower."

"There are towels in the bin next to each stall. And be quick. We can't waste water."

"I didn't notice you being all that speedy with your shower."

He grinned. "I'm the boss. It's my water."

"And if I want to . . . *take my time*?"

His grin grew wicked. "If you find yourself in that kind of need, I can help you out—there's no reason to be in the shower."

She'd always hated flirting with the enemy, but she was actually enjoying the oral foreplay between her and Logan.

"How generous of you to offer," she said lightly.

"All in the name of conservation, babe."

Snorting, she moved off. Quickly, she gathered her clothes, took her shower, and by the time she was finished packing her rucksack, the team was ready to go. Before she forgot, she tucked her tiny texting device into her pocket—once they found the chupacabra, she'd update Dev on their situation.

They headed out into the jungle. Logan, Dax, two men who appeared to be scientist types, and half a dozen men armed with both deadly and dart weapons. Logan led the way, and he insisted that she follow directly behind, sandwiched between him and Dax.

"I'm not worried about you taking off," he'd said, as he handed her a dart gun. "I just want to keep you safe."

Like she was some delicate flower. Then again, he didn't know she'd been trained by ACRO to near–special operations standards. Annoyingly enough, she got the feeling that even if he were aware of her background, he'd still treat her like she was a damned glass figurine.

Still, she supposed that was a good thing, because if he was protecting her, he wouldn't be thinking about killing her.

IF SELA NEVER SAW A JUNGLE AGAIN, SHE'D DIE HAPPY. AFTER this mission, she doubted she'd even watch Animal Planet.

The GWC team had been combing the jungle for two hours and hadn't found so much as a footprint. Lots of mosquitoes and biting flies, but no sign of the chupacabra.

Now, as they approached the site where the SEAL team massacre had taken place, Sela's pulse picked up. Shoving through a tangle of branches and vines, she moved out of formation without waiting for King Logan's permission. He uttered a raw curse, but she ignored him as she knelt next to a log that had been clawed apart by something very large. All around, giant splinters of wood littered the ground, and embedded deep in one was the hard outer shell from a claw.

"Oh, excellent." She reached into her pack for pliers and a specimen bag.

Logan peered down at the six-inch-long black claw. "Nasty thing, isn't it?"

Nasty was right. Those claws had gone through the hard wood like it was Styrofoam. The SEALs hadn't had a chance.

"Where did you track the creature after you found Chance?" she asked, and Logan gestured to the west.

"We found the remains of a deer about two miles from here, and another mile away, we found a monkey with two holes in its throat. Drained of blood."

Carefully, she used the pliers to work the claw from the wood. "Did you bag it?"

"It's on ice at the camp."

She dropped the claw into the baggie and straightened. "Why the hell didn't you tell me that sooner? I could have studied it last night."

"You were busy last night," he drawled, and Dax snickered.

Glaring, she dabbed sweat from her forehead with the back of her hand. "I hate you both."

For some reason, that made them smile. Infants.

Logan hefted his rifle, his incredible biceps bunching and flexing beneath tan skin. "We'll head to where we found the monkey and start tracking from there."

"Wait." She nodded at the clawed log. "Have you found anything else like this? Trees, branches, logs?"

"Yeah, why?"

She took in the surroundings, the sun-dappled clearing hugged by ancient, gnarled trees, crimson and yellow blooms that tipped broad-leafed plants—a deceptively beautiful setting. A man-eater had been here, and it would most likely be back. "Chupacabras are likely territorial. This one could be marking the boundaries of its territory."

"Dax," Logan said, "grab the map we used to log the killings. We'll add the territorial displays and narrow down our search grid."

Dax drew a wrinkled map from his pack and spread it on the ground. Once they'd plotted out the markings and kills, and she supplied the locations of sightings of odd creatures and livestock deaths she'd recorded, they found a distinct pattern within forty square miles.

Logan crouched on his heels with his forearms draped over his thighs and whistled, long and low. "That's a lot of area to cover."

"But now we won't be wasting time searching outside of it." Dax gave Sela a grateful grin. Idiotically, she smiled back like a damned geek happy to have the cool guy's approval.

Logan shoved to his feet and held out his hand to her. She didn't want to take it—at least, that's what she told herself—but she needed to get close to him. So she placed her palm in his, tried to ignore the spark of electricity that shot up her arm at the contact.

He lifted her effortlessly, his fingers lingering on hers for longer than was appropriate as she found her footing.

"Thank you," she said, somehow managing to speak through her constricted throat.

His eyes glittered with both amusement and hunger, as though he might laugh as he threw her down and stripped off her clothes. He leaned into her and put his mouth to her ear. "You're welcome."

Her knees nearly gave out at the husky murmur, and then he was moving, his stride fluid and sure, while she felt like a gangly colt as she hurried into formation.

And why the hell was it so hot in the damned jungle?

Cursing—at herself, at the plants, but mostly at Logan—she fell into step with the men. They moved quickly, stopping now and then for water, or so Sela could study tracks or territory claw marks. Some had been made by jaguars, and their weathered, smooth edges indicated that they weren't fresh. Which made sense. With a predator like a chupacabra in the area, the big cats would probably move out.

"We're getting close to the monkey site," Dax said, and Logan's steady gait instantly shifted into a stealthy prowl, and his already hard body bunched up like a coil.

His sharp gaze scanned the jungle ahead. "Last time we were here," he said to her, "we nearly ran into a squad of FARC guerrillas. We need to be on our toes and keep quiet."

Her heart stuttered. She knew more about the Revolutionary Armed Forces of Colombia than she wanted to. The mission that had nearly gotten her killed had been about infiltrating one of their cells, and in a lot of ways, their brutality was on par with Itor's. People who tortured children to get to the parents were simply beyond evil.

"Sela?" Logan's voice made her jump, and some damned monkey or bird or something in the trees made a screeching sound that was too much like laughter.

"What?" Her voice was humiliatingly squeaky.

"You okay? You look like you've seen a ghost." A curious expression flashed on his face. "You're jumpy."

She smiled and hoped it looked genuine. "Low blood sugar. I'm getting hungry."

Dax slapped at a bug on the back of his neck. "It's lunchtime anyway."

"You always think it's time to eat," Logan muttered.

"What can I say," Dax said, as he drew a brown MRE pouch from his backpack, "I love these things."

Clearly, Dax was touched in the head, but Sela really was hungry, and one thing she'd learned over the years was that when you were on a physical mission like this, you ate whatever and whenever you could. Plus, the MREs sometimes came with candy.

Hers had a bag of M&M's.

She took a seat on a rock in the full shade of a tall, broad-leafed tree and tried not to be annoyed when Logan sat next to her. He said nothing, but then, he didn't have to. His presence alone was a statement—he either wanted to protect her or make sure she didn't take off.

She wasn't sure which one she would rather it be.

The team ate in silence, the security guys and Logan never taking their eyes off the jungle surroundings. Nothing was getting past them. Hell, Logan zoomed in on every freaking insect that flew into their airspace. Alertness and confidence oozed from every pore, and even though he was sitting with one foot lazily perched on a mossy log as though he didn't have a care in the world, she knew he was a lit fuse, ready to explode into action in a heartbeat.

She was used to being around warrior types—ACRO had its share of nonmission personnel, but even they had been trained to the limit of their mental and physical abilities so that, if needed, they could handle anything. Hell, the cooks in the cafeteria knew about a thousand ways to kill someone with common utensils, not to mention their training with various ways to make people sick—or dead—with food.

But even though Sela worked with the best of the best, Logan stood out. There was just something . . . unique about him. She couldn't put her finger on it. She only knew that the way he moved and the way his fiercely intelligent eyes took in the world seemed too impossibly efficient, almost mechanical in nature.

All that caged power sent a shiver of appreciation through her.

"What are you staring at?" He spoke softly, his words directed at her, but he didn't look away from the forest.

"I'm not staring."

"Really? Because your eyes have been locked onto me for the last five minutes, and you haven't eaten more than a few bites of your mystery meat and gravy."

She glanced at the pouch in her lap and shooed away an oddly colorful fly. "Maybe I'm thinking about how much I hate you."

One corner of his sinful mouth tipped up. "Nah. You're wondering how good I am in bed."

That hit too close to home, and heat scorched her cheeks. "You are the most arrogant man I've ever met, and that's saying something." She eyed his spread of food. "You going to eat your Skittles?"

She expected a cocky comeback, but in a movement too fast to track, he'd lunged to his feet and trained his rifle on a dark expanse of jungle. His men followed suit, and three of the security guys peeled off, melting into the trees like shadows.

"What is it?" she whispered, as she came to her feet.

He pushed her behind him, and the blood froze in her veins at his chilling reply.

"We're being watched."

CHAPTER *Nine*

Marlena was being watched. She might not be chained, but she was most definitely a prisoner in this camp, and she had the unshakable feeling that something was going down.

It hit her not long after Sela, Logan and some of the other men had geared up and taken off for the jungle. Sela had waved to her and Logan had simply nodded. When she went back to Chance's tent after breakfast, the doctor had still been in with him, and so she'd taken that opportunity to shower.

Now dry and feeling human again, her stomach growled and she realized it was close to lunchtime. The mess tent was uncharacteristically quiet—granted, Logan had taken men with him into the jungle, but everyone left at camp seemed tense, as if anticipating something.

She ate quickly and then fixed a tray for Chance.

She wasn't sure where to begin with him—after their initial fight last night, they'd done little more than give in to their primal urges. Several times. She'd conked out, waking every hour when staff came in to take Chance's vitals and blood.

Now she called, "Chance, is it okay if I come in?" through the door, and heard a sharp "Sure" in response.

As she elbowed her way in, Sela's warnings continued to echo in her ears.

Stay with Chance. Keep him calm. Don't tell him what's happened to him.

Chance was sitting on the edge of the cot, dressed in sweats. His restraints had slightly longer chains now and his hair was damp from a recent shower.

But it was the way he stared at her that truly made her blush.

"I, uh, wasn't sure if you'd gotten lunch brought to you already," she started lamely.

"I did, but I'm still starving."

The familiar blush heated her body as she drew closer to him. She put the tray down on the table between them, which was about two feet from his cot. His restraints were long enough that they allowed him to sit at the table to eat.

He could fall in love with you.

You could be mated for life to this man.

Stop it. Dammit. It was time for Convincing, to find out about his family, to find out if he continued to remain off the radar, disappearing totally, would anyone notice?

Well, beyond the U.S. Navy, and Devlin had a way of taking care of that. "So, have they let you call your family?"

He shook his head.

"I'm sure they'll be worried."

He shrugged.

"How many people are in your family?"

He stared at her across the table, asked, "What's with the twenty questions?" and shit, why did she suck at this with him?

Questioning and information-gathering was something she could normally do. Easily.

But with Chance, she was tripping over her tongue, while her insides did flips.

Chance, whom she'd slept with. Who didn't hate her after.

Who turned into a chupacabra when anyone tried to touch her because she was mated to him. For life. Maybe.

Did ACRO agents hyperventilate? Because she was pretty sure she was going to. "Sorry. I didn't mean . . . I'm not used to . . . this."

"Hey, it's okay. I'll answer your questions if that's what you need to stay calm. If that's what it takes to keep you from freaking out about me."

"It's not that. Exactly." She looked at him, was grateful that he'd taken her nervousness well. She wasn't as forgiving of herself, but despite her screwup, it looked like she'd get the information. "Maybe a little."

"Yeah, well, me too. And I don't admit to being freaked out very often." He ran his hand through his hair, longer than a typical military cut, and his eyes, the color of sea glass, raked over her with an intensity that made her squirm.

Who was she kidding—she squirmed the second she came within twenty feet of him. "So, about the family thing . . . "

"Well, there's no one who'll miss me, if that's what you're asking. No one to send a rescue squad, except the Navy. My closest friends were part of my team." He looked up at the ceiling for a second. "I guess they're watching over me now."

She'd never been particularly religious and she was more than a little curious at his words. "You believe in God?"

"Gotta believe in something."

"Someone must be worried. Your house—"

He sighed. "I pay everything online; it's automatically deducted. No paper trail. My neighbors know me as the guy who's never there, but they're all military too, so they get it. Don't ask questions."

"You weren't dating anyone?"

"No one special. My momma made sure of that. I don't trust well, Marlena. Especially not women."

Why did her heart surge at the fact that his transition to ACRO might actually be easy for him? That maybe when all this was over, he wouldn't totally hate her, because even though he didn't trust easily, he seemed to trust her. Or at least it seemed as though he wanted to.

"My turn. Are you really a cryptozoologist's assistant?" he asked between bites, and she froze. For someone confined to this damned tent, he certainly knew a lot of what went on around this camp.

Yes was the safest answer—the only one. "You could say that."

He stretched then, the muscles in his chest and arms flexing, and her body stirred again. She was almost insatiable around him.

"So you're here to hunt down the creature that killed my team," he continued.

Tread carefully, Marlena. "We heard rumors and our boss sent us here to check things out."

"You can't go anywhere near that thing. It's strong and smart and bullets don't seem to do shit to it." His voice hardened as he spoke.

"Do you remember what happened to you?" she asked, hating to see the pain return to his face at the mere memory.

"Yeah, I do." He swallowed hard. "This thing—it looked like a goddamned horror show monster. Came out of nowhere, a blur of destruction. And when it came after me, I swore I wouldn't go down. I fought, and the next thing I knew, I was waking up in a tent in this camp."

"Were you in a lot of pain?"

"No, I wasn't." He lowered his voice, and she could barely hear him. "I've always healed unusually fast. When I was a kid, I got hit by a car and broke my leg—it healed in a quarter of the time it should have; and once I got stabbed in the thigh and should have bled out, but by some miracle I didn't, practically watched the wound seal up."

"And this time . . . ?" she prompted.

"This time, that thing should've killed me almost instantly, the way it did the others. There's no rational explanation for why I'm still alive. He attacked me for a long time, Marlena. And when I woke up weeks later, all I had to show for it were superficial bruises and cuts." He paused, looked back at the door as if he expected someone to jump out any minute.

"So you healing fast might not have anything to do with the fact that you were bitten," she said slowly.

He shrugged. "Other weird things are happening, but that . . . I'm not a hundred percent sure but the healing thing isn't new." He took her hand in his. "You're not going to tell anyone, are you?"

"Sela—my boss—she needs to know this to help you."

He took his hand away. "How the hell can she help?"

"The more she knows . . . I mean, we've been pulled away from our jobs, this might be the only way she can get her research done. The only way to help you."

But he'd stopped listening to her. He put a finger to his lips and stood as if prepping for battle.

She froze, waited for men to burst in, but nothing happened.

"Do you hear that?" he asked.

"I don't hear anything."

He stared at her as if she were crazy. "Marlena, they're talking so loudly—they're right outside the door."

She cracked the door open. Shep and the doctor were at least thirty feet away. Unless Chance was wearing some kind of listening device, there was no way he was hearing them.

Unless . . . maybe, since he was part chupacabra, maybe he could really hear those men. Maybe this was one of the weird things happening to him that he'd mentioned.

She walked back to him. "What did they say?"

"Shep was talking about *the mission*—he said some guy from Itor Corp's been calling here nonstop, wants to speak to Logan."

She felt a chill go up her spine as his gaze met hers. *Think fast.* "What's Itor?"

"I overheard Logan talking about them earlier. I guess they're some sort of paramilitary company that sells their services to the highest bidder. It didn't sound like he thinks very highly of them."

He rubbed a hand along the back of his neck and then stopped, listening again. "The doctors say they want to run some tests on me."

Another pause while he listened, and then, "They said... they've gotten orders from some man named Richard to run the tests. He just arrived at the camp and he insists there's no time to waste."

Maybe they were going to take some blood—something simple.

But if GWC was involved with Itor, then the tests very well could be more involved than taking blood samples.

His expression hardened and her fears were confirmed. "They're talking about heavy sedation. Stronger chains. Cerebral and spinal fluid tests."

Marlena's heart pounded—what the hell were these men thinking, attempting to test an unstable entity? Didn't they see what happened to Chance yesterday when he was threatened?

No, none of this could end well. And there was no way for her to get in touch with Sela.

Chance had turned his full attention to her now. The chains clanked as he moved until mere inches separated them.

"I know something's going on with me, Marlena. Because, these?" He held up his arms and indicated the chains. "We both know I can break these if I wanted to, just like I did earlier. That's not normal. I was never able to do that before I was attacked. I mean, Jesus, I've heard of adrenaline being responsible for superstrength, but this... this is weird as shit. And then there's you. Fuck, you're beautiful, don't get me wrong, but it was, like, if I didn't have you immediately, I would die."

She didn't say anything. What could she tell him? The truth? And risk flipping him out more?

He deserves to know. "What have the doctors told you?"

"Not much. What have they told *you*?" he countered. "Because I've got a really bad feeling about this testing. And you do too—I can see it. You can't lie to me. Whatever bond we've got now, I know you. I know that you're scared of me and want me at the same time. And that you're holding back something major from me."

She took a deep breath, tried to think of a way to stall. "You might want to sit down."

When he spoke, she knew he was repeating what he'd heard, word for word. "Cerebral and spinal fluid from Chance can be compared to the original chupacabra. If we kill him, we're in trouble, so take it slowly."

Dear God.

He held up a wrist and yanked the chain. With seemingly little effort, it broke apart. He did the same to the other one and then worked the ones on his ankles off too, leaving them in a pile on the floor. "Fuck sitting. Fuck everything. Tell me what you know."

There was no turning back now. "The animal that attacked your team is called a chupacabra. Sela's a cryptozoologist—she studies phenomena like that. Near as we can tell, when the chupacabra bit you, it—for lack of a better word—infected you."

"What do you mean, infected me?"

"Yesterday, when you attacked Shep, you turned into a chupacabra. I saw it happen with my own eyes."

He took a step back then, as if she'd punched him hard in the gut, pivoted away from her. She heard his breathing turn harsh and she wondered if she'd made a huge mistake by telling him.

And then, with his back still to her, he asked, "What does this have to do with what's happening between us?"

"According to Sela, chupacabras . . . possibly mate for life."

"Mate for life?" He repeated the phrase slowly as he turned to face her. Narrowed his eyes. "You are fucking kidding me. What the hell—like a goddamned swan?"

"Kind of." She blew out a long, drawn-out breath and prayed he kept his temper under control. Probably would've been better to let Sela explain everything, as she'd wanted to.

Damned twenty-twenty hindsight.

There was a combination of fear and anger in his eyes when he said, "And I've mated with you."

She nodded slowly. "I feel it too, when I'm near you. It's a pull. But I think it's worse on your side. Because if I hadn't come to you yesterday—"

He held up a hand. "Don't say it." His voice was hoarse.

"Chance, I know this is all . . . " Freaky. Hard to hear.

"Completely fucked up?"

"Okay, yes." What now?

"You shouldn't be here. Jesus Christ, I can't believe they left you alone with me, knowing what I could turn into—knowing what I am."

"You didn't hurt me when you changed," she pointed out. "You were angry because Shep was trying to take me away from you."

"You think that's the reason I . . . turned?"

"It makes the most sense. You didn't change when you were with me, and you're not changing now."

He stared at her, an intensity in his eyes she hadn't seen before. He swallowed, hard, and she prayed that her theory was correct.

A FUCKING CHUPACABRA. ONE OF THOSE . . . THINGS . . . FROM horror movies and speculative documentaries. Chance's head spun—he didn't want to believe it, but why the hell would Marlena lie to him?

He almost laughed at that, because in his experience, women lied about everything. It was a heavy lesson for a kid to learn from his mom, but the harsh education helped him in a variety of situations.

Except this one, where he was a mated-for-life *chupacabra*.

Maybe Marlena was different. She smelled of pure honesty . . . and yet, somehow, he knew she was still holding things back, maybe for his own good.

Or maybe for hers. "I'm sure you get a lot of things by just walking into a room. But I learned a long time ago that pretty packages can house a whole lot of bad shit. I've seen what a woman can do, the ways she can manipulate in order to get what she wants. And I promised myself I would never get sucked in by a pretty face who spoke even prettier words," he told her with a growl. "But now I think I'm getting sucked in by you, Marlena. In more ways than one. So tell me, what secrets are you hiding behind that pretty face?"

She swallowed, hard. "I can't say I haven't taken advantage of my looks in the past. But I'm not making this up, Chance. You had physical symptoms when I didn't stay with you. And now they're gone."

It would certainly be a small consolation if her theory was true, that he'd turned last night because he was protecting her. It would mean he wasn't a vicious murderer like the monster that killed his friends.

He stared at his hands as if they were still clawed. There wasn't a trace of the beast left on him, except for the fact that all his injuries, pre-chupacabra shift, had healed.

That alone left the doctors scratching their heads.

It also left him with chains that couldn't hold him, and considered far more dangerous than this camp was ready to handle.

Logan was hunting down the original chupa to kill it. What the hell were they planning to do with him? That thought alone was enough to keep him from spiraling into a pity party. Because even though he was part monster, his survival instinct was strong.

And he'd known something was happening to him, from the second he'd regained consciousness. Still, nothing could've prepared him for what he'd just learned about himself.

He had so many questions—maybe Marlena's friend had more answers, more scientific data. But could he trust either one of them?

Logan had told him yesterday that he was safe. But Chance didn't know these people from Adam. There were a lot of men with big weapons running around in the middle of the Amazon jungle. He'd figured drugs or guns. He'd also figured that Logan was ex-military; Chance could recognize it a mile away.

He ran a hand through his hair, his voice sounding tired when he spoke. "They definitely don't have Logan's approval for the testing they want to do on me. Any idea when Logan's coming back?"

"Sela said before dark—it's too dangerous in the jungle after that."

"It's just as dangerous here," he murmured, his gaze dropping to her full breasts even as he acknowledged the inappropriateness of the action. "Something's happening to me, Marlena. My senses are on overdrive. It's only a matter of time before I turn into a beast again. What if I don't change back to human?"

"You can't think like that."

That set him off, because how the hell could he *not* think like that? "What do you care? What the hell is in it for you?" He was yelling now, grabbing her shoulders and fighting the urge to shake her. "Why are you staying here unless you're collecting data? Is that it? Is it part of your job to fuck a half man, half beast?" He let her go and she backed away from him. "That's it, isn't it? That's why you're here, to study me. I must be very interesting stuff for a crytopzoologist's assistant."

She took a tentative step forward, and this time it was he who backed up. "You don't understand."

"Yeah, actually, I do. You're scared of me. You should be. And you should go now."

"I don't want to leave you alone, Chance—it's not safe. You said yourself they plan on testing you."

"You can't stop them. Neither can I. Maybe if you go be nice to them, they'll give you their data." He heard the harshness in his tone and saw her flinch as if he'd slapped her. Not like someone who was hanging around him simply looking for scientific evidence.

But he couldn't believe she might actually . . . like him. Not when a big part of her was still terrified of him, of the monster that lurked inside of him.

"I'm not worried about data. I'm worried that if I leave you alone for too long, you'll get sick again."

The problem was, every fiber of his being ached at the thought of her leaving him. "How the hell will this ever work? I don't want to be your science project. But I do want to be with you, inside of you, fucking you again." He rubbed his face with his hands, felt stunned. Numb. "They're going to take me soon. There's nothing you can do to stop them."

"I'll stay. Try to talk them out of it."

"This might be the only way to reverse whatever's happened to me. If I submit, they can test everything. Come up with some kind of cure. Be able to give me some answers." He paused. "If you're with me when they come for me, I might . . . "

"Turn again," she finished for him. And yeah, as much as he didn't want Marlena to leave his side, he had no intention of changing back into that monster—not if he could help it.

But still, the thought of sitting here alone, for hours, waiting . . . that was too much to handle.

"They're not coming for me for a few more hours—at least from what they said," he said finally. The new guy and the doctors called it *making preparations.* "I could, ah, use the company for a while. If you want."

"I can do that," she said quietly. "I can definitely do that."

SELA HAD BEEN AFRAID FOR MUCH OF HER LIFE. WHEN SHE was a child, her mother had put them both into a lot of shit situations with very bad people. As an adult, Sela had made some reckless choices. And working for ACRO was a bag of adrenaline, mild anxiety and pants-pissing terror.

Right now, Sela was in danger of needing a change of underwear.

They'd all remained absolutely still for several minutes, but now she moved closer to Logan, who was inching toward a copse of trees where the shadows were so dark and expansive, the Loch Ness Monster could be hiding in them.

"You know," she whispered, as she raised her dart gun, "if you'd given me a real weapon, I might be of more help."

"Just stay close."

No worries about that.

He signaled to his men, who spread out in a coordinated pattern. All around them, the rain forest was silent. No birds, no monkeys, not even frogs or insects dared to make a noise.

Slowly, Logan's team crept deeper into the tangle of vegetation, where the canopy above was a tight weave of leaves and branches, choking even the narrowest rays of light. Sela nearly lost her footing when she stepped on something slimy, but Logan's hand shot out and caught her elbow. Damn, he was fast.

Maybe he was an excedosapien. It certainly would explain a lot. There were different kinds of the biologically enhanced humans—people who were superfast, superstrong, or who possessed overdeveloped senses—and most of those with lower-level abilities hadn't been picked up by ACRO, Itor or The Aquarius Group, ACRO's sister agency in England. It was possible that Logan was one of those.

But that still didn't explain his extraordinarily precise movements and mannerisms.

They continued on, sinking deeper into the forest. Clawed branches grabbed at Sela, snagging her clothes, and thorny vines cut through them, until her arms and legs were a mass of scratches. Every now and then, glowing eyes pierced the darkness as curious creatures spied on them from the safety of the trees.

A soft, low growl rose up from nowhere and everywhere, and Sela's heart stuttered. A hot breeze rattled the leaves, bringing with it a fetid odor, one of death and decay, and Logan halted so quickly she bumped into him. The next ten seconds were a blur of action and terror.

Something shot through the brush. Someone screamed. Shots rang out. Logan's men scattered, disappearing silently into the forest. Logan slammed her to the ground and covered her a split second before a bullet shattered a branch where her head used to be. Leaves, thorns and shards of wood rained down on them.

"Is someone *shooting* at us?" Sela tried to wriggle out from beneath Logan, but the guy weighed a ton.

"Looks like." He pushed off her into a crouch, sharp gaze scanning as he tried to get a bead on the activity, but he seemed as confused as she was. "This is chaos."

All around them, men were shouting in English and Spanish. Gunfire popped in constant bursts. "Isn't that the state of battle?" she shouted.

He squeezed off a round with icy calm. She heard a grunt and thud. "This is different—" He broke off, shoved her down again, face-first into wet moss and dirt, and another tree fell victim. "There's a third party."

And that was when she heard it. Smelled it. A shriek that shriveled her soul. An unmistakable stench of a rotting corpse that stung her nostrils.

The chupacabra.

It burst from out of the shadows, a grayish, man-sized beast with a gaping mouth full of fangs. Its saucer-sized red eyes locked on her. Terror screamed through her as she whipped the tranq gun up. It swiped the weapon out of her hand with six-inch claws, propelling her into Logan, whose shot went wild at the impact.

Logan lunged, smashing his fist into the creature's throat, and though it rocked backward, it didn't seem to be injured. If anything, its eyes grew redder, its skin gray, and foamy drool sprayed from its mouth as it hissed.

They faced off, a split second of terror and tension arcing through the air among the three of them, broken when three heavily armed men crashed through the brush. The creature fled, and the guerrillas turned their weapons on Logan. He came to his feet in an explosion, smashing one in the face with the butt of his rifle even as he slammed his foot into another guy's gut. Sela caught the remaining one by surprise, nailing him in the balls with her knee and then crunching his face with that same knee when he doubled over in pain.

Three—or maybe more—men crashed through the curtain of vegetation at them.

"Son of a—" Logan seized her arm and hurled both of them into the brush. Gunfire sprayed the forest floor, and shit, they'd dived into a ravine, and suddenly they were rolling like logs down an impossibly steep rock face. Bullets strafed them even as they landed in a tangle. Pain screamed through Sela's shoulder, and she cried out as Logan dragged her behind a moss-covered pile of stones.

Logan's face was scratched, and mud smeared his cheeks, forehead and chin, but his eyes were as sharp as ever as he rapidly assessed her for injury. "You shot?"

Agony and nausea made her stomach churn. Just breathing became an impossible effort. "Don't . . . know." She did know that she couldn't move her left arm, and trying made her want to pass out.

Logan gripped her shoulder gently, but even that slight contact made her suck air. "Sorry. No blood—but I think it's dislocated."

"Great," she gritted out.

"I can fix it, but it's going to hurt like a mother."

The sounds of pursuit, men barreling through brush and skidding down the ravine, sent her heart rate into overdrive. "Yeah. Do it."

He pushed her gently against a tree. "Hug the trunk. You're going to brace yourself while I pull." He took her hand and gripped her biceps. "On the count of three. You ready?"

"Just hurry. They're coming."

"Okay." He looked into her eyes, held her immobile with his steady gaze. So calm, as if men and monsters weren't bearing down on them. "One . . . *two!*" He yanked her arm, smashing her into the tree, and pain, like she'd been hacked by a sword, sliced through her shoulder.

The world spun, but Logan caught her as she slid to her knees. Even as her senses came back, she realized the extreme pain was gone. There was a dull, throbbing ache, but nothing she couldn't handle. She still couldn't breathe, though.

"You . . . said . . . on three."

"I lied. Come on. We gotta go." His voice went low, as though he was embarrassed. "I lost my rifle."

Sela scanned the ground. "Shit. My tranq gun is gone too." And her pack had been torn away on the tumble into the ravine.

"Yeah, we're a little fucked." He unsnapped his holster and drew his handgun, a high-class HK USP, and she knew he also had a knife strapped to his arm. They weren't totally defenseless, but they were definitely outgunned by the FARC assholes who were between them and the camp.

Logan led the way, moving like a panther through the dense jungle. They kept ahead of their pursuers, but no matter how fast Logan and Sela ran, they couldn't widen the distance between them and the guerrillas. They knew this land, and evading them wasn't going to be easy.

A shot rang out. Too close. Logan cursed, and Sela's heart stopped. He had a bullet hole in his sleeve.

"You've been shot." She reached for him, but he blocked her.

"It's fine. It didn't hit me. Went through the cloth."

Well, there was no blood, but she didn't see an exit hole anywhere in the fabric.

"We're not going to be able to lose them," he said, and she forgot about the bullet hole. "This is their territory, they have the advantage."

"So what do we do?"

Logan peered back the way they came. They'd left no trail; the jungle had closed up behind them, almost as though it was trying to trap them. "I want you to keep going. Head for the mountains. I'll catch up."

"What? No! I can help you—"

He rounded on her, teeth bared like a jungle cat. "This isn't up for debate. I can handle these guys, but not if I have to worry about you." She must have looked frightened, because his expression softened and his voice lowered. "Look, it'll be okay. Find us shelter, and do your best to cover your tracks. Walk on rock and through streams. If I'm not with you by nightfall, hide yourself, then try to get back to camp in the morning." He reached into his pants side-leg pocket and handed her his GPS unit and knife.

And then he kissed her. The contact was fleeting, but damn if she didn't feel a rush of warmth all over her body.

"Go." He shoved her away and melted into the shadows like a ghost, the rain forest swallowing him entirely.

Tempted to stay and help, but realizing she might be more of a liability, like he'd said, she headed for the mountains that occasionally peeked through the rare breaks in the trees. She ran hard, but ran smart, using the evasion skills she'd been taught at

ACRO. By the time she heard shots again, the sounds were distant.

The sun had just dropped below the tops of the trees, giving way to late afternoon by the time she made it to the base of the mountains. The landscape had changed, becoming more open, more rocky, with more ground-hugging vegetation that hampered her steps. But it didn't take long to realize why Logan had sent her this way. The rocky outcrops were rife with caves, many of them well concealed by years of foliage growth. She explored several, praying the whole while that she didn't find a starving jaguar, or the chupacabra, inside.

Heart jolting at every stray sound, she crept into one narrow passage. Or, more accurately, she fell into it, and even as she winced at her twisted knee, she realized that this was the perfect cave to keep her safe from bad guys.

Safe from the chupacabra was another story.

Aching and sore, she used the greenish light from the GPS to make her way toward the sound of running water. Packed earth and porous pebbles crunched beneath her feet as she walked, and a few yards into the cavern, she found a trickle dripping down a crack in the wall, which collected in a shallow pool. *Thank you, God.* She nearly dove in she was so thirsty.

After she drank and washed her face and hands, she made her way back to the mouth of the cave. Dim light filtered inside at the entrance, just enough for her to find a place to sit and listen for anyone who might approach.

Exhaustion set in, and she found herself nodding off.

She came awake to the sound of breathing. Startled, she screamed and struck out in the darkness, her fist slicing through empty air. A palm clapped across her mouth, cutting off her scream. She was shoved to the ground, a heavy body coming down on top of her. A cascade of terror crashed down on her, obliterating thought and logic and leaving behind only survival instinct. Snarling, she jammed her assailant between the legs with her knee and bit down on his finger.

Logan's low-pitched groan echoed inside the cave. He rolled off her, clutching his crotch. "And to think," he rasped, "I was worried about you."

Silently thanking her lucky stars, she scrambled over to him and knelt at his side. "I'm sorry, Logan. You scared me."

"Obviously." He levered into a sitting position so suddenly, she threw up her arm to defend a blow. Frowning, Logan gently pushed her arm down. "Hey. What's wrong?"

Feeling like a fool, she smiled, grateful for the darkness that would hide her trembling. "Nothing. Guess I'm just jumpy." That much was true. God, she didn't think she'd ever been so stressed out or tired in her life.

He snapped the casing on a glow stick, and in the eerie green light, she saw the skeptical expression on his face. But thankfully, he didn't push for more of an answer. "You did a good job picking a shelter."

"I live for your approval," she said dryly. "So I'm guessing you got the bad guys?"

"They're chupacabra food now."

She nodded, and he narrowed his eyes at her. "You don't seem very upset."

"Why would I be?"

"Because women have a tendency to go all soft and shocked over stuff like that. You know, like these guys could have been rehabilitated or some shit if only I'd tied them up instead of taking them out."

She snorted. "When it comes down to my life or theirs? I can get pretty ruthless."

He smiled, that damned blinding one that made her go all mushy inside. "My kind of woman."

"I have a feeling *any* woman is your kind of woman."

"I do have standards," he said, sounding offended.

"What? She has to be breathing?"

His chuckle rumbled deep inside her, stirring up sensations she shouldn't be feeling. "Breathing is a bonus."

She couldn't help it. She laughed. God, how long had it been since she'd actually had fun with a man? Fun . . . in a freaking cave, hiding out from men who would probably shoot him and rape and kill her.

Yeah, good times.

Sobering, she hugged herself. "How long do we need to hunker down?"

"Probably overnight. I got rid of the guys who were close on our tails, but more will be looking for us. If my men don't find us tonight, we'll head out at first light. I also found a patch of berries outside the cave and picked some. They're wrapped in a leaf near the entrance if you get hungry." He nodded at her shoulder. "How is it?"

"Sore, but much better." She reached up to rub the knotted muscles. "I didn't get a chance to thank you . . . so, thank you."

He gestured for her to move closer. "Let me. I give good massages."

"I'll just bet," she muttered, but she eased around, and the moment his strong, warm hands came down on her shoulder, she groaned with relief.

And strangely, that's when she realized she'd allowed him to touch her because she wanted it, not because she needed to seduce him.

Fuck. She was in a lot of trouble.

CHAPTER *ten*

They sat in silence for a while, Chance resting on the cot, Marlena sitting at the table, mainly because Chance continued to listen to the men on the other side of the camp.

He said that sometimes conversations came through clearly, other times, if too many people were talking at once, in a jumble. And she could tell when it all became too much for him, because he shook his head as if clearing it of everything he'd heard, and sat up. Looked at her, the familiar burn of desire in his eyes.

God, that was nice. Despite everything.

She spoke first. "I'm sorry about all of this, Chance."

"Why? You didn't bite me," he said, and then he shot her a small, albeit wicked grin. "Well, not like that anyway."

The man could still make jokes—even after all he'd learned. The familiar heat flooded her body. He was aroused too—she could see it. But she supposed their mutual panic took precedence over that desire for now.

"*Your* family must be worried about you," he said after a few more minutes had passed.

She'd considered ACRO—Devlin—her family for ten years and, yes, he always worried about her. As for her biological family . . . "I don't have one. My dad, stepmom and stepsister were all killed in a car accident."

The raw hitch in her voice surprised her—she'd thought she'd come to grips with her past a long time ago. She'd never known her mom—Marlena was the product of good-bye sex between her parents on the day their divorce had been finalized, and her mom had died during childbirth. Her father had remarried, had a new wife and a ten-year-old stepdaughter. Neither Kelly nor Gillian had welcomed the newborn baby girl into their lives.

Marlena's father had done his best to compensate for the loss of her mother, but he'd *over*compensated, and the bitterness that had taken root inside Kelly when Marlena was born had bloomed into insane hatred as the years passed.

"I'm sorry," he said softly. "What about your biological mother?"

Marlena wasn't sure why she was choosing to share this with him, could've easily come up with some lie. But ever since she'd had to break the news about the chupacabra situation to him, she felt the urge for honesty.

If she could tell him about ACRO, that she was one of the good guys, that maybe they could even help him . . .

No. She couldn't share that now. Not yet. "I don't remember her. She died when I was born. But my dad always said I looked just like her."

Chance's face tightened. "You've been through a lot—no wonder you're so tough. Where'd you grow up?"

She knew what he was doing, trying to make conversation to take their minds off what was going to happen. Thank God for that. "Kansas."

"I'm a Vegas boy myself."

"Worlds apart," she murmured.

"Not so much now," he countered.

"That's the sex talking." *Mated. For life. Holy crap.*

He must've seen the look of panic cross her face, because she felt panicked when she thought about that. She'd desired to fall in love for real more than anything in the world—and now she'd met someone she *wanted* to fall for. And he was turning into a monster. Who'd mated with her.

Yeah, someone upstairs was laughing their ass off at her.

Chance's voice was steady when he next spoke. Firm. Strong. "I hate it that you're with me out of pity. I hate that you've seen me turn into something ugly. Because I'm not that fucking monster, Marlena. I'm a Navy chief. A good man."

"I know that."

"If I can learn to control this—if it can't be cured entirely—I can still . . . " He trailed off, shaking his head. "I don't want to talk about this now."

"You fought for your life, and you won," she whispered. "You can do it again. I've seen miracles happen."

"That's what I keep telling myself. After every mission, whether they went right or wrong, I put one foot in front of the other, lived one day at a time, because I realized early on there's no other way. Spending time appreciating what you've got is much better than bitching about what you don't."

"Those are words to live by."

He smiled. "Yeah, well, someone's got to be the optimist of the group. On my team, that was my role. Loved my job."

"I can tell."

"What about you?"

"My job is . . . it's just a job. And somehow, it's also my entire life. My world. I know that doesn't make any sense."

"It makes sense if you're lonely."

She opened her mouth to protest, to tell him she was just fine, but all that came out was a small sob. Horrified, she turned away and sat on the cot, her back to him, and pulled herself together. "You don't know anything about me."

"I know you bite your bottom lip when you get nervous. I know you twirl your hair when you're amused. And when you get shy, your smile is lopsided."

How had he noticed those little things about her? No man beyond Devlin had known so much about her, and that had taken a long time to happen. She'd been so busy under a fog of lust, so busy wondering why she hadn't fallen head over heels for Chance, she hadn't taken much time to notice anything about him.

He was rubbing her back. She wiped the tears away with a fisted hand and whispered, "I'm supposed to be comforting you."

"Ah, is that how it works? I've never done well with being fussed over."

She leaned back against him and he put his arms around her. They stayed like that until he said, "Marlena, it's time. You need to leave me. Go to your tent and just stay there, okay?" She turned to him, the pained look on his face heartbreaking. "Please. Make this easy on me."

How could she deny him that? She twined her fingers through his hair, drew him in for a deep kiss. And when she broke away, she couldn't say anything, for fear of crying. So she forced herself to smile at him before she left the tent, and then she hurried across the compound to the smaller tent where Sela had found her last night, and watched out the window.

If she couldn't be with him, she could at least keep an eye on his tent and hope he remained safe.

She put a hand to her belly to quell the butterflies—*butterflies*—at the thought of Chance. Her heart raced, her face warmed, and although she was afraid for him, what she felt most definitely went beyond fear. Beyond lust. Sure, when she was with him, that pull was unmistakable. But this . . .

This was what caring deeply for someone was really like when it happened naturally instead of as the result of a malicious curse. The feelings were there, inside her, not circling just outside her grasp or crushing her with artificial intensity.

And so Chance—part man, part beast—was part of her mission, and she might be mated to him for life . . . but there was now the strong possibility that she was actually also able to fall in love with him.

She wasn't sure whether to laugh or cry, and so she did both.

LOGAN SLID HIS HANDS ALONG SELA'S SHOULDER. "DAMN, you're all knotted up."

"That's what happens when you get slammed against a tree," she said dryly, but there was no complaint in her voice. Girl was tough.

Girl was *hot*.

He let his fingers slip under the crew neck of her T-shirt, skin on skin, and she let out a moan she didn't bother to muffle. "You have magic hands."

"You don't know the half of it," he murmured, continuing the massage until she became relaxed, nearly purring.

God, he wanted her. Needed her. And there was no way they were leaving this cave without him taking her at least once, maybe twice, and closer to four times, because they had an entire night ahead of them. A nice, long, dark night, and a nice, cool cave, which would require body heat.

His erection pressed into her lower back and he made no attempt to hide it. She leaned against him and a harsh groan rose in his throat. The friction was good, really goddamned good, and she knew it.

She turned into him then, and he tightened his arms around her, and without preamble, he kissed her—a deep, hot kiss that reverberated through his body. She tugged at his T-shirt, and the feel of her hands on his shoulders was like licks of fire along his skin. He hadn't had such a heightened reaction to a woman since he'd been fitted with the bioware, didn't think he was capable of feeling so good . . . or feeling much of anything.

Her hands were in his hair now, twisted there to keep him from pulling away as the intensity between them built. He wanted her so much, and not just physically. His emotions were actually functioning, and it was odd and crazy and wonderful.

It had been so long—he couldn't remember wanting this badly. Truthfully, before the accident and the bioware, he'd taken arousal and the swirl of emotions that came with it for granted.

He hadn't realized what he'd been missing—and he had no idea why it had returned now, with Sela, but hell, he was going to enjoy it.

She shifted her hips against him, ankles catching together behind his lower back, and was kissing him as if her life depended on it.

Everything fucking depended on him—getting the chupacabra for Itor Corp, thus saving a major contract for GWC, figuring out what the hell to do about Chance, keeping Sela alive . . .

She'd pulled back, took his face in her hands. "Now's not the time to be thinking."

"That's one of the smartest things you've ever said."

"You're just lucky you're sexy."

"Yes . . . lucky." Quickly, he skimmed her shirt off, had her in his arms in seconds, his tongue flicking an already hardened nipple. She buried her face in his hair as she rocked against him and he could come this way—didn't want to, but he could easily.

He tore his mouth away for a second. "Are you wet for me, baby?"

"Mmmmm."

He tugged the nipple between his teeth and she groaned. He sucked again, hard, and she brought his hand between her thighs and began to rub there. "Logan, the things you make me want to do . . . you have no idea."

He had an idea—many, many ideas. Including her hot sex sheathing his cock tightly—and oh, yeah, he needed that, and soon. Could take her any way and every way she wanted, pictured her up against the wall and under him and on him, and all of those ways included him coming inside of her. "Tell me, then."

"I want to feel you, inside me, filling me. Making me scream."

"Consider it done, Sela." His hand slipped inside the front of her pants, but he couldn't get far enough down to touch.

"I want to feel how wet you are. I want to see it. Smell it. Taste it. Take your clothes off for me—all of them." His voice was husky now, thick with lust, and when she stripped her pants and thong off, he drew a slow breath at her beauty.

She had the kind of toned, slim body that was still lush enough to bring a man to his knees. He was already long past that. And when she walked back to him, he grabbed her hips and brought her sex to his mouth, licked her wet heat while her soft moans bounced off the cave walls. His tongue probed her clit—it was hard and throbbing and he knew he could push her over the edge easily.

He buried his face against her, sucked and lapped until everything was sticky and sweet and she was grabbing at him hard as she came.

He continued to kiss his way down her thighs while she rested her hands on top of his head and then she was ordering him to strip. He barely got his pants unbuttoned before she was straddling him.

He didn't have time to get completely out of his BDUs, and they remained open as she took him inside of her. Her back arched and she let out a low keening moan that bounced off the stone walls and echoed beyond.

He needed to tell her to keep it down, not to draw attention to their hiding place, but he loved watching her, hearing her . . .

He was making her crazy and happy and pleasured and it made him swell with a primal pride. "Ride me, Sela."

And she did, hands on his shoulders, a fierce, sexy smile of pleasure as she took him—and oh, yes, it had been years since sex had been this good.

He buried his face against her breasts as his balls tightened—and as she cried out in a release, he prepared to lose himself in her.

"DEAR . . . *GOD*." SELA'S ENTIRE BODY SHOOK WITH PLEASURE as she came down from an orgasm that had blasted her apart right to each individual cell.

Since she'd been at ACRO, sex with men had been about the job, about their orgasms. She'd faked hers, partly because the guys she'd fucked had been scum she could barely pretend to be attracted to, and partly because when she came, she was too busy concentrating on her pleasure to get a good read on her partner.

But Logan was different. He was the sexiest man she'd ever seen, and for once, having sex for the job wasn't a hardship.

Beneath her, Logan surged, his big body arching and retreating as he held her hips so she was at the mercy of his thrusts. "You're so fucking hot when you come." His voice was ragged and raw, his eyes glinting in the darkness.

Her sex was still clenching around his thick cock, her tissues sensitive and swollen and ready for another release. But Logan had the control of a machine, and he ceased moving, lay there motionless. Even his breathing was slow and steady, and the only visible sign that he was turned on was the fine sheen of sweat that coated his throat, making the straining tendons stand out.

She so wanted to lick it right off him.

"Lean back. Brace yourself with your arms." His command shot through her in a shiver of excitement.

Unsure what he had planned, she put her palms flat on the ground behind her, making her spine arch and her thighs spread wide. His heavy-lidded gaze dropped to where they were joined, and . . . ah, she got it. He wanted to watch his shaft slide in and out, wanted to create their own little porn show.

The idea got her wildly hot, and she felt a warm rush between her legs. His thumb dragged through her slit, spreading her cream up to her clit.

"Tell me what you see," she said, and his eyes darkened even more.

"You're so wet," he said roughly. "You're swollen and pink, and your juice is making my cock glisten."

She moaned as his words sparked the beginnings of another orgasm. Crazy, since they were both utterly motionless. Motionless until he began that maddeningly slow sweep of his thumb again. Her clit pulsed with need every time he skimmed it. She whimpered and rolled her hips in an attempt to catch his maddening, fleeting touch, but he grasped her thighs and held her still.

"Don't move." His voice was a hot whisper as he held her in that exposed position and thrust up. Slowly. Deliciously. His retreat was just as prolonged, and at the same time he lifted her so the head of his cock nearly came free.

Again he thrust and drew back, with the same torturous, lagging strokes, all the while watching their joining. His cock stretched her opening so she could feel every texture along the shaft, the velvet skin, the firm, ropy veins, the ribbed striations of muscle. Shuddering with pleasure, she ground against him, clenching her sheath around his erection.

With a groan, he picked up the pace and pumped into her with increasing strength and speed until the quick-time double slap of his ass against the cave floor and his legs against her butt echoed off the rock walls in an erotic soundtrack.

Still he watched as he fucked her hard, his expression intense and dark. Fire burst in her belly, spreading through her pelvis so fast she couldn't stop the orgasm. It crashed into her and she cried out as Logan did the same. She felt him swell and pulse, and he kicked his head back as the pleasure took him.

Fuck... she bit her lip, forced herself to let go of the physical sensations in order to get inside his head and get a read while his shields were down.

It happened quickly—his thoughts swirled in a jumbled mass, but once again, they were all of a personal nature. More images of childhood, and then the military—a few things she was pretty sure were secret missions, but nothing that was relevant to *her* mission. There was a fight with a friend... he'd accused his buddy of fucking his girlfriend, but he'd been mistaken; scowling, she pushed harder, because he was jerking beneath her with the last spasms of pleasure.

Again, she ran into a wall that was much more solid than any psychic could put up. It didn't feel like a psychic wall at all. Didn't have the soft give. Truly, it was as though her mental probe struck a titanium shell around his mind.

And then there was nothing. His orgasm had faded away, along with her ability to get a read. Confused and exhausted, she fell forward and collapsed against his chest. For a couple of heartbeats, he lay there, frozen, as if he didn't know what to do, and then his arms came around her.

The intimacy should have bothered her—*would* bother her later—but right now she only wanted to rest. To revel in the feel of a connection with someone, something she hadn't experienced in... well, never. Maybe they could lie like this for a while. No talking, no thinking. Just enjoying basic human contact.

Oh, man, she was seriously thrown off her game here.

Logan drew in a ragged breath. "Get off me."

"I don't have the strength," she muttered.

He went taut beneath her. *"Now."*

The hard tone of his voice startled her, and she lifted her head to see what the hell was wrong with him, but he didn't give her the chance. Roughly, he shoved her off him so she was left sitting in the dirt.

Humiliation spread like a sunburn from her cheeks to her entire body as she grabbed for her pants. Clearly, his thoughts hadn't taken him down the same connection trail she'd been on. The rejection stung with poisoned memories; she'd seen her mother completely trashed by men she'd slept with. "What got up your ass?"

He picked up the glow stick and moved toward the rear of the cave. "I need to clean up."

Like she was dirty or something. Shaking with anger, she jumped to her feet. "What? You can't just—"

He wheeled around. "I need a minute. Give me a goddamned minute, okay?"

She felt her jaw go slack, and had no idea how to respond, which wasn't normal. At all.

Logan closed his eyes and blew out a breath. "Jesus. I'm sorry, okay? I just . . . I need a second." He spun back around and stalked off.

Sela stood there in the last, faint rays of sunlight, confused and pissed. Once he was out of sight, she did what any agent in her situation would do. She followed him.

Silently, she crept toward the back of the cave, hoping the trickling water would mask the sound of her footsteps. It didn't mask the squeaks of bats and the skitter of unidentifiable creatures in the cave, however. She just hoped none of the creatures were poisonous. Or huge.

She eased up to the bend and carefully peeked around the damp wall of stone, expecting to catch him taking a piss or maybe washing himself in the tiny pool.

None of the above. Holy shit, Logan had taken off his shirt and was injecting himself with the black sludge, like she'd seen him doing last night. Except his arm, the one he'd said hadn't taken a bullet, was . . . shredded. A bullet had definitely struck him in the triceps—or what should have been his triceps.

There was nothing there but metal. Metal and wires, instead of veins and muscle.

She must have made a noise, maybe a gasp, because his head whipped around. Fury lit up his face as he threw down the syringe and crushed it beneath his foot.

"I told you—"

"Yeah, you told me," she snapped. "You fucked me and then tossed me off of you like I was a whore you picked up while drunk, and now you're sober and have realized what you've done. So fuck you. And fuck you for being so secretive about this. So you have a fucking artificial arm. You think you're the only person on the planet who has lost a limb?" Except she got the feeling this went way deeper than just a limb, and she also suspected that his arm was no ordinary piece of machinery.

"It's a hell of a lot more than that," he growled, confirming her suspicions.

"So does this have something to do with your *diabetes*?" For some reason the fact that he'd lied to her about that rankled. Hurt, even. God, she'd actually believed him! The knowledge that she'd basically forgotten all her ACRO training and believed a bad guy fried her temper to a crisp. It was definitely time to get back on track and do her damned job. "Is there anything else you've lied to me about?"

He stalked toward her, fists clenched and eyes sparking. "Excuse me for not telling a complete fucking stranger that I'm half machine."

Half? Jesus. "I . . . ah . . . Are you serious?"

"No!" he shouted. "I always tell that to the whores I pick up while drunk." He raised his arms, and alarm shot through her, an instant of panic she regretted but couldn't stop, and she flinched, brought her hands up to shield her face.

When no blow fell, she risked a peek at him, and instantly wished she hadn't. He looked . . . devastated. Pale and worried.

"Sela?" His voice cracked. "Hey, I'm sorry." He eased toward her, but she shook her head, smiled like nothing had happened. Like she hadn't just had a flashback to her near death.

"It's okay. I got spooked. You know, dark, scary cave." Skepticism flashed in his eyes, but she aimed for distraction by grabbing his hand and turning his arm to expose his injury. "Now," she said firmly, "tell me about this."

CHAPTER *Eleven*

They took him sometime in the late afternoon. Chance had been in a restless, fevered sleep because, although he'd let Marlena go willingly, his inner chupa seemed to know it was still a forced separation.

He'd barely heard the footsteps, the hushed voices. Then he'd felt something sharp in his arm and had woken up again strapped to a stretcher, with an overhead light shining into his eyes.

He'd told himself it would happen, but nothing could've prepared him for this.

A steel band ran across his forehead, so he couldn't even turn to see what was going on around him.

And Christ, the pain . . . He could handle pain, it came with his job, but holy mother of God, it hadn't been like this.

There were needles placed into his eyeballs, his spine. He heard talking around him as if they yelled directly into his ears.

Some voices were familiar—like Shep's—but there was one voice he didn't recognize, someone new to the camp. Most likely, that man Richard they'd spoken of earlier. He was urging the doctors to take the testing as far as they could go.

Without killing him. Yet.

And then another voice, saying, *The woman could be infected too. We'll test her next.*

Chance heard himself howl at the threat to Marlena, and then he clamped down hard as the light faded and a wash of crimson slammed down over his vision. Suddenly his skin wasn't big enough for his body, the bones in his arms and legs were stretching, and there was a God-awful ache in his skull.

He heard snapping, wondered for a second if his bones had broken, and then he was free from the restraints.

THEY WERE HURTING CHANCE.

Marlena knew that, felt it keenly, had been pacing the medical tent they'd taken him from a couple of hours earlier. Watching him walk with the men had been heartbreaking. Knowing she'd been helpless made it even worse.

She'd fisted her hands as she moved, so tightly there were crescent marks in the tender skin of her palms. Had almost left to find him, several times.

It wasn't until she heard the bloodcurdling screams coming from the admin tent that she ran in the direction of the yells.

Shep was coming out of the tent, and even in the growing dusk she could see the blood running down the side of his face. "Stay the hell out of there," he ordered her, but she didn't listen, slammed past him and into the room where Chance—at least, she thought it was Chance—was crouched over one of the doctors.

He turned to her and let out a powerful, roaring growl that shook her confidence, and this was getting more dangerous than she'd ever have imagined—for her heart and soul.

Her palms began to sweat and her stomach clenched and she cursed herself for not being stronger, for being afraid of Chance when he took this form.

The chupa prowled toward her and she heard a low, stuttered breath escape her, felt her knees start to buckle. The clawed hand stretched out toward her . . .

"What are you doing? This thing could kill you," a man she'd never met before yelled even as she took a step toward the chupa and the chupa took a step toward her.

"It's not a thing," she snapped. "What did you do to him?"

No one answered. No one except Chance, with a screech that threatened to shatter her eardrums.

She took a step back and hated herself for it. "Have you given him a tranquilizer?"

"Four," the doctor said from the corner of the room.

"Try a fifth," she said as Chance roared toward her, with no sign that he recognized her at all. Frozen to the spot, she closed her eyes and waited, felt the cold breath on her neck as the beast leaned in and sniffed her.

She opened her eyes and looked at the red ones Chance's had morphed into, tried to find something in the animal who stood before her that was the man she'd been with.

The whir of the tranq gun cut through the air, followed by a dull thud of the dart piercing flesh. The chupa's eyes widened and then his body began to sway, his legs ready to give out.

She couldn't grab him before he fell, but Chance began to change back almost immediately.

She knelt beside his prone body, stroking his hair and taking his hand as she spoke to him softly. "Chance, are you okay?"

His fingers tightened around hers even though his eyes remained closed. Bruises mottled his skin from where they'd stuck him with needles, and there were heavy circles under his closed eyes. She knew he was awake, although he kept his eyes closed.

The man she'd identified as Richard had left the room while she was talking Chance down. Goddamned coward. One of the doctors who'd remained in the tent approached her now. "Ma'am, I think—"

"*I* think you should leave," she interrupted. "When he wakes, the last person he'll want to see is you."

The doctor nodded. "I'll be right outside the door, then."

When the tent door closed softly, Chance opened his eyes and looked up at her. "Thanks. I don't think I'd have turned, but I kind of want to wrap my hands around his neck for a bit."

"I figured."

"You shouldn't have risked your life like that," he murmured. "You don't know for sure that I wouldn't hurt you. And, I don't trust any of these men."

"I couldn't let you suffer. I heard you screaming. I felt it."

"They talked about testing you," he said. "I had to make sure that didn't happen."

Again, he'd worried about her. Put himself at risk because of her.

In a sense, he'd been cursed himself, forced to live with a beast inside of him he neither wanted nor could control.

She understood how he must be feeling, better than he knew. But she certainly couldn't share that with him. Not now. Maybe not ever.

This was all such an impossible situation. Unbelievable. And there was nothing else she could think of doing beyond kissing him. Avoidance for sure, but between the primal heat she felt when she was near him and his kisses—oh, they made everything else seem completely unimportant.

A shiver went through her as he rolled her to her back, his heavy body on hers. His hands were swift and sure, unbuttoning and unzipping her BDUs, his fingers finding her core.

He pulled his mouth from hers. "You're so wet for me. You want me . . . still," he murmured, as if he couldn't believe it.

"Make me come, Chance . . . just like this." Her hands gripped his shoulders as he complied, slid one finger along her sex, another sliding inside of her in a maddening rhythm.

He had no problem complying with her request. The imminent danger and adrenaline rush combined with Marlena's scent made it impossible for him not to want her. And the soft smile of pleasure on her face was enough to make him forget all the pain he'd just endured.

But she'd risked her life for him—again. And as much as he hated knowing she was afraid of him when he turned, he loved the way she held him when he was back to being a man.

He lost himself in her kiss, until his cock was steel against her. He wanted her and there was no way he could wait. He didn't know if it was the beast in him, but he didn't care about anything else but having her, right then and there.

Of course, he didn't want her on display if any of the doctors or guards walked in. There was a small area in the corner that was curtained off—a changing room, of sorts—and he picked her up and placed her on the bench before pulling the curtain around them for a modicum of privacy.

"Chance," she whispered, but he was tugging at her BDU pants, pulling them down around her knees, along with her black thong, while she was attempting to kick off her boots without untying them.

He was only able to get one pants leg off, but it was enough to give him full access. He spread her legs and knelt between them, licking her core, tonguing the tight pillow of nerves until her fingers dug into his scalp. He couldn't remember wanting someone more—it was as if he needed to memorize her taste, to inhale it . . . to make sure he was so bonded to her that he could never, ever hurt her, no matter what form he took.

He buried his face against her sex as though it could save both their lives. She tasted sweet, like honey, her musk rising around them in the small space. She was already slick from want and he couldn't get enough.

A single finger traced her slit—he used it to enter her, then added another, sliding them in and out as he suckled her clit, hard.

When her orgasm hit, fast and intense, it was all that much more satisfying for him. She contracted her thighs around him—and he refused to stop, even as she whispered that it was too much, too much, Chance . . .

Because it could never be too much. He knew that now with the clarity of a man whose life and death was a precarious—and hourly—balance. And even though it was better for her to be far away from him, it was too late for that. He'd chosen—and he wasn't letting go.

Well, not until she finally pushed him away, her body weak from orgasm, her face flushed.

He didn't give her the opportunity to recover before he was pulling her urgently to the floor, their bodies tight together in the small space. "I want more."

"More," she whispered, and she smiled and touched his cheek.

He rubbed the day's worth of whiskers against her hand. "Fuck me like . . . fuck me like it gives you pleasure."

She looked uncertain, and at the same time guilty. "You do give me pleasure—but I want *you* to feel good."

"Baby, I do. But I want you to feel amazing. I want to make you feel the way no one else has."

"You already have."

"Trust me, you haven't seen the half of it." He averted his gaze for a second, until she brought a hand under his chin and forced him to look into her eyes.

"What's wrong? Where did you go?"

He squeezed his eyes closed. "I want to be able to tell you that when we get out of here, I'll take you away someplace nice—someplace with a big bed and champagne and room service and anything else you want. But I can't promise you that . . . or tomorrow. Or the next fucking hour."

"Talk about it like you can," she insisted, and he smiled.

"I'm not all that good at fairy tales."

"Everyone can use some fantasy."

"Yeah?" His voice was rough with desire, his fingers still stroking between her legs as he spoke. "So what's yours?"

"I've never thought about it."

"Bullshit."

She hesitated, then blurted, "It's you."

His heart thumped and he didn't know what to say, but it didn't matter because loud voices outside the tent startled them both. No one appeared to be coming inside, though, so Chance took the opportunity to roll her, quickly, quietly, entering her in one swift stroke.

He'd opened her with his tongue, but still, the hot pulsing of his cock took her breath away momentarily. She locked her legs around his as she groaned against his palm. And as he took her furiously, she forgot everything she'd been taught—forgot her job and ACRO and simply let herself be fucked, hard and well, and she was fucked and loved and there was nothing orchestrated about it.

He was close to release—she could tell by the way his body strained against hers, strong and silent—and he went deeper, plunging in and out until her legs were rubber and she could do nothing more but give in to anything and everything he wanted, right here on the changing room floor.

LOGAN HADN'T EVEN FELT THE BULLET GRAZE HIM. AND NOW Sela was staring at the rip in the synthetic skin that had been implanted underneath his own thin epidermis.

With a tentative finger, she touched the exposed wires and then stared at him. "Are you really half machine?"

"Did I feel like a machine?" he asked, barely able to contain the fierce anger that tore through him. "Because when I was fucking you, there was nothing mechanical about it. That was all me."

"I'm not judging you, Logan."

"Shit." He pulled his arm away from her as the rage ebbed slightly. He felt off balance, like the injection hadn't worked well.

And maybe because of the wound, it hadn't. "I'm in trouble here. The reason I'm yelling at you . . . it's not you. I think some of my bioware is malfunctioning. The shots keep me alive. And I'm not feeling . . . right." Uncontrollable rages were a seriously shitty side effect of the malfunctions.

She looked concerned, and concern too often led to pity, and he didn't want either. Not when he was half naked and trying to enjoy the post-orgasm haze.

Although, truth be told, that was pretty well gone the second she got pissed at him.

Since he'd met her, it was like his emotions were hijacking his better judgment—and that never happened. He never gave away intel this freely. Or ever. He blamed the fact that his bioware was compromised from the wound. That he might not have enough serum to make it through the night. That he might break down completely and be unable to control himself.

But really, he wanted to tell someone. Not just someone—*her*. Because if she was disgusted, if she was going to walk away, better he know now.

Because he liked her a hell of a lot. She was smart. Sharp-witted. Called him on his shit.

He felt like a normal man around her. The problem was, there was nothing normal about him.

So he knew what Chance was feeling. He'd been where Chance was now. He got it. The guy must be freaking out, and Logan knew GWC had to do everything in its power to try to cure the SEAL.

The guy had turned into a chupacabra and, judging by the sounds Marlena had made, she didn't seem to mind.

But Sela was not Marlena. She was watching him carefully, and when she spoke again, her voice was gentle, like she was trying to keep him calm. "Can you give yourself another shot?"

He sighed. "I've always got backup—always. But I lost my

pack during the fight and the backup with it. If you weren't here, I'd head to camp."

"I don't want you risking your life for me."

"Too late, Sela." He stared out into the darkness. "I'll last through the night. We'll hump it back at first light. And I'll try to control myself . . . well, my temper, at least."

That earned him a wan smile. She moved away, under the pretense of washing her hands, as he tried to get his shit together.

He sure as hell didn't feel like explaining all of this to her. But there wasn't a choice now. Especially because she was suddenly pointing the gun at him and backing toward the cave entrance. "Where the hell are you going to go, Sela? It's the middle of the night—do you think you'd fare better with the FARC or a chupacabra than with me?"

"I don't know," she said. "All I know is that you got pretty angry before, and if you lose control again . . . "

"You weren't worried about that when you were coming."

"I didn't know you were . . . unstable."

He swallowed, hard. Because, yeah, he knew *that*, even if he didn't know what the hell he really was. All he knew was that he'd never felt like more of a man than he had in Sela's arms, and he didn't want that to end.

But she was nearly to the mouth of the cave.

"Sela, you can shoot me, but it won't stop me. You've seen a little of what I'm made of. You have to know that if I wanted to, I'd already have you down on the ground and out of commission. But I haven't."

"That makes me feel a lot better."

"I'm not trying to make you feel better. I'm trying to explain. Now, are you going to stand with the gun pointed directly at me the whole time I talk? You need me to get out of the jungle alive," he reminded her, and she lowered the gun to her hip but didn't let go of it. And she stayed on the other side of the cave.

He began the story, reluctantly, his voice flat, distant, as if he was talking about someone else. "Up until about four years ago, I was in the Navy."

"Let me guess, you were a SEAL."

"Now you're telling the story?" he shot back, and she flinched. Dammit. He hated what his mechanical malfunctions did to his temper. "Okay, yeah, I was a SEAL. And I was on a mission in the jungle—like Chance was. My team was ambushed by a group of tangos. We were outnumbered, which happens, but this was bad. At the end of the day, I was the only man left alive—and *alive* was a really fucking relative term."

He didn't remember anything after taking a round of ammo to the head. Later, he'd learned how bad things were for him, how his legs had been rendered useless, as had his right arm.

"I was in the hospital, on life support—my brain was swollen, so they couldn't perform surgery." He sank down to the ground, settling in for the confession. "And my dad—he owned and ran GWC—he came in and had his lawyers get me out of the military hospital and transferred to his facility. At that point, the military thought—figured—I'd be headed for some kind of long-term care, so they didn't fight him."

Sela swallowed hard and he looked away as he continued, because he didn't want sympathy from her. Wasn't sure what he wanted, except he didn't want her to know about his internal wiring, but it was too late for that. "When I woke up, I'd lost six months of my life."

"But you woke up . . . How?"

He pointed to the left side of his head. "Bioware. It was all an experimental procedure—my legs, my right arm, my head. It's what saved me. During those months—really, the first year after my bioware was installed—I was the GWC's living, breathing science experiment. Sometimes they performed surgeries on me whether I consented or not. What choice did I have? And the more they experimented, the more they learned how to help me."

He thought about the operations; they were like torture. The pain was both physical and mental—one night, they killed him on purpose, just to see how long it would take to bring him back from the dead.

During those months, he grew cold and distant from everyone, didn't know if it was from the accident or the bioware, but if it wasn't for the fact that his sister could still make him laugh, he would've sworn he was dead on the inside. The doctors told him not to expect much in terms of emotion. The most life he could muster was during sex.

So yes, he used sex for the pure pleasure of being alive, but the emotional connection had not been there since the accident and the surgeries. Not until this spitfire of a woman marched into this jungle and his life and turned everything upside down.

"The one thing that kept me going was my sister. I thought maybe my love for her was more about memory, about knowing how I should feel about her, remembering how close we were before. I didn't think I was capable of real love anymore. Of any emotion beyond constant anger." Even now, he had to pause for a deep, calming breath when he thought about his past. "In the beginning, I felt like a slave to the serum that keeps me alive. I was told that I should feel lucky, but all I could feel was rage. The doctors insisted it was a side effect of the implant. The psychologists claimed it was the aftereffects of almost losing my life, of losing a big part of myself."

"And what do you think?"

"I think that when I'm with you, all that shit falls away and I'm just me—the old Logan. So when I told you earlier that I wasn't a machine . . . I don't know, I probably lied. I have no idea what the hell I am anymore. A real-life version of the Six Million Dollar Man. But I'm not going to hurt you—that much I know."

"Logan."

It was all she said. She walked toward him, putting the gun down before she reached him. She knelt next to him on the ground and wound her hand into his, and he felt the combination of anger and shame rush through him. He breathed deeply, because he'd promised her he'd control himself, that he could.

Truth be told, he wasn't sure—wasn't sure of anything at all.

WOW. LOGAN'S STORY WAS STRANGE. HEARTBREAKING. AND IF she hadn't seen crazier things during her time with ACRO, she'd say it was unbelievable.

"So, this technology... are there more people like you out there?"

"Not that I know of. The company wants to perfect it more so the next chump doesn't get stuck having to inject himself with a quart of motor oil every day."

"Is that what it is? Oil?"

He tore the bottom of his shirt into a long strip. "It's a lubricant base combined with antibiotics, hormones, immunosuppressant drugs and a few other ingredients I don't care about."

She eyed him. "So where are all the parts? Are they more than functional on a basic level?"

"You mean, do they give me superstrength or -speed or anything? Yeah." He sighed. "Look, I don't want to talk about this anymore."

She ignored him. "You don't like having to depend on anything, do you? It must kill you to have to be a slave to your injections."

He seemed surprised by her words. "You sound like you know something about that."

"I watched my mother go through something similar."

"Did she have medical problems?"

"You could say that." She leaned back against the cave wall and closed her eyes, the day's events suddenly overwhelming her.

"Hey." Logan's hand came down on her leg. "You can tell me."

She snorted. "You mean that since you spilled your guts, I owe you. Tit for tat, right?"

"I won't force you to talk. I'm just saying that you can."

"Thanks for the offer, counselor," she said dryly.

She listened to the incessant drip of water near the cave entrance, the trickle of the spring at the back of the cave and the muffled sounds of insects and birds in the forest. Through all of that, the sound of Logan's soft breathing came to her, more soothing than anything she could remember.

She rolled her head toward him. "Need help with that... laceration?" Could you call it a laceration when the injury involved mostly machinery?

"Nah. Just need to hide it from prying eyes. The injury itself is minor. The skin on top is mine, but the vessels are small. The bleeding has already stopped." He looped the strip of cloth around his arm and held one end with his teeth so he could tie it.

"Here," she said, taking the ends. "I'll do it."

He watched her with heavy-lidded eyes that might appear drowsy, but she had a feeling he was missing nothing, was merely powering down to conserve energy but not turning all the way off.

"You never said which parts of you are... upgraded."

A bitter smile turned up one corner of his mouth. "Upgraded. Interesting way to put it."

"That's me. All kinds of creative." She finished tying a secure knot. "So? You didn't say."

"Nope, I didn't."

She ignored his brush-off and slid her palm down his injured arm. "We know this one has been upgraded."

"Obviously."

Scooting around behind him, she ran her hand down his other arm, admiring the tight ropes of muscle, the thick veins, the warmth that flowed beneath the surface of his tanned skin. "This one is the original."

"Yeah." His voice sounded a little strained.

Unsure if she was touching him out of scientific or personal curiosity, she slid her hands up his shoulders, kneading and massaging. He was tense as stone, but as she worked the curve between his shoulders and neck, his muscles loosened, slowly becoming pliable, yet firm. When her hands moved up, her thumbs rubbing circles over his cervical spine, he dropped his head forward with a moan.

His pulse slammed into her palms as she caressed his skin, using her fingertips to work out the knots in the deep muscle. He smelled good, like jungle and man and earth, and she suddenly wanted to taste him. Her breasts pressed into his back as she leaned forward and slid her lips over the back of his neck.

"These are all original parts," she murmured against his skin, and he grunted in acknowledgment.

Slowly, she ran her fingers through his hair, over his scalp. "What about here?"

"Some of it is new," he whispered.

"In your brain?"

He tensed again, and she silently cursed. He didn't answer, but she knew. Which could explain why she couldn't read him during sex. Maybe the circuitry was messing with her psychic airwaves.

"It's okay." She nuzzled his hair, the fading ocean scent of his shampoo seeming so out of place in the musty cave. "You don't have to tell me."

She eased her hands down, over his shoulders to his chest. The hard slab of muscles layered on top of his rib cage twitched when she touched them. "What about here?"

"Some." His voice was husky and raspy, as if he didn't want to talk but was afraid she'd stop touching him if he didn't. "Inside."

Closing her eyes, she rubbed her cheek against his back, a reward of sorts, for opening up. It was a Seducer trick, and she might have felt guilty if not for the fact that she was taking pleasure from touching him, something she rarely felt. She liked that she was enjoying this, because somehow it made her feel like less of a user.

Less of a whore.

She wrapped her arms around his waist, slipped her hands beneath his shirt and caressed his abs. God, they were hard, rippled, so cut that her fingers disappeared into the grooves between the muscles.

"These," she purred, "have to be fake."

His soft chuckle rumbled through her and lifted her heart. She doubted he'd ever laughed about the things that had happened to his body.

She spent several minutes exploring his stomach and chest, all the while kissing his neck and nibbling the tendons that rippled in the curve of his shoulder. Logan didn't move, but his breathing grew more ragged the longer she played. Her own body heated, burned, until she needed to touch more. What had started as a fact-finding mission was becoming a pleasurable jaunt over his perfect body.

Eager for more, she eased around him on the uneven ground, feeling the sizzle of his gaze as he watched her. When she was at his hip, she laid both palms on his thigh. It was hard, and through his pants she could feel that it wasn't as hot as much of the rest of him.

"New?"

"New." His jaw was clenched, as though he was either in pain or having a hard time tolerating her touch.

She ran her hands down his leg, all the way to the top of his boot. "Can you feel me?"

"Yes, but sensation is dulled on the parts that are bioware."

She moved her hands to his other leg. It felt the same, and she knew it was artificial as well. "What about pain?"

"I can feel pain in my limbs, but it's mild, because the only nerves are in the skin."

God, she wanted to tell him she was sorry—but she remembered how people had looked at her when they learned who her mother was, what she was. She knew what pity felt like. It made you feel small and helpless. And Logan was anything but that.

With a firm touch, so he could feel her hands, she massaged her way up his leg until her fingers brushed the bulge at the juncture of his thighs. His entire body shuddered, joining her own shiver of pleasure.

Boldly, she cupped him. "Real?"

He sucked air. "What do you think?"

"I don't know," she mused, as she trailed her fingers up the fabric-covered ridge of his shaft. "The way you used it earlier can't have been natural."

"Is that so?"

Smiling, she tore open his fly. His erection sprang free, the dusky column swollen, and even in the dim light she could see a drop of moisture glistening at the tip. Her mouth watered and her core went utterly wet.

She didn't tease or stall. She took him into her mouth. His response was instant and fierce as he drove his hands into her hair and let out a raw curse. She swirled her tongue over the smooth cap and dipped it into the slit before taking his cock to the base and swallowing the head.

Another curse broke from him as he arched up. She was good at this, a true professional, and she knew it. His earthy, male flavor tingled on her tongue, and Logan's reactions, everything from the heady sounds of his breathing to the way his cock bucked against the roof of her mouth, delighted her.

Gently, she scraped her teeth down the underside of his shaft, following the thick, winding vein to his sac, which had drawn up, the satin skin tight and textured against her lips. Soft, springy curls tickled her as she slid her tongue beneath his balls, separating them, bouncing them lightly while humming. He let out a tortured hiss. Everything inside her that was female melted, loving the ability to control this big male's pleasure.

"Can't . . . take . . . much . . . more," he groaned. "Fuck me—fuck me *now.*"

She dragged her tongue up the length of his shaft. "This is for you. Just you." Rolling his balls between her fingers, she closed her mouth over him again and sucked hard. A muffled shout accompanied a tensing of his fingers against her scalp and a sudden pulsing against her lips. He was close.

"Touch yourself, then." His voice was distorted with pleasure, deep and rough. "Please."

"I can't resist a man who begs," she said, smiling as she tore open her pants and drove her hand between her legs.

She was wet and slick with need, and the instant her fingers slid past her clit, the beginnings of an orgasm caught her off guard.

Not yet . . .

Desperate to taste his orgasm as she came with him, she flicked her tongue across the head of his cock and returned to the firm up-and-down rhythm that made him rock into her. She scraped her teeth gently on his glans on the upstroke and swirled her tongue into his hole on the downstroke.

"Yes," he rasped. "Fuck, Sela . . . I'm gonna come . . . "

She appreciated the warning, but she intended to swallow. She'd always hated the act, but as a Seducer it had been required. For the first time, she was going to do it because she wanted to. Wanted to give him a blow job he'd remember forever.

As his hands tightened in her hair and he began to lose control and fuck her mouth, she rolled her clit between her fingers and lost it. Ecstasy washed over her. Logan shot his hot seed into her mouth in an endless rope of salty cream. When it finally eased off, she continued to suck him, and though he begged her to stop, she didn't.

She had another trick up her sleeve.

Using her own slick moisture, she slipped her fingers behind his sac to the smooth, sensitive skin there. She rubbed there, tight circles as she kept up gentle suction on his cock. Curses tumbled out of his mouth, sounds of agonized pleasure, and in moments, he was climaxing again, his hips coming completely off the cave floor.

She sucked on him while she pumped her fist on his shaft and slid one finger to the tight, puckered flesh between his cheeks. He roared in release, arching his back and bucking so hard she had to pin down one of his legs to keep from being thrown.

Gradually, he eased, and his flow trickled away. "Jesus," he breathed, flopping onto his back. "That was . . . just . . . *Fuck*."

Smiling, she crawled up his body and snuggled down, half on, half next to him.

And that was when she realized that for the first time in her life, she'd been with a man without experiencing any psychic sensations that had always accompanied orgasm. No external noise, no horrible thoughts, feelings or scenes. She'd forgotten to even try.

There had been only blessed silence, and two people taking pleasure in each other.

CHAPTER *twelve*

Sela woke, feeling like she was lying against a hot stove burner. Disoriented, she sat up, blinking in the shadowy darkness until she realized she was in the cave with Logan.

He was beside her, sleeping. Breathing a sigh of relief, she sank down next to him again—and hissed when her hand came down on his arm. His real one. It was on fire.

"Logan?" She put the backs of her fingers on his forehead. Same thing. He was hot to the touch, clammy. "Logan!"

He groaned. "Yeah?"

"You're burning up. I'm going to get you some water." They'd used up their one bottle of water last night, but she could refill it with water from the spring at the back of the cave.

Logan didn't respond, and since she needed an excuse to get away so she could contact Dev, she made her way to the spring and stuck the bottle in the trickle of water running down the wall. Keeping an eye on the bend, she dug the tiny texting device out of her pocket and tapped out a message to Dev, doing her best to fill him in on everything she could in the short time she had.

A twinge of guilt pricked at her; she hadn't asked for backup, but she knew he'd soon send in agents to extract them and take down GWC, and Logan would hate her after that. Then again, he'd probably hate her for lying to him all this time anyway.

Sighing, she hit the Send button and tossed the one-use device into the water. After it sank into the murky pool, she headed back to Logan, who was sitting up, one arm draped over his knees and resting his forehead on his wrist.

She knelt beside him, urged his head up and put the bottle to his lips. He drank gratefully, until the water was gone.

"I wish I had some aspirin or something for you."

"Wouldn't help." He cleared his throat. "I need my injection."

"That's what's causing this?"

"Yeah."

"Are you going to be able to travel? I could always—"

"I'm fine," he snapped, and she couldn't help flinching. He cursed, and his voice softened. "Who hurt you, Sela?"

A ball of adrenaline drop-kicked into the pit of her stomach. She didn't want to talk about it. Hadn't talked about it even after ACRO had patched her up and forced her to go to a bazillion therapy sessions.

She screwed the cap onto the bottle, more to busy herself than anything. "It's in the past and not important."

"Bullshit. If it were in the past you wouldn't cower every time I raise my voice."

She threw down the bottle and shoved to her feet. "I don't cower." Though she did notice that before they'd been intimate, none of his angry or threatening actions had truly frightened her. It was only after she'd begun to know him that suddenly every move he made had her flinching. The fact that he'd noticed bothered the shit out of her.

Lightning fast, he grabbed her hand. "I'm sorry. I didn't mean it like that. But you do react, like you expect me to hit you. Someone did a number on you, didn't they?"

Sighing, she sank back down, because there was no point in denying it. He knew. "Yeah."

"Who? Tell me, and I'll kill him."

"How sweet," she said dryly. "But he's already dead. Car crash." The car crash part wasn't true, but Arnaud *was* dead. After the Itor agent had nearly killed her, Dev had sent Akbar after his ass, and within hours, the guy was ruing the day he'd been born.

"Tell me."

She shrugged. "We dated for a while."

They'd fucked for a month while she'd read his mind during sex and communicated the sensitive information to her supervisor. The guy had been fond of sharing, and she'd been forced to entertain some of his buddies as well. After she serviced his friends, he'd go into violent, jealous rages. But if she refused to fuck them, he beat her even worse. It had been a nightmare she couldn't escape . . . not if she wanted to get information for ACRO.

Afraid that the psychic Triad assigned to her for that mission would report the abuse and have her extracted from the situation, she'd pleaded for their silence—Arnaud had been using the drug operation's profits to plan coordinated dirty bomb attacks on a dozen major U.S. and European cities, and ACRO needed to know where.

And then, just as his beatings were escalating, she began to get more out of him regarding the terrorist attacks, so she stayed. Which had turned out to be a huge mistake.

"And?"

"And one day he got mad at me. Beat me into a coma. Broke every rib, my jaw, my left orbital bone, my skull, my leg, both arms . . . Do I need to go on?"

"No," he rasped. "Jesus. How did you survive?"

Actually, she'd fought back, her ACRO training allowing her to hold her own for a little while. But he'd been equally well trained, stronger, and he'd gained the upper hand with a vengeance. Thankfully, her Triad had picked up on her failing vital signs and had alerted the local authorities. In the meantime, as she lay on the floor of Arnaud's bedroom, dying, the psychics had banded together and kept her alive with their own life forces.

"I was just lucky, I guess."

Before she could blink, he folded her into his arms and held her against him. "You're so strong. God, Sela, what you must have endured."

Her? His experience made her hell seem like nothing, and while she might have some mental scars, his were emotional *and* physical.

"Did you have family to take care of you?"

She'd had ACRO, but obviously, she couldn't tell him that. "Not really. My mom died of AIDS ten years ago."

"I'm sorry." His soft voice drifted down to her, barely audible. "Is that what you meant by your mom going through something similar to me?"

She sighed against his chest. It felt good to be leaning on him, and though she should probably fight the feeling, she was tired, and honestly relieved to have someone to talk to.

"Sort of," she said. "She was dependent on people and medications in all aspects of her life. She was bipolar, so she needed medicine to keep her normal. And she was dependent on men. God, she was so dependent."

His hand stroked her hair gently. "What do you mean?" When Sela didn't answer, he kissed the top of her head. "Let me help. Nothing you can tell me will shock me. Trust me."

Tears stung her eyes. She didn't want to trust him. Couldn't. And yet, she found herself desperate to confide in him in a way she'd never done with anyone. Somehow, he'd wormed his way into her heart, and if he got much deeper, she'd be in real trouble.

But she didn't have the energy to care right now.

"She was a stripper. Part time anyway. She tried other jobs, stocking shelves at Wal-Mart, flipping burgers at fast-food joints, but she was a single mom, and she had to feed me. Put a roof over our heads. And she . . . " Sela trailed off, swallowed hard before finishing. "She sold herself for those things."

"She must have loved you very much."

Sela blinked. She'd expected disgust, or at the very least some sort of shocked response. But he almost sounded like he understood. "She did love me. I don't judge her for what she did. It was all for me. Everything."

"I guess you didn't have a very stable home life."

"I can't count the number of places we lived," she said, surprising herself with the amount of bitterness in her voice, even after all this time. "I don't remember ever living anyplace that was ours except the times we lived in the car. Mostly, Mom shacked us up with guys she was sleeping with. Once, I tried to list all the different places I've lived, but I gave up at thirty."

His palm rubbed slow circles on her back, lulling her, comforting her. "You must have been living out of suitcases."

"Garbage bags. We couldn't afford suitcases."

She remembered hauling around big black Hefty bags full of their belongings, which pretty much amounted to some clothes, a few photos and two or three toys. With only a few exceptions, they'd never even unpacked. Most of the guys her mother hooked up with weren't looking for her kind of baggage—a mental disorder and a snot-nosed kid.

"I can't imagine how hard that must have been for you."

She shrugged. "I didn't know anything else. When there's a new 'uncle' in your life every week, you get numb to it. Only the 'uncles' who were extra-nice, mean or too touchy stuck in my mind."

He stiffened. "Some of them touched you?"

"A few. But my mom taught me to take care of myself, and she didn't leave me alone with them for long, so they never got further than a hand down my pants. A couple creeps whipped it out in front of me and tried to get me to touch them, but I managed to wiggle my way out of those situations."

"Sick bastards," Logan muttered. "What did your mom do when you told her what they'd tried?"

"She beat the shit out of them with Mr. Ruth—that was the baseball bat she took everywhere we went—and then we'd get the hell out of there."

"Good for her."

"Oh, don't be thinking she was a saint or anything. She believed me every time I ratted out some scumbag, but she was incapable of seeing a good thing when it was right in front of her." Logan continued the soothing strokes, and words kept spilling out. "There was one guy. Gary. He had a trailer in the middle of nowhere, but he was one of the few guys who gave me my own room to sleep in. He was nice to Mom and me, and he gave us the first real Christmas I'd ever had. With a tree and presents and everything."

"Sounds nice," he murmured. "What happened?"

Sela's stomach growled, and she eyed the berries they hadn't eaten last night. "Do you really want to hear all this boring crap, or do you want to eat?"

"Both." He stretched for the leaf-wrapped packet. "So? What happened with the nice guy and your mom?"

Sighing, she took a small purple berry from him. "I don't know. My mom was with him for six months, and then she left him one day while he was at work." Sela had hated her mom for a long time after that, for ruining the one good thing that had ever happened to them. "I think she was having bipolar issues, or maybe she got scared because he loved her . . . "

They'd spent the next two years with more guys than Sela could count, almost as if her mom had gotten even less picky after Gary. Sela had grown more and more bitter as time went on, more uncontrollable as she hit her teens. "I made my mom pay over and over for leaving Gary. I was a horrible teen. And then she was diagnosed with AIDS."

Logan took the berry uneaten from her and put it between her lips. The tender gesture tugged at her, made her heart squeeze a little. "How old were you?" he asked quietly, after she began to chew. Only then did he eat a berry himself.

She swallowed the sweet fruit, grateful that he'd had the forethought to forage for food even as he'd sought her out last night.

"Fourteen," she said, taking another berry. She noticed that he waited until she'd eaten it before he ate another. "I didn't get what it meant, and I wasn't very understanding. I was still upset that she'd left Gary. I mean, how could she leave someone who loved her? Someone who had given her a way to get out of the life that was killing her?"

Sela swallowed on a lump in her throat. She'd freaked out on her mom, had screamed at her, told her that the AIDS was her fault for being such a slut. "God, I was so cruel. And you know what's so funny? I called her a whore, and then went out and did the same thing. I lost my virginity to some guy I didn't even know." She'd been so self-destructive, so ready to end it all. "I think I just wanted someone to love me, and after years of watching my mom fuck every dick she ever met, I figured that love and sex were the same thing, you know?"

And then her ability had reared its ugly head, and it hadn't been long before she discovered how awful sex was when you learned every horrible secret your partner had. Why she'd allowed Dev to talk her into being a Seducer was beyond her—no, actually, she understood why she'd let it happen. She'd been given a chance to be accepted by a big family, people who had turned their gifts into something useful. Sela didn't regret her time as a Seducer, but she'd definitely been happier since joining the Cryptozoology team.

"You didn't know any better, like you said." Logan held another berry to her lips, but she shook her head, appetite gone. Besides, he needed the nourishment more than she did. "Take it. I won't eat unless you do."

"Damn you," she whispered. He was disarming her slowly but surely, his method of breaking down her walls gentler but no less effective than a battering ram. She ate the fruit, letting him feed her until her portion was gone.

"You haven't forgiven yourself, have you?" he asked, thumbing juice off her lip. His fever had eased a little, but his touch still made her burn, not with sexual longing, but with rapidly growing emotion.

"No. My mom died thinking I despised her, when nothing could be further from the truth." She sagged against him, feeling rubbery and road-rashed from being dragged down memory lane. "This is going to sound so sappy, but I just wish she'd been able to find someone she loved before she died. I always wanted that for her."

"What about you?"

"You mean, do I want love for myself?"

"Yeah." His voice was scratchy, as though he was uncomfortable with the subject. She certainly was.

"More than anything," she admitted quietly. "But I'm not cut out for it." Not when everyone she slept with gave her nightmares with what was in their head.

Everyone except Logan and Creed, but she shoved that thought away as fast as it had come in.

"I'm so sorry, Sela. You went through hell and back."

Warmth seeped into her chest. She shrugged nonchalantly, though she felt anything but. "Guess we all have our traumas to deal with, huh?" She peeled herself away, feeling suddenly vulnerable. She'd just shared more with him than she'd shared with anyone, ever. And now he had a lot of ammunition if he wanted to hurt her.

He let her stand and move away, but he also pushed to his feet and stepped close. "Hey. I won't make you regret telling me those things."

She paused, thinking things out before she said something stupid, like she already had. But ultimately, she was here for a job, and maybe she could foster the bonding they'd done. Her stomach turned a little at the thought, because he didn't feel like the enemy anymore. He felt like a lover. A friend. And damn, she was an idiot.

"I believe you," she said softly, and strangely enough, she found herself buying her own bullshit.

"And I trust you to keep what I told you to yourself. There are a lot of assholes who would love to get their hands on the technology I've got all over my body."

"It'll be our secret." Bile filled her mouth at the lie, because she'd already texted Dev about it. Silently, she swore, calling her boss the vilest names she knew for sending her here. After this mission, she was never, ever going undercover again. She really would rather wrestle the chupacabra than get close to someone she had to deceive. "Are you feeling better?" she asked, not only to change the subject, but because she was genuinely concerned.

"I feel like shit," he said. "But the water and sugar helped a little." He checked his watch. "We need to get back. I need a shot before I rage out, and we could both use some real food."

"And a shower," she added.

He waggled his brows. "Together?"

She punched him in the shoulder—his real one. "Not a chance, big boy. The camp doesn't need a show."

"We'll see." Before she could argue, he headed toward the mouth of the cave. "Let's go. We have showers to take, food to eat and chupacabras to catch."

"Logan?"

He pivoted around. "Yeah?"

"What happens then? After we catch the chupa?"

He gave her a sly smile. "While the camp is celebrating, we take that shower, because everyone will be too busy to hear us."

He was avoiding the real question, but he sounded serious enough. And she wouldn't mind . . . "That's not what I mean, and you know it."

His expression turned serious. "I know. But I can't talk about that, Sela. Company business is private."

A blast of cold stabbed her. "You don't trust me." *Which is smart.* That thought stung as much as the fact he didn't trust her.

"It's not that." He checked the wrap on his injured arm, tightening the knot. "My company works for powerful people. Breaching their trust could put you in danger."

"I can handle myself."

"I know."

"Then let's cut the bullshit. You don't trust me. That's why you won't tell me what you plan to do with the chupacabra."

A bitter laugh escaped him. "I told you—"

She jammed her fists on her hips. "I don't believe you."

"Yeah, well, maybe you'll believe that I don't want to tell you because I'm not always proud of what my company does and who they're involved with." He averted his gaze, reached up to rub the back of his neck. "So yeah, there you have it. Question answered."

Sela nodded numbly. He was ashamed of his company's actions. This was not the behavior of a man who was in bed with Itor for fun. There was a whole lot more to Logan, and the more she learned, the harder this job got.

ANNIKA POUNDED ON THE DOOR OF THE HOUSE WHERE FAITH and Wyatt lived. For a while, they'd had a place off base, but after Faith had been nearly killed by an Itor agent—who now worked for ACRO—Wyatt refused to take any chances with her safety, and had moved them to the luxurious old officer quarters on the north side of the compound.

Faith answered, dark hair pulled up into a ponytail and black sweats rolled up to her knees. She blinked when she saw Annika standing there, because, yeah, they weren't exactly the best of friends. But they had similar backgrounds, similar thought processes, and if anyone could possibly help Annika make sense of her current mess, it would be Faith.

Annika really would much rather talk to Haley, who was pretty much the only woman she considered a friend, but Annika's home pregnancy test had popped a positive, and though Haley had a kid, she wasn't a field agent, and she had no special abilities. She wouldn't understand some of Annika's unique issues.

"Ah, hey, Annika. Wyatt is at work—"

"I'm not here to see Wyatt," Annika said quickly, before she lost her nerve. "If you have a minute, I need to talk to you."

Faith hesitated, confusion and suspicion darkening her expression before she finally stepped aside. "Come on in. Can I get you anything? Coffee? Tea?"

The thought of either made Annika's stomach roll over. "Thanks, no." She followed Faith to the living room, where a three-month-old baby girl was sleeping in a playpen.

"Don't worry about waking her," Faith said in her lilting British accent. "She can sleep through anything. She's just like her dad."

Annika sank down on the couch. "Is she showing any signs of being telekinetic or biokinetic?"

"Not yet, but both abilities tend to emerge later." Faith snorted. "Good thing too, because her tantrums are bad enough without her throwing things across the room with her mind."

"I'll bet." An awkward silence stretched, because Annika wasn't sure what to say next, and clearly, Faith was just as unsure.

They really didn't have a peaceful past. Finally Annika blurted out, "Why did you have a baby?"

Faith's eyes shot wide, and Annika had to wonder if that had been a rude question. Then she decided she didn't care. She'd never really been one for subtlety.

"Well," Faith said slowly, as though she suspected a trick, "I've always wanted a family."

"But, I mean, how are you going to keep working? Aren't you afraid it'll screw up your life?"

Faith smiled at the dark-haired infant. "I'd rather be home with her than off getting myself into danger. I still plan to work, but I'll be more careful about the missions I accept." She turned back to Annika. "Why? Are you and Creed thinking about a family?"

"No!" Annika lowered her voice and hoped her panic hadn't come through as blatantly as she thought it had. "It's just that we'll have to discuss it at some point, you know?"

"Do you both want kids?"

Annika folded her hands in her lap and looked down, her stomach churning. "He does. I don't. But then, the other day, he flipped out when he thought I might have been lax on getting my birth control shot." She dragged in a long breath, as if that would relieve the tension that had sprung up between her and Creed since then. They hadn't fought, but they hadn't talked much over the last couple of days, let alone made love. "I guess I'm just confused. Figured it couldn't hurt to talk to someone who loves the work as much as I do, but who had a kid."

"He might be worried that if you don't want kids, getting pregnant could drive a wedge between you two."

It already had, and she hadn't even told Creed she was knocked up. "Maybe," Annika said. Faith watched her expectantly and, unnerved, Annika looked away. But the sight of diapers, baby powder and a breast pump didn't help. Coming here had been a mistake. "Look, I should go. Thanks for the talk."

"If you need anything, let me know." Faith walked her to the door. "Come by anytime."

Annika's eyes stung. Stupid hormones. "Yeah," she rasped. "I will."

She took off, heading straight for home, where Creed's hog was parked in the driveway. Nerves rattled her so badly her hands shook. She didn't know what to do or say—she definitely didn't want to tell him she was pregnant. Not until she got her mind unscrambled.

Maybe not ever.

He was sitting in front of the TV watching a *Seinfeld* rerun. "Hey, babe," he said.

She walked over to the TV, turned it off and stood in front of it. "We need to talk."

"Okay . . ." He reached for the longneck beer on the coffee table. He always made sure he had something in his hands when it looked like things were going to get uncomfortable.

"You said we should talk about kids."

He nearly choked on his beer. "Yeah. Later."

"I don't want to wait until later. You freaked when you thought I was behind on my shot. Why?"

"I just know you don't want kids."

"Do you still want them?"

He shoved to his feet. "Look, ah, let's not talk about this now."

"We *are* talking about it now."

"No, we're not." Creed headed off toward the kitchen, but she darted to him, grabbed his arm and swung him around. His elbow struck the bookshelf, knocking over a picture of his dead brother, Oz. Figured. The guy had been a pain in the ass when he was alive, and now that he was dead, he continued to stick his nose in everyone's business. Somehow, he still communicated with Dev, and he used Creed's spirit guardian, Kat, to talk to Creed too.

"I want to know what got you freaked out," she said, ruthlessly shoving Oz from her mind, because he had no say in this. "Do you want kids, or not?"

"Dammit, Annika." He jammed his fingers through his hair. "Why is this important right now?"

"Stop avoiding the question. Answer me!"

He slammed the beer bottle down on the bookshelf, rattling the whole thing. "Not with you, okay?"

"Oh." She stumbled back, her brain churning to process what he'd said. He seemed to realize he'd just stepped in it big-time, because his face lost some color.

"I didn't mean it like that," he said quickly, backpedaling. "I don't want them at all."

"But . . . you said before you did." The room spun a little, and she threw out a hand to brace herself against the wall. "If you were with someone else . . ."

Creed seized her shoulders and got right in her face, his eyes darkening with his intensity. "Listen to me. I would rather not have kids and be with you than be with anyone else just to have kids."

"But you want them." Her voice was barely a whisper.

"Stop it, Annika," he said, palming one of her cheeks tenderly. "Just stop it. We're not having them, so it's a pointless discussion."

"What if I change my mind? What if I want kids?"

"You won't, and you don't." Releasing her, he straightened to his full, imposing height. "Remember how you said you don't have a maternal bone in your body? How you'd just screw a kid up the way your CIA fake-parents screwed you up? You don't want to risk it."

She stifled a bitter laugh. She'd been raised by people who'd given her knives and guns as toys, while Creed had grown up with loving, family-outing-type people, who, if not for the fact that they were ghost hunters, could have been the freaking Cleavers. "You mean *you* don't want to risk it."

"You're right. I don't."

An irrational anger surged through her. "So you don't trust me to be able to let go of my past and take care of a kid properly? Is that what you're saying?"

His harsh exhale was a sound of pure frustration. "Why the hell are you turning this around?" His dark eyes narrowed. "This is about Sela, isn't it? You're still upset about her."

He stared at her like she was insane, which was exactly how she felt. She had no idea why she was baiting him like this or what she wanted from him. If he fell to his knees, begging her for a baby and telling her what a great mom she'd be, she'd be just as upset as she was to know he *didn't* want a baby with her.

"Sela?" she spat. "She wasn't even on my mind, but obviously she was on yours. Maybe *she* would want to give you a baby. You should ask her. Bet she could raise one without totally warping it."

"Fuck." Creed threw up his hands. "I give up." He grabbed his jacket off the back of the couch and headed toward the door. "I'm going for a ride. When I get back, things are going to be normal again, and we're done talking about kids, got it?"

Before she could answer, he slammed out, leaving her alone with her insanity.

CREED SPED ALONG THE BACK ROADS OF THE ACRO COMpound, ignoring limits and Kat's screeching at him to slow down.

Sometimes, having a spirit attached to him for life was a real fucking drag. She'd been there as long as he could remember, along with his tattoos—both of which provided him a certain measure of protection.

Neither would protect him from what Oz had predicted last year.

He tried to tell himself that Ani was simply being moody, that she was still worried about Dev, but neither of those explanations fit.

Ani had frustrated him many times before; typically, it was nothing he couldn't handle, but hot damn, she'd never been like this before, so freaking emotional.

Pull over, Creed.

This time, he listened to Kat—steered to the side of the road, parked his bike and got off. "Don't say it, Kat. Don't you dare say it."

She didn't, simply put her hands on his shoulders in an attempt to calm him. He was shaking.

And Ani was pregnant.

"How did this happen, Kat?" He paused. "Yes, I know how it happened, but how did it *happen*? She's on birth control. She doesn't want kids."

Fate always has a way of intervening, Creed. You know that better than anyone.

"What am I supposed to do?" he asked, and listened to the deafening silence. "Great—now she decides to shut up."

He sat on the ground, palms down behind him in the dirt, and he pictured Oz, last year, sitting on his couch, dressed in all black. He'd come back to help Devlin again. Such a long and tortured road for those two men.

At that point, Creed hadn't a clue that Oz was his biological brother.

If I'd known . . .

Nothing would have changed, he supposed. It was the reality he'd come to after months of mourning. Oz had always been there for him, no matter what. And he'd given Creed Kat and his tattoos for those times he couldn't protect his brother alone.

At the time, Creed had thought what Oz had told him had been bad enough.

"So, you and Annika."

"Yeah, me and Annika," Creed agreed.

Oz smiled, leaned his head back against the couch. "That's different, but hell, I guess it works."

"When it works, it's damned good." Creed actually had been readying to go over to Annika's house when Oz showed up.

"Yeah, I know what you mean." Oz smiled, but it faded quickly—he leaned forward as if pushed from behind, his eyes went wide and his mouth opened, but no sound came out.

Creed had been around Oz before when he'd had a vision come through. Oz's souls—the posse that traveled with him—would send him visions from time to time. Clearly, Oz was seeing something now. He stared at Creed without really seeing him at all.

"I'm here, Oz" was all Creed could say, grabbed the man's hand. It was useless to try to pull him out of the spell—Oz always said it was like being trapped between time, heaven and hell.

Finally, after ten minutes, Oz sat back, breathing heavily. "I don't know how to tell you this, but I've promised Dev I'm going to stop holding things back from people for their own good," he started gently. "It's about you and Annika."

Fuck. "Tell me everything."

"I don't have a lot of detail, it's all fuzzy—the vision kept showing the same thing over and over again, like it was stuck. Like the universe isn't even sure how this one could play out." Oz paused and then, "You can't get pregnant."

"Christ, I hope not."

Oz stared at him, sobering Creed up again. "There's something about pregnancy that's not good for you and Annika. I don't know if it's something about you being together, or if it's only you or only Annika. To be safe, you can't ever get Ani pregnant, okay? Like, go get sterilized right now, and Annika too."

"What the hell are you talking about? Half the time Annika and I can't even be in the same room with each other, let alone have kids together."

"Someday you'll want to," Oz promised. "And you can't."

"You've got to be a little more specific about the consequences here."

Oz's eyes went darker than Creed had ever seen them. "If you get Annika pregnant, one of you could die when the baby's born."

Ani hadn't wanted kids. Ever. It was a no-brainer. And she was always on top of things with her birth control—all the female agents were. It wasn't so much a part of protocol as it was common fucking sense.

Annika always had an overabundance of common sense. But now she was pregnant with his child. A part of him swelled with pride, with excitement. In spite of her worries, he knew Ani would be a damned good mom.

They'd have a son or daughter. And one of them wouldn't be around to see the kid grow up.

You've got to go back to her, Kat prodded. *She's confused. Angry.*

"I know, Kat, I know." But he didn't move, kept his ass on the freezing cold ground and called out to Devlin instead.

CHAPTER *Thirteen*

It was late morning—they still hadn't arrived at camp, but not for lack of trying.

Logan had forced himself to move fast and sure over the past four hours; years of Special Forces mental conditioning helped him overcome an awful lot. Except, of course, the total mechanical failure of over half his body.

The jungle was a trying place under the best of circumstances—wet and dark and hot and full of enough red herrings to throw even the best of men off their game. He knew he'd have to maintain full mission mode to make it back to camp.

"Let's go. Keep behind me and keep up," he'd told Sela right before they'd left the relative safety of the cave and ventured out into the jungle. She'd snorted softly at his words, and she'd been keeping up with him.

God, she'd been through hell. The story she'd told him—stories—vibrated through his head and could easily prompt an angry rage. If any of the men who'd hurt her were put in front of him now . . . Well, they'd have a better chance with the chupa.

He cut some of the branches and vines so she'd have an easier path through the thickest of the foliage—his skin was full of cuts and scratches and bites, but he was better able to handle it, thanks to his bioware.

He heard Sela's harsh breaths behind him—and when he turned to check on her, he noted she was sweating nearly as badly as he was, but she hadn't complained once. He'd been about to ask if she needed to take a break, when Sela tugged at the back of his shirt.

"Did you hear that?"

He turned to face her—her eyes were wide and she was pointing behind them.

"I think we're being followed," she mouthed, and shit, with his body running on half strength and no comms to call to camp, this wasn't going to be a good thing at all.

"Let's keep moving," he mouthed back, and she nodded, even as he tugged her to walk ahead of him.

The hairs on the back of his neck prickled for the next half mile. Sela was right—this thing was tracking them, methodically. Quietly. Like it was . . . practicing.

And then it growled, and Logan stopped dead, drew his gun.

The growl hadn't come from behind him so much as it seemed like it came from everywhere, surrounding them, and he circled slowly, trying to locate it before it could make a surprise attack.

Sela had turned so they were back to back and moving together—four eyes circling continuously, an excellent instinctive safety move.

Except it wasn't instinctive. Someone had taught her quite well, and he didn't have time to think about why a cryptozoologist needed to know combat moves, because the snarling, red-eyed chupa leaped out of the tree directly in front of him with no further fanfare, as if tired of hiding.

As if it knew it was unstoppable.

Well, fuck that.

Logan shot four rounds at the beast, but the damned thing was fast as well as strong, and suddenly it took him by the throat and threw him, violently.

Sela screamed as Logan landed with a jolting crash against the trunk of a tree. He willed himself not to pass out, because the beast had stopped focusing on him and was moving toward Sela.

With a roar, he used the momentum from pushing away from the tree to fling himself toward the chupacabra.

His mechanical arm still functioned, despite the break in the wires, but it felt weak and his legs weren't much better. He needed an advantage, and as much as he hated to do it, he let the rage that had been slowly building since he was injured yesterday take over.

It was a risk—he couldn't be sure if he'd be able to bring himself back from the edge.

"Sela, get to camp," he managed to yell before he saw red—literally.

The next moments were a blur. He had a vague awareness of grabbing the creature by the throat, the cold, scaled skin crumpling under his fingers. His emotions were out of his control completely for those moments, and he felt the urge to kill race through him. He rolled with the beast, both fighting for the upper hand—he heard his own grunts mix with the chupacabra's, the metallic taste of his own blood in his mouth from when he'd been slammed by the creature.

Sela's yells brought him back to a lucidity of sorts, and it was then he remembered Chance and the infection, and he managed to stay out of reach of the thing's teeth. And he knew that if he didn't pull back his fury immediately, the bioware malfunction would take over the human emotion . . . and he'd be as much of a danger to Sela as the chupacabra.

Bad enough she'd seen him so out of control.

He wasn't sure if he let go or if the chupa got away, but he saw it disappear into the thick brush. "Why did it run? Something must've spooked it. Unless I did manage to hurt it—if it's weak, now's the perfect time to go after it."

He heard himself babbling, felt his disorientation. Dammit, he needed his injection, and soon.

"Logan, it's okay—you must've scared it."

He stared at her. Her eyes held concern not fear, and good, that was good. "I can get it. I have to."

"No. Let's go." She pulled at him and he let her help him drag himself to his feet. His body felt depleted, like he'd run too far too fast, and he leaned against her.

When he was finally upright, she told him, "If you go after it now, you'll die."

He stared at her. "I didn't want you to see me like that. I didn't want to scare you."

"It's okay, Logan. Really. You saved me."

"I hate this. Hate that I'm built with fucking parts." He closed his eyes and swayed, didn't open them until her palm brushed his cheek.

"I don't hate anything about you. And those parts are what saved us." Her words were soft, but sure. "But if we don't get you back to camp, I'm not going to have the chance to prove that to you. And you're not going to live to capture the chupacabra."

She was right. And her words made him smile, despite the weakness. He lowered his mouth to hers for a brief moment, holding her and wishing that this could be real. Hoping it was.

"Okay," he sighed. "Let's go."

"Just one second?" Sela gave him a sheepish look as she picked through the forest floor to pluck a couple of the beast's scales from the dirt. Then she very carefully broke a blood-coated leaf off a branch, rolled it up and stuck it in her pocket.

She was still smiling like a kid on Christmas day as they humped it back to camp.

* * *

DEV WAS AT HIS DESK, FIRMING UP PLANS TO SEND IN OPERATIVES to back up Sela and Marlena in order to accomplish the physical takedown.

He wanted both Akbar and Stryker for this mission. The men made a good team, and Stryker knew the Amazon jungles and had a skill that no one could rival, so he'd be the perfect choice to help Sela and Marlena.

Stryker had just returned from a four-month mission in the Middle East—he'd bitch about going back out again, but if Dev plied him with a twenty-four-hour Seducer-fest, his operative would come around.

Now Dev ran his hands through his hair as his entire body felt as though there was electricity rising off it. Worse than pins and needles, this was a sense of foreboding, as if he'd suddenly become a divining rod leading straight to something that had gone fucking wrong. And it had nothing to do with the Seducers' mission.

No, this was something different.

He barked for Christine—*barked* because she wasn't Marlena, and that was frustrating the hell out of him.

God forbid any of the agents kept up on paperwork since Marlena stopped being his assistant, and Jesus, Christine needed to learn to kick some ass, and fast, or ACRO would go to shit.

It wasn't all her fault, of course. She was just too . . . nice. Too accommodating. And she couldn't read his goddamned mind.

"Give her a break, Dev, she's trying."

Dev swung around, to find Gabe sitting on his couch, feet up. "How long have you been here?"

Gabe smiled, the same smile that made Dev want to throw him over the back of the couch and fuck him until they were both exhausted—which was a real possibility.

"I'm in training—I can't stop for sex," Gabe told him, and Dev wondered if the younger man really *did* have mind-reading abilities. "I just stopped in to show off my newest skill."

"I know you can make yourself invisible," Dev muttered as he stared at the beautiful blond man. But his lover hadn't ever been able to sneak into his office undetected. Dev wasn't sure he liked it, but hell, this could come in handy. "How long have you been here?"

Gabe shrugged. "Long enough. I like watching you."

Devlin pulled the man to him fiercely. "I plan on doing more than watching you."

Gabriel melted against him as the two men fought for control—neither won, and they ended up slamming onto Dev's desk, sending a plethora of objects scattering to the floor, loudly.

Christine finally buzzed in, but bad fucking timing, and Dev told her to belay his order before he turned the radio on, since Gabriel tended to get loud and God fucking knew Christine would call in security if she heard yells.

She was the daughter of one of his oldest and most trusted agents, a psychic who was second in command in that department only to Sam. Christine had no special powers of her own, beyond an intricate understanding of the ACRO structure and its need for secrecy and discretion. So far, Devlin hadn't been worried about her in those areas.

But in others . . .

"Stop thinking. Fuck me," Gabriel murmured breathlessly, stripping himself naked as Dev contented himself with sucking the side of his neck, bracing his hands on the mahogany desk as he lay on top of the younger man.

Content until he heard the voice float into his consciousness.

Dev, fuck—I need help.

"Dev, what's wrong?" Gabe's voice mingled with Creed's—Dev raised a finger. And Creed's voice came through loud and clear.

"Devlin, I need your fucking help. It's Ani. We're in trouble."

"Where are you?" he asked out loud. Gabe cocked his head and watched him for a second and then he disappeared.

Smart man. Dev knew Gabe wouldn't hide here under the cloak of invisibility—no, his lover was a hell of a lot savvier than that. Though he might hang out long enough to see who Dev was dealing with.

"Behind your house, the first road," Creed was answering him. "I can't go back home to Ani until I talk to you."

Just then the line on Devlin's desk buzzed. Christine. "Devlin? Annika's here, asking to see you."

"Shit," Dev said fiercely. "Creed, she's here."

"She's pregnant, Dev. And she doesn't know that I know."

Dev felt his heart drop to his feet as Annika stormed into the office. "Gabriel's not here," he said, well aware that his standard-issue black BDU shirt was unbuttoned to his stomach.

Annika smirked for a second. "I'm not here about him. Although he's a royal pain in the ass." She shut the door—on Christine's face—and Dev felt Gabe melt out of the room. Through the wall this time. Interesting. His lover's skills were getting stronger, but Gabriel still wasn't able to touch anyone, or anything, when he was invisible. He claimed that his hand—indeed, his body—would pass right through any object he attempted to reach out and grab.

Every ability always came with its own issues.

Which of course meant that Gabriel's clothes were still on the floor. Dev surreptitiously kicked them under the desk.

Annika clapped her hands together. "Earth to Dev. I've got a huge problem. Astronomical, bring-down-the-house huge."

Don't tell me, Annika. Have some sense—think about how pissed Creed will be knowing you told me first instead of him . . .

"Where's Creed? I'm sure he'd want to help you."

At the mention of Creed's name, she bit her lower lip and went silent.

Dev took that opportunity to give her a subtle once-over; if he didn't know about her condition, he wouldn't have guessed. She still looked slim and strong, although her face did look slightly drawn. And there were some telltale circles under her eyes as well.

If she was pregnant, it could be a real problem for her, mission-wise. And health-wise.

He remembered what happened to Faith when she'd been pregnant—she'd nearly died on a mission because her powers had been affected, had grown progressively weaker with every month of gestation.

They hadn't been sure she'd even get her powers back after she'd given birth. Thankfully, she had . . . but they weren't as constant a danger as Annika's were.

Dev had never thought any of this would be an issue. Annika had never ever wanted children and she wasn't the type to change her opinions about things.

Even now, as she stood in front of him, he could see that nothing had changed. That brought a slight relief, but he still held his breath as he waited for her to speak.

ANNIKA'S STOMACH ROLLED OVER AS SHE STOOD THERE, DEV'S question about Creed hanging in the air. Fuck. She'd come storming in, unsure where else to go, prepared to tell him she was pregnant so she could beg for advice on how to deal with it. But at the mention of Creed, she froze.

She and Creed had been through so much, and a big part of their problem had been Dev—Creed's jealousy of her relationship with their boss, her dependence on him. For a long time, she relied on Dev when she should have leaned on Creed, and she'd caused her lover a lot of grief.

And here she was, reverting to old habits.

But what else could she do? Dev had saved her a long time ago, had taken her out of a life where she'd been nothing but a cold-hearted killing machine. He'd been there for her whenever she needed him, had been more of a parent to her than the people who'd raised her.

Still, she couldn't betray Creed like this. Not after all they'd been through. If she was going to tell anyone she was pregnant, it would be Creed.

Shit. Now what? Dev was expecting her to say something.

"It's, ah, Baker. He's causing all kinds of trouble at the firing range." She'd actually planned to talk to both Ender, who ran the shooting program, and Gage, the Trainee department head, instead of jumping the chain of command to Dev, but she needed a cover for coming here, and fast.

Dev buttoned up his shirt. "Shouldn't you be talking to—"

"Ender and Drummond. I know. But Baker isn't in shooting instruction yet, so Ender can't really do anything about this. We're just on basic weapons training, and we're cycling through the M16 right now. And Drummond is on a mission." She swallowed a wave of nausea and continued. "Baker is a hazard. Every time he fires the rifle, he melts every weapon within ten feet of him."

"I know he doesn't have control of his gift yet."

No, he didn't. His pyrokinetic gift was a little unique. He couldn't make flame. Instead, he created some sort of subsonic frequency that created intense heat. "It's not that. I think he's doing it on purpose. He's, like, some sort of Greenpeace nut."

Dev cocked a dark eyebrow. "You suspect he's a plant?"

She blew out a long breath. Groups like that had been known to infiltrate the very organizations they protested against in order to bring them down from the inside. "I don't get that vibe. I think he's just trying to do little things here and there to protest." She shrugged. "I could be wrong."

"Okay, we'll keep an eye on him. I'll send him to Samantha and see if she can get into his head and look around a little."

A sudden wave of nausea rolled over Annika, and she threw out a hand to brace herself on Dev's desk. Instantly, he was there, catching her—even though she was still on her feet, thank you very much.

"I'm fine," she ground out, though the room was spinning a little.

Dev gently guided her toward the couch. "Have a seat. Let me get you something to drink."

"I said I'm fine!" She shrugged out of his arms. Her skin was suddenly sensitive and her eyes were watering and she wanted only to climb into bed, with Creed holding her.

Dammit, the waterworks were truly starting now. She dashed away her tears with her BDU sleeve.

"Annika, maybe you should see a doctor."

She scoffed. "It's nothing. I just missed dinner." She'd thrown up dinner, actually. "Look, I need to go. I have a class tonight."

"Ah . . . no, you don't."

She spun around. Forced herself to not fall over. "What?"

Dev squared his shoulders and spread his legs as though preparing for battle, and she knew this would not be good. "You are no longer going to be teaching self-defense and offensive combat."

"Say again?" She could not have heard that.

"Annika, you've been teaching those subjects for two years. It's time to rotate to a classroom setting."

Her blood pressure was going through the roof, making the backs of her eyes throb. "You did not just say that."

"Akbar has been asking to take over—"

"*Akbar?* He's a pussy." Okay, that wasn't true in the least—the guy had trained in Pakistan before joining Mossad, the Israeli intelligence and special operations organization. He was an incredibly skilled fighter, and that, when coupled with his poisonous wrist spurs, made him fucking deadly as shit.

But physical training was her baby. And— *Her baby.* She sucked in a harsh breath. Did Dev know?

"Dev," she said slowly, "what are you not telling me?"

"Nothing. I've been contemplating this move for a while. You know you should have rotated out months ago."

That was true, but the coincidence didn't sit well. Or maybe she was being paranoid. Everything else inside her was fucked up. Why not that?

"No. I'm staying where I am." Which was basically being a stubborn bitch.

"I'm putting my foot down on this. People already think I indulge you too much."

"Since when have you given a shit about that?"

He ignored her. "And let's face it, you and Gabe are butting heads—"

"Gabe?" Her rage hit the next level. "*This is about Gabe?* You're kicking me off the job so your boy toy isn't inconvenienced? Why not him? Why doesn't *he* have to go? Oh, right. Because he sucks your dick." Yeah, she knew she'd gone way over the line, was heading straight to Irrational City, but hey, this was starting to be normal for her. "What are you going to do when Akbar pisses off Gabe? Fire Akbar too, just to make your lover happy?"

"Enough." Dev's voice was low and sharp, a tone he rarely used with her. "You've now earned a suspension of your mission status, until further notice, as well."

She stopped breathing. He'd just spanked her, harder than he ever had. "Fuck you, Dev," she whispered. "Go to hell." Tears spilled onto her cheeks as she stormed out of the office, slamming the door behind her. Christine stared, wide-eyed, but wisely kept her piehole shut.

If this wasn't the biggest piece-of-shit day she'd ever had, she didn't know what was. All she could do was thank God she hadn't told Dev she was pregnant, because in addition to taking away her classes and mission status, he'd probably have revoked her armory pass, restricted her work hours and relegated her to a wheelchair.

She'd die. *Die.* He'd gotten so weird after Faith's near-fatal attack while pregnant, but the thing was, she'd been on a support mission only. No action. And she'd been on her home turf, just outside TAG headquarters in England. All she'd been doing was taking a walk. It was a freak incident, but Dev suddenly seemed to think that pregnant operatives had eggshells for skin.

Well, Annika's skin might be extra-sensitive, but it wasn't fragile. Dev could kiss her ass.

Trembling all over, feeling like she was flying apart and barely grasping a rapidly unraveling thread of sanity, she headed for her Jeep. All she wanted was bed. Maybe tomorrow she'd wake up and find that this big nightmare was over.

CHAPTER *Fourteen*

Finally, camp loomed in front of them, and Logan felt himself sway. The last twenty feet seemed to take hours, but then Dax was rushing toward them, calling to the other men over the walkie-talkie. "Jesus, Lo, you look like shit."

"Yeah, thanks," Logan mumbled, his grip tight on Sela. She held him even tighter than before and that made all of this worth it.

"I've got men looking for you—everyone was worried, wanted to search for you last night, but I followed your orders," Dax continued while he got on the other side of Logan and took on most of the weight Sela had been carrying.

"Call the men back now. We need a better plan," Logan said as the three of them walked to the med tent.

On the way, he caught a glimpse of Shep. "What the hell happened to him?"

Dax shot him a worried glance. "There were some problems while you were gone. Some experimentation."

Logan stopped dead in his tracks. "I didn't order any experimentation."

"No, but your father did," Dax said. "He's here—arrived yesterday, late morning."

"And Chance?"

"He's been better."

"What about Marlena?" Sela broke in, but before Dax could answer, Logan pushed both of them off him and walked toward the med tent, the familiar rage sending enough adrenaline through him to propel him forward.

His father must've been alerted that Logan made camp—he rushed out of the med tent toward him. "Logan, what happened to you?"

"What the hell did you do?" Logan growled.

"Please, we can talk about everything later. For now, you don't look well," his father reasoned.

"Logan, you need to come with us, let us patch you up," one of the doctors urged.

Logan knew he was right, felt the uncontrollable rage skimming the surface. He'd fought it all night with Sela's help—but now the wound was sucking too much of the serum, when the rest of his body needed it. He felt stiff and weak and angry—so angry.

He walked into the med tent with Dax and Sela, and that's when he saw Chance. The man was chained in a corner on the floor, Marlena curled next to him. He looked battered, bruised. "What did you do to him?"

"We ran a few tests," a doctor began hesitantly, cutting a look at Logan's father, who'd refused to answer the question himself.

"Under whose authority?" Logan asked.

"Your father's."

"He's not in charge here!" Logan picked up a chair and hurled it across the room. Chance startled and sat up and Logan forced himself to regain control, for the injured man's sake. "I'm sorry, Chance. It's okay. There will be no more experiments conducted on you without your consent. You have my word on that."

He glanced at Sela, who wore the same expression she'd had in the cave when he'd lost control. She was scared of him, maybe even disgusted, and he couldn't blame her. Fuck.

"Logan, you need to let us help you," the doctor said, glancing between Logan and Sela.

Sela, who'd saved his life, who'd made love to him and made him feel fucking whole.

Sela, who already knew far too much about his bioware. And the company's mission here in the Amazon.

"Dax!"

Dax was by his side in seconds. "Yes, sir?"

He didn't hesitate. "Take Sela and Marlena and put them in lockdown together. Two men guarding at all times. From the outside. And they don't come out until I say so."

He heard the sharp intake of breath from Sela at the sudden betrayal, and out of the corner of his eye, he saw Marlena rub Chance's arm in an effort to keep him calm.

"If you have to sedate Chance to get Marlena out of here, do it," he barked. And then he stared down at his arm and mumbled something even he couldn't understand, as the world began to shift out from under him.

ONCE LOGAN FAINTED, EVERYTHING WENT TO SHIT FAST. Chance reacted quickly, rising to his feet and taking Marlena with him as Dax and the doctors picked Logan off the floor and placed him on the table.

Logan was Chance's only shot at getting out of this hellhole without further experimentation. But once the man had ordered Sela and Marlena contained, Chance knew his own reaction would not be a good one.

He stood with Marlena tucked protectively against him, staring at Dax. "Put the gun down, asshole. I know you're not going to shoot me. Even if you do, it won't kill me."

Not that Chance knew that for sure, but hell, he'd shot at the chupa who'd attacked him, and nothing happened.

"Chance, listen to me, I'm going to be fine. Please don't get angry or upset, don't do that to yourself." Marlena stared at him steadily. "Let me go with them."

"I'll make sure she's okay, Chance," Sela assured him. "Really."

Okay, yeah, he could play this. The monster inside of him was strong as shit, but he, the man, was still damned smart. And so he nodded and moved aside, watched as Sela and Marlena were escorted out of the tent.

Dax was watching him warily, gun still drawn. Behind him, a doctor was holding a syringe, one no doubt filled with tranquilizers.

Chance's jaw tightened. "You don't need that. I said I'll stay put. As long as you don't touch Marlena, I'll be fine."

He sat in the chair and let Dax drag over the long chains for his ankles and wrists. When Dax was done, he took the syringe from the doctor and told Chance, "We'll be outside with this, just in case."

They carried Logan out as Chance watched, and then he was alone in the tent.

These men had to realize that they had nothing in this camp that could hold him for long—and if they didn't, he'd bring it to their attention.

CHAPTER *Fifteen*

Creed breathed deeply and tried to slow his roll as he strode across the parking lot toward Devlin's office and was seriously glad he did so when he caught sight of Ani fuming her way to her Jeep.

She stopped when she saw him and then continued her pissed-off stride until she ended up toe to toe with him.

Ah, the memories of the old days came flashing back to him—the fights, the Annika anger, the never knowing if he was on solid ground.

Fuck, he loved this woman more than he'd ever thought he could love anyone. Could take her right here in the parking lot—that's how much she turned him on.

She, however, seemed less than enthralled to see him.

"What are you doing here?" she demanded. "What, did Dev call you in so you could comfort me?"

"What the hell are you talking about?" he asked, keeping his voice low to avoid drawing stares from some of the other ACRO employees.

Jesus, he hoped Dev didn't say anything about the preg—

"He's treating me like I'm suddenly breakable or something, just because I almost fainted."

"You almost fainted?"

She rolled her eyes. "I'm fine. But Dev took me away from teaching martial arts with some lame excuse that I've been in the position too long."

No, Ani wouldn't take that well at all.

"So I told him I knew Gabe was getting special treatment."

"Aw, Ani, you didn't go there, did you?"

"I might've said something about Gabe sucking his dick." She shrugged, like it was no big deal, but Creed knew it was, to both her and Devlin.

"If anything, Dev indulges you a hell of a lot more than any other agent here—including Gabe."

She eyed him with a pissed-off look, but he'd take that over crying any day of the week. Pissed-off Annika could be handled. "Why are you here?"

"Devlin wanted to see me. I'm assuming it has something to do with my job, because I do fucking work here, okay? You're not the only agent in this relationship."

"Actually, *you* are."

He frowned. "What are you talking about?"

"Dev suspended me from mission status until further notice. Because of my comments about his lover, I'm sure."

Oh, man, this was not good at all. Dev didn't even know about Oz's prediction, and he was still freaking about Annika's pregnancy. He felt Kat's hands on his shoulders, her insistence that he confront Annika, and shrugged her off.

Now wasn't the time to tell Annika he knew . . . better to let her tell him in her own time.

Unless she got too close to the end of her first trimester.

"Do you really think Dev makes more concessions for me than he does for Gabe?" she asked.

"Absolutely." He put an arm around her shoulder and guided her toward her Jeep. "Ani, look, you've definitely held your position longer than you were supposed to. You'd be the first one to bitch if it was someone else."

Reasonable and calm . . . and a small prayer helped.

Maybe Oz was wrong about this. Maybe the pregnancy would be a good thing.

Tell her, Kat insisted.

"Tell me what?" Annika asked, and shit, he'd forgotten that when Kat wanted to, she could make herself heard by Ani.

"Tell you I'm sorry that I'm being an ass," he said smoothly. "I made you mad before, with the past girlfriend thing. The whole fight was my fault."

Annika crossed her arms and eyed him suspiciously, Kat continued to chant, *Tell her,* and then the only thing Creed could think of to get out of this conversation was sex. Lots and lots of sex.

He grabbed Annika and kissed the shit out of her, right in the middle of the parking lot, kissed her until her resistance melted and his tattoos—and his cock—throbbed with need. She responded in kind, the electricity buzzing through them both until she pulled back.

"I thought you needed to go see Devlin."

"He can wait." He picked her up and carried her to the Jeep.

THEY ALMOST DIDN'T MAKE IT BACK TO CREED'S PLACE OFF base. Well, Creed *didn't* make it. He'd been driving, and Annika had been fondling him from the passenger seat. When she leaned over and took him in her mouth, he'd shouted at the top of his lungs and shot his load all the way down her throat.

Damn, she loved the way she could make him blow with hardly any effort, and how he came so hard he could barely breathe afterward. Good thing he could drive, because it would have sucked to end up in the ditch and have to explain to the police how it happened.

Creed pulled to a smooth stop in their driveway, but as she reached for the door handle, he lunged across the space between the seats and pinned her to the door. He was gentle but firm and he wrapped her hair around his fist and took her mouth while tucking her beneath him. It was an awkward position, with one of her legs crammed up on the dash and the other skewered between the seat backs, but his cock was still hard and he was rocking it against her sex, and oh, yes, she so needed this.

"Creed," she moaned, "I'm so sorry about our fight. I was wrong—"

"Shh." He quieted with a tongue lashing against hers. He slipped his hand under her BDU shirt, his palm leaving pleasant tingles in its wake. Her skin had been so sensitive recently, and her breasts—if he touched them, she was sure she'd come . . . *Oh, God.*

He cupped one breast, flicked his thumb over the nipple, and even through the fabric of her bra the sensation was incredible, and she exploded, bucking wildly, and banging her head on the window.

When she could see through the sparks in her vision, Creed was looking down at her with an expression of awe. "Holy shit. You've never come from me touching your breasts before."

"I know." She was panting like she'd run a marathon, but her body was still strung tight, her sex throbbing and aching to be filled—with his fingers, his tongue, his cock . . . she didn't care. "Fuck me, Creed. Fuck me *now.*"

A slow, lazy smile touched his lips. "In the house. I want a bed."

Bed? They weren't going to make it to the bed. She was going to take him down on the driveway and ride him until he begged for mercy.

Geez, hormones were weird.

"Come on." He peeled himself off her, even though she tried to cling to him. "I'll take care of you inside."

"But, Creed . . ." That was the whiniest thing she'd ever said, and it made him laugh.

"Come inside, Annika, and I'll do whatever you want," he cajoled, crooking his finger as he eased out of the Jeep. "Want my mouth between your legs? Want me to suck you off again and again?" His voice grew deep and husky, and she knew he was as affected by his graphic talk as she was. "I can taste you already. You're wet for me, aren't you? I'm going to bury my tongue in your pussy and eat you until my cock is ready to explode." He backed toward the house as she climbed out of the vehicle. "And then I'm going to flip you over and fuck you, long and hard."

She growled low in her throat and stalked him, thinking she could pounce when he stopped to unlock the front door. Good thing they didn't have neighbors, because she was ripping off her top and he was rubbing his dick, and fuck, they'd had some intense sex over the last couple of years, but this was going to blow the lid off all those other times.

"You want it, baby?" he murmured, as he jerked himself with long, tantalizing pulls. "You want this buried so deep you can taste it when I come?"

A wave of silky wetness flooded her. She ran at him. And damn him, the door was unlocked. He bolted through the doorway and pounded up the stairs. She gave chase, and as she topped the landing, where the huge loft bedroom was, he caught her and spun her onto the bed.

He came down beside her, careful not to squish her. They ripped their clothes off so fast she heard the tearing of fabric, and when he lay back on the bed and pulled a leg up to unlace his boots, she finally pounced. Before he could protest, she straddled his face so she could look down the long length of his gorgeous body.

"Do it, Creed," she demanded. "Do it like you said."

At the first stab of his tongue in her slit, she cried out. She managed to hold it together so she could take off his boots as he licked at her, and once his boots were off, she eased down on his mouth, threw back her head, and let him do what he did best.

His tongue swirled in her core, round and round, and then pushed deep, thrusting in and out. Her nervous system whacked out, shooting electric tingles all over her body, and she knew he was tasting her sparks like a battery. He moaned and spread her wide with his thumbs. He was ruthless with his technique, keeping her on the edge and anchoring her thighs in place when she began to pump her hips, fucking his face with the need to explode.

"Not yet." His mouth hummed against her core. "I need more of you . . . " He closed his lips around her clit and sucked, and she screamed with pleasure.

Annika fell forward and gripped his hips. His cock lay stiffly on his abs, the tip dripping with pre-cum, or maybe it was leftover from his earlier orgasm. She swiped her tongue across the broad head, and his smoky flavor exploded on her taste buds. He bucked, but he didn't stop his ravaging rhythm. He devoured her, every decadent lick, suck, thrust bringing her so much pleasure she thought she might die.

Whimpering with the need to come, she captured his heavy sac in her mouth and sucked, letting him know she was done playing. He got the hint, and immediately, the tip of his tongue danced on her clit and took her straight to the ceiling. Her orgasm took her apart, rattling her bones and stretching her joints, until the only thing holding her together was her too-tight skin. She shouted so loud she knew her voice would be gone in the morning.

Before the climax had fully melted away, Creed lifted her and rolled out from beneath her with a speed and grace that always surprised her when it came from a man so big. But in a matter of a heartbeat, he was impaling her from behind, his cock scraping over already sensitive tissues and igniting another intense release.

"God, Annika," he breathed. "I love you."

She barely had the ability to speak, but she managed a husky "Love you too. So . . . much . . . *Mmm . . . yes . . .* "

Slowly, and much more controlled than she expected, he withdrew and plunged inside her again. Her tissues burned at the invasion, but it was a good burn. She could feel the pulse of his shaft as her channel spasmed around it, could feel the soft slap of his balls against her tender, swollen pussy lips.

"You're so wet, so slick. Soaked." His voice was a raw rasp that rolled through her sweetly. "You feel so good." He wrapped his muscular arm around her belly and hiked her hips higher as he increased the tempo of his thrusts.

This was bliss. This was perfect. Beyond perfect. Fire shot through her core, spreading from where they joined all the way to her fingers. His panting breaths came faster, and she knew he was only a few pumps of his hips away, which was good, because she was right there too.

Their orgasms crashed into them at the same time, his hot splashes intensifying her release.

They collapsed on their sides on the bed. As always, she'd lit up like a lightning storm during orgasm, something that would kill any other man, but it only made Creed come harder, and they both lay there and twitched as their orgasms went on and on, her electric current keeping them going even longer than normal.

Was this a pregnancy thing? She hoped so, because there had to be some benefit to offset the crying jags and mood swings and morning sickness, which was a stupid name for it, because it happened all day and night.

Fifteen minutes later, when they could move again, Creed hefted his arm over her waist and tugged her as close as they could get. A sheet of paper couldn't get between them right now.

No, the only thing that could possibly get between them would be a baby.

STRYKER WILLS WAS SIX FEET FIVE INCHES OF LEAN MUSCLE, with a broad back and shoulders and eyes that women got lost in. They were nearly crystal clear with a hint of blue and green—kaleidoscope eyes, his first girlfriend, in kindergarten, had dubbed them. They'd made him the object of scorn and, at times, fear, but for the most part they got him laid on a regular basis. The angular jaw and chiseled cheeks and blond hair didn't hurt either. But Stryker never really thought about those things—he was usually too busy trying to keep his temper in check so he didn't set off a string of earthquakes that could swallow the United States whole.

A pretty heady thing for a kid to learn when he was in the if-I-want-it-I'll-take-it, it's-all-about-me phase of his life.

Luckily, with two parents who were agents with special abilities and working for ACRO, he had the best help imaginable to learn to channel any and all anger from his body.

The fact that his gift also came with, ah, hormonal side effects was unsettling, to say the least. His libido was directly affected by his gift—and vice versa—so his temper wasn't the only thing he needed to keep under control.

His abilities as an agent kept him well in demand. His gift was extremely volatile and had the potential for mass destruction, and so he was forced to use it sparingly when on assignment. You never knew how the earth would react to a quake, what the ripple effect would be, no matter how small he tried to make it.

The unofficial ACRO motto, *Don't piss us off, we can kill you with our minds*, was never more true than when he was out on a mission. He was back home now though, on leave and hitting the gym—the second best way to deal with stress.

He'd find—and do—the first later on tonight.

He set the weights and began to bench the three hundred pounds on the bar. Fuck the excedos and their superstrength, he could take any one of them in a fair fight.

Then again, he could take out half the civilized world if he really wanted to.

Good thing he was a pretty easygoing guy these days.

He lifted the weight, got to eight reps before he saw Dev standing over him.

"I didn't call for a spotter."

"I'm not here to be one." And yeah, Dev made no attempt to help him put the bar back in place.

When Stryker did, he sat up and swiveled to look at his boss.

"Stryker . . . "

"You told me I could have some time off."

Dev cocked an eyebrow. "I never make promises about leave. You know that."

Stryker sighed. "What is it this time?"

"I need someone who knows the Amazon well. You fit the bill."

Stryker did, had spent plenty of time there adventure-seeking in his late teens and early twenties. "Who's going with me?"

"Akbar."

"When do I leave?" Stryker asked, and then looked toward the door of the gym, where Dev's glance had gone.

Two of the most beautiful Seducers stood there, waiting. One of them pointed and then motioned to Stryker.

"You've got a couple of hours. Make good use of it," Dev told him.

"You didn't have to bribe me, Devlin."

"But it's so much more fun that way."

GABE SLIPPED INTO DEV'S OFFICE SECONDS BEFORE AKBAR slammed through the door. And since Akbar wasn't the invisible one, he got Dev's immediate attention.

Gabe knew he should leave immediately, that he shouldn't be sneaking in and out of Devlin's office at all. But hell, it wasn't like he was planning on gossiping about any of the intel he'd learned on these recon missions. No, he considered it all a part of training, as he'd told Dev earlier.

And far more interesting than the training the other agents, like Annika and Akbar, wanted him to do. He'd done enough goddamned fighting to last for a hundred years.

"Devlin, we must talk." Akbar was all business. The man stood well over six feet tall, with deeply tanned skin and black hair—handsome and menacing all at once.

Devlin gave a small frown. "So talk."

"I do not want to step on any toes."

"That's never stopped you before. Besides, if you step too hard, I'll beat the shit out of you." Dev's voice was steady but a half smile softened the words.

Gabe had only been at ACRO a few months but he knew as well as the other men and women who worked for Dev that his lover was a fair and semi-patient man. And yeah, this was going to be a good show, especially because Gabe found himself turned on by the authority in the man's voice—aw, hell, he could get turned on just watching Dev do paperwork.

"Gabe is a fuckup," Akbar said bluntly, and Gabe stood, as if to defend himself. This was suddenly no longer a fun floor show.

Dev didn't say anything more than "Go on."

"He is not taking the training seriously. Not working on his skills. I am unsure if it is because he thinks he can get away with murder because of you or something else, but that is certainly not helping."

"You know I don't give special treatment to anyone who's fucking up at their job," Dev growled, and Gabe's heart sank.

"Of course. But the kid needs discipline, or I will never take him on a job with me." Akbar's Middle Eastern accent usually softened his words, but now it delivered a hard, cold promise few other agents could match. "I will never clear him. I know you have big plans for him, but I would not trust him with any responsibility right now."

Gabe shook with anger. He was trying, dammit. It was just that coming to ACRO was finally like being home. He wasn't the oddball. He could relax, didn't have to be on guard all the time.

Then again, he had to learn to back up his fellow agents so they didn't all look at him with inherent suspicion because of his newness and the affair with Devlin.

And what the hell were the big plans Devlin had for him?

"If Gabriel can't cut it as an ACRO agent, he won't go anywhere, plans or no plans." Dev's voice was firm; he meant it.

What the hell did you expect, Devlin to stick up for you?

Fuck. His breathing was so harsh he was sure the men could hear it, but they were engrossed in their conversation. Gabe wanted to leave the goddamned room now, but when he was pissed or upset, the walk-through-walls thing didn't happen.

He was stuck. Trapped. Deserved what he got too, for being where he shouldn't.

"I know Annika spoke to you about Gabe already," Akbar continued, "but I needed to reiterate. Kid is a pain in the ass. It is going to take a hell of a lot for him to impress me."

"You do what you have to do," Dev said. "Write him up. Make him train overtime. He deals with it or he's out."

That hit Gabe like a punch in the gut. *Out*.

"Your flight to the Amazon leaves in two hours," Dev continued. "I've already briefed Stryker."

"I can get the intel from him, then." Akbar started to leave, but paused at the door. "I am sorry, Devlin. I know you want Gabe to work out. He's got a hell of a talent, but he is not earning anyone's respect."

"I understand."

Gabe watched as Dev stared out the window and wished to hell he could read minds. Then again, maybe it was better right now that he didn't know what his lover was thinking.

He slid out of the office, didn't materialize until he was back in his room. Sat for a few minutes on his bunk and thought about what he could do to prove himself—and fast.

Your flight to the Amazon leaves in two hours.

Yes, and Gabe would find a way to be on it.

CHAPTER Sixteen

When Logan surfaced, he found himself faceup, strapped to a table in the command tent, the familiar panic welling inside his chest. His father and Dr. Ives were next to him.

"Logan, you're okay," his father said. "We've given you a mild sedative and we're repairing your arm."

"Turn off the fucking light." He put up his free hand to shield his eyes until the overhead lamp was angled away. He kept his hand there, his mind racing as his dad asked, "Who are the two women?"

He remembered feeling faint, remembered getting extremely paranoid . . . ordering Sela and Marlena contained.

It's for their safety, and for ours, he reassured himself. Sela knew enough now to really do some damage to the company if she wanted to.

He had to find out who she was really working for. Who'd trained her to fight. What she'd shown him in the jungle, those weren't simple reactions that could be explained away by her childhood and other traumas. Those moves weren't taught in self-defense classes.

She'd been trained by someone in Special Ops. During her truth-telling session, she'd conveniently left that part out. Finally he answered his father. "We came across them in the jungle. Sela's a cryptozoologist."

"Who just happened to be in this jungle looking for a chupacabra?" his father asked.

Logan ground his teeth, irritated by his father's sarcasm. "I took precautions by bringing them to camp."

"And now she knows about the bioware. Who does she work for?"

"I don't know," Logan growled, and his father snorted. "Don't give me shit, Dad. You don't have the right to get on any kind of fucking high horse right now." His father held up both hands in a sign of surrender, and why the hell was the room spinning? "What exactly did you give me?"

"Just something to calm you down, to take the edge off," the doctor explained, looking up from where he was starting work on Logan's arm. Fuck it all, those meds hit him too hard most of the time. He hated the fuzzy feeling around the edges of the still human half of his brain. If it weren't for the bioware portion, he'd be a drooling mess on the table.

A hand—his father's—came down on Logan's good arm.

"Logan, you're going to be just fine."

"Is Chance?"

His father didn't answer at first, and then, "I wanted to help out. Itor's been putting pressure on the company to get the chupacabra recaptured quickly."

"And what? You'd give them Chance instead to appease them?" he asked, and his father didn't deny it. "Chance is a SEAL. Just like I was. How could you do that to him? He's still a man."

"Logan, you don't understand."

"Damned straight I don't. What, I'm not enough of an experiment for you?" Logan saw his father wince, and he hated the satisfaction that settled in his own gut.

Not your fault—it's the wound.

Indeed, his arm was twisted at an awkward angle, wires exposed as the surgeon worked. They'd pumped him full of the familiar black sludge, but with opened skin, he was bleeding it out faster than they could give it to him. "Why are you really here?" Logan demanded.

His father looked pained. "It's about Caroline."

"What's wrong with her?"

"I don't want to . . . I thought I could take care of it before you had to know."

It was only sheer will that kept Logan flat on his back on the table. "Tell. Me."

"Itor has her."

Suddenly, it all made sense. His father might have questionable values and standards, but he couldn't imagine he would've morphed into such a monster that he would perform horrifying experiments on an innocent man.

But for his daughter . . . "When? How?"

"They took her from college on Friday—they told her they were from GWC. They said you were hurt."

Of course Caroline would go without question. Shit. "What are their terms?"

"If they don't have the chupacabra within a week, they'll—"

"Don't say it." Logan rubbed his forehead with his free hand. Contracted by Itor, GWC had been studying the chupacabra's weapons potential, but when Itor changed the game and insisted on being given the animal, GWC's shareholders panicked. The weapons potential the creature represented could bring billions of dollars into the company. Its loss was not an option. Logan's father had figured if GWC could find another chupacabra and start a breeding program, they'd be able to give Itor one of the creatures, and problem solved. Richard had taken a gamble by sending a team back to the Amazon with the animal, hoping the creature would attract another, but when the chupacabra had escaped two weeks into the mission, clearly Itor's patience had run out.

Fuck. "How much longer do I fucking have to lie here?"

"Another few hours, at least." The doctor barely looked up from the delicate repair, and Logan sighed in frustration. He tried not to let the bitterness overwhelm him, but then he thought about Caroline . . . and Sela, who was pissed at him, no doubt.

Logan's father rubbed the back of his neck. "When they took her—threatened her—I thought about Chance. A trade. I ordered the tests to make sure he possessed the qualities of the original animal, so Itor would be satisfied. You have to understand," he pleaded, and Logan tried to forget the way Chance had looked, lying on that floor, holding Marlena.

Because, unfortunately, Logan did understand. "That's still no reason to torture an innocent man. We'll get Caroline away from Itor."

"How? You're no closer to recapturing the chupacabra than you were a month ago. And now you've got two women here who could be spies from a competitor or the government—and one of them knows about you, what you are."

"What the hell am I, Dad?" he asked, his voice low, and dangerous enough that the doctor froze.

His father had once been SAS—the British Secret Service. He understood what Logan had been through in the military. When Logan was younger, he'd wanted nothing more than to follow in his father's footsteps.

Now he was sickened that he almost had. Logan didn't wait for his father to respond to a question no one knew the answer to. "What does Itor know about Chance?"

His father's hesitation told Logan all he needed to know. Itor knew all about Chance, that he could change into a chupacabra. Which made him very valuable to Itor.

Chance's life was now in danger in more ways than one. Most of all, he'd become a prisoner in his own body. And, as Logan glanced at his arm, he felt the pressure of that knowledge settle over him like a lead weight.

"THAT BASTARD." SELA PACED THE LENGTH OF LOGAN'S PERsonal tent while Marlena stood near the entrance, arms crossed over her chest and just as pissed. Fortunately, she hadn't fought being taken away from Chance. She'd been smart enough to realize that if she caused a scene, Chance would freak and Logan's men would be forced to sedate him. Or worse.

As Sela passed by, Marlena grabbed her arm and spun her around. "What the hell is going on? What happened while you two were in the jungle? Didn't you—?" She cut herself off before she said it and risked the men waiting outside overhearing.

Didn't you seduce him?

"Of course I did," Sela snapped. "Don't fucking blame me for this. I know what I'm doing, and I've been doing it for a hell of a lot longer than you have."

Marlena's chin came up so she was looking down her perfect nose at Sela. "Then why are we locked up and under guard?"

"Because Logan is an asshole. He betrayed me." Sela almost laughed. Here she was, all indignant because he'd betrayed her, when *she* was the one who had been deceitful all along.

Instead of letting out the bitter laugh condensing in her chest, she jerked away from the other woman and took a deep, calming breath. Fighting with her partner was counterproductive, especially when there was an element of truth to what Marlena had said.

Sela had failed. She'd gotten very little usable intel from Logan, and she apparently hadn't gotten close enough to him to make him trust her. Either that, or he suspected she wasn't who she said she was. Maybe both. In any case, she'd fucked up.

Guilt tore through her, a big, knotted jumble of it. She'd let herself get too close to Logan, which had compromised her mission and failed ACRO. And she'd been lying to Logan, which hadn't been a problem at first, but she'd stopped seeing him as a bad guy at some point, and now . . . well, she actually felt bad about deceiving him.

Except that she was also furious at him for locking her up.

"I'm sorry," Marlena said quietly. "I realize this isn't your fault. I'm just worried about Chance."

"I know." She knew, because despite her fury, Sela was just as worried about Logan. He hadn't looked good for a couple of hours, and then, right before he'd given the order to have her and Marlena put under house arrest, he'd gone as white as a sheet and started swaying. And as she and Marlena were escorted away, he'd collapsed.

Sela had tried to run back to him, but she'd been restrained and he'd been surrounded by doctors, and there had been nothing for her to do but bitch and curse as she was herded to the tent.

Marlena sank down on Logan's cot and looked longingly at the bottle of Scotch on the table. "Did you learn anything?"

Sighing, Sela sat next to her so they could speak in a whisper. "Logan is half machine. His company developed the hardware for soldiers or something, and he's the prototype."

"Oh." Marlena looked taken aback. The woman whose boyfriend was a fucking chupacabra.

"It isn't like he's the Terminator or anything. But I can't read him, and I think that's why. Part of his brain is a hard drive."

Marlena looked even more surprised—not terrified, but now Sela understood why Logan was so defensive about his condition, if this was what he was used to dealing with. Shame washed over her; had he seen the same expression on her face when he told her the truth?

Shit. She didn't want to talk about this. "Did you get anything from Chance, or the staff?"

"Not much," Marlena admitted. "They took him. Experimented on him or something." Her voice hitched, and Sela decided she didn't want the gory details. "I don't think they were doing it to help him."

Sela nodded. "Logan wouldn't tell me what the company plans to do with the chupacabra once they catch it, but given what GWC does, they'll probably want to use it as a weapon, and I'll bet Itor's involved. He said it would be dangerous for me to know too much."

"Bastards," Marlena spat.

"GWC or Itor?" Sela dug the scales and blood-covered leaf from her pocket and set them on the table. They might not have gotten the chupacabra, but these were still amazing samples and would be worth their weight in gold at the Crypto lab. She also needed to get hold of all of GWC's research on the chupacabra they'd had in captivity, as well as all medical records pertaining to Chance.

"Both." Marlena clenched her fists at her sides, her gaze sharp and fierce. "I want Logan and his damned company to pay for what they've done to Chance."

A protective instinct reared up in Sela from out of nowhere. "Logan isn't responsible for Chance being attacked or experimented on." Not directly, anyway. Sela was sure of it.

"Oh, my God," Marlena whispered. "You've fallen for him."

Sela's heart clenched as Marlena's words sank in. Because yes, she'd fallen for him, and that could only lead to disaster.

CHAPTER *Seventeen*

The gynecologist appointment was a disaster. Dr. Davies had confirmed Annika's pregnancy, and had also shared her concerns about Annika losing her power.

"I can't predict exactly what will happen if you go through with this pregnancy," Davies said. "Almost every woman with special abilities experiences changes. Some lose their abilities completely and never get them back, others see a slight increase in power that lasts even after the birth."

The idea that Annika could lose her powers forever made her break out in a cold sweat. "When?" she rasped. "When will these changes happen?"

The doctor shifted her stethoscope as if she was nervous. "Again, it varies. Some start seeing changes at conception. With others, it happens in the second or third trimester. And it can be gradual or sudden."

"That is not a helpful answer," Annika snapped.

And then she'd made sure Davies understood that she'd learn the meaning of hell if she spoke a word about her pregnancy to anyone, including Dev.

She'd left the office, only to get a call from the director of the Training division with details about her new duties.

Despite being thoroughly pissed off, she was heading to Dev's office to apologize to him. Probably not the best idea, given her mood, but she couldn't wait another minute. She hated fighting with him, and their argument kept playing over and over in her head, hijacking her appetite, her sleep, her mind.

Annika stormed into the outer office, where Christine was sitting at the desk, her puffy eyes and sullen expression saying she'd had a recent cry. Maybe she was pregnant too.

"Is Dev in?"

"Yes, but he's busy with someone."

"Who?"

"I'm not at liberty to say."

Annika slammed her palms on the desktop. "Tell me or I'll shock you into next week."

Christine swallowed. "Creed."

"Thank you." Annika smiled. "Now, in the future, when someone asks you what I asked you, tell them, 'I'm not at liberty to say, but you're free to have a seat and see who leaves.' And if they threaten you like I did, push that little button under the desk. Dev will come out and kick their ass."

Christine returned the smile. "Thank you."

"No problem." Annika turned away just as Dev's door opened and Creed walked out.

"Hey, babe," he said, and pulled her into his arms. "If you're here to apologize, it might not be the best time."

"I know. But I have to do it."

He kissed the top of her head. "Just don't get yourself worked up."

She snorted. "As if I would do that."

"Yeah, it's crazy talk."

"Smart-ass." She socked him in the shoulder and went into Dev's office, closing the door behind her.

Dev looked up from where he was sitting at his desk, his hair a spiky wreck, his eyes bloodshot and framed by dark crescents from lack of sleep. "I'm not changing my mind about your training assignment or your mission status."

"That's not why I'm here." She looked around his office, which was as wrecked as he was. "I'm here to apologize."

His eyebrows shot up in surprise. "It's not necessary."

"Yes it is."

"Annika—"

"I'm not good at this," she broke in, "but I need to do it. And you need to hear it." She inhaled raggedly. "I'm really sorry, Dev. I haven't been myself lately, but that's no excuse. I crossed a line and was more than a little disrespectful. You didn't deserve that. Not as a friend, and certainly not as my boss."

For a long moment, he just stared at her. "Thank you. I know that wasn't easy."

"And about Gabe—"

He held up his hand. "We're not discussing him."

"Yes, we are." She started pacing, careful to avoid stepping on crumpled files, a stapler and the broken shards of a coffee mug. "Look, I've been jealous, okay? It's stupid, I know. But for a long time you were all I had. You were the only family I've ever known. I have Creed now too, and I'm still getting used to balancing the both of you. Hell, I'm still learning how to have any kind of relationship. No one ever told me that the problems don't end with those three little *I love you* words." She dragged her hand through her hair. "And it's all the dumb little things I catch on, because I've never had to share with anyone. I mean, the other day I bought toothpaste, and I wondered if couples are supposed to share or get their own. Dumb, huh? I still don't know the answer to that one."

She didn't give Dev time to respond. She kept going before she lost her nerve. "So I'm learning and stumbling and doing my best to not screw up or lose you or Creed, and then suddenly, there was Gabe, taking up all your time, so you didn't come over for dinner anymore . . ." She cut him a meaningful look. "And it didn't help that Gabe's an asshole. I don't know how to add another person into my life. I mean, look how long it took me to let Creed in, and I *love* him. It takes time for me to adjust, and you know I have a tendency to strike out first and ask questions later."

"Annika, you're handling your relationships very well, considering your past."

She almost laughed. "Everyone at ACRO hates me. I wouldn't say I handle any kind of relationship well."

"That's not true. Everyone wants to work with you."

"That's because I'm good. But no one wants to be in the same room with me outside of work." No one except Haley, ACRO's head parameteorologist, with whom Annika had forged a strange friendship over the last couple of years. Which was fine with her, the way she wanted it. She just didn't know how to deal nicely with most everyone else. She was too awkward when it came to social situations, and she was always making stupid mistakes, which created self-doubt, and if there was one thing she couldn't handle, it was not being confident in herself.

Dev leaned back in his chair and folded his hands over his abs. "You're being too hard on yourself."

"Whatever." She stopped pacing and faced him. "I was wrong to say the things I said about Gabe. He makes you happy, and I'm a shit for being an ass about it."

He sighed. "It's okay. You actually helped me confront something with him that needed to be handled."

Oh, shit. "What did you do?"

"Nothing that concerns you."

She drew in a harsh breath, because she had a feeling Dev and Gabe had fought, maybe even broken up, and if so, it was her fault. "Look, I can talk to him."

"Don't."

The tone of his voice said he was done talking about Gabe, so she gave up. For now. She planned to hunt down Gabe and find out what had happened though. "Okay . . . but . . . can I go back on active mission status now?"

"I thought you said that wasn't why you were here."

"I swear I was going to apologize anyway. But . . . I need it. Please."

"I'm sorry," Dev said firmly, "but the answer is no."

"Dev, I'm begging you." Fear that he'd truly not change his mind made her emotions start swimming in that crazy soup again. "I'm so lost right now. My moods are all over the place, and I can't control them. Creed doesn't want kids with me. I'm not training anymore. Miles just called and he's not even putting me in a classroom. Since I'm not on active mission status, he thinks I should fill in for other instructors when *they* go on missions. And in the meantime, he wants me to fucking inspect trainee quarters. My life is going to consist of endless hours of making sure beds are made and underwear is folded properly. I'll die, Dev. *Please.* You don't have to actually send me on missions. Just let me have my active status back so I can feel a little normal."

Dev pinched the bridge of his nose as though warding off a headache, and then his gaze snapped up at her again. "Wait. Go back to Creed and the kids. You said he doesn't want any?"

"No, I said he doesn't want any with *me.*"

Scowling, Dev shoved to his feet. "When did he say this?"

"Couple of days ago."

His expression darkened. "God, Annika. No wonder you've been so upset."

"It's no biggie." She jammed her hands in her pants pockets and looked down at the floor. "I'm sure he thinks I'd be a shitty mom, and he's right. I mean, a few months ago he thought maybe we should have a pet, so he got me a goldfish, and I managed to kill it within three weeks."

"What do you think he'd do if you got pregnant?"

Her throat closed up so tight she had to swallow half a dozen times before she could speak. "I think he might... leave me. He'd take the kid and leave me."

"I doubt that would happen, but you need to talk to him."

"I already did. He was adamant." The tremor in her voice was humiliating. "I can't lose him, Dev. On top of everything else, I can't lose him."

Dev's arms came around her. "Your fear is making you doubt him and yourself. Talk to him, okay?"

She braced her forehead against his chest. "I will. And the mission status? Please, can I have it be active again?"

"Tell you what," he said. "You go to medical and get a full physical, and if everything looks good, I'll put you back on active duty."

Disappointment sapped her strength, and she stepped away from him on wobbly legs. "Why?"

"You said yourself your moods are all over the place. You nearly passed out in my office yesterday. I want to know you're healthy."

"But—"

"This isn't negotiable. You want to go on assignments, I need to know you're in top form."

Fuck. There was no way he'd clear her for missions if he knew she was pregnant. Not unless the mission was something lame, like posing as the wife of another agent—an agent who would get to do all the fun stuff.

"Fine," she sighed, as though she intended to get that exam. But what she intended to do was find Gabe. She couldn't fix any of her own problems right now, but at least she could try to fix Dev's.

Yep. Avoidance mode was definitely engaged.

Annika searched practically every nook and cranny on the ACRO grounds, but Gabe was nowhere to be found. He hadn't been in the tiny base bar where he liked to hang out after class, he wasn't at the gym, in his dorm room or even at the little park where she sometimes caught him lying on the grass in the sun.

No one had even seen him, and she was about to give up when her cell rang. She dug it out of her BDUs' leg pocket—an awkward trick while driving a stick.

It was Kira, an animal psychic who worked at ACRO's massive animal complex. Gabe had been assigned there months ago, mainly just doing odd jobs when he wasn't in a training class. Both Dev and Kira had thought that working with animals would focus him, and okay, Annika had definitely seen improvement since he started working there . . . but not enough.

He still tried to weasel out of lessons and half-assed his studies of past missions that were supposed to teach him about successes and mistakes. His detail work was sloppy, because the only thing he wanted to do was practice with his abilities. He hadn't yet learned that there were reasons the recruits were taught seemingly crazy things, like folding their T-shirts into perfect squares.

People who didn't follow orders got killed.

"Yeah?" Annika asked, by way of greeting. She eased the Jeep to a stop at an intersection near the medical clinic. "Did Gabe come in?" The animal facility had been the first place she'd looked, but that had been an hour ago, and she'd asked Kira to call if she heard from him.

"He stopped by to visit Jag—"

"Who's Jag?"

"Border collie. Bomb sniffer. Gabe has kind of bonded with him." Kira paused, and Annika heard a snort from something that sounded like a horse. "Anyway, I didn't hear what Gabe said, but he took off when he saw me. So I asked Jag what was up."

Kira didn't actually hold conversations with the animals, but she was able to communicate through images, scents and projected words, if the animals understood them. "And?"

"Jag indicated that Gabe was taking a holiday. Something about a plane. And a jungle? I don't know. It wasn't very clear."

No shit. That wasn't a lot of help. Wait. "Jungle?"

"I think so."

"Thanks, Kira. I owe you." She hung up and flung her phone into the passenger seat as she sped toward the base airport.

ACRO's fleet of custom aircraft included three helicopters, two jets and one C-130 cargo plane, the latter of which was on the tarmac, its rear cargo ramp down, and Annika had a sneaky suspicion that Gabe was on that plane. The crew might not know it, either because he was pulling his invisible trick or because of the thick bulkhead separating the crew and passenger section from the cargo hold. He could hang out with the supplies and no one would know he was there until the plane landed.

Cursing, she slammed the Jeep into a stall in the hangar parking lot. She leaped out and ran toward the plane.

The whir of an engine vibrated the air, and the cargo bay ramp began its slow crawl upward. Without thinking, she leaped onto the ramp, sprinted into the rear of the plane and dove for the control panel. The ramp couldn't be stopped, but the door could, alerting the pilots to a problem.

As her fingers brushed the toggle switch, something hit her shoulder, and she wheeled into a steel crate. *What the—*

Gabe stood there, between her and the control panel. The bastard had been doing his damned invisible thing. "Oh, no, you don't."

"Gabe," she snapped. "Get off the plane. Now."

"Fuck you."

The ramp was a third of the way up. "If you get off now, I'll make sure your punishment is minor."

"What part of *fuck you* are you not getting?"

Annika clenched her fists to keep from knocking Gabe's teeth out. "This plane is heading on a mission. A mission you are definitely not ready for. You'll get yourself killed. Or worse, you'll get someone else killed."

She'd obviously struck a nerve, because his eyes flashed and he took a menacing step toward her. She smiled. Bring it on. She'd kicked his ass so many times in training that she knew every move he'd make before he even made it.

"I need to do this," he growled.

Oh, she was tempted to deck him, but once the ramp closed, the door would shut, and they'd be screwed. There was a custom-made, thick wall between the passenger section and the cargo hold, with a door that could only be opened from the other side. The moment the cargo doors closed, Annika and Gabe were in for the ride.

She was done being nice.

"You," she said crisply, "had your chance. You are now in so much trouble, you're going to need a backhoe to dig yourself out of the deep shit you're in. And this time, I guarantee that no amount of dick-sucking is going to get you out of it."

She shoved him aside and reached for the panel again, but he snagged her arm and spun her back to him. She wanted to light him up, but the sudden motion had made her head spin and her stomach churn, and it took everything she had to keep from passing out.

"You little bitch. I have no idea what a cool guy like Creed sees in you, but I hope one of these days he gets wise and dumps your ass."

The buzzing in her ears muted his words. Saliva filled her mouth and a cold sweat broke out on her skin as nausea rolled over her. Swallowing sickly, she jerked out of his grip and went for the switch once more, a little sluggishly.

This time, when he grabbed her, she lit herself up—or tried to. Nothing happened. Even as Gabe shoved her toward the bulkhead, panic flared. Her power . . . gone. She tried again, nausea making her weak and fear making her clumsy, and her feet hit something and then she was falling. Her head slammed into the corner of a crate, and blackness took her.

OH, SHIT. FUCK, FUCK, FUCK!

Gabe knelt next to Annika, disbelief clouding his brain. Annika couldn't be hurt. He was pretty sure she was indestructible.

"Annika?" He shook her shoulders, gently at first, and then with increasing urgency. "Annika!"

Behind him, the cargo door closed with a clang and a hiss, and darkness filled the bay. Only one recessed light illuminated the forward section of the huge space, but he could see well enough to note the blood streaming down Annika's temple.

"Shit! Annika?" No response. He had to get her help.

Desperate, he scanned the bay. The control panel. She'd been trying to trip the switches, which obviously must control the ramp and door. He stood, but the aircraft shuddered and lurched forward, and Gabe stumbled into the crate Annika had hit.

Awkwardly, he shambled to the panel and flipped the switches. Nothing happened. He glanced at Annika, who still lay motionless.

Think, dammit. Right. He'd never been in the fucking cargo hold of a plane before, but there had to be an alarm here somewhere... or an intercom to the pilot. As the plane gathered momentum, he felt around the walls, scanning the floor, the ceiling, everywhere he could think of, but there was nothing. What kind of damned planning was this? Whoever designed this death trap should be shot.

He pounded on the metal wall that separated the passenger compartment from the cargo hold, shouting for help. No response. Was the thing soundproof? Or maybe the engines drowned the noises. Could be superthick metal too—the fact that it was metal at all meant he couldn't dematerialize through it.

He scrubbed his face with both hands as he considered his pathetically few options.

Maybe a phone. But he didn't have one—trainees weren't allowed cell phones. That had been something Dev hadn't budged on, no matter how often Gabe had bugged him. But surely Annika had one.

Carefully, because he didn't want Annika waking while he was feeling her up or he was liable to be shocked into the next century, he searched her black BDUs, but he found only car keys. His throat grew tight as the reality of their situation began to sink in. Fuck, he was in so much trouble. He hadn't been worried about Dev's reaction to his little stowaway mission idea, because he'd planned to show his boss and lover that he could handle himself.

But because of Gabe, Annika was injured. And if she didn't kill him when she came to, Creed would. Dev would make the funeral arrangements.

Hand shaking, he put pressure on her head wound, but the bleeding appeared to have already slowed. "Annika? Come on. I know you hate me, but I need you to wake up."

She moaned, and he blew out a relieved breath, which cut off as the plane rose, knocking him off balance again. Annika rolled—he caught her, dragged her against him and held her as the aircraft climbed skyward.

He was officially screwed. All he could do now was hope to hell Annika loved the Amazon. He looked down at her and also hoped that she was a cheerful morning person.

Somehow, he doubted it.

CHAPTER *Eighteen*

At some point in the evening, a couple of hours after Marlena and Sela had been put under house arrest, Dax brought them food. Marlena had begged for an update about Chance, but Dax wouldn't say anything. He'd looked at Sela as though he expected her to ask about Logan, but she remained silent. She wasn't about to give him the satisfaction.

An hour later, he returned and allowed them to shower and change before shoving them back in the tent. Marlena instantly fell asleep on Logan's cot. With darkness engulfing the camp and a rough day behind her, Sela rolled out the sleeping bag and collapsed into a deep sleep.

She wasn't sure how long she'd slept when she woke to a hand shaking her shoulder. In the darkness, she could make out Dax's form. For a second, she considered feigning a nightmare and punching him, but a glance told her Marlena was still sleeping, and she didn't want to wake her.

So Sela hefted her backpack over her shoulder and groggily

followed Dax across the camp, to a large tent adjoining the medical facility. Inside, Logan was prowling back and forth like a caged animal, his big body throwing shadows in the light from a single lantern. He'd showered, and his hair was still damp, wildly grooved as though he'd run his fingers through it repeatedly. He wore BDU pants, but his feet were bare, and so was his upper body, save for a bandage around his right biceps.

On the table at the back of the tent were papers, clipboards and folders, and every time Logan passed, he'd glance at them, curse and turn away.

She remained at the entrance, unsure what to do or say. And she had a rare, annoying attack of self-consciousness that made her hastily comb her fingers through her tangled mop of hair.

"Come in," he said gruffly, without looking at her.

"With or without my guard?" The bitterness in her voice surprised her. She thought she had more control than that. Apparently, not when it came to him. "What the hell, Logan? I thought we were in this together. Why did you have Marlena and me locked up?"

He rounded on her. "I thought you were a cryptozoologist."

"I am."

"Really?" He came at her, and she forced herself to stand her ground. He didn't halt until they were practically nose to nose. "I didn't know chupacabra experts need combat training."

"What are you talking about?"

Darkness clouded his expression. "Come on, Sela. I saw how you handled yourself in the jungle. I'm not a fucking idiot."

Shit. Time to kick in her acting skills. "No, you aren't a fucking idiot. But you are highly suspicious and you jump to conclusions." Casting a glance at the papers on the table, she shoved him away. Bingo—GWC's chupacabra research. "Maybe you could have asked me about it instead of making wild assumptions? What in the world do you think I am? An agent for one of your rival weapons development companies, sent to steal your supersecret designs?" She narrowed her eyes at him and wondered how she was going to get her micro-camera out of her pack. "Wait—is your company involved in something illegal? Dangerous? Do you think I'm a cop or something?"

"What I think is that you've been lying to me."

"Why? Why would I possibly lie to you? Need I remind you that you found me, not the other way around? And why would you think that just because I can handle myself, I'm lying to you about something? Do you want my entire life story? The things I left out when I told you about my mom the stripper and my childhood spent mooching off strange men? Do you want me to tell you that my foster father was an Army Ranger, and after the shit I went through as a child, he taught me to fight? To hunt? To shoot?" Actually, that was true, but ACRO had taken her training to a whole new level. "Is any of that a crime?"

"No, but—"

"But what?" She was mad now, thoughts of getting pictures of the files forgotten. Her guilt about lying to Logan was mixing with residual anger from a childhood she'd left behind and rarely revisited. But Logan had stirred up that pot, bringing all her worst memories to the surface, and she was lashing out in the only way she knew how at the only person within striking distance. "You're accusing me of being dishonest, but why haven't you told me what's going on in this camp? What you've done to Chance?" She snorted. "You didn't lock me up because you think I'm some sort of cop. You locked me up to keep me from learning your secret. So let's cut the hypocritical bullshit, huh?"

He looked a little shell-shocked, opened his mouth to say something, but she jabbed her finger into his chest. "You want proof that I'm not here to spy on you . . . whatever it is you're doing? Fine. I'm out of here. You can find the fucking chupacabra on your own, and I won't be around to learn your precious secrets." She spun away from him and stalked toward the exit, knowing he wouldn't let her leave.

"Sela, wait." Sure enough, Logan grabbed her arm and turned her around. "Just hold on."

"Oh, that's right. I can't leave. I'm your goddamned prisoner. Want to tell me why that is, exactly, if you're so fucking innocent that you can be accusing me of shit?"

"I'm sorry," he said quietly, turning away from her. "You're right. I jumped to conclusions."

"Yeah, you did. You'd think you would have learned your lesson after accusing your best friend of fucking your girlfriend."

Logan whirled around. "What did you say?"

Oh, shit. He heard and there was no point in talking her way out of this. Instead, she raised her chin. "I wouldn't think that after losing them both, you'd be so casual with the accusations you throw around."

"How do you know about that?" He'd gone pale, and his fists clenched.

"I just do."

"How?" he bellowed, and she took a step back in the face of his rage.

"It doesn't matter. What matters is—"

She found herself pinned against the center support post, his forearm over her throat, his hard gaze keeping her there even without the restraint. "Answer me. Because they're both dead, and I've never told anyone that. Not a single soul."

Dammit. "You were talking in your sleep—" Her breath cut off, only for a second, but long enough to shut her up and make her realize that lying wouldn't get her anywhere.

"Not. A. Soul."

Her mind worked furiously, searching every nook and cranny for a believable lie. Nothing. There was nothing. At this point, all she had left was the truth. The truth, twisted a little to hide her ACRO status. "You're not going to believe me if I tell you."

"I don't believe you now," he said through clenched teeth. "So you can only go up from here."

"Really? You think?" She took a deep breath. Exhaled. "Fine. I'm psychic."

"Bullshit."

"You asked."

He shoved away from her. "Okay, I'll play. What am I thinking?"

She was pretty sure it wasn't anything flattering about her. "It doesn't work like that."

He laughed. "Of course not."

"I'm telling you the truth. It only works under certain circumstances."

"Like what?"

No way was she going to tell him. "Periods of... high emotion. Now, if we can just—"

"High emotion? Like now? Because I'm pretty damned pissed. Is that coming over your psychic airwaves?"

Ass. "It hardly needs to."

"So what are you talking about? Sex?"

She looked away, but too late. He'd seen something on her face, and he pounced. "Fuck me, it is. You get your readings during sex. No wonder you've been humping me like a cat in heat. You've been getting information."

Anger flared like a flame in her chest, and she moved toward him. "Information? I don't think so. The hardware in your head seems to be blocking memories of everything that happened since it was installed." She snorted. "But wow, your childhood is really fascinating. A dog named Popeye? And could you have been any geekier as a teenager?"

"You do not want to push me right now." He took a menacing step toward her. She held her ground. "Who do you work for?"

Again, she lifted her chin. "Listen to me—"

"Who?" he barked, and this time she took a step back. "Who have you been whoring yourself for?"

The words, and the venom in his voice, hurt more than they

should have, sliced right into her, but she kept her expression neutral. "I'm here to learn about the chupacabra. Nothing more."

"And you decided to do it by fucking me?" He backed her against the pole again. "Did you get everything you wanted? Or do you need something else?" He tore open the fly of his pants with one hand and palmed her breast with the other. Even angry, she felt her body respond to him with a wet, honeyed rush between her thighs, and she didn't push him away. "How about it? Want more information?"

"Logan," she whispered. "I—"

He cut her off with a punishing kiss. It didn't even occur to her to protest. Instead, she closed her eyes, and opened her mouth for the thrust of his tongue. Their teeth clashed, but he didn't let up. His hands dropped to her waistband, and he roughly jerked open her pants. His fingers dove inside, slipped between her swollen folds and into the silky evidence of her arousal. The brush of his touch over her clit made her groan, and against her will, her hips rolled toward him, and he smiled against her lips.

He had her exactly where he wanted, and he knew it.

Humiliation and anger swirled together, because she'd never been this weak. She couldn't do this. Wouldn't. Wrenching her head back, she tried to squirm away, but Logan fisted her hair and held her for his kiss.

She bit him. The tang of blood hit her tongue at the same time his snarled curse hit her ears. "Really, Sela?" he growled. "You really want to play it that way? Because I can do rough."

His words shouldn't have turned her on, but they did, in a wild, primal way she couldn't understand. She got all hot and achy and she didn't want to talk anymore. She wanted to fuck.

Smiling coldly, she fisted his cock—and her knees nearly buckled. Apparently, their sparring had worked him up as much as it had her, because he was huge, hot, throbbing in her palm. "Rough gives me more information," she said snottily, though she was lying.

"Then let's not waste any time." His tone was as nasty as hers, but there was an underlying lust that licked her right between the legs as he bent to yank off her pants. And then, as he stood up, *he* licked her between the legs. One hot, long stroke up her slit that nearly had her coming.

And then he was in her face again, his tongue in her mouth, his body crushing hers against the pole and his cock poised at her entrance. He didn't wait—there was no room for finesse and teasing in this tent. Roughly, he lifted one of her thighs and hooked it over his hip as he impaled her.

They both grunted at the to-the-hilt joining. He filled her so completely, so deeply she felt him all the way to her heart, which had no business feeling him at all. God, she'd turned into Marlena, falling in love with the man she'd slept with.

No. She wasn't in love with Logan. Lust, yes. Even as pissed as she was, she wanted him. Wanted his body. That hard tool he used with brutal skill.

"More, Sela?" he rasped, as he ground against her. "Do you want more?"

"Yes. God, yes." But even as she said that, she wasn't sure what she meant by *more*. More sex? More roughness? More of him? She lifted her other leg so they were both wrapped around him, holding him tight, bringing her as close as she could get.

"You feel something for me, don't you?" He dragged his mouth away from hers and kissed a trail along her cheek. "You didn't want to, but you do."

"Stop it." This was supposed to be a hard fuck. Not some sappy session where she admitted she was softening up. But that's what was happening. He was still angry, but she'd lost her edge and was melting into him, wishing he'd hold her like a lover instead of screwing her like the whore he'd accused her of being.

Like the whore she was.

He pumped into her roughly. Fiercely. Pleasure coiled tighter with each thrust, the ecstasy condensing and gathering until it had nowhere to go but out. She came in a blazing explosion of delicious spasms that had her crying out his name and not caring if the whole camp heard. Which they probably had.

"You getting what you need?" he growled into her ear. "A lot of juicy information? Or do you need me to come? Because I'm about to. So get ready to raid my brain."

She cried out again, but this time in shame and hurt.

His thrusts became more frenzied, but oddly, his grip gentled, and his mouth opened against her in a deep kiss. She felt him swell, and then his hot splashes filled her.

I love you.

She gasped. That . . . couldn't have come from him.

Love . . . you . . . Sela. Did you hear that, Ms. Psychic?

Oh, God. The words, his voice, pierced her brain, and pain speared her heart. She'd gotten images from him before, and emotions, but never direct messages. He'd projected those words intentionally, to hurt her.

And it had to be to hurt her, because he couldn't mean it. Could he?

Of course he didn't mean it, idiot. She'd always prided herself on being good at using her gift—she might not like having it, but she knew how to use it. But Logan had scrambled her judgment, and for just a second there, she'd almost fooled herself into thinking he actually cared about her.

He jerked once, twice, and then he went still, a low groan erupting from his chest. She didn't even give him time to catch his breath before she dropped her feet to the ground and shoved him away. Sobbing, hating herself for it, she stumbled to her pants and hurriedly jammed her legs into them. Her toes snagged on the hem and she tripped as she staggered toward the exit.

"Sela?"

His voice was a knife through the heart. She tried to button her pants but her hands were shaking too badly. "You bastard," she rasped. "You sick bastard." Fuck the pants. She left them unbuttoned and tore open the door.

"Wait!"

She paused, but the tears didn't. Her vision swam as she gazed blindly into the darkness. "I knew you were a hard man, but I didn't think you were cruel. You know that the one thing I've never had, the one thing I want, is love, and you threw it in my face with your lie. No matter what I've done, I never wanted to see you hurt. But you intentionally tried to hurt me. Well done, Logan."

She grabbed her backpack and fled. Darted out into the night. Followed, of course, by two guards, who herded her right to Logan's tent, where Marlena was still sleeping. Crying like a scared little girl, Sela climbed onto the cot and stretched out against the other woman, because for the first time since her mother died, she needed a friend.

AFTER SELA RAN OUT, LOGAN SANK DOWN, FLAT ON HIS BACK on the cot in the admin tent, pants still open, his body bathed in a thin sheen of sweat.

What the hell had he done? More important, what had he been thinking, telling her he loved her like that, like it was some kind of high-powered weapon.

She was right about one thing—he'd wanted to shock her with the information. But what she didn't understand was that he'd meant it.

He'd really meant it. And he didn't pretend to understand women any more than the next guy, but now he kind of figured that screaming *I love you* during sex, from his mind to hers, wasn't the best way to broach the subject.

A freaking psychic.

At least she can't read your whole mind. A small concession of relief, to be sure. But he couldn't imagine how much he would've unwittingly given away.

He could tell she was still lying to him about who she worked for, but that wasn't his concern at the moment. His concern was that he'd just pissed off one of the few people who could help him with the chupacabra. And so he buttoned his pants and strode, barefoot, out of the tent and toward his own tent, where Randall was guarding Sela and Marlena. Staying outside and far away from Marlena, as ordered.

The last thing Logan needed was to piss off Chance and make him turn. The guy had been through enough hell over the past weeks, especially the past twenty-four hours. Logan had already put GWC's doctors and scientists on finding a cure.

He held up a hand to Randall and prepared to walk inside. Except he heard the low sobs from outside the tent and he brought a hand to his nose, squeezed the bridge of it as the guilt ran through him.

She wasn't the type of woman who cried easily.

"She's been doing that for hours," Randall offered.

Shit. He hadn't realized that hours had passed while he'd been ruminating. Checked his watch and saw it was close to three in the morning before heading into the tent, which was dark save for a small lantern on a side table. The two women were sharing the cot, and any other time, it could be the stuff of most male fantasies.

But not him, not today, because his didn't include a sobbing woman—one he'd upset, no less. "Hey, Sela?"

Sela sat up quickly, faced away from him as she wiped her eyes. Marlena glared at him, and yeah, he deserved that.

"Chance is okay," he said, as if that would appease her. "No more experiments."

"But I can't see him," Marlena shot back.

"Not tonight, no," he told her. "Sela, I need to talk to you."

"No."

"It's not a question. I'll have Randall bring you to command tent if you won't come on your own." A dick move, yeah, but it was the only way to get her alone.

There was a long pause while he turned to the door. He heard shuffling behind him, and sniffling, and cursing him under both women's breath before Sela was at his side.

She kept her head down as she walked next to him. When he started to open the door for her, she jerked it away from him and did it for herself, stomping into the command tent. And then she stood, nowhere near the bed, arms crossed, eyes reddened, mouth twisted. "You got me here, Mr. I Like Giving Orders. So talk."

He sighed, ran his fingers through his hair and wasn't sure where to begin. So much was fucked up—and just plain fucked—that he was having trouble unraveling it all. "I didn't mean to upset you. I shouldn't have let you hear my thoughts like that."

Her chin rose and she didn't say anything.

"I was angry with you. I wanted you to know—"

"So you thought you'd test me and shove the love lie in my face," she bit out.

"Sela, listen to me. I wasn't lying to you. I would never use what you told me against you. Do you really think I could be so fucking cruel?"

She didn't answer him. Yeah, she thought that. "I'm in love with you, Sela. It just happened. I didn't want it or expect it, but it happened. You treat me . . . Christ, you make me feel . . ."

He couldn't continue, hadn't had this much emotion running through him since before the accident. And it didn't matter, because she fucking hated him now. He'd pushed her too far—pushed her away. "I meant it. I couldn't hold it back . . . I've never actually felt this way about a woman. I guess I screwed up."

He didn't know what else to say. If there was anything more he could do. And so he turned away from her and stared at his laptop, where Caroline's email sat, unanswered. He tried not to think about the hell she was being put through, and all because of his damned company. "I'm in a lot of trouble, Sela. I'd like nothing more than to spend the next twenty-four hours convincing you that I'm in love with you, making you trust me enough to tell me why you're really here. But I have something else going on that needs my full attention come morning."

"Logan, what's wrong?" Sela had moved closer to him, actually put a hand on his shoulder. He couldn't bring himself to look at her, though.

"My company—well, let's just say you're not wrong about me being ashamed of what's been happening behind the scenes. I didn't know how deeply my father was in a bad deal until today, when he tested Chance like that." He paused. "These people he has a contract with—Itor Corp—they have my sister and they're holding her until we bring them the chupacabra."

"Oh, my God. Your sister? Does she work for GWC too?"

He shook his head and finally looked her in the eye. "No, she's in college. Completely innocent. She knows nothing about the family business. Well, I guess now she does." He laughed a little but it sounded harsh and felt like his chest was ripping apart.

When he'd left the med tent, he'd been declared fine. Healed. Good as new. But he sure didn't feel that way.

"What do they want from you?"

"The chupacabra. That's why I've been looking for it for the past month, trying to bring it in alive. And now they know about Chance too."

THE SITUATION KEPT GETTING DEEPER AND MORE CRITICAL BY the minute. Sela sank down on the cot and drew her knees up to her chest. Her mind was a jumble that started with Logan's profession of love and ended with the fact that he'd opened up a little about his company's involvement with weapons development. Which was why she was here, but now things were much more complicated than they should have been.

Right now she had to ignore the love thing and concentrate on the job. A job she was never, ever doing again. Once she got back to ACRO, she was going to tell Dev that if he ever asked her to seduce someone, she was walking. She loved ACRO, loved working in the Crypto department, but fuck if she was going to whore herself out for anyone or anything.

"Logan?"

"Yeah?"

"What do these Itor people want with the chupacabra?" She knew, but the more information she could get from him, the better the chances at a good outcome once her backup arrived. Though Logan would have to know the truth eventually, of course, because ACRO had to get GWC out of Itor's pocket.

He scrubbed his hand over his face. "Originally, GWC found the creature when we were here doing plant research."

"So you weren't lying about that," she muttered.

He gave her a tolerant sigh. "No. We're a weapons company, and bioweapons and treatments from natural sources are a huge part of that. Anyway, the creature attacked our scientists, and it was a stroke of luck that we managed to contain it. Right away, our scientists saw potential in the thing as a weapon—a component of armor, defense, whatever."

"So how did you lose it?"

Bitterness wafted off him in waves. "Apparently, my father gave permission to have it brought back to the jungle, as bait to catch another one. Before that, we'd used its saliva to create a biological weapon capable of destroying only adult male humans. Some of our developers thought how great it would be to kill off enemy soldiers and not have to worry about killing innocent kids and women. Word of the prototype viral weapon leaked, and before I knew what was happening, there was a bidding war, and an organization called Itor won. But they wanted the chupa in addition to the weapon."

"And GWC didn't want to give it up."

"No. My father figured we'd get another one or two so we could start a breeding program and be able to give one creature to Itor."

"Okay, so your plan went bad and the chupacabra got away . . . "

"Yeah. That's why I'm here. To capture it before Itor got wind of its escape. But apparently, it's too late. And they took my sister."

Oh, damn, this was bad. "How long do you have?"

"A week."

She closed her eyes. Itor never kept to their time line. They always—*always*—moved the timetable to catch their opponent off guard. "We've got to get that chupacabra." She opened her eyes, only to see Logan look away. "Logan?" She narrowed her eyes at him, a sick feeling of dread swirling in her gut. "What are you not telling me?"

"I can't let her die, Sela."

"Oh, my God," she breathed. "You're going to give them Chance if you can't catch the animal."

"My father wants to." He scrubbed his hand over his face, looking suddenly exhausted. "I think we can find another way."

"But if worse comes to worst it . . . "

"She's my sister."

Sela got that, but she couldn't let it come down to a choice between Chance and Logan's sister. Sela had to contact Dev and step up ACRO's time line of getting help in here. And she had to come clean with Logan. Nausea swirled in her stomach at the thought. After all her denials and lies, she was going to have to admit she'd been here as a spy the entire time.

"Hey." Logan moved toward her, cautiously, as though he was unsure where they stood. "What's wrong? I know what I did to you was shitty . . . "

"It's not that," she sighed. "I guess I'm glad you at least believe me, though."

"That you're psychic?"

She nodded. "It's not something people generally believe or understand."

"I wasn't sure I did either."

"I was telling you the truth when I said I didn't get much from you." She folded her hands in her lap and looked down at them. "Honestly, I'm glad. I hate what I do, Logan. Sex has never been real fun for me. I mean, you called me a whore—"

"God, I'm sorry, Sela." He sank down beside her on the cot, and his warmth engulfed her like a blanket. "I didn't mean it."

Yeah, he did, but she couldn't be angry, because it was the truth. "I'm not asking for an apology. I'm bringing it up because I told you all of that stuff about my mom, how she slept with guys so she could put food on the table and a roof over our heads. What I didn't tell you is that I swore I would never be like her. But I got angry when I was a teen, when she left Gary, and I did some pretty stupid things. I slept with some guys I shouldn't have . . . and I learned real quick that I didn't like sex. The men would climax and my brain would get invaded by the things they'd done. Things they wanted to do."

She shuddered, and Logan took her hand. The strength and comfort that came from that simple gesture put butterflies in her stomach. She'd denied it before, but she really was falling for this man.

Taking a deep breath, she continued. "It's amazing how normal people can look on the outside but be so twisted on the inside." He squeezed her hand, and she smiled before squeezing back. "Anyway, I stopped having sex for a long time because of that." Until she'd spied Creed in a bar and had been fascinated by the tattooed, pierced man. Then there had been a string of men because of her Seducer assignments, each one eating away at her soul and self-worth.

"Then there was the asshole who beat me. That was three years ago. You're the first since then. And . . . you're only the second who hasn't traumatized me with visions."

The other was Creed, and though she'd gotten a reading from him, she hadn't seen anything horrible in his head. He'd been decent, honorable, and his nature had been reflected in the images and thoughts she'd gotten from him. It had been such a relief, such a wonderful experience—not to mention the fact that the man was an incredibly skilled lover. Annika was one lucky woman.

Sela eyed Logan, because he'd proven to be as talented as Creed, just in a different way. A way that made her burn hotter each time they came together. Creed had been amazing, but there had been a distance between them—not surprising, given that their time together was supposed to be a one-night stand. And he'd held something back, whereas Logan had given everything, even that first time, when they hadn't known each other any more than she and Creed had. Hell, she and Creed had at least talked for a couple of hours before they'd done the deed, and she'd liked him.

She couldn't say that about Logan. She'd barely known him and had hated him on sight.

"Who was the other guy?" Logan's voice was a little rough, laced with a thread of jealousy that was sweet.

"Just someone I work with."

"So you see him? A lot?" The jealousy had thickened in his tone. "With your cryptozoology job?"

Her mouth went dry. "Yeah, about that . . . " Oh, God, this was going to hurt. He was going to hate her.

Logan's eyes narrowed, gaze alert, and for a second she thought he'd figured it out . . . but then his head came up. "Do you hear that?"

She frowned. "Hear what? Do you have bionic hearing?"

He gave her a clipped nod, and then he was on his feet and from nowhere he'd drawn a pistol. "Stay here."

"Logan—"

"Stay!" he barked, and darted out of the tent.

She didn't listen. She wasn't a helpless girl. She was a trained ACRO agent, with more skills than the average person. Covertly, she slipped out into the early morning darkness. She eased to the rear of the tent, to where a group of newcomers stood in the middle of the camp, surrounded by Logan's armed men.

The newcomers didn't have weapons. But that didn't mean they weren't armed. No, these people were far more dangerous than anyone in the camp knew or could imagine, and an icy chill ran up Sela's spine.

These people were Itor.

CHAPTER *Nineteen*

Chance called to her softly through the rolled fabric window, and Marlena moved quickly across the tent, stood on her cot so she could see him through the sheer fabric.

"What are you doing here?" she asked. "Are you alone?"

"Yeah. I'm okay. I needed to be free, to figure out what the hell I can control about this thing living inside of me. What I can't."

"Did you?"

"I'm not a chupacabra right now, if that's what you're asking." He managed to make it a joke and she laughed a little. "I haven't been going far. I can't go that far from you."

"I know," she said quietly.

"I don't mind that, you know." He paused. "I keep thinking, if we'd met before this, maybe . . . maybe things would've been okay. Maybe we would've ended up together."

Oh, God. Her throat tightened and she put a hand to her mouth. Finally, she managed, "I know I would've liked you no matter when we met, Chance."

At this point, she wondered if she should tell him about who she really was before she wasn't able to hide it any longer.

ACRO would soon send agents in to save the day. It would be great for Chance—if anyone could cleanse his blood from the infection the chupacabra had given him, the ACRO scientists could. But would he see the opportunity for what it was if he was blinded by anger at her for lying? "I've got to ask you something."

"Go ahead."

"If there was a way for you to stay the way you are—half man, half chupacabra—would you?" It was such a stupid question—she knew that. Knew he'd have no way to understand why she'd ask it.

Especially when she knew the answer.

"Why would I want to be half an uncontrollable monster who scares the shit out of everyone? There's not enough money in the world to make me stay the way I am now. It's not fair to you either."

"I could really fall for you, Chance."

"The way I am now? You'd have to be some kind of saint."

"Far from it."

"Marlena, I'm going to hunt the chupacabra down myself. It's the only way to ensure nothing like this happens to anyone else."

Tell him about ACRO, about everything. He needs to be here when the ACRO rescue team arrives. "You can't do that," she said urgently. But there was no response. He was already gone—and she knew what she had to do.

CREED WAS IN A MEETING WITH THE OTHER GHOST HUNTING department staff when Dev burst in, no warning, and yanked him out. Raised eyes from Creed's supervisor followed them both out of the room and Dev didn't give two shits.

He only knew that Creed was hurting Annika—and that was something he'd sworn to Dev he'd never do.

"What the fuck, Devlin?" Creed demanded, once they were outside.

Dev fisted his hands and kept his voice low. "What the hell aren't you telling me, Creed?"

Creed raised his chin—he knew exactly what Dev was talking about, and that wasn't a good sign.

Dev continued. "Annika came to me, apologized. She's falling apart, and that's when you decide to tell her you don't want to have kids with her?"

Creed paled. "It's not like that."

"Then you'd better start telling me what it *is* like."

"I don't want anyone else to know this, not even Annika."

Dev nodded—Creed was asking Dev to do a mind shield over their conversation. The psychics who worked here were all above reproach—both men knew that. This was more out of respect for Annika, that she wouldn't be the last to know about something that concerned her. "My office," he snapped, began walking.

As Creed followed, he tried to channel Oz, the way he'd done countless times since his brother died. Of course, it was hard to hear anything through Kat's incessant chatter of *I told you so,* and fuck it all, it appeared Oz's spirit wasn't going to come out and help him now.

All too quickly, they'd walked past Christine and into Dev's office, the door closing ominously behind Creed.

He felt like all the air had been sucked out of the room, felt it spin a little, and shit, he hadn't felt this bad in a long time. He reached for the arm of the couch, and Dev was helping him to sit and ordering him to *breathe,* and that almost made Creed smile.

For a few minutes, he simply sat there, following Dev's orders and ignoring Kat, until he knew he couldn't put off his confession anymore.

Finally, he spoke directly to his spirit. Out loud, because Dev knew all about her. Everyone at ACRO did. "All right, Kat, I know I'm supposed to tell Ani," he muttered. "Shhh for now, okay? Devlin and I have to talk."

Kat quieted down, but she stayed close. Creed shifted on the leather couch under Dev's scrutiny. "I was going to tell Annika, I was just waiting for the right time. Fuck, I knew she was upset."

Dev waited—none too patiently at this point.

"Oz . . . made a prediction," Creed blurted out.

Dev blinked. "He never told me about a prediction concerning Annika and pregnancy." Dev's jaw tightened. "Tell me everything, Creed. Is Annika in danger?"

"She could be. So could I. Oz wasn't specific, dammit." He scrubbed his hand over his face. "I was hoping . . . you could ask him."

Dev didn't answer, stared at Creed, unblinking.

"I'm sorry—I know that would be hard on you, contacting him. You probably don't—"

"I have, when it's necessary," Dev said softly.

Creed leaned forward. "There's something about pregnancy that's deadly for either me or Annika. I never thought it would be an issue—she didn't want kids. So I don't know if I'm going to die when she gives birth, or if she will. And I want kids—shit, I think, if Annika was ready, she'd be a kick-ass mom. And I should've told her and now everything's fucked up."

He leaned back against the couch, his head beginning to throb. "I'll find her now. I'll tell her everything. But how the hell could I ask her not to have this baby if it's what she really wants?"

Dev didn't answer, not immediately. And then Christine was knocking on the door frantically, not waiting for Dev to answer before barging in.

"The pilot, ah . . . Captain Walker, he radioed—Akbar and Stryker found Annika and Gabe on the plane."

Dev's expression went deadly, as did his tone. "The plane to the Amazon?"

Christine took a step back. "Um, yes."

And just then, Kat screeched so loudly, Creed fell to his knees and covered his ears in a futile attempt to stop the sound. He was vaguely aware of Dev touching him, talking to him, but he could only focus on what Kat was telling him.

It was nothing he wanted to hear. Ever. Shit. "Dev . . ."

"What is it?"

He looked up at his boss and friend. "A message . . . Kat got a message from Oz. He said . . . four are going in, but only three are coming out."

Only three are coming out of the jungle alive.

ANNIKA'S HEAD WAS KILLING HER. THE PEOPLE YELLING AT her didn't help much. And what the holy hell was all that shaking and jolting?

"Annika? Get up!" Akbar's thickly accented voice drifted down to her, along with the distinct smell of engine smoke. Were they on a mission? In what, a truck going over a dirt road littered with logs?

Groaning, she sat up. Blinked. There were crates all around her. Akbar was kneeling in front of her. Stryker was digging static line chutes out of a storage crate. Gabe was watching with the expression of someone who was in a fuckload of trouble for something. *Gabe!* Everything came back in a rush, and she realized that she hadn't stopped him from stowing away on the cargo jet, and in fact, they were now in the air in said jet.

"You fuck!" She lurched to her feet, and then nearly went down when a wave of nausea bitch-slapped her. Both Gabe and Akbar caught her, which was good, because the plane was pitching and rolling. Were they in a storm?

"FARCs nailed us in the right wing with an SA-7 or 14 . . . some sort of surface-to-air. Both engines are out," Akbar said. "Pilots have climbed and leveled so we can jump before they put down." He peered into her eyes with his dark ones. "You have been injured."

"You think?" She touched her bandaged temple and winced. "How bad?"

Akbar, the only one among them with formal medic training, ran his thumb over the bandage. The thick leather cuff on his wrist that kept his spurs hidden brushed her cheek. "Hard to tell. You have been in and out for hours. But it is nothing compared to the knocks you will take if you go down with the plane."

Good point. And now that some of the fog had cleared, she remembered waking up a few times before falling back to sleep.

"We gotta go!" Stryker shouted. "We're too low for the thousand-foot min for a HALO—we're going for a static line jump."

Shit. Annika hated those. HALO chutes allowed for steering precision landings. With static chutes, though, you hop and they pop, and you were at the mercy of the wind. Groaning, she engaged her internal autopilot, donned her jump gear and loaded up with weapons.

Gabe had done a couple of jumps, so he wasn't totally clueless, but just in case, after Stryker finished gearing up, he made sure Gabe was ready. Akbar double-checked Annika, which would have annoyed her under any other circumstance, but right now she just wanted some painkillers. Could she take them while pregnant?

Akbar hit the toggle for the cargo ramp, and as it leveled out, letting in the first rays of the morning dawn, Annika braced herself against a crate. "How did I get hurt?"

Stryker shot Gabe a glare. "Apparently, you were trying to stop him from riding along, and you slipped and hit your head."

Right . . . but she was never so clumsy. Why would she—she sucked in a harsh breath, remembering that she'd tried to electrify Gabe, but failed. She reached for her power, but she might as well have been digging for water in the desert. Oh, God.

The plane shuddered, sending Gabe wheeling into her. She

grabbed him, almost grateful for the distraction. The intercom crackled, and the pilot's voice, calm and cool, told them that he'd have a jump zone for them in two minutes.

"Okay," Annika said. "You have two minutes to brief me on what the fuck is going on."

Stryker slid a hunting knife into his chest-harness's sheath. "We're going into the GWC camp to extract two agents, take down the operation and seize a mythical, man-killing creature."

She snorted. "Is that all?"

Akbar grinned, exposing straight, white teeth that contrasted with his tan skin. "Itor might be there."

"Ooh," she said, returning his grin. "Things are looking up." Well, maybe not, since her power seemed to have left the building. Oh, and she had a head injury. And was pregnant. Crap.

She shook herself out of the pity party, because no matter what, she was in fucking awesome shape, was deadly as shit, and being pregnant didn't turn women into glass figurines. She'd known agents who had run freaking marathons well into pregnancy.

Akbar lost the smile and turned to Gabe. "Kid, if this plane were not going to be making a crash landing, I would make you stay with it, and when we got back to ACRO, I would have your ass thrown in a detention cell for a year, and the only action you would see is when you got tasked for hard labor around the base." Gabe stiffened, but wisely kept his mouth shut, and then he dropped it open when Akbar handed him a Sig P226. "But you are here, and we have to work together. No screwups. Try to remember every drop of your training, and do not be a hero."

Wow. Akbar was a lot nicer to Gabe than Annika would be, given that she wanted to shove him out of the plane without the benefit of a parachute. But she got what the man was doing. If Gabe didn't feel like he was part of the team, he was going to make mistakes, his confidence shot.

Akbar clapped a hand on Gabe's shoulder. "We have each other's backs, yes? I have yours, and I trust you to have mine. You good with that?"

Gabe swallowed shakily but his nod was firm and strong. "Yeah." He turned to Annika. "Look—"

"No." She held up her hand, because now wasn't the time to get into what had happened. They had to survive the mission first. And then she'd kick his ass. "What Akbar said. For now, that's good enough."

Stryker gave a thumbs-up, and then he signaled that it was time to go.

BEFORE HE'D GONE TO TALK TO MARLENA, CHANCE HAD BEEN hanging around, trying to gain any intel he could.

He discovered that when he was close enough to the subjects who were talking, it was much easier to filter out the excess noise. He'd moved silently, years of training on his side, and heard part of a conversation he wished he hadn't.

Logan and Sela were talking in the command tent—about the chupa, Logan's sister . . . and him.

And some company named Itor.

What do they want from you? Sela was asking Logan, who said, *The chupacabra. That's why I've been looking for it for the past month, trying to bring it in alive. And now, they know about Chance too.*

It didn't take a fucking genius to figure out how the rest of this would go down. Logan's dad planned on trading Chance for Logan's sister. And hell, Chance could almost fucking understand that . . . but he was sure as shit not going to let the original chupacabra continue running wild.

He couldn't have that on his conscience.

He'd already grabbed one of Shep's knives when the man wasn't looking and poached Randall's rifle as he sat outside of the tent's door, and he was off, into the jungle in the dark of night.

He ran, fast and sure-footed, but came to an abrupt stop when he realized someone—or something—was following him. They were slower, to be sure, and too fucking loud to be much good as recon.

"Who the fuck is there? Come out before I shoot you," he called quietly. Within seconds, there was more crashing and Marlena stumbled out of the brush. Under the glare of the flashlight, she looked scratched and bruised, and she was out of breath.

But she'd tracked him. It was something he wouldn't have expected from a cryptozoologist's assistant, but he'd suspected there was so much more to her than that—which was why he'd been trying to get her to admit it. He'd been praying she hadn't been part of Logan's team, playing him this whole time.

"What the hell are you doing?" he demanded.

She moved toward him. "It's too dangerous for you to be out here alone. If I can't talk you out of it, I'm coming with."

"How did you get away from the guard?" he asked, and she shrugged.

He narrowed his eyes at her. He'd fallen in love with her, but that didn't mean he completely trusted her.

She knew a hell of a lot more than she was telling him.

In one quick motion, he had her back against the nearest tree, his body pressing into every soft, sexy curve of hers. He was instantly aroused, but it didn't matter—couldn't. Not this time. "Tell me who you are. Tell me now."

She rolled her hips against his groin in a long, slow grind, and Christ, it was getting harder to think. "Chance, baby—"

"No." He put a hand over her throat, palm touching the hot skin, feeling her pulse beat wildly beneath it. She was doing that thing again—the amazing, sexy thing that made him hot, that made him feel the real Marlena wasn't behind those eyes at the moment. "Who the fuck are you right now? Because this isn't the woman I made love to in the tent that first night, or this afternoon. So. Who. Are. You."

She swallowed, hard, and no doubt realized her options regarding the truth were severely limited. Especially when his hand squeezed harder. "I'm an ACRO agent. One of the good guys."

She'd choked the words out, and he released his grip a bit.

"Fuck me." He'd heard rumors of a paramilitary agency that recruited agents with special abilities—and some not-so-special ones too—for years. But he'd never looked beyond the rumors, since all his abilities were purely man-made. And because he'd loved his job as a SEAL.

Now his blood ran colder than it had been, thanks to the infection from the beast.

"ACRO is . . . agents who are like X-men," she said, confirming the rumors, making them a reality. "We're a secret organization by necessity, but we're here to help. Agents are on their way to help us right now."

His laugh was low but harsh. "Yes, just like the doctors here were trying to help me. Itor too."

She paled, and he continued.

"I heard Logan and Sela talking about them. Apparently, they've taken Logan's sister hostage and won't release her until they have the chupacabra. Or a near facsimile of one."

He released her then, but she grabbed his arm. "I won't let Itor take you. ACRO won't let them."

"But ACRO *will* take me—right, Marlena?" He leaned in close to her, whispered in her ear. "Will this be a nice feather in your cap, Agent? Earn you a medal or a promotion?"

"It's not like that."

"What's it like then, honey? Are you going to keep telling me you love me . . . and then freak out every time I turn into a monster?" He lowered his mouth to her neck, kissed her and felt her jump. She was half afraid of him, of the possibility that he could turn at any time. And yet, she was excited by him—he knew that if he dipped his fingers between her legs, she would be wet.

"Chance." She struggled but he picked her up and brought her back to the tree, held her there roughly.

"What is your job with ACRO, exactly?"

"I back up other agents. I wasn't lying when I told you that Sela is a cryptozoologist." She panted slightly—from the run, from fear, because his hand was caressing between her legs through the BDUs. "Chance, please . . . "

"Please what? What's your special skill, honey? Your secret ability?"

"I don't have any special powers," she told him, even as his hands slid down the front of her pants.

Two fingers inside of her and she squirmed, bit a moan back—but oh, no, he wasn't having that. "I want to hear you."

They were far enough from the camp now—she'd followed him for a good mile, which at night in jungles like this might as well be twenty.

Her moans intermingled with the sounds of the jungle and he bit her shoulder lightly. "What's your job, Marlena?"

Her hips rocked against his hand as she sought relief. "I'm an assistant. That's all."

"Most assistants I know can't take out a guard and follow a Special Ops operator through the jungle so efficiently." Impatiently, he tore down her pants and then his own.

"Everyone at ACRO is . . . trained." The last word was a sigh as he replaced his hand between her legs.

His other hand was wrapped around her throat. "Trained for what, exactly?"

And then her hand snaked out and fisted his cock. She wasn't giving an inch, but neither was he.

"I'm trained for anything," she told him as she began a slow stroke that almost made his brain—and everything else—explode. Christ, he was quick on the trigger with this fucking chupa blood. Maybe the creature was mean because it was always horny.

She wasn't letting go. When he increased the pace of his rhythm, so did she, until his knees threatened to buckle.

"I want to fuck you. Please," he murmured against her neck. And then he moved his hand from her throat and leaned in to kiss her, his tongue dueling with hers, their skin sweaty and slick from the humid night.

She was nodding against his mouth and he pushed her thighs open with one of his. She responded by climbing him, ankles locked around his lower back.

He thrust inside of her, not caring if her back scraped against the bark. The walls of her sex were tight and hot as he plunged his throbbing cock back and forth, until his breath came in short, harsh gasps that echoed in the still of the jungle night.

I'm trained for anything.

"Are you trained to know how to fuck an animal?" he murmured harshly against her ear.

Her head was thrown back, eyes closed, and still she didn't answer him. But then she was calling out his name into the dark night—a begging, keening sound that almost made him stop interrogating her.

But he had to know, once and for all, if he could trust her. She'd saved his life multiple times, even now—but at what price, and for whom?

He couldn't hold his orgasm back any longer, held her hips tight and spilled inside of her as she contracted around him with her own climax.

His release could only be described as ferocious—he felt as if he might've blacked out when he came, but when he regained focus, he was still standing, holding a worn-out Marlena against him.

Her arms wrapped around his shoulders, her nose nuzzled against his neck, and yeah, it was time.

"You know all about me—the ugly side of the beast I live with now. You've seen it. Do you have an ugly side, Marlena?" He'd growled the words against her cheek, and now, as she drew in a quick breath at his surprise attack, she simultaneously unlocked her legs and dropped to her feet.

She pulled up her pants as he buttoned his, and then she walked in a slow circle around him. He remained stock-still in the darkness, watching the soft glow of her eyes, and his stomach clenched.

"I seduce for a living." She spat the words brazenly in his face and cupped his ass, caressing boldly. "Is that what you want to hear? That I've been trained to sleep with men in order to get information from them? That I'm damned good at my job? Because none of that negates how I feel about you. Man or beast, I'm in goddamned love with you."

It wasn't what he'd wanted to hear, or what he'd expected to. But he'd initiated the damned interrogation and had no one to blame but himself.

Hands shaking, he shoved her hand away. "You fuck men for ACRO."

"You've probably fucked people for your country," she retorted.

He laughed then, long and loud and not giving a shit who—or what—heard him. "You're going to sell me down the river, just like Logan and his father."

"No."

Suddenly, there was a jumble of voices coming from the camp. Chance moved away from Marlena so he could concentrate. Everyone was confused, excited—no, not excited. Scared.

"What is it?" Marlena asked him urgently.

He could make out one word, repeated over and over by several different people. "Itor."

"What about them?"

"I think they're here."

CHAPTER *twenty*

Phoebe Milan got off on pain. Giving or taking, didn't matter. She just liked it. She often wondered what her other half thought when she took over the body they shared. No doubt Melanie freaked every time she came to in a body covered with bruises and cuts. The wuss loaded up on OTC painkillers, which was annoying, because Phoebe liked the prescription stuff.

Or the illegal stuff. Both of which Itor provided.

Once, Melanie had tossed Phoebe's stash when she found it hidden under their bed, but Phoebe had quickly ensured that would never happen again. She left a note for Melanie taped to the bathroom mirror—which was one of only three ways they ever communicated—and then she'd stabbed herself in the leg with a boning knife.

Rarely did Phoebe willingly give up possession of their body, but she'd instantly snapped into the background, forcing Melanie front and center. Phoebe had no idea what had happened when Melanie found herself writhing in pain and bleeding on the bathroom floor, but never again did Melanie fuck with anything of Phoebe's, even when Phoebe intentionally left things lying around to irritate the bitch. It was just too bad Phoebe couldn't see the look on Mel's face when she got up in the morning to find lines of coke arranged neatly on the coffee table or sex toys in the kitchen cupboards. And Phoebe would kill to know how Melanie reacted when she came to in a foreign bed with one or more people doing wicked things to her.

Oh, yes, fucking with Melanie was a load of fun, but even more fun was when Phoebe got to fuck with complete strangers.

Complete strangers like these Global Weapons Corporation idiots.

She rolled her head, moaning at the release of tension in her neck. It had been a long trip from the icy wastes of Ukraine, where one of Itor's bases was set up, to the jungles of South America. And now she was standing in the middle of the camp, surrounded by men with automatic weapons.

Little did they know that she and her six colleagues *were* weapons. Any one of them could take out the armed idiots before they could fire off a shot.

"I want to speak to Logan or Richard Mills."

"I'm Logan."

The deep, rich voice came from behind her, and when she turned, a shiver of hunger went through her. Though she generally preferred women over men, she could appreciate the male form when it came in a package like Logan's. Yes, she was an equal-opportunity lover when it came right down to it. Had to be, since sex charged up her pyro abilities, and without it, she couldn't so much as light a match.

Thanks to two of the excedosapiens, Mick and Dane, who had accompanied her on the private jet, her battery was at a hundred percent and ready to blaze.

"I'm Phoebe," she said, taking note of his bearing, the way he held his weapon as though it was part of his body, and decided that he was who he said he was. She knew he'd had military training, and she also knew it wouldn't do him any good if she decided to squash him.

"I'm guessing you're with Itor." Logan gestured to his men, and they lowered their weapons and backed off, though they remained watchful. Another man approached, older, and by his looks she deduced that this would be Logan's father, Richard.

"Where is my daughter?" Richard took a menacing step toward her, but Logan wisely held him back.

"She's safe," Phoebe said. "For now. The sooner you give us what we want, the sooner you can have her back." Her gaze swept the camp. "Where is the creature?"

Richard clenched his fists. "I told you, we need to perform more tests—"

"You lie," she snapped. "Itor believes you've either lost it, killed it or sold it to someone else. So I want to see it. Now."

"It's in the jungle," Logan said smoothly. "We staked it out as bait to catch another one. It's perfectly safe."

Yes, and she was the fucking tooth fairy. Oh, he appeared to be telling the truth—his voice was steady, his gaze fixed on hers and he was as calm as a frozen pond—but Phoebe had never trusted a soul in her life, and she assumed everyone was lying about everything. Melanie was the sap who would believe grass was purple if someone told her it was.

"You'll take us to it."

"No," Logan said, "we won't. The sun is barely up and the jungle is still dark. We'll have to wait until this afternoon."

"You're stalling."

"I'm being practical. This jungle is crawling with guerrillas and drug cartels and their booby traps. Messing around without full light is suicide."

He wasn't worried about any of that and she knew it. Neither was she. "We can handle ourselves. You will take us within the hour." When he opened his mouth to say something, she cut him off. "Need I remind you that we have your sister?"

"You bitch," Richard rasped. "This was never part of our agreement!"

"We're paying you more than enough to alter the agreement." She smiled at Logan, thinking that maybe she'd add one more item to the contract. After all, you could never overcharge a battery.

LOGAN QUICKLY ASSESSED THE ITOR WOMAN. SHE LOOKED LIKE she could damned well handle herself, but she was, no doubt, dispensable to Itor. Capturing her and insisting on a trade for Caroline wouldn't work. His best bet was to head into the dark jungle and hope to capture the fucking chupacabra, which was exactly what they were doing now.

Once Phoebe discovered Sela was a cryptozoologist, she'd immediately chosen her to come along. Logan's father remained back at camp with the Itor men and all the others, including Dax.

Sela was directly behind him, with Phoebe behind her.

Phoebe's last words before they left camp still rang in his mind.

Your father will be the first one killed if you try anything stupid in the jungle. Caroline second. And the cryptozoologist, she's third.

When she'd pointed at Sela, he'd refused to allow himself to have any kind of reaction. Letting this Itor agent know he was in love with Sela meant certain death for her.

Thankfully, his father had kept his mouth shut, didn't mention Chance at all. And it was the only thing to hold on to as they tramped through the jungle floor in the near dark of the early morning.

Six miles in, Phoebe stopped. "I don't think any of you know where this thing really is."

Logan turned to her. "That's not true," he said, his heart freezing when she grabbed Sela around the neck and pointed the gun at her head.

"Really? Prove it."

Fuck. He gestured to the north. "In that clearing."

"Then you go draw it out," Phoebe said.

Logan didn't hesitate. He feinted left, then turned and kicked Phoebe's legs out from under her. Both women—and the gun—went flying, and within seconds Logan had Phoebe on her feet, his arm around her neck.

"Stop fucking with me—you need me as much as I need you right now. And don't think for a second that I won't kill you because I'm worried about other people," he growled, before he pushed her away from him.

She smiled, as if she'd enjoyed the choke hold, and yeah, this chick was fucking nuts. "We'll see if you're spewing truth," she told him as she clicked her radio to call her minions back at the camp.

Just then, Logan heard sounds he would've been more than happy never to hear again.

Sela shoved to her feet and moved to his side.

As they drew closer to the growling and snarling, Logan held a hand up and Phoebe lowered her radio. It sounded like the beast had... perhaps it had gotten hold of another wild animal. Or a drug runner.

But as they broke into the small clearing, the reality proved to be much more dangerous.

Two chupacabras were locked together in mortal combat, a dance of death that could easily extend to all of them if they weren't careful.

"Two of them," Phoebe whispered.

Logan's blood ran cold—the lie he'd told Phoebe earlier, about staking out the chupa in order to catch another one, had come true... in the worst way possible. Because one of those chupacabras engaged in a death battle on the jungle floor was Chance.

How the hell had the guy escaped?

Sela was clutching his arm. "Marlena," she mouthed when he tore his eyes off the snarling beasts, her eyes shifting to the right, where the beautiful woman stood in the relative safety of the trees, holding a tranq gun.

Marlena would have to know which chupa was Chance, although for the life of him, Logan couldn't tell the two beasts apart.

He would have to give away Marlena's position if he was to save Chance's life.

"There's a woman in the trees across the way," he told Phoebe. "She's with us."

Phoebe's eyes trained on Marlena. "Shoot her."

"No!" Sela yelled.

"You don't get a say." Phoebe raised her gun to take a sniper-like shot at Marlena, but Logan palmed the barrel and shoved it down.

"One of the chupacabras is half human—he was infected when bitten. She's the only one who can identify him." Logan hoped so, anyway.

"Really? Two chupacabras—and one is a half and half. I like that," she murmured. "Tranq them both. Now."

"The tranq doesn't work on the full chupacabra," Sela said urgently. "Tranqing Chance now ensures his death."

"Chance? Stupid name. And I'm supposed to stand here until one of them kills the other?" Phoebe stifled a yawn. "Seriously, you people need to find better ways to have fun."

A scream straight from the depths of hell silenced everything in the jungle, and then one of the chupacabras suddenly leaped toward Logan, snarling and screeching, and *fuck me,* this was going to end badly.

Logan had no idea which beast was now half on top of him, jaws snapping, threatening to rip his throat out. He kicked and rolled, but even with the strength of his bioware, the thing was stronger. Fetid breath stung his eyes and claws ripped into his skin. Panic, the heart-stopping realization that he could die, swamped him. And then, with no warning, the other chupa was jumping on the first one's back, taking it to the ground right next to Logan. He rolled, fired two tranqs at point-blank range into each creature's flank, but not before he heard a horrible crunch.

One of them had broken the other's neck.

CHAPTER *Twenty-one*

For several long seconds, no one moved. Not even the birds in the trees. And then, gunfire shattered the air. The whiz of the bullet vibrated Logan's ear, followed by the surviving chupacabra's bloodcurdling scream.

It rocked backward from the force of the slug's impact, its blood exploding from the hole in its abdomen. Its red eyes fixed on Logan, hatred burning like coals as two more bullets slammed into its muscular body.

Then two more.

The beast stumbled sideways, its legs wobbly, its chest heaving, and as it collapsed, the gruesome sounds of bones snapping and muscle stretching joined Marlena's horrified cries.

The chupacabra's body writhed on the ground, and with agonizing slowness, Chance emerged, his breaths shallow and rattling, his skin morphing from grayish scales to pale, bruised flesh. The transformation would have been incredible if Logan didn't know that Chance was dying.

Bullets couldn't kill the purebred chupacabra, but Chance was only half... and obviously not bulletproof.

Logan released a breath and pulled himself to his feet. He heard Marlena's screams behind him, and Phoebe's laughter, and he curled his hands into fists, because he knew that trying to kill that bitch would lead to both Sela and Marlena getting hurt.

He was at Chance's side before Marlena, checking for a pulse, and heard Sela attempting to keep her friend back.

There was so much damned blood that Logan couldn't tell where all the bullets were. He applied pressure to Chance's abdomen in an attempt to stanch the bleeding, knowing full well it wouldn't be enough.

They were hours away from camp. He could run with Chance, leave the women with Phoebe, but...

"Save him, Logan," Marlena was telling him now. She'd struggled away from Sela and was rushing to Chance. Her eyes glistened as she bent down to whisper in Chance's ear.

The usually bustling Amazon seemed so quiet now, the noise deadened by the sudden, gaping loss of life, as if the jungle were in mourning.

Suddenly, inexplicably, Chance drew a shuddering breath and opened his eyes.

"Holy Christ," Logan muttered. Marlena continued whispering, and son of a bitch, Chance nodded as if in response to whatever she said to him.

"Thank God," Phoebe said. "I need one of them alive."

Logan stared in amazement. The blood that had been running through his fingers had slowed, turned dark as if coagulating.

If he didn't know better, he would say that Chance was... healing. Right in front of his eyes. He was dying and healing at the same time.

He heard Sela catch her breath behind him, felt her hand on his shoulder, and he wondered what the hell on God's green earth was happening. None of this was natural and yet...by the way Marlena looked at Chance, she didn't care.

Just like Sela looked at him.

"Chance, can you hear me?" he asked, and Chance nodded. Logan took his hands away and stared at the hole in Chance's gut. It was puckering, closing, right before his eyes.

"This one's dead for real, unless that return-from-the-dead thing is something all chupacabras can do," Phoebe called from where she was nudging the chupacabra with her boot.

Behind him, Sela shifted, called back, "You can still get a lot of information from it—probably more than you can from a live one, since you can perform a necropsy. That chupacabra will still be a big asset to Itor."

Phoebe snorted. "Nice try."

There was no way Itor would walk away empty-handed, not when they had a half man, half beast they could turn into some B horror movie supersoldier who miraculously healed from life-threatening bullet wounds to the chest.

Logan leaned down, told Chance, "We're in some trouble, but I won't let anything happen to you."

Chance nodded, closed his eyes again.

"We'll carry him back. Both of them," Phoebe ordered.

Marlena launched herself at Phoebe, slamming the other woman to the ground. She was no match for the Itor agent, but the fierceness of her intent couldn't be denied.

The women rolled, hitting trees and grunting, as fists flew. Marlena got in a nice right hook, and blood spattered from Phoebe's nose before Phoebe pinned Marlena, a knife to her throat.

Logan glanced at Chance—the man was fighting so hard to get up that the veins in his neck and forehead bulged.

"Let her go!" Sela kicked Phoebe in the ribs, and as much as Logan enjoyed watching her kick the shit out of the woman, alarm trickled down his spine—one wrong move would get his sister killed.

Cursing, he took Sela in his arms, restraining her against his chest, even as she spat obscenities at him and Phoebe. Phoebe stood, keeping her boot on Marlena's chest.

"She's very pretty. Itor would have many uses for her," Phoebe said as Marlena jerked out from under the boot. Phoebe smirked—clearly, she'd allowed Marlena to escape. She gestured to Chance. "If he can't walk, we'll drag him to camp."

Logan took a deep, calming breath. "I'll carry him. He shouldn't be jostled."

Phoebe shrugged. "It's your back."

"You're a font of compassion," Logan muttered as he gathered the SEAL up, easing him over his shoulder.

Phoebe cocked her head at the dead chupacabra and pointed at Sela and Marlena. "You two will carry the creature."

His fury must have shown on his face, because Sela covertly held up a hand and mouthed, "It's okay."

No, nothing about this was okay, but he kept his cool as she and Marlena hefted the beast, and they marched, single file, out of the jungle, the way they'd come in.

IT WAS LATE AFTERNOON BY THE TIME THE ACRO FOURSOME reached the outskirts of the GWC camp after hiking the thirty or so miles from the crash-landing site.

As always, the Amazon wasn't like Stryker remembered. When he wasn't here, he tended to romanticize the jungle, think about the cool adventures he'd been on. When he was here, he realized that it was sort of like being in the middle of hell, except he was pretty sure hell would be more fun than this.

Not that hanging out with Akbar wasn't an adventure. His mentor was one of the fiercest fighters Stryker had ever encountered.

They'd worked together from the start, with Akbar teaching

him things about combat and patience, and Stryker would never have come this far without Akbar's steady encouragement and rock-solid work ethic.

Our gifts are work—you're not taking the easy way out, Akbar would say. *You need to develop every aspect of your power—harness it, rein it in, never let it control you.*

It hadn't been easy—Stryker knew it never would be—but men like Akbar made things a lot more bearable.

His parents first realized he had his gift during a typical four-year-old temper tantrum. He'd terrified the shit out of everyone, including himself, convinced that the house was falling down on him.

Which, of course, it almost did.

He was pretty much scared straight from that point forward, and although the ACRO scientists and doctors talked with him about what happened, he didn't ever go there again—until he was seven, and that too was an accident.

It had taken a long time to gain precise control, and it didn't always work. Stryker always had to be especially careful here—the Amazon was already uncontrollable, wild, and he was never sure how the jungle would react to his powers. And really, taking out a chunk of the Amazon was something Dev would be royally pissed at . . . he was trying to take ACRO green as much as possible.

He looked over his shoulder at Gabe, who was sitting near Annika. Akbar had forced Annika to lie down and rest and hydrate and she had grudgingly complied. She'd done a fine job of chuting down into the jungle and had handled the hike like the pro she was.

He turned back to the camp, assessed the situation with his high-powered binoculars. Some GWC guys, being guarded by some Itor ones. Perfect. Itor had always found a way to spoil a party.

"They're all yours," Akbar said quietly.

"I thought we'd draw straws to see which one played captive," Stryker grumbled.

"*I* thought I'd just pull rank." Akbar flashed his easy, familiar grin. Anyone who didn't know what the man was capable of could easily underestimate him—and end up dead, thanks to one flick of a wrist.

Akbar's gift came in the form of poisonous spurs that shot out of his wrists.

Stryker and Akbar planned as much as they could, leaving room for the inevitable fuckup, which could happen at any time. Stryker would provide most of the muscle, with Akbar jumping in with the element of surprise at the end. If needed, Annika and Gabe could play a role as well.

He stood and prepared to head to the camp.

"Stay safe," Akbar told him.

"Always," Stryker answered, the way he had hundreds of times before. But this time, when he began to walk away, a feeling of unease hit him and he almost turned back.

Just your nerves screwing with you, he told himself as he worked through the thick jungle. His clothes helped with the worst of the bites and scratches in dealing with the underbrush, but man, what he wouldn't give for a cold pool. And a beer.

And women. Not ones who could kill you if you touched them either.

Focus, man. He got to the edge of camp and checked out the competition. He could take them all down pretty easily, but it would be nice to have the GWC guys on his side. And so he strode in from the jungle like he owned the place. "Hey, why the hell didn't anyone relieve me?"

All the men turned to stare at him. He walked straight up to one of the GWC men—easily differentiated from the Itor bastards because of the look of annoyance on their faces. "What's going on here, guys?" he asked loudly, and then mouthed, "Work with me," to one of the men.

"Who the hell is he?" one of the Itor guys demanded, and Stryker pivoted around.

"I work for GWC. Who the hell are you?"

The Itor guy—fucking excedo, of course—slammed him to the ground with one closed fist to the side of his head. Stryker bit the dirt and held his temper in check. It wasn't the time to give away the fact that he could play the special-abilities game. Yet.

But he'd have fun with payback when it was—because, fuck, that hurt every single time. Fucking overkill—excedos loved that shit.

For now, he sucked the dirt and pretended he was down for the count while they jacked his hands up behind his back with plastic disposable cuffs and dragged him across the ground. He waited for a while, at least an hour, until he heard footsteps stop next to him.

He rolled and groaned.

"It's okay, man... you're okay," one of the men whispered. He opened his eyes and stared at a man with half his face bandaged.

"Where's Logan? And Sela?" he asked quietly.

"Some woman's got them in the jungle, searching for the thing—the beast," the man said as he helped Stryker sit up.

He chafed against the restraints. He could get them off, but it would come with a price—the price of his temper, and it was way too early for that part of the plan.

Instead, he assessed the GWC men around him; few seemed worse for wear, and he'd guess that none of them had any special abilities beyond being ex–Special Forces. Which, he had to admit, came in pretty damned handy in a pinch.

Except for the old guy—identified by pre-mission briefing photos as Richard; he didn't look like he was willing to do anything but get in the way. "Who are you?" he asked, crouching next to Stryker.

"I'm here to help." Stryker kept his voice low and his gaze on the Itor bastards, some of whom patrolled the perimeter of the camp, and others who maintained a watch of the GWC people.

The old man's eyes crinkled as they narrowed. "You government? Military?"

"Something like that. You're going to have to follow my lead and we'll all get out of here alive."

"Itor has my daughter." Richard gripped Stryker's shirt in his fist. "If you've jeopardized her safety, if they transmit trouble back to their headquarters . . ."

Stryker stared into the man's eyes. "They're not calling in shit. We'll be ready when the rest of my team arrives if you shut up and do exactly what I say. If you don't, I can promise you'll be sorry."

CHAPTER *Twenty-two*

That Phoebe bitch scared the crap out of Sela. Mainly because when Sela looked into her baby blues, the only thing she saw was evil. The uncommonly gorgeous blonde had a body to die for and eyes that said she'd be happy to help with getting you dead.

How she'd do it was the question. Sela had no idea what the woman's special ability was, and she really didn't want to find out. So she kept quiet as the group hiked through the jungle with the chupacabra's body, Chance still draped over Logan's shoulder.

A fierce rainstorm caught them about halfway back, making the last three miles even more miserable. When it was over, steam rose up off the forest floor, mingling with the streaks of intense sunlight that pierced the cap of tree branches, and Sela might have thought it was beautiful if not for the fact that she was soaking wet, hot and feeling like she was living in a pressure cooker.

By the time they straggled into camp, the afternoon heat and humidity had taken its toll on everyone—except, seemingly,

Phoebe. The woman smiled brightly at her crew, and Sela took the opportunity to nonchalantly move toward Logan's tent, while everyone else dealt with Chance and the dead creature—a dead creature Sela would love to study. If she could get to Logan's sat phone, she could call Dev and find out where the hell her backup was. She needed boots on the ground, and fast. She had a sneaking suspicion that Itor wasn't going to leave anyone alive once they got everything they wanted all packaged up.

Sela was almost there when a hand came down on her shoulder, and she was roughly jerked around by the female Itor agent.

"If you were planning to call for help, you should know that all tents have been cleared of electronic devices."

"Well, goody for your efficiency," Sela snapped. "But I wasn't planning on calling anyone. Who are you anyway? Is Itor a government agency? For the United States? Another country?" Yep, Sela could play dumb pretty well.

Phoebe laughed. "We work for many governments."

Yeah, you work for any sleazy government with enough money to pay you to do their dirty work. Probably best not to say that. "What do you want with Global Weapons Corporation so badly that you had to hunt them down in the middle of the jungle?"

Phoebe's hand trailed down Sela's arm in a playful caress, and Sela had an instant suspicion that, sexually, the agent played for the home team. "You ask a lot of questions for a cryptozoologist."

"You barged into camp, took over and threatened our lives. I think I'm asking questions anyone would ask."

A half smile turned up one corner of Phoebe's mouth, and she let her hand drift to Sela's breast. "I suppose you're right." She paused when one of her men approached.

"What are your orders?" he asked.

"I want the unconscious man and the creature prepared for transport," she said, her fingers plucking at Sela's nipple now.

"Confiscate all research materials, and call Jackson. Tell him to bring in the rest of the team. I want to be gone within the hour."

The agent nodded and jogged off.

"The rest of the team?" Sela asked, stepping away from Phoebe's groping hands, but the other woman caught her, backed her against a tent, and this time slipped her hand under Sela's shirt. Sela's skin crawled at the feel of the hot palm sliding around her waist.

"We didn't want to alarm anyone, so we've had half our team staged outside the camp."

Hopefully they'd been killed by the guerrillas or eaten by another chupacabra. Because Phoebe wouldn't be calling them in if they weren't a cleanup crew. Which meant that everyone in the camp was about to die.

"Ma'am? Is everything okay?" The familiar male voice had Sela whipping her head around. Stryker stood there, and though Sela couldn't tell for sure, she thought his hands were bound behind his back.

He was watching Phoebe, completely expressionless.

"This is none of your concern," Phoebe growled. "Go away."

One eyebrow cocked up, but Stryker didn't move. He merely looked to Sela. "Ma'am?"

"I'm fine," she assured him. "We're just talking. Killing time before the rest of Phoebe's crew gets here."

Phoebe's nails dug painfully deep into Sela's hip, punishment for what she'd said. But Stryker had gotten the message, and he dipped his head in a brief nod before walking away.

"I didn't realize it was a secret," Sela said, lowering her voice, putting her Seducer tricks into play.

As a Seducer, she'd been trained to reel in men and women, had been instructed in all the ways to pleasure both sexes. On the job she'd done what—and who—she'd had to, and when it came right down to it, fucking a woman she hated was just as easy as fucking a man she hated. It was all a matter of putting your mind in the right place and detaching yourself while engineering their pleasure.

Problem was, Logan had ruined her, and she didn't know if she could get to that place with anyone else ever again. But if she could keep Phoebe busy in a tent for a while, maybe she could buy Stryker some time to call in help or plan something. Better, if she could get the Itor agent to climax, she might get some good intel.

But the only person she wanted to make climax was Logan, and as Phoebe's hand drifted down the back of Sela's pants, the images that popped into her head were those of Logan, his head thrown back in ecstasy, his eyes closed, tendons in his neck straining.

Maybe that would be how she could deal with Phoebe; keep Logan in her head as the person who was stroking her ass, inching fingers down between her legs.

"That's it," Phoebe purred into Sela's ear, and that fast, she was jolted out of it. This wasn't going to work. Roughly, she shoved the Itor agent away.

"I'm not playing your game, lady." Sela had to raise her chin to meet the other woman's stare, but she didn't let that intimidate her. "I'm a scientist, not a whore. I want to study the chupacabra." True enough, but maybe she could buy ACRO some time.

Phoebe's ice-cold eyes revealed nothing, but her voice rumbled with annoyance. "What you want is irrelevant."

"I'm the world's leading chupacabra expert. No one knows as much as I do about them. Sounds to me like you need some help with whatever you're doing, and I can be that help." Sela could see the wheels start turning in the gorgeous woman's brain.

Finally, Phoebe inclined her head. "You might be useful. How do you feel about travel?"

Sela didn't answer the rhetorical question, and she knew as well as Phoebe that this would be a one-way trip.

* * *

TEAM TWO HAD BEEN WELL BRIEFED. OF COURSE, THEY WERE professionals, so Phoebe expected them to perform their jobs quickly and without creating panic. Obviously, the GWC staff were terrified; Team Two looked like something out of a science-fiction military movie. But the team, consisting mainly of exce-dos, knew how to gather people up and offer reassurances that everything would be fine as long as they cooperated.

They were excellent liars.

Phoebe dragged Sela with her to the staging area, where Mick was supervising the packaging of the dead animal and the guy named Chance. The animal had been stuffed into a body bag, and Chance was sitting quietly inside a cage. The Marlena woman watched with red-rimmed eyes, but she stood stoically, making no trouble, which was smart. Huh. Beauty *and* brains. Shocking.

Well, it might have been shocking if Phoebe didn't possess both of those traits too.

Dane was standing outside the medical tent, whose canvas sides had been rolled up to prevent any of the GWC staff from trying something cute. Inside, Logan was attempting to keep his father calm. Maybe now was the time to bring in Caroline. She'd either die in the camp or she'd die where they'd left her in the jungle, so it didn't matter to Phoebe. But if she was here, Richard and Logan might be easier to control.

The small hairs on the back of her neck stood up, and the sensation that someone was watching her rolled over her like a cold wave. Slowly, she turned, locked gazes with the man who had interrupted her and Sela. He stood near the open command tent, wrists bound behind him in flex-cuffs, like eighty percent of the camp. But even so, there was nothing restrained about him.

He had to be nearly six and a half feet, and she had a feeling his jungle camos were hanging on a solid frame of muscle. But it was his eyes that really gave him the impression of power. Crystal orbs flecked with blue and green, they were almost hypnotic.

They gave absolutely nothing away. He could be terrified, or he could be enjoying himself.

Leaving Sela with the animal and Chance, she approached the man, halting just a foot away, well within his personal space. It didn't seem to bother him. Too bad. "What is your name?"

"Guess," he drawled, in a deep, rich voice that hit her in places men didn't usually touch, unless she was desperate.

She struck his face with her open palm, leaving a pink handprint on his cheek. "Next time, I draw blood."

"Look closely," he drawled.

She narrowed her eyes at him. "Why?"

"You might see me tremble."

Snarling, she hit him again, this time with her closed fist. A satisfying trickle of blood formed in the corner of his mouth. "Name."

He bared his teeth, now streaked with red. "How about... Bob."

This time, she buried her fist in his gut. His hard abs hurt her hand a little, but his soft grunt was satisfying. "*Your* name, not *a* name."

"Hit me again, and you're going to regret it." His voice was eerily calm and flat, but the flecks in his eyes were flashing like glitter in the wind. Weird. And in her world, weird meant special. As in *special abilities* special.

Fuck. That was all she needed. He might be a free agent, hired by GWC, or he could be ACRO. Either way, if he was special, he was a shitload of trouble.

"Dane!" She gestured to the tall redhead. "I want this one packaged to go. He'll need to be tranquilized." She eyed "Bob." "Don't be stingy with the meds either. And just to be sure, dose him with Nullox."

Dane cocked his eyebrow at the mention of the special-ability nullifying drug Itor had developed, but he nodded. "You got it, Phoebe."

She turned back to Bob. "Nullox will temporarily render useless any special ability you have."

"Special ability?" His perplexed expression might have fooled anyone else, but Phoebe had always been good at picking out others like her. "Oh, you mean like my talents in bed?" His voice had lowered to that delicious husky drawl again. "Because I do have a lot of special abilities there."

"I'm sure you do." And if she had her way, she'd find out firsthand—with or without his consent. "Now, why don't we try the name thing again."

"Why don't we not and say we did?"

She hated him. So she hit him. Right in the nose. Blood sprayed his cheek and her hand, and tiny droplets hit the dirt at their feet.

Bob's head dropped, so she couldn't see his eyes as he shook his head slowly. "I warned you."

Suddenly, a strange rumble rattled the air, as if a jumbo jet was flying overhead at a low level. And then the ground beneath her began to shake. Phoebe didn't have time to be terrified, because Bob launched at her—his fucking hands were somehow free.

She dodged, blocked his strike with a forearm, but the power behind his throw knocked her backward. Awkwardly, she swept her foot out, catching him in the shin. He wobbled but didn't go down.

All around them, chaos erupted. Fighting broke out between the GWC people and Itor, but at least the ground had stopped shaking.

Bob's hand came down on her biceps, crushing her arm as he yanked her toward him. "You are so dead, you little—" Hissing, he jerked away from her, and stared at his blistered hand.

Yeah, she'd fired up her gift, a lovely ability to cause second- and third-degree burns. "That's just for starters, asshole." She lunged. "I'm so going to barbecue you."

* * *

IT WASN'T VERY OFTEN THAT ANNIKA WENT ON AN ASSIGNMENT where she wasn't in charge, and it was annoying as hell not to be calling the shots.

Then again, she wasn't supposed to be on this mission.

Akbar had ordered no guns in close proximity to the civilians unless necessary, and he'd ordered that Annika and Gabe stand back until his signal. When it came, she was ready.

She and Gabe burst out of the jungle and into the fray. She *thought* Gabe had gone out anyway—he'd turned invisible. About ten seconds later, she saw him materialize behind an Itor agent and take him out with a surprise blow to the kidneys and head.

Annika sprinted toward Sela, who was struggling with one of the male Itor agents, when an orange flash seared her peripheral vision. She spun, and there, between two tents, the female I-Agent was hurling a fireball the size of a Humvee tire at Stryker. He dodged, hissed as it brushed his arm and fell into a group of GWC personnel, his BDU sleeve smoking.

And then Akbar was there, ripping into the female in a blur of arms and legs, the poisonous spurs in his wrists cutting tears in her clothes. She lit up like a damned torch, and Akbar fell back, his skin blistered.

Jesus. That woman was a fucking walking rotisserie.

Gabe darted toward Akbar and the I-Agent. Stryker tried to, but a lightning-fast excedo attacked him, and the two traded blows, fists and feet flying.

The woman slammed a coffee-cup-sized fireball into Akbar's chest, and he yelped, fell back even more as he slapped at the flames. Gabe was almost there when the woman turned toward him. Instantly, he dematerialized, and she snarled, whipping around and locking her sights on Annika.

Bring it on, bitch.

Annika fired up her power. A light tingle ran over her skin and faded away in a weak sizzle, leaving behind the knowledge that she could do nothing more than initiate a static shock. Devastation rocked her, and the moment of hesitation at the lack of power cost her. In almost slow motion, she saw the woman's hand glow, and a Jeep-sized ball of crimson fire blasted through the space between them.

Akbar lunged, knocking Annika out of the way, and then he was... oh, God... oh... *dear God*... he was engulfed.

His screams rent the air as he hit the ground, his body completely encased in fire. Annika's own screams tore from her throat as she ran toward him, knowing as she did that it was too late. Out of nowhere, she was thrown to the ground, and Gabe's heavy body came down on top of her, pinning her to the damp earth.

"No, Annika, no. It's too late." His voice was shredded with horror and pain, his eyes wide, liquid, haunted.

"Let go!" she yelled, but Gabe only held her tighter as she struggled to get up, to get to Akbar, whose screams had died away, and whose body still burned, though now it lay in a heap, barely twitching.

"No!" She sucked in a lungful of black, greasy smoke and choked. That taste, she knew, that smell, would never leave her, and even as she sobbed, she plotted.

Plotted the Itor woman's death, because by all that was holy, Annika swore that the next time they met, one of them would die.

PHOEBE DIDN'T HAVE TIME TO REVEL IN THE DYING MAN'S FINAL twitches. The first asshole, Bob, was coming at her like a tank, the glitter in his eyes spinning like blades of death. Obviously seeing his buddy get barbecued didn't sit well with him.

"You fucking cunt!"

Smiling, she blasted him with a small fireball—the large one meant for the blond bitch had sapped a lot of power, and she needed to conserve now.

He wheeled away, and as before, there was a rumble, but this time, the earth seemed to buck in protest. Beneath her feet, the ground rippled like a shaken carpet. No longer amused, she cried out. Terror such as she hadn't felt since she was a child screamed through her as she was flung through the air. She hit a tree, and then rolled and dodged as another came down, landing where she'd just been.

Fear and horrific memories crippled her, sucked her into a dark place where she could hide . . . but *no*. She had to fight the panic. Stay calm, or Melanie would take over. Phoebe struggled to remain in the light of consciousness, but all around her, trees were falling and tent poles were coming down and people were screaming.

Inside, Phoebe felt Melanie shoving against the walls of her mind, an expanding pressure on the inner surfaces of her skull. The little bitch sensed weakness, but she couldn't know what situation she'd be awakening in. Melanie would get them killed.

A fist slammed into Phoebe's face, and then a wall of solid muscle was on top of her. Bob. The ground buckled, and just feet away, a mountain of a rock boiled up out of the soil like a tombstone. Once more, terror took control, and this time it won . . .

MELANIE BLINKED, HER VISION FUZZY AS HER CONSCIOUSNESS came online, as if from a deep coma. It was always this way when Phoebe retreated and let Mel out. Waking was an interesting experience, because Melanie never knew where she was coming to. In a strange bed, a strange country, the middle of the ocean.

She smelled smoke, heard shouts and gunfire. She blinked again. And then she screamed. A man was lying on her—an extremely pissed-off, bloody man, with pure murder in his eyes. His hands were around her throat, squeezing—she charged up her gift. His eyes shot wide in surprise, and he flew off her like he'd been thrown from a rodeo bull.

That was the power of her icy blast—a gift that couldn't be more opposite of her sister's, and usually a whole lot less useful unless someone needed ice in their lemonade.

Scrambling to her hands and knees, she crawled away from the man. Her heart thudded against her rib cage as though wanting to break out and get her moving a hell of a lot faster.

"What the fuck?" His angry roar joined the rumble of noise all around her. An earthquake? Wait, where was she? This was a jungle of some sort. Jesus, what had Phoebe gotten them into?

The earthquake explained why Melanie was here, though. Phoebe was terrified beyond reason of them thanks to a childhood tragedy.

Mel somehow made it to her feet, but the rolling ground sent her crashing into a tree. The force of the impact bruised her chest, and she had to cling to the trunk to stay upright as she caught her breath.

The angry man was standing a few feet away, his gaze as fury-filled as something right out of hell, and she could practically see steam coming out of his ears. Behind him, people were fighting, and a charred body lay on the ground, smoke and small flames coming off it.

Phoebe.

"Get away from me." Mel's voice was humiliatingly shaky and weak and the angry man didn't react at all. "Just . . . leave me alone."

"Oh, now you want to beg?" he snarled.

She nodded. Vehemently. "Look, whatever I did . . . I'm sorry. Okay?"

"Not good enough." He took a step toward her, and a dread skittered up her spine. He was going to kill her.

Swallowing, she threw out her hand, sending a hard-core cone of icy wind at him. In humid climates like this one, water in the air froze with the wind, turning her blast into a weapon full of tiny shards of ice. The cone of cold struck him full in the chest, neck and shoulders, shredding his clothes and his skin. Hissing, he wheeled backward several steps.

His curses cut through the air, and the earth shuddered and tore. A gaping fissure opened up in front of Melanie. Screaming, she scrambled backward, but the crumbling dirt fell away beneath her feet, sucking her into the bottomless hole. With all her strength, she clawed at the edge, and just before she plummeted to a certain death, her fingers found a vine.

The angry man reached for her from the opposite side of the growing crevice. Desperate, she held out her hand.

"Help me," she breathed, and for a moment, she thought that was what he was trying to do, but when she looked into his eyes, she gasped.

He didn't intend to save her. He wanted to pull her to safety so he could kill her with his bare hands.

Dear God, what had Phoebe done to him?

Melanie clung to the vine, scaling the crumbling dirt cliff and barely throwing herself to solid ground before a three-foot-wide section of earth fell away, into the fissure.

"Motherfuck!" the man shouted. His gaze swept the area, and she knew he was looking for a way to cross the gaping crevice that now separated her from the rest of the camp.

"Stryker!" A young man sprinted toward Stryker and tossed him a pistol.

Shit! Melanie scrambled into the jungle, shots blasting after her. All around her, tree bark exploded, and then a hot bullet burned a streak across her cheek.

His outraged voice followed her like a monster from a horror movie, and she knew it was something she'd never forget. "You're dead, Phoebe! I will hunt you all the way to your goddamned grave."

Melanie ran. She didn't know where she was, she had no survival skills and she didn't know anyone here. All she knew was that certain death awaited her back at that camp. Better to take her chances out here in the middle of... Asia? South America?

Panting, her side aching, she slowed near a ravine. A noise caught her attention. Below, she could hear rushing water, but to her right... Was that a woman? Shouting for help? Slowly, Mel crept through the brush, shuddering at the giant spiderwebs that stretched between the trees and the colorful yet creepy bugs climbing broad leaves.

"What were you doing in this godforsaken place?" she muttered, as though Phoebe could hear her. But she couldn't, and when she took over the body from Melanie again, she wouldn't know anything that happened while she was locked inside the head they shared.

"Help! Anyone out there? Help me!"

Mel brushed aside a branch and drew a harsh breath at the sight of a young woman tied to a tree. She was standing, her back to the bark, her dishwater-blond hair clinging to the sweat on her face.

Melanie stepped out from behind the bush.

Fury turned the woman's cheeks crimson. "You bitch! You fucking piece of shit!"

Melanie sighed. "I see you've met Phoebe."

"What?" the woman screeched. "You're insane, you know that?"

Yeah, that was a news flash. "Look, I'm going to let you go. But I need to ask you a few questions."

"We already covered this," she spat. "I don't know anything, and even if I did, I wouldn't tell you."

Clearly, Phoebe had gone light on the young woman, or she would have spilled her guts, and maybe anything else she could. Oh, she had been beaten. Badly. Her lips were swollen and split, her face was bruised, and she had two black eyes. Multiple burns lined her arms. But Mel had seen photos of Phoebe's handiwork before, and this was nothing. Still, nausea rolled through Melanie's gut.

"I'm so sorry," she whispered, as she worked the knot binding the woman's wrists. "Are you here because of something going on at a camp?"

The young woman didn't answer, and the moment her hands were free, she leaped away from Melanie, rubbing her abraded wrists.

Knowing she wasn't going to get anything out of this girl, Melanie pointed in the direction of the camp. "It's that way. Big battle going on. At least the earthquake has stopped, though."

The woman looked at Mel like she was crazy, but wisely she didn't stick around. She went crashing through the jungle as if her feet were on fire. Which they very well might be if Phoebe came out anytime soon.

Blinking against the sudden sting of wetness in her eyes, Melanie sank to the ground. As much as she hated to admit it, only Phoebe could save them now. So she rested her head against the tree and relaxed, hoping her evil twin would hurry up and take back the body, get them the hell out of here.

THE BITCH HAD GOTTEN AWAY AND IT WAS HIS OWN DAMNED fault.

Stryker stared across the chasm in the earth he'd created. He hadn't let his temper get the best of his gift in as long as he could remember, but seeing Akbar die like that...

Fuck.

Stryker covered his eyes with a palm even as he squeezed them shut, but it would never erase the picture in his mind. He knew Akbar's screams would remain a constant echo in his ears for a long time to come as well.

That Phoebe bitch was crazy. Maybe even certifiable. And talk about running hot and cold—one of his hands had third-degree burns and he was pretty sure he'd suffered frostbite to his chest. If he hadn't seen the change take place directly in front of him, he'd never have believed it. When ice woman emerged, he'd noted both confusion and resignation in her eyes—and she hadn't been faking either emotion.

Not that he gave two shits. He would still kill her with his bare hands if given the chance.

You still have to complete the mission.

Akbar would never want him to let his guard down now, or to risk other lives.

"Gabe, you stay close to Annika," he called. Gabe nodded and Stryker ignored Annika's glare—the woman was working with a concussion, burns and a possible loss of her gift. Whatever was going on there, she needed cover, and the kid was doing a damned good job of providing that.

The battle raged all around him, and Stryker prepared to unleash his power and put a new chasm between his group and Itor.

Two men stumbled from the debris of a fallen tent, the younger one, Logan, helping Richard walk toward him. One hulking excedo with a body that looked made of steel rushed Logan, who, without hesitation, leaped at him. As Stryker watched, ready to step in, Logan wrestled the excedo to the ground, before breaking his neck.

That type of takedown didn't happen easily; there was no way Logan didn't have some kind of special ability. He wouldn't have survived a fight with an excedo otherwise . . . no, he most likely never would've walked again, unless he was an excedo himself.

Sela, her upper arm bleeding, raced to Logan and Richard, and together they approached Stryker.

Anger and grief was a hell of a potent combination, and he closed his eyes and concentrated with the fierceness necessary, so as not to take out the entire jungle with his powers.

First, he imagined the break starting about twenty feet deep. Within seconds, the sound of rumbling earth moved through his body like a shot of adrenaline that made him want to scream. It was part pain, part fear, all rolled together with a surge of power he was never completely comfortable using, even when it was to save lives.

The ground began to buck under everyone's feet. The Itor assholes retreated, and GWC personnel scrambled away—only Stryker stayed still as the ground broke open ten feet in front of him, wide enough that the I-Agents who weren't fast enough tumbled into the fault, and to their deaths.

All conversation behind him had come to a halt. Causing an earthquake—even a small one—had the tendency to be a real showstopper.

Now he turned to Logan, because the real show was about to begin.

"What the hell is this guy?" Logan demanded of Sela as he pointed to Stryker.

"I work with Sela," Stryker told him. "Who the hell are you?"

Sela answered, her palm over the gash in her shoulder. "Logan's GWC. But consider him special like us. He'll be a help taking out Itor."

Who could still have agents close by, planning another attack. Sticking around longer was not a smart idea.

"How do you know this guy?" Logan asked Sela, and Stryker frowned, hated being talked about like he wasn't in the room. Jungle. Whatever.

"I've got a way out of here," he interrupted. "I'll take you and your father, the women and that caged guy. Send the rest of your men out of here. I'm assuming you've got a plane at the airport."

Logan nodded. "Yeah, we do. But who the fuck are you? You aren't taking anyone, especially the women."

Sela gripped Logan's biceps urgently, even as the sound of incoming vehicles reached his ears, and fuck, that was all they needed. Either more Itor or the damned guerrillas were coming.

"Logan, Stryker is with me," Sela said. "With my company,

ACRO, which I'll tell you all about later. For now, you need to trust him. You need to come with us. You still have something Itor wants—you can't take Chance back to GWC headquarters, because they'll follow you, and you aren't equipped to deal with them."

"I'm not going anywhere until I find Phoebe," Logan snarled. "She knows where my sister is." He shot Stryker a you're-dead glare. "If Caroline dies because you did something to Phoebe—"

Stryker aimed his pistol at Logan's chest, and the earth began to shake from the force of his anger. It didn't help that he'd caught sight of Akbar's body again. "Doing things your way got you into this fucking mess. We're doing things my way now."

CHAPTER *Twenty-three*

Even over the continued rumblings of the earth and the Stryker asshole trying to take charge of the situation, Logan heard his name screamed out from somewhere in the jungle.

Caroline. "That's my sister," he said, more to himself than to anyone else, and within seconds he was drawing his Sig and taking off in the direction the scream had come from, careful to jump over the heavy grooves left in the earth, apparently from the asshole's temper tantrum. Granted, it had saved all their asses, but still, Logan didn't like the guy.

He heard the heavy footsteps behind him but he wasn't stopping for anything.

"If that bitch Phoebe is back, she's mine," Asshole barked.

Logan ignored him, barreled into the tangled brush, not caring about getting scraped and bruised to hell. He only had rescue on his mind.

He stopped short when he saw Caroline in the merciless grip of an Itor agent.

If he hadn't recognized her long blond hair and the watch she always wore, he might not have believed it was her.

Her eyes were swollen, as was her bottom lip . . . her cheeks bruised. Logan felt the rage well up inside of him.

"Don't come any closer," the Itor agent warned; he had the barrel of his gun pointed at Caroline's head.

"Your men are dead—there's no way out for you," Logan told him. "Let her go."

The Itor agent laughed, loudly and inappropriately. And then he began to mutter in a language Logan had never heard before.

Suddenly, next him, Stryker went deadly silent, as did Caroline in front of him. She simply stared into space, her body stock-still.

What the hell? He hadn't seen the guy give Caroline anything, and the I-Agent certainly hadn't gotten to Stryker. Something told Logan to pretend he was as affected as they were, and so he stood still, looked straight ahead and waited.

"Stupid ACRO agents. No match for my hypnosis," the Itor agent muttered. "They make it too easy."

Mind control. Hypnosis. And because of his bioware, Logan wasn't affected, but he continued to pretend, stood with the stiffness and the stare, until the agent began to drag Caroline away.

Logan waited until they were almost out of sight, and then he charged the agent, who never saw him coming.

Within seconds, Logan had broken the man's neck and caught Caroline as she fell from the dead man's embrace. Stryker shouted from behind him, the hypnotic spell broken.

"We're here. We're okay," Logan called as Stryker crashed through the snarled vegetation.

"Fuck. Fucking hypnosis." Stryker rubbed the back of his neck and then shook his head. "How's your sister?"

Caroline was whimpering, eyes still slightly glazed. "Not great."

"It takes non-specials longer to recover," Stryker assured him, moving to rifle through the dead man's pockets while Logan spoke to Caroline.

"Caroline, it's me—it's Logan—you're safe now," he told her. Stroked her cheek until her eyes lost the glazed look.

"Caroline, did you see anyone else around here?" Stryker asked, his voice gruff.

She shook her head vigorously. "The woman—the one who kidnapped me—she untied me and told me to run, and then that guy grabbed me," Caroline sobbed.

Logan hugged her tight against him. "I'm so sorry, sis. If I'd had any idea you would've been in danger..."

He trailed off as she sagged against him, exhaustion and trauma sapping her strength. Gently, he picked her up and brought her to the clearing, Stryker right behind them.

Sela had already organized the men—his men—and they were loading up the GWC vehicles with the camp's equipment. She kept pressure on her arm wound and didn't even glance at Logan as she spoke with Stryker in a clipped, professional voice that reminded him he didn't know her at all.

"There's a helo waiting ten miles out in a clearing," she said. "It'll take us to a jet, which will take us to ACRO."

Logan shook his head, confused, pissed and so fucking betrayed by the woman who'd sworn up and down that she was nothing but a damned scientist. "I'm not going anywhere until one of you explains how the hell ACRO will help me deal with Itor."

"Logan, it's okay," Marlena started, but Sela stopped her with a hand on her shoulder.

"ACRO is sending in more personnel to finish breaking down the GWC camp," she said, as Chance eased into a Hummer next to them. "Your men will be taken care of and allowed to return to GWC by this evening. But ACRO is the only place *we'll* be safe for now. Please trust me—I can explain everything."

"You can explain on the helo," Stryker said, as he opened the vehicle doors. "Let's roll."

THE TEN-MILE RIDE THROUGH THE JUNGLE WAS CRAMPED, mostly silent and slow going. Logan sat with his sister and father in the middle row of seats, spending most of the hour trying to comfort Caroline, who had apparently gone through hell. Itor had kept her mostly blindfolded, and they'd interrogated her, brutally, about things for which she'd had no information. Whether she'd talked or not, they'd beaten her. Or, more accurately, Phoebe had beaten her. And burned her. Refused to feed her.

The poor girl would need time to recover, but with Logan helping her, Caroline had a head start.

Stryker, in the front passenger seat, had made Chance drive, probably giving him something to do in order to keep his mind off turning into a beast, and it left him free to handle any issues that might pop up with Logan. It was pretty clear that Stryker didn't trust anyone in the car besides Sela, Gabe, Annika and Marlena—but then, the non-ACRO people didn't trust him either.

Even Sela was a little wary of him, especially now, when he looked about two seconds from going into a rage that would reach all the way to the earth's core. Damn, she'd known he was some sort of elementalist with powers over the land, but she hadn't seen him in action. She'd been terrified... which had come on the heels of being horrified at what had been done to Akbar.

She'd barely known the man, but the sight of him dying the way he had would stick with her for life.

From the haunted look in Gabe and Annika's eyes as they sat next to each other in the backseat, she knew they'd be having nightmares for a while too. Sela had definitely never known Annika to be so quiet, or to look so tired.

When they arrived in the clearing, the chopper pilot started up the bird—ACRO's long-range transport, specially outfitted to seat a dozen agents in comfort, or twice that in less comfort, plus carry a ton of gear. They piled in, and once the dead chupa was secured in the back, along with the medical equipment and files they'd brought along, everyone settled in. Logan eased Caroline into a seat next to their father, gave her a bottle of water, and then moved to the very back near the bathroom, signaling for Sela to follow.

Stryker started to protest, but she cut him off with a glare. She was grateful for his help—okay, he'd saved their asses—but when it came right down to it, this was her mission. And if she wanted to slink into the shadows in the back of the helo with Logan and ignore takeoff buckle-up procedures, she would.

Annika and Gabe had chosen seats next to each other again, and Annika sat quietly, fingers wrapped tightly around a can of 7UP.

Sela paused in front of her. "Is everything all right?" Sela asked, though she had no idea why, and she was shocked when, instead of a biting response, Annika merely nodded and looked down at her soda. Even more shocking was that when Gabe touched Annika's hand reassuringly, she didn't flip out.

Weird.

After playing stewardess one last time and making sure Marlena was okay—sitting near Chance to keep him calm while Stryker started a sedative IV drip—Sela reached Logan. He pointed to the bench seat that lined the bulkhead, and nodded at her shoulder, which had been grazed by a bullet. She'd barely felt it, but now that he'd pointed it out, it began to throb.

"Where's the med kit?"

"Right behind you." She sank down, grateful to be off her legs, which had gone rubbery with exhaustion, an adrenaline crash and the knowledge that she was going to have to come clean with Logan now.

While she removed her BDU shirt, he fetched the first-aid kit from its secured box and took a seat next to her. "Doesn't look too bad."

"It's not." Stung like hell, though.

Gently, he rolled her T-shirt sleeve up, and dug gauze and antiseptic solution out of the bag. "I need to clean it. Won't feel good."

"I've had worse."

His gaze snapped up to hers. "Are you talking about the asshole who beat the shit out of you? Or does this have something to do with these people you work with?"

Sela's mouth went dry, and she suddenly wished she'd grabbed a bottle of water before she'd come back here. "I guess we should talk about ACRO."

"I guess we should." He held a gauze pad below her wound to catch the antiseptic as he irrigated the groove the bullet had made in her flesh. "I'd like to hear about what this company is and how you know about it."

She clenched her teeth against the bite of the liquid. "I'm an operative with the Agency for Covert Rare Operatives. ACRO."

"And that is?"

"It's like the CIA. Except it's staffed by the X-Men." When he nodded, she frowned. "You don't seem very surprised."

"After what I've seen—a man who turned into a chupacabra, another who can make earthquakes, Itor people who can throw fireballs—I'm willing to believe you." He cut her a hard look. "About this, at least."

"I couldn't tell you about ACRO, Logan. We thought you were in Itor's pocket. I came to find out what kind of weapon you were making for them."

"So the cryptozoologist thing really was bullshit." His voice was too level, too calm, and Sela began to sweat despite the air-conditioning, which otherwise made the inside of the helo feel like a giant refrigerator.

"No. That's what I do for ACRO. I'm an expert in the field of unknown species. And," she added, wincing, "that really fucking hurts."

"Sorry." He gentled his touch as he used tweezers to dig bits of her shirt out of the wound. "So what is Itor? Really."

"What did you think they were?"

He shrugged. "A private paramilitary agency that sold their services to the highest bidder."

That's right, GWC would have vetted Itor for legitimacy—probably. And yeah, Itor was known to the world as nothing more than a private security agency. The reality was far more sinister, but GWC would have had no way of knowing that.

"They're an agency much like ACRO, except they play for Team Evil. They work differently than we do, they're set up differently than we are and they have absolutely no ethics. They're all about the profit and power." Though in recent years, they'd stepped up their game, and speculation within ACRO was that Itor was building to something big. Something very big.

A warm trickle of blood ran down her arm. Logan pressed a pad to her wound and applied pressure. "You doing okay?"

"Yeah."

"A little sting . . ." He rinsed her cut with saline solution, and yep, it stung. "Was the man who was, ah, killed . . . one of yours?"

Though many had died during the battle, only one had died so horrifyingly, and she knew exactly to whom Logan was referring. "Yes," she rasped, her throat as raw with emotion as it was from breathing the smoke that had come off Akbar's burning body.

"I'm sorry." He sighed. "So how much of what you told me about your background is true?"

"All of it."

"What about Marlena?"

"What about her?"

The helicopter banked hard to the right, and Logan braced her by throwing a strong arm across her shoulders. When the bird straightened out, he pulled back, his movement brisk and impersonal, as though he'd been keeping a sack of flour from falling off a shelf. "Is she really your assistant?"

"No," she admitted. "Can you bandage my shoulder now? We should be approaching the airstrip."

"So what does she do at ACRO?" he asked, not falling for her distraction. Though he did dig a bandage out of the kit.

"Logan, we need to get ready to land—"

"What does she do?" His voice was sharp now, cracking even over the loud thump of the rotors.

Sela grabbed the bandage from him and shoved to her feet. "I'll finish this myself."

Trembling with nerves, annoyance and about a million other emotions she couldn't name, she yanked open the bathroom door and slipped inside.

But when she went to slam it shut, Logan's arm blocked it. Then, with icy deliberation, he filled the tiny space with his body, his presence . . . and the force of his anger.

"There is nowhere to go, Sela." Logan's expression was dark, his voice low and dangerous, but as he crowded her in the small space, his body hardened with more than anger.

Instantly, her traitorous body ignited with a slow simmer of heat at her core. Angry sex was not a good idea right now. Hell, sex in any form was not a good idea—not with Logan. He already had a lot of control over her heart, and sex would only bind her to him even more tightly.

And then, when he learned the complete truth about her, he'd cut those tethers and leave her broken.

"Get away from me," she rasped.

Instead of complying, he closed and locked the door, then took back the bandage. His face might be a storm cloud, but his hands were gentle—if brisk—as he opened the sterile package and smoothed the bandage onto her shoulder. His touch sparked more heat, and she actually quivered with desire. Not good.

She shoved at his chest, desperate to get out of the bathroom before she did something stupid, but he struck like a snake, somehow gripping her wrists in one hand and lifting her onto the sink with the other as he stepped between her spread thighs.

"I said, there's nowhere to go." His breath was hot and desperate in her ear, the scrape of his teeth on her lobe bordering on erotic.

"All I need to do," she whispered, "is scream."

His hips pushed against her, his arousal in hard contact with her sex. "You going to let your friends kill me, Sela? For what? Bandaging your wound?" He ground his hips, and she gasped as her core became molten. "Making you hot?"

The last time they'd been like this, had screwed while angry, he'd said he loved her. She didn't know if that was true anymore, but she did know it wouldn't be once he found out what she really used to do for ACRO.

This would be her final chance to be with him, so no, she wasn't going to scream. At least, she wasn't going to scream for help.

Jerking her hands out of his grip, she reached between them and tore open the fly of his pants. He growled in approval, and then somehow, in the cramped space, he managed to peel her BDUs and panties down to her ankles and then step between her legs while her pants were tangled around her boots.

His expression was wild, feral, as he thrust his finger into her wet pussy, and she had to bite her lower lip to keep from crying out.

"I love the way you respond to me," he gritted, his jaw so tight she suspected the exact opposite, that he hated it, that he was as much a slave to her physical response as she was.

She arched her back, needing him deeper, and he complied, adding another finger and pushing them in up to his knuckles. His fingers thrust and swirled, rasping over nerves that screamed with pleasure.

They didn't have time to play, but Logan knew that as well as she did, and in the space of a breath, he replaced his fingers with his cock. The broad head of him stretched her, slowly, almost painfully, and then the tenderness was over.

He slammed into her with a grunt. His hot gaze collided with hers as he angled his head to kiss her. The helicopter jolted, but Logan kept his balance easily, holding her steady with both hands on her hips. Needing more of him, she gripped his hair in her fists, forcing his head down to keep his mouth on hers.

There was no talking. No trying to get information from her. This was about releasing the horror of the day's events, about confirming that they were alive, because even if they were furious with each other, they *were* alive.

Logan began to move faster, the veined ridges of his cock stroking her sensitive flesh with each thrust. Heat curled upward from her sex, spreading like wildfire through her muscles and over her skin.

Powerful surges sent lightning strikes of pleasure into her clit, and she moaned into his mouth. He pumped harder, his thrusts becoming frantic as he neared the peak, taking her with him.

Just as the first ripples of climax struck, he pulled away, his eyes focusing on her like searing lasers. "Yes," he ground out, "or no?"

For a second, she just blinked, too dazed to get what he was asking. Then it struck her—dear God, he was . . . he was asking permission to come. He didn't want to hurt her with his thoughts. The knowledge destroyed her. Made her eyes sting and her heart sing.

"Yes," she gasped. "Please!"

He closed his eyes and threw back his head. His jaw was clenched, the tendons in his neck straining, and then molten jets splashed inside her, turning the ripples of pleasure into a tsunami of ecstasy. She would've screamed, except his hand shot across her mouth, so she was biting down on his palm as the release took her.

Images swamped her, but they were beautiful—Logan's fantasies of them together, on a beach, in a forest, in front of a fire with snow falling outside.

She came again, and when it was over, she had to clamp her teeth together to keep them from chattering at the amount of intense emotion washing over her.

Logan said nothing as he buttoned up and stepped out of the cage of her legs and pants. But he surprised her by helping her tug up her pants, and when they were dressed, he opened the door and ushered her out.

"I still need to tape up your bandage."

"It's okay. Really. I'm going to get a seat up front. You can sit back here if you want."

He gripped her waist and guided her back into the seat she'd been in before she fled to the bathroom, and this time, she knew she wasn't getting away from his questions. They'd had a brief moment of escape, but his expression was hard again, his body tense.

And her? Yeah, she was a mess. She didn't bother glancing into the main cabin, because everyone in there probably knew what had gone on in that bathroom.

"How many times do I have to tell you that there's nowhere to go? So you might as well answer my question." His voice was a deadly rumble that reminded her of Stryker's earthquake. "What. Does. Marlena. Do."

Sela's stomach clenched. He really wasn't going to let this go. She could put him off if she truly wanted to cause a scene, but he'd find out eventually anyway. He might as well hear it from her.

"She came with me to seduce you."

Logan's head snapped back in surprise. "She what?"

"She's what's called a Seducer," Sela said. "Her job is to—"

"Fuck information out of someone," he finished. "So you came for the chupacabra, but ended up fucking me, and she came for me, but ended up fucking the chupacabra." He laughed bitterly. "Ironic fucking world, huh?" He reached for some surgical tape, then froze . . . and turned back to her. "Wait. You can read people during sex. Can she do that?"

"No." Her stomach turned over, because she knew where this was headed.

"But you can. Which seems like a damned handy skill for someone who works for a secret agency that employs Seducers."

"I guess."

His expression went flat and cold enough to make her shiver. "I think it's time to cut the bullshit. You're a fucking Seducer, aren't you?" She shook her head, and his fingers tightened around her wrist. "I am so sick of your lies, Sela. I want the truth, and I want it now."

Anger flared, a welcome heat to replace the icy dread that had centered in her chest. "You are not in charge here. You're on my turf now, so I'd be careful about demanding answers I don't want to give you."

"So that's a yes," he said, eyes flashing with fury. "You denied it over and over, but you really are a goddamned corporate prostitute, so dedicated to your job that you fucked me on a company flight." He laughed. "I apologized for calling you a whore, but now I realize I was right all along."

Stung, she leaped to her feet and slapped him as hard as she could. "You don't have a lot of room to talk, you bastard. At least I have never sold my services to the highest bidder. I don't think you can say the same thing about your company."

She spun around, and nearly collided with Stryker, who must have been keeping a close eye on what was going on in the back of the helo and had come to help her. His eyes were chips of ice as he glared at Logan, but spoke to her. "You okay?"

Not at all. When she'd actually worked as a Seducer, falling in love hadn't been a concern. She'd been intimate with so many people and had never even come close to love, so it just figured that she'd succumb while on a mission that wasn't even intended to be about seducing.

And now her past had come back to haunt her in a way she could never have predicted.

"I'm fine. I'm just going to take a seat with Marlena." They'd be on the plane and in the air within half an hour, and thank God Dev kept the thing stocked with expensive alcohol, because she planned to drink the past few days away. With any luck, she'd wake up and find that the whole mission was nothing but a bad dream.

CHAPTER *twenty-four*

After a fifteen-hour flight, thanks to bad-weather diversions, they landed at the ACRO compound at seven in the morning. Logan helped his sister off the jet with the medics, who wanted to keep Caroline in the infirmary overnight for observation.

Neither Caroline nor he was happy about it, but Logan knew his sister needed to be checked and treated more extensively. "I'm going with her."

No one argued, and so Logan and his father followed the medics and Caroline into a waiting Hummer. He felt Sela's eyes on him, but he refused to turn around. The anger at what she'd done, what she'd kept hidden, would reach another boiling point if he looked at her.

Within five minutes, they were in front of a brick building where there were four more men waiting. Two of them ushered his father away for a debriefing; Logan didn't bat an eye. Let the old man explain what he'd done. Logan needed to stay with Caroline. The remaining men escorted Logan and his sister inside an extensive medical facility and to an exam room.

"Sir, we've got to change her into a gown," one of the nurses said. "Which means you need to leave."

Reluctantly, he did, but stayed right outside the door in case she called for him. The guilt, which had built from the second he'd learned she'd been kidnapped, now threatened to overwhelm him. He slid down the wall and sat on the floor, buried his face in his hands as he did so.

It was only then he realized he'd need to call GWC for more of his daily injections. He'd managed to grab a week's supply from the tent after Stryker's great earthquake matinee, but he had no idea how long they'd be here.

"Sir, I'm going to be the doctor in charge of Caroline."

He looked up at the soft-voiced, slightly older woman in a white coat and small, round glasses standing in front of him.

"I'm going to examine her thoroughly, decide if I need to order tests—and, of course, I'll have to find out exactly what happened to her," she continued. "It might take a while, and you look like you need some food and rest. I can have one of the agents escort you to a sleep room."

"I don't need sleep. Or food. I just need to make sure my sister is all right."

The doctor nodded. "Of course, I understand. But for safety reasons, you cannot wait in the hallway."

Logan stood, because arguing was useless. "I'll be back in half an hour."

He began to walk down the hall toward the door, well aware he was being followed by an agent, sort of like having a bodyguard in reverse. It made sense that he wouldn't be allowed to roam this compound unattended, especially since he was sure Sela had filled ACRO in on the secret of his bioware.

Sela, the first person he'd told his secrets to. Which had been the stupidest thing he could've done; should've known that trusting her was wrong.

God, his instincts were fucked. He blamed the bioware. And Sela's training. And this entire ACRO world.

When he'd taken her in the bathroom, he was actually thinking about a future together with her. About beaches and long walks and normal things that couples do.

But you're not normal. That always seemed to come back and slam him between the eyes as a harsh and stunning reminder. When he'd been normal, he'd taken it all for granted. Thought he'd had all the time in the world for family, for children . . . for everything.

Now he knew life was too damned short and nothing would ever be the way he'd thought it would. But he'd had enough of this pity party; there was still a lot more to be done to dig GWC out of this mess. With ACRO's help, of course.

The thought made his fists tighten.

As he walked outside, he tried hard to keep it together. It would do no good to put on a show of temper here, if Stryker's powers were any indication of what kind of men—and women—worked here.

"You're right. You're strong, Logan, but we don't let our agents, or our guests, use their powers against one another." A tall, brown-haired man, wearing the familiar black BDUs, fell into step with him.

Great, a fucking swami mind reader.

"I don't need to read your mind to know what you're thinking." The man stopped and so did Logan. "I'm Devlin O'Malley. I'm in charge of ACRO."

Logan stuck out his hand. Dev shook it with the firm, easy grip of someone completely in command, of himself and his team.

"Yes. Let's keep walking, okay?" Dev didn't bother to wait for

Logan to agree before he was moving at a fast clip along the winding paths, nodding at the men and women he passed.

Logan kept up the pace next to him and for about five minutes, neither of them spoke. Finally, they came to a well-kept building.

"If we're to talk about Itor, I'd rather do it here in my office. It's protected," Dev explained, holding a door open for him.

"Protected?" Logan repeated as he entered a plush lobby.

"You don't have a mind-shield yet. Itor can read you—break into your mind and grab information." Dev led him past a desk and into a large office. "This building has recently had extra shields put in place."

"So they know I'm here."

Dev closed the door and remained standing. "They knew that the second they saw Stryker. What concerns me is that you might be thinking things Itor can use—against you and against us."

"Great. I want to take Itor down. Which means I need to get out of here and make a plan. I'm happy to let your organization in on—"

Dev shook his head. "It's not that easy. Itor can't be stopped in one fell swoop. At least not yet," Devlin muttered, ran his hands through his hair and stared at Logan. "You, your father, your sister—none of you will be safe at GWC now."

"So I'm supposed to close my company?" Logan demanded.

"I didn't say you have to close it. But you'll have to run it in a far more protected environment than where it is now."

"What, here?" Logan heard the sarcasm in his own voice. "Yeah, sure, we'll become an ACRO-run company. So I can supply you and your agents with weapons. And how the hell do I know you don't have the same evil intent that Itor does?"

"Because I'm telling you. We rescued you, didn't we? And we haven't done anything but keep you safe." Devlin's voice grew hard. "Itor will never stop looking for you. Now that they know what you're made of, what Chance is—"

"Can you cure him?" Logan interrupted.

"There's a small possibility. Very small."

"I want him at GWC—we can probably help him, the way they helped me," Logan insisted.

"If you go back, it's without Chance. He's too... vulnerable for us to let him fall into the wrong hands."

"Yeah, he was in great fucking hands with your Seducer agent," Logan said roughly. "Just like me."

In one swift move that spoke of military training, Devlin had him pinned against the wall, a knife across his throat.

"Bioware or not, I'll cut you from stem to stern if you talk about my agents like that," Dev told him through gritted teeth. "We respect the agents—and their jobs—here. Not all the work is pretty or fun or easy. What Sela and Marlena took on for the safety and security of the world—for the safety and security of you and your firm—you should be thanking your lucky stars they're as trained and skilled as they are."

Logan didn't struggle. In fact, he felt like a total fucking ass for... well, acting like one to Sela.

"It happens." Dev released him. "We've all got our pride, want to do the protecting. No one likes to be deceived, even if it's for our own good."

Logan didn't respond to that, stuffed his hands into the pockets of his camo pants and said instead, "I'm going to need to call GWC—the scientists, they have to send me injections."

"They can send us the formulation—we'll re-create it here."

"Fair enough."

"You'll need to submit to an examination as well. It's SOP whenever we bring new people with special abilities into the compound."

There was no leeway in Devlin's words. "I'd like to go to Sela first, if that's permitted."

"You hurt her, half the agents here will want to kill you."

"What about the other half?"

"Take *want* out of the sentence and you'll have your answer."

* * *

By the time the plane landed, Annika was ready to sleep for a month. She'd never been so tired in her entire life. Creed had been waiting on the tarmac—being held back by Ender, because it was pretty clear Creed wanted a piece of Gabe, but the moment she'd stepped onto solid ground, he'd kissed her, swept her into the Jeep and sped straight to medical, even though she tried to explain that her head was fine.

"You're not fine," he growled, as he carried—yes, *carried*—her through the infirmary halls. She didn't have the strength or will to fight him, though she did grouse a little. "It's just a bump on the head, Creed."

"It's more than that, and you know it," he said, and for a split second, she wondered if he knew she was pregnant. "I heard what happened to Akbar."

She clung to him, relieved, because the last thing she wanted to do right now was fight with Creed about a kid. She'd been able to forget their problems for a couple of days, what with her concentration being on not getting killed, but now their issues were all flooding back, and she wasn't ready to talk.

Not that talking about Akbar was any better.

"It was awful." She shuddered as a nurse whisked them into a prepared room. So many ACRO agents had died over the years, and she'd witnessed much of it. But after a brief moment of grief, she wrote off their deaths as a risk they all took. But Akbar... God. She didn't know why losing him made her want to cry, whether it was the horrific way in which it had happened, or whether it was her stupid hormones.

Or maybe it was just the fact that she was a very different person than she'd been before she committed to Creed. He'd awakened a lot of things in her, and unfortunately, some of what he'd awakened were sappy emotions she'd buried long ago.

Creed set her on a bed, and immediately, medical staff swarmed. She swatted at them, not in the mood to be poked and prodded by dozens of people. "Get away from me!"

"Annika," Creed said gently, with a squeeze of her hand, "let them check you out."

"Fine," she grumbled, "but I only want Dr. Davies." Hopefully, since Davies was new, Creed didn't know that she was a gynecologist. Annika planned to tell Creed she was pregnant, but only after the doctor confirmed that everything was okay.

Davies ordered Creed out, and he kissed Annika on the forehead before he left. "I'll be right outside the door. When I come back in, I want to know everything that happened in the jungle." His palm gently cupped her cheek. "God, Annika, I was so scared. Don't ever do that again."

"I promise I will never again get knocked unconscious and flown to the Amazon, where my plane gets shot down and I have to bail at four hundred feet before taking out a camp full of Itor agents and chupacabras," she said solemnly, and he just shook his head and left.

Dr. Davies made Annika change into a hospital johnny, and then she performed a brief general exam before concentrating on the cut on Annika's head. "What happened here?" she asked as she cleaned the wound.

Annika looked down at her lap. "My ability failed." It was so humiliating. She'd now lost pretty much everything. Her job, control over her emotions, the ability that had been a part of her since birth. She'd rather lose an arm.

"It's possible that it'll return as soon as you are no longer pregnant. But I'll be honest with you, the likelihood of it returning as strong, or at all, decreases with every passing day."

Tears welled in Annika's eyes, and she kept her gaze in her lap. This pregnancy was costing her so much, and very likely, she could lose Creed too. He'd said he didn't want a kid with her. Didn't want to risk it.

And Annika . . . she'd screw that kid up in so many ways. She didn't know how to play or nurture—she'd killed her *goldfish*.

The doctor smoothed a bandage on Annika's head. "Feet in

stirrups. I want to do a pelvic exam—just a precaution. Have you decided what you want to do?"

Gut twisting, Annika put her feet in the metal cups at the end of the bed. "As in, do I want to have this baby or not?"

"Yes. If you want to terminate, it has to be done soon."

Oh, God. Annika hadn't even gotten that far in her thoughts about the pregnancy. Though it made sense that Davies would ask—Annika had been furious and distraught at learning she was pregnant and might lose her powers . . . which she had.

Annika stared up at the ceiling while Davies put her fingers in places only Creed had been, and when she was done, she snapped off her gloves and took Annika's hand.

"It's a simple procedure. TAG medical staff recently shared their method of psychic purging, which rids an agent of all foreign bodies. You'll spend about sixty seconds with Dr. Graves, and your period will start right away. It's very quick and easy."

Easy. Should it be *easy*? Something inside her screamed at what the doctor was saying. Which was weird, because she'd always been ruthless, heartless, cold. Bad shit happened in the world, and that was that. No use in whining about it or letting it get to you.

But somehow this was different.

Hormones. Had to be hormones. Because normally Annika's heart was a frozen stone that had thawed just enough to let in Creed and Dev. Could she let in a baby too? Could she live without her powers? After all, the lack of her electrical ability was what had landed her here. How could she be effective as an ACRO agent without it? Sure, her combat skills couldn't be topped, but when you were going up against people with superpowers, fighting skills sometimes didn't amount to jack shit. She'd never go on a mission again. She'd be putting herself and others at risk.

But then, having special powers didn't make you invincible either. They hadn't saved Akbar. A sob built in her throat at how he'd given his life for her. In an instant, he was gone. Just like any of them could be. Even Creed.

The thought of Creed being killed struck her like a punch to the gut. She couldn't lose him, but she also couldn't lose any part of him, including the life he'd planted in her belly.

"No," she rasped. "I can't do it." She couldn't even *think* about doing it.

Dr. Davies smiled kindly. "We'll make sure you and your baby get the best of care."

What was she getting herself and some poor kid into? Tears streamed down her face as the door opened and the doctor let herself out. Creed, followed by Dev, entered, both rushing to her like she was bleeding instead of crying.

"What is it?" Creed grabbed one hand, and Dev took the other.

"I'm just tired." She sniffed, and Dev handed her a tissue. "It's been a long couple of days."

"What happened, Annika?" Dev asked, and she knew he was talking about the fiasco that had gotten her on the plane in the first place.

"Gabe was being an idiot. He was hiding in the cargo section. I guess he figured he was ready for a mission."

Dev's brown eyes turned muddy with anger, and his voice went very, very flat and cold. "And?"

"And I tried to stop him. We got into a scuffle, and I hit my head and was knocked out."

Creed made a low, dangerous sound that would have had her shivering with appreciation in any other circumstance. He was such an easygoing guy that he rarely got worked up, but when he did, it was something to behold. "I'm going to kill him, Devlin."

"No," Dev snapped. "You won't. Because I am."

Annika rubbed her temples. "He didn't mean to hurt me. It was an accident—"

"It was an accident that happened because he was being impulsive and irresponsible," Dev said. "Because of him, you ended up in a situation you shouldn't have been in."

"True." She sighed. "But don't be too hard on him. He probably feels guilty about Akbar, and what he saw . . . Dev, he's been punished. Besides, he stopped me from doing something really stupid that could have gotten me badly hurt." God, she was going soft.

Dev cursed. "Yeah. Okay. I'll think about it."

"And I want that bitch who murdered Akbar," she said softly. "I want to spend days making her fry." And if her powers never returned . . . well, in lieu of Chutes and Ladders, her CIA parents had taught her all kinds of Fun with Car Batteries.

Yep, she'd be a *great* mom.

"We'll get her, Annika. I swear." Dev checked his watch. "I gotta go see Stryker and Marlena. You sure you're okay?"

"Yeah. Go."

Dev left, but Creed was still pacing the room, worry etched on his face. Shadows framed his nearly black eyes, and the tattoo on the right side of his face stood out starkly against his pale skin. Fierce, possessive need clawed at her. Her arms were way too empty.

In a tangle of sheets and hospital gown, she struggled to her knees on the bed and threw her arms around him. "I'm sorry I worried you."

Creed caught her in a huge bear hug. "No, I'm sorry, Annika. I'm so sorry. I should have told you sooner . . ."

She frowned. "Told me what sooner?"

The long pause that followed froze her breath in her lungs. Finally, just as they began to burn with the held breath, he blurted out, "I know you're pregnant. And if you'd known that I knew, maybe you wouldn't have taken chances with yourself by trying to stop Gabe or in the jungle."

Holy shit. "You knew? How?" she asked against his chest, ignoring the poke of his ACRO badge in her cheek.

"Kat."

Of course. She should have known that meddling ghost would figure it out and spill everything to Creed. Fuck. How long had he known? she wondered . . . and suspicion stirred.

"You told Dev, didn't you?" She pushed away from Creed, saw the truth in his eyes. "That's why he took me off all my duties. It wasn't because I mouthed off."

"Well, you did piss him off—"

"Creed . . ." Her warning tone made him sigh.

"Yes, that's why." He sank down next to her on the bed. "I'm sorry. I didn't know what else to do. I didn't want to tell you I knew because I thought you needed to be the one to come to me."

"You would have been pissed if I told Dev and not you," she shot back.

"Yeah. I know." He squeezed her hand. "I'm sorry. I freaked. I didn't want to pressure you, and I didn't know who else to go to. Guess I know why you always went to him before."

"Creed, I—"

He cut her off with a shake of his head. "Why didn't you tell me?" He didn't sound mad, just . . . sad.

"Because . . ." She looked down at her bare feet, now dangling off the edge of the bed. "I didn't know how you'd react. I tried to talk to you about it." Her eyes began to sting again as she thought back to their argument. "But you didn't want to. You said you didn't want kids with me."

He lifted her chin with a finger and turned her face to meet his. "I'm so sorry for that, Annika. I didn't mean it. Not like you think. It didn't have anything to do with your ability to raise a kid."

"I thought . . . I thought I would lose you if you knew I was pregnant."

"Oh, Jesus." He folded her into his arms and held her so tight she had to struggle to breathe.

"Creed," she gasped and he loosened his grip. "Creed, what's wrong?"

"You wouldn't have lost me," he whispered into her hair.

"Good, because I told Davies I wouldn't terminate the pregnancy."

Creed's expression was a strange mix of joy and panic, and she swallowed against the dryness in her throat. "We'll deal with this, Annika. We will."

"I know. I freaked out for a couple of days. I'm still freaked. What if I'm a sucky mom—" She broke off, because the word *mom* just wasn't in her vocabulary, and even though she'd made the decision to keep the baby, she still didn't think she could handle it.

She was such a selfish piece of shit.

Creed took a deep breath, but his voice cracked when he spoke. "You won't be a sucky mom."

"Creed? What's wrong?"

"I'm happy, baby. I am. But . . . Damn, I'm scared."

"Me too."

He shook his head. "Not of being a parent. I can do that. I want to do that."

"Then what's the problem?" She couldn't believe she was the one trying to convince him that everything was going to be okay.

"Oz."

She blinked. "Oz? Oz is the problem? He's dead!" She growled low in her chest. That bastard had been the bane of her existence for years, and even in death he couldn't leave her the fuck alone.

Several seconds ticked by before he finally spoke. "I didn't want to tell you this. It's why I talked to Dev first . . ."

"Spill, Creed."

Creed raked his hands through his hair. "It's about one of his visions. He had it right after I told him we were together. Fuck." He gripped fistfuls of his hair as though he was trying to keep his head on.

Gently, she peeled his hands away. "Tell me."

"He said if you got pregnant, one of us could die."

"Seriously?" Annika laughed. Like, a deep down belly laugh. "Creed, come on. You believed that bullshit?"

His cheeks colored, turning his face markings dusky maroon. "He's never wrong."

"He's wrong all the time! He's always misinterpreting shit. Remember that time he freaked out because he'd seen Dev bleeding and stumbling around crunched cars on a highway? He was sure Dev had been in an accident. Turned out Dev had come upon the accident and got himself all bloody trying to help people. He was perfectly fine."

"But what if Oz is right this time?" Creed asked.

She rolled her eyes. "He's not. Need another example? The dickhead kissed me once. Didn't mean anything—he hated me and I hated him, and we'd been fighting about Dev." Annika had gone to a local bar to drag out an agent who was causing trouble, and she found Oz in the middle of it. He and Dev were broken up, and Oz was blowing through town with no intention of visiting Dev. Which was fine by Annika. But he'd started mouthing off, and she'd done the same, and the next thing she knew he had her backed up against the wall with his mouth on hers. "He was trying to teach me a lesson or hurt me or something—he said it would be the only real kiss I'd ever get. And look how wrong he was."

"He was being an ass," Creed growled. "That wasn't a vision."

"I don't care. My point is, he's an ass who isn't always right. He could have told you those things about pregnancy and dying because he hated me."

"He wouldn't have lied to me."

"Why? Because he's your brother?" She shook her head. "Come on, Creed. That's the best reason to lie to you. To protect you. He lied to you for years when he failed to mention you were brothers."

For a long time he was silent, and then he smiled. She knew he wasn't convinced, but she recognized his attempt to agree to disagree and get past the discussion. Good, because he was a little blind when it came to Oz.

"You could be right," he said, in that I-don't-believe-a-word-I'm-saying tone.

"I am right. And I'm certainly not going to let some hokey Oz prediction change my mind about anything." She raised her chin stubbornly. "I got screwy for a while, but once I make up my mind, it's done."

"Don't I know that," he muttered, and then he cupped her cheek and frowned at the bandage on her head. "You left something out about how you got that. I know Gabe couldn't have managed to make you bleed."

Humiliation crawled over her skin. "My power failed. The surprise of it caught me off guard, and I lost my balance—"

"Your power is *gone*?"

"Yes." So embarrassing. "The doctor said that's normal for pregnancies in people like us. But I don't need it to kick Gabe's ass," she added quickly. "If I hadn't been so surprised, I could've taken him."

"I know you could."

That was one of the reasons she loved him so much. He was always willing to humor her. She sighed. "So what now?"

He grinned, but she could still see a spark of worry in his eyes as he said, "I guess we're having a baby."

AFTER THE DOCTOR FELT COMFORTABLE RELEASING ANI FROM the hospital, Creed took her home in her Jeep. He'd waited around the hospital room all day, watching her sleep, talking to the doctors about various tests she needed to have because of the baby. Dev stopped by frequently during those hours as well.

By the time Creed hit the driveway, he didn't want to think

about anything, didn't want to talk . . . well, dirty talk would be fine.

And so he went around to Ani's side and lifted her out and carried her into the house.

"I can walk, you know," she complained.

"Yeah, I know, but I need to get you to bed as soon as possible."

"I'm not on bed rest."

"Fuck resting, I want you naked in bed with me," he growled as he raced up the stairs to the loft, where the bed was. Ani had moved in with him a few months ago and ever since then they'd been talking about getting a bigger place. But there was something about the house—the loft bed—that neither of them was ready to give up.

But now . . .

He dumped her unceremoniously on the feather bed and landed on top of her. No kid gloves for Ani—she would hate that, especially from him. Although really, he'd braced himself on his arms so the only thing touching her was his cock, solid as steel through his BDUs.

He needed to taste her—before anything else. It was his favorite way to drive her up-the-wall insane.

Okay, one of many of his favorite ways. And so he slid down her body quickly, preparing to make quick work of her pants.

"Creed, wait."

Yeah, not the words he wanted to hear. And not words he ever heard from Ani at times like this—she'd never choose talk over sex. He lifted his head. "What is it, baby?"

"Suppose . . ." She swallowed hard. "I've lost my powers because of the pregnancy. And suppose . . ."

"You're thinking it's only your powers that make us good together in bed?"

If she didn't look so serious and sad, he probably would've been angry at her for doubting that—for doubting them.

"What's between us has nothing to do with special abilities, Ani. Trust me. And besides, your powers might be gone, but don't doubt the power of the hormones they've been replaced with."

"How do you know so much about pregnancy?" She narrowed her eyes at him.

Instead of answering, he slid her pants off. Her thong came next, and his tongue, with its piercing, found her core with a vengeance.

She came as soon as he thrust it inside of her, cursing, clutching at him, her fingers only catching the fabric of his shirt as he held her hips firmly in his grasp. He continued his assault of pure pleasure, not letting up, his tongue flicking her now-engorged clit, until Annika was seriously calling out his name in vain.

But in a good way.

"Creed . . . don't stop . . . fuck me again . . . with . . . your tongue."

He had no intention of stopping, ever. Because stopping sex meant he would have to think again, about the pregnancy, Oz's prediction . . . death.

For right now, pleasure would override everything. He actually found himself humping the bed as Ani came again, the friction on his cock, from his pants and the mattress, was delicious, and he had to get inside of her, like now.

As if she knew, she was pulling and pushing at him, and this time he let her, flipped to his back as she frantically tore at his clothes.

Her breasts were bigger—slightly swollen, nipples darker. Gorgeous.

Don't think. Just fuck.

Her belly was still flat—no signs of baby there yet.

But it was in there. His son or daughter.

Stop thinking.

And then Ani's soft, hot mouth circled his cock and he nearly shot to the ceiling, and yeah, thinking was definitely impossible.

* * *

"WE'VE GOT A REAL FUCKING PROBLEM WITH A NEW BREED OF Itor agent."

Those were Stryker's first words, not *I'm sorry about Akbar,* or even *Mind if I come in?*

Of course, Devlin could more than understand—he watched Stryker carefully, looking for the signs of the breakdown he knew would happen eventually. A good friend and mentor getting killed in one of the most horrific ways possible right in front of you was not something agents dealt with on a daily basis, even though the threat was always there.

Stryker stood, fists clenched, not ready to talk about anything else beyond revenge, and so Dev rubbed his forehead and motioned for Stryker to continue.

"I think she's a split personality. Name's Phoebe."

"I've never seen a report of anyone like that—under Itor or any free agent."

"I saw it with my own damned eyes. One half tried to roast me and the other wanted to freeze me to death. Logan's sister reports the same thing: kidnapped, worked over by a sadistic bitch, left tied in the jungle with no food or water for hours; then the same exact woman came back, had no clue who Caroline was or why she was there, apologized and let her go." Stryker played with the bandage on his hand. He'd already been to the healer—and Dev could almost guarantee that by tomorrow the severe burn on his palm and the cuts on his chest would be a mere memory.

But the split-personalitied agent . . . Stryker wouldn't be able to shake her. Didn't want to, from where Dev stood. And that's where the problem lay. "I'll send Ender after her."

Stryker nearly hit the ceiling. "No!" Obviously fighting to hold back his emotion, he spoke next through clenched teeth. "This. One's. Mine."

"We're going to need to find her first."

"Last known locale: running through the Amazon jungle. Send me back in now. I'll find her."

Dev took two steps, bringing him face-to-face with Stryker. "Last time I looked, you do not give me orders. This isn't the field. This is my goddamned office. I know you're pissed, but you need a little time to cool down and get your shit together. I don't want you getting killed too. Understood?"

Stryker nodded, but he didn't look happy.

Dev thought for a second. "Go see Ryan Malmstrom in Comms. He spent time inside Itor and he's remembering more and more about it every day. Maybe you can jog his memory and get his help finding this agent." He leaned across his desk and typed something quickly on his computer. "Go now," he told Stryker. "They're expecting you."

Stryker closed the door behind him, and ten seconds later Christine buzzed in.

"Mr. O'Malley, Marlena West is here for her debriefing."

He didn't wait for her to finish before he was striding across the room and opening the door.

Marlena sat, legs crossed, wearing the same black BDUs from the jungle, as evidenced by the rips and dust. She looked gorgeous—and tired. And conflicted. And fuck, he'd missed her.

Christine waited nervously at her desk, hands folded, looking between them as Marlena stood and walked past Dev into his office.

"You've been a real bear to her, you know," she told him after he'd shut the door behind him.

Dev grinned. "I've never liked bears—you know that."

She rolled her eyes and shook her head slightly as they fell into the routine, comfortable and familiar.

He fought the urge to tell her that she never should've taken the Seducer job, that she could come back to her old job, that he needed her to. He didn't say any of that, simply motioned for her to sit down on the leather couch, rather than one of the stiff chairs across from his desk. "Tell me what's going on."

She proceeded to explain about Chance, the SEAL turned chupacabra. She told him everything, as was required, and he didn't see anything out of the ordinary for her job as a Seducer. Of course, sleeping with a half man, half beast went above and beyond, but . . .

"Chupacabras mate for life," she blurted out. Dev nodded slowly and wondered if everyone had gone a little crazy in the jungle. "Chupacabras mate for life, Chance is now part chupacabra, and he's mated. With me."

Oh, shit. Not good. "We'll fix it."

She shook her head, covered her mouth with a palm for a second. This was not the Marlena he knew. Sure, he'd seen her emotional at times—he was probably the only one she let her guard down around—but something was really different about this.

"I slept with him, Devlin," she said. "Chance likes me and we've slept together multiple times. And I like him, but not in that crazy, cursed way, and he needs the cure and then this chance—no pun intended—will be gone, but—"

He all but put a hand over her mouth to stop her babbling; she was in a state of near panic. "I'm guessing Chance doesn't know about the curse."

"No. And he won't. You save him, Devlin, if it's the last thing you do—save him and change him back into a man. A fully human man."

"But then—"

"I owe him that. Want the best for him. And I don't want a man who only wants me because he's got this crazy urge to mate for life."

"Most animals—most humans—don't mate for life randomly, Marlena. They choose based on attraction."

"Maybe."

Dev narrowed his eyes. "You're scared."

"For Chance."

"For yourself." He paused. "I'm not saying I'd like to keep the man the way he is—it's safer for all involved if he's cured."

"Exactly. He needs the cure. There's no way anything could work between Chance and me anyway. He knows what my job is. He knows I'm a Seducer. I told him. So he thinks I fucked him to get him to ACRO. And you know what? That's what happened, to a certain extent."

"You need to tell him everything about the curse."

She shook her head stubbornly. "It's better this way."

"And what happens if we can't cure him?"

Marlena stared at him. "You can do it, Dev. ACRO can do anything."

"We couldn't do anything for you. That magic happened all on its own. Sometimes things are meant to be."

She snorted. "You've got Oz helping you with your magic, Devlin. I don't have anyone. And maybe it's better that way."

She walked off and he let her go—for the time being. He'd have to assess Chance on his own, after Sela and the other scientists gave him a full workup and tested his triggers. He hadn't lied to Marlena—he'd been told by Sela herself on the phone from the plane that a cure was so far unheard of; even Logan's company, which had been studying the chupacabra for months before it escaped, had no success in figuring out its complicated DNA structure.

WHEN CHANCE WOKE, HE WAS ALONE, TERRIBLY ALONE, IN A hospital bed in the ACRO clinic.

He'd made it easy for Marlena on the helo, and again on the jet, by pretending to be asleep, which hadn't been difficult. Sela had explained that it would be best to run an IV of tranquilizers for the flight. Just in case.

They'd barely worked, but they took enough of the edge off

for him not to give a shit where he was going or what would happen to him.

"She used me," he'd heard himself murmur during the long flight, shifted to find Sela staring at him.

"Chance, you don't understand," she'd insisted.

"She told me everything. I know everything." Marlena had slept with him because she had to. Anything she said outside that was a well-done lie. A testament to ACRO's training.

But a big part of him refused to believe that. He told himself it was the chupacabra mating crap talking. That it made him vulnerable and jealous. That Marlena hadn't lied to him.

But it all hurt too much to deal with right now.

Sela had stared at him with a silent pain in her eyes and Chance wondered what she'd done in the name of ACRO, whether Logan felt as betrayed as he did.

Because Chance didn't know much, but he knew that when a man looked at a woman the way Logan did Sela . . . well, that man was pretty well destroyed.

Now he glanced around the small, clean room, complete with monitors and cameras—so he could see the team of people in the hallway . . . and so they could see him, he presumed.

He'd been impressed by the facility when they'd arrived. There hadn't been much time for a tour, though, because of course he'd been whisked away with Sela for an extensive examination, which had thankfully been nothing like the one he'd received from the docs at the GWC camp.

He'd gotten the distinct impression that he was being treated with the same cautious respect he'd always had for grenades.

Both the doctors and the scientists told him there was no known cure for what ailed him. Half man, half chupa was obviously a new chapter for the medical books labeled "Crazy."

"Just do what you can," he'd said wearily, and he'd been assured by the head of ACRO, Devlin O'Malley, that they would do just that.

"Have you thought about what you'll do after this?" O'Malley had asked him early yesterday morning during his debriefing.

"I haven't thought ahead more than two hours since all of this happened, sir," he'd admitted. "I'm assuming I'm being reported as MIA, or suspected KIA."

O'Malley had nodded. "They discovered what was left of the remains of your team. I'm sorry."

"Yeah, me too. Look, if you can cure me and get me the hell out of here, that would be great."

Dev had stared at him for a long moment, as if he wanted to say something. But he didn't, simply stuck out his hand, which Chance shook, and then left.

And Chance lay alone, in a hospital room with the tranquilizers still coursing through his bloodstream, and he thought about Marlena and cursed the fact that the meds took away his resolve to hate her for what she'd done to him.

She did her job, asshole—you're the fool who fell for it. And her. And her amazingly hot body, her beautiful face, and if he stroked himself, he could almost pretend it was her doing it, could picture her mouth opening to take his cock deep inside, to drive him crazy with her tongue, her teeth...

"It's time." One of the doctors had walked in without knocking, and yeah, what a way to blow a fantasy.

Chance nodded, watched as the doctor produced a syringe and plunged the contents into his IV line. It was the first of several injections that he would need, and then they would lighten up on the drugs and try to get him to turn into a chupacabra. The drug stung his arm as it entered his bloodstream.

"We'll cage you first, of course," the doctor said casually. "You'll be safe, and so will we."

"Sounds like a blast."

"We'll try to replicate what's made you change in the past," the doctor continued. "From the debriefing, we've learned that you're quite protective of—"

Chance heard the growl, and for a moment didn't realize it had come from him.

"Whoa—easy . . . we don't have to re-create the scene exactly." The doctor kept his voice calm, but his hands shook.

Chance squeezed his eyes shut and concentrated on not changing. Of course, what stopped him from changing was thinking about Marlena—she appeared to be the key to everything in his life right now. "I think it's better that we don't."

The door opened, revealing Marlena, dressed in a curve-hugging blue blouse and black skirt, on the other side. A nurse pushed past her. "I'm sorry—she insisted."

"It's okay. I want to see her. Need to," Chance said. Because his body had heated the second he'd seen her.

"Five minutes," the doctor agreed. "We can't put this off much longer. And you know better," he told Marlena as he walked out of the room and she walked in. She remained near the door, and he wondered if she felt like she might need to make a quick escape.

"I had to see you. To explain." She stared, and, man, she looked gorgeous. And sad. And a little turned on, but that had to be bullshit, because he'd been a job. She'd told him as much.

And then she tried to save your life in the jungle. "Look, I get that you work for the good guys. I know that you're what they call a Seducer. You're trained to give it away in exchange for intel. I hope you got everything you were looking for."

"I did," she said quietly. "And with you, I got something I thought I'd never have."

He shook his head slowly, lighting up inside with an angry fire. "You're going to have to do better than that."

YOU'RE GOING TO HAVE TO DO BETTER THAN THAT.

Those were her stepsister Kelly's snarling words to her after Kelly found her boyfriend flirting with Marlena, and after Marlena had made a token, mocking apology.

Because Marlena had been flirting right back. With a vengeance.

Seventeen years of dealing with Kelly's growing bitterness and constant abuse had finally brought Marlena to the edge, so when Michael had come with Kelly to Thanksgiving dinner, Marlena had, for the first time, decided to get back at her stepsister, if only in a small way.

Except Kelly hadn't seen it as small.

For years Kelly had told Marlena that she'd cursed her as an infant. Cursed her to not grow, to be ugly, to be stupid. It was all bullshit—Kelly had believed herself to be a witch, or maybe she just told Marlena that. Didn't matter; none of it had come true.

But then . . .

Marlena blew out a long, bracing breath before looking Chance in the eyes. "I'm cursed," she blurted.

Chance cocked an eyebrow. "Cursed." His tone dripped with skepticism, and her resolve dimmed. "As in . . ."

"As in, a curse was put on me and it doomed me to a loveless existence. Well, I fall in love, but no one can fall for me." Her voice was a low murmur, because this all sounded so lame when she said it out loud. "Remember I told you I had a stepsister?"

Chance nodded. "She died in a car accident? With your dad and stepmom."

"Yes," she said. "I think their deaths were . . . punishment."

Silence stretched, broken only by the incessant drip of the IV machine's contents. Chance must think she was crazy. Finally, he cleared his throat. "I'm not following."

Marlena moved a little closer to the bed, close enough that she could have taken Chance's hand if she wasn't so afraid he'd push her away. "Kelly hated me," she began. "From the day I was brought into the family as a baby. She was awful, always saying I shouldn't have been born, and that if it weren't for me, my dad would love her and her mom more."

Sadly, Kelly was probably right. Once, when Marlena was six,

Kelly pushed her down a flight of stairs and then claimed it was an accident. Marlena knew the truth, told her father, and he'd believed her. That had caused a huge rift between him and her stepmom, which nearly ended in divorce. After that, Marlena had kept Kelly's torments to herself.

Chance's eyes gave nothing away, but he was still there, listening, which she took as a good sign.

Heart in her throat, she continued. "One Thanksgiving I'd reached my limit. Kelly had moved out years before, but she came back for holidays and she brought her boyfriend. I flirted with him just to piss her off. She went crazy. She swore she'd make sure I was miserable for the rest of my life. I wasn't a scared kid anymore, and I laughed at her." Her voice became unsteady, because this was where things got a little hard to believe. "A couple of days later, I lost my virginity to the boy I'd been dating. The moment it was over, I was madly, deeply in love with him. I mean, before that I'd liked him in that high school crush way, but I wasn't *in* love, you know?"

Chance snorted. "Not really. Thanks to my mom, I was pretty adept at avoiding relationships."

"Yes, well, I'm sure you must've broken a few hearts in your day." *Maybe you'll break mine too.*

He didn't answer, simply waited for her to continue. She did, quickly, before she lost her nerve or threw up or something.

"Anyway, after sex, the crush was replaced with this insane kind of love. Obsession, really. But he suddenly loathed me. The second he pulled away from me, Jared was a different person. Hateful. Disgusted." He'd called her names and kicked her out of the backseat of his Mustang and made her walk the two miles home.

Chance's lips tightened into a hard, grim line. "He was an asshole."

"That's putting it mildly. But I still loved him. Humiliated myself over and over trying to get him back. A couple of weeks later, in a stupid attempt to make him jealous, I slept with his best friend. Before I could even pull my pants up, I fell in love with his friend with the same intensity I'd felt for Jared." It had been so strange, confusing. Her feelings for Jared were gone, but she instantly wanted Brad even though she'd despised him before the sex. "And just like it had been with Jared, Brad hated me. That's when I got suspicious. I went to Kelly, and she gloated about this love spell she'd cast on me. Said I'd finally gotten what I deserved. The next day, the day before my eighteenth birthday, the car accident killed her, my stepmom and my dad. Someone here at ACRO told me her dark deed had come back on her with a vengeance, and my dad and stepmom got caught in the cross fire."

"Jesus H. Christ," Chance whispered. "And since then?"

She shrugged. "Since then, it's been the same story. I never feel anything for any man unless I sleep with him. Then what I feel is this horrible, consuming love that at once seems so real and yet artificial." She squeezed her eyes shut, felt her emotions shift inside her as though urging her to finish her confession. When she opened her eyes again, Chance's expression was warm, caring, and her heart skipped a beat. "All of that has changed. Now there's you." She managed a small smile. "So that's the story. Pretty unbelievable, right?"

Before turning into a chupacabra, Chance never would've believed that shit like this really existed. "So I broke the curse?" He sounded humiliatingly hopeful, and when Marlena's smile turned sad, his gut sank.

"Not exactly. I mean, I *am* in love with you," she added quickly. "And it's real. I know it is, because I didn't fall for you after we had sex. I don't have any of the insane, obsessive feelings. I know it sounds sappy, but what I feel for you is pure, not tainted."

As relieved as Chance was, he sensed she was holding something back. "But?"

She shifted her weight. Stalled. Finally blurted, "But I don't think the curse is broken. I think you got around it. A loophole my sister never thought of when she said I'd feel only obsessive love for a man, and that no man would ever love me."

Chance went cold. "Fuck me. The curse doesn't apply to me because I'm not a *man* anymore."

"That's my guess," she whispered.

Realization ripped through him, tore right through his heart. *God . . . no.* "If I'm cured . . ."

Her throat worked on a hard swallow. "You'd be human again. All man. And happy. And you can go back to your job and your life."

He narrowed his eyes at her. "That's why you asked me that question, about remaining part beast."

"Stupid, I know." She sighed. "I mean, of course you'd jump at the opportunity to be cured. I know I would. I'd kill for a cure."

"But with me, you don't need one anymore."

"Oh, Chance," she breathed, taking a step back. "I admit it, I fell for you. I know you don't believe that and think it was all for the mission. And it started that way. But you might only care about me because of the mating thing. And I know what it's like to be locked into something you can't control, something you don't want. I could never let you live with the infection, not if there's a possibility you can be helped."

Before she could take another step closer to the door, Chance shoved the covers off him and stood in front of her. Looking ridiculous in a hospital gown. Not that he cared. The pull was most definitely still there between them. He could easily take her here, on the bed, but he knew that there was more to it than just sex.

They'd connected. She'd saved his life. Maybe he'd saved hers as well. "Suppose we give this a shot. Suppose you think you could be with me because I'm the first guy who could love you.

Because here's the thing. I don't give a shit how we got to this point or how I came to care for you. I do, and that's all that matters."

He yanked the IV catheter out of his arm.

Marlena's gorgeous eyes shot wide, and she rushed to him, slapped her hand over the bleeding wound. "What are you doing?"

Cupping her cheek, he said softly, "Staying the way I am."

"You can't. Devlin won't let you."

"We'll deal with that." He drew Marlena to him and she fit so well in his arms—and, yes, they'd deal with it somehow. They had to.

DEV WASN'T READY TO DEAL WITH IT.

Correction, he was over the moon that Marlena wanted to come work for him again—on one condition: She would train Christine so the two women could back each other up.

But Chance remaining a chupacabra? Not so onboard. "You have to try for the cure," Dev said.

Marlena and Chance stood in the middle of Devlin's office, with Chance wearing only scrub bottoms, with a determined look in his eye that Dev knew all too well. "I don't want it."

Dev shook his head. "I can't have you running around here, potentially getting angry and infecting my agents."

Chance jutted out his chin. "I can control myself, sir. I've been doing it since the day I joined the military."

"But the animal side of you might not be able to control itself—it's dangerous."

"Just because the other chupacabra infected Chance doesn't necessarily mean Chance can infect others," Marlena broke in. "We can test that."

"So if he can't infect people, he can just kill them," Dev said dryly.

"Most of your agents could've done the same thing when you first brought them in—still can, I'd guess," Chance said evenly.

Dev turned to Marlena. "What other argument do you have?"

"Rik and Kira can work with him. And the scientists. They just can't cure him."

"What happens if the infection progresses?" he asked quietly of both of them, his eyes on Chance. "What if, one day, you change and there's no changing back?"

"We're not there yet." Chance took Marlena's hand and gave her a tender smile. "We're both willing to see this through, to see where it leads us."

Marlena's eyes shone, and she was so strangely content. Happy. How the hell could Dev take that away from her?

For her own good, and the good of ACRO.

He sighed and ran his hands through his hair. "Chance, give Marlena and me a minute."

Chance complied. A good sign.

"Something big is going down, Marlena. Huge. I feel it in my bones, and it gets stronger every day," Dev told her once they were alone.

"Itor."

He nodded. "I'm going to need everyone up and running at one hundred percent."

"There are plenty of agents who are in relationships and do their jobs. And we've had far more dangerous people than Chance here. And you always tell them, *Your gift is special and it's been given to you for a reason—ACRO can help you find a reason.* Is that bullshit?"

He felt the anger rise inside of him at the way she called him out. "It's not the same—this isn't a gift."

"It is to me."

What the hell was he supposed to say to that? With a drawn-out sigh, he nodded. "We'll find a way, Marlena. We always do."

CHAPTER *Twenty-five*

The dream thing Sela hoped for didn't pan out. She had downed a few small bottles of vodka on the plane and fallen asleep, but when she'd awakened, nothing had changed, except she'd had a headache the size of New York. This was definitely *not* a dream.

After the jet landed, Gabe had been taken away by Ender, who had been the only reason Creed hadn't ripped Gabe apart right there on the tarmac. It had been clear that he'd wanted to for some reason, until he saw Annika—and then the murderous light had left his eyes and he'd whisked her away, probably straight to medical.

Sela had waited with Marlena while Chance and the dead chupa were unloaded. Immediately afterward, Caroline and Logan had been escorted off the plane.

He hadn't even looked at her.

Sela had gone immediately to the infirmary—the first required stop after a mission of this nature. After that, she'd gone to Psychic headquarters to have her Triad disbanded, followed by a visit to the mission supervisor. She and Marlena would also be meeting with their department heads later, and with Dev if he requested it.

He'd called Sela last night, just to make sure she was okay, and to update her on Logan and his family. She was glad to hear that GWC was going to be working with ACRO now, but she wondered what it meant for her and Logan.

Now, a day after returning from the jungle, she was sitting in her office, futilely trying to catch up on paperwork. After every mission, agents were given a minimum of three days off, but she hadn't been able to sit around in her base apartment, doing nothing but thinking about Logan, who, according to Christine, had been assigned quarters in billeting with his father. Caroline had been admitted into the infirmary, but that was yesterday. She should be released today, and then... would Logan be leaving with her?

The thought that Sela might never see Logan again made her stomach tighten into a knot. She wrestled with the desire to find him before he left, but what would she say? She had no idea how to make him understand that not everything had been a lie. What she felt for him was so real she could taste it, like salt in tears.

She hadn't been the only one to come away from this assignment emotionally damaged, and she thought about checking on Marlena, but she knew the woman would be deeply engaged in Seducer de-stressing. Seducers often came back from missions an emotional mess, so a program had been developed to help them deal—everything from receiving psychic meditation therapy to massages.

Sela could use a little Seducer treatment herself. Maybe tomorrow—

Someone tapped on her office door, snapping her out of lovely visions of a deep-tissue massage. "Come in."

Ulrika stuck her reddish-blond head through the crack in the door. "There's someone here to see you," she said, in her faint German accent. "Big guy wearing a visitor badge."

Logan. Sela's heart started bouncing around in her chest, all happy, conveniently forgetting that he was the big asshole who had broken it.

Squaring her shoulders, Sela nodded. "Fine. Oh, have you been to see Chance yet?" The shape-shifter was the closest thing ACRO had to a half man, half chupacabra, and the special team assigned to his case had been hoping she could either provide some insight or help Chance adjust.

She nodded. "He was kind of out of it, though. So I didn't get much of an opportunity to talk to him. Which was probably for the best. Cujo was really nervous around him. She could sense the danger."

Cujo was Ulrika's beast that lived inside her, and though she'd gained control over the huge wolflike creature, it was best not to agitate it.

"Are you going to try again?"

"Probably. He'll need help adjusting." She smiled. "I'll get your visitor now. He's really hot, by the way."

"Yeah," Sela muttered. "I noticed."

Ulrika left, and thirty seconds later, Logan walked in, his expression one of cool professionalism, looking like he belonged in black BDUs, but wearing a visitor badge and no doubt being escorted around the base by a security guy or ten. The BDUs suited his powerful, masculine frame, and though she'd seen him just yesterday, it seemed like months, and she drank him in as if he was a stiff drink and she had just fallen off the wagon.

He looked tired, but the dark circles under his eyes didn't diminish how handsome he was, how his big body was coiled with leashed power she knew could break her in more ways than one. Hell, it already had.

"Hello, Logan," she said tightly. "Are you here to watch me

whore for the company?" It was a bitter, spiteful, childish thing to say, and she immediately wished she could take it back. To his credit, Logan didn't respond to her baiting. No, he remained completely unruffled and distant, as though he were here to inspect the office.

"Actually, I was hoping you could tell me more about ACRO."

"Why me? I'm sure you've been assigned someone to answer all your questions."

His cheeks colored as he glanced around the room. "I wanted an excuse to see you. To see where you worked."

For some reason, his words released her anger, as if she'd had it all nicely contained and he'd opened the box holding it. "Ah. You wanted proof that I worked where I said I did, in a building full of weird creatures and research equipment, instead of in a room with only a bed." She shoved to her feet and stalked to a shelf lined with jars containing various odd specimens. "Well, here is a whole rack of creatures—some anomalies by birth, others of unknown origins. Maybe you think they're sex toys." She gestured to another shelf, this one lined with small skeletons and skulls. "Bones, obviously. But the things you could do with them in bed . . ." Her fury built as she yanked a map off the wall, tearing it and not caring, because by now she was worked up and letting loose about ten years of anger. "And this is a map logging all sightings of chupacabras in the last five years. I was thinking of going to all of them and fucking the witnesses—"

Logan moved so fast she didn't see him until he was in her face, his hands on her shoulders and gripping tightly. "Stop it, Sela. I was mad and I said things I shouldn't have. Can we move past it?"

"If that was an apology," she snapped, "then it was the lamest one in history."

"That's because it wasn't," he snapped right back at her.

"So you shouldn't have said it, but you did mean it."

"Yes. No." He swore. "I don't know. That's why I'm here. A

lot of shit happened and you told me a lot of lies. Itor told me a lot of lies. I don't know which way is up, and I want to get straight again. I fell for you, and afterward I found out you were lying. And then I found out you fuck guys for your job. Does it really surprise you that I'd be upset?"

Well, when he put it that way . . .

She hadn't really thought about it from his perspective. He'd lashed out, striking at her in the only way he could, but only because he'd been hurt—and she could only lay the blame for that at her own feet.

Deflated, feeling like the air had gone out of all her tires, she turned away. "You're right. You have every reason to be upset."

"It's just . . . how many guys are out there right now, in love with you after you played with their heads?" His fists clenched and unclenched at his sides. "How many guys do I have to kill?"

Startled by his jealousy, she swung back around to him. "What did you just say?"

"Fuck. Forget I said that." He jammed his fingers through his hair. "How often do you do this? Are there others like me?"

"No," she whispered. "It never got personal with any of them." She sank down on the desktop, scattering papers and nearly knocking over her coffee cup. "It's been years, Logan. The last one was the guy I told you about. The one who nearly killed me. After that, I couldn't do the job anymore. I asked to be assigned here, in the Crypto department. I didn't lie about my history doing this. After my mom died, I went to live with a wonderful foster family who owned a cryptozoological research company. I kind of grew up studying cryptids."

Even now, her foster family believed she worked for a private cryptozoological firm. ACRO had given its Crypto department legitimacy by naming it Creature Search and allowing contact with any citizen or agency. Actually, that was how the staff got much of its information and leads.

"So was that how you found out about ACRO?"

A surge of guilt rose up in her, because she wanted to fib, to say yes, but there had already been too many lies. But what if this one last truth was the straw that broke this fragile camel's back? Her heart began to pound as she braced herself for his reaction.

"No," she said, forcing herself to meet his gaze steadily. "I slept with an ACRO agent. I learned about ACRO when he . . ."

"Came." Logan practically spat the word. "You read him when he climaxed." His brows lifted as a thought dawned on him. "The guy you said you worked with. That's who you were talking about."

She managed a nod. "Yeah."

His fingers caught her chin, forcing her to look at him, when all she wanted to do was study those nasty jars. Or a map. Or maybe the contents of the trash can. His gaze was fierce, flashing with jealousy. "Was it Stryker?"

"Does it really matter?" She knew it didn't. But since he couldn't physically lash out at her past, he needed an outlet, and he wasn't very fond of Stryker to begin with. Gently, she pushed his hand away. "Look, I slept with that agent a long time ago, and it was the last time I had sex because I *wanted* to—until you. You probably don't believe that—"

His mouth came down on hers. She gasped in surprise, and he took advantage, sinking his tongue into her mouth with predatory intent. He gentled almost immediately, using his lips and tongue to caress hers as he tugged her body against him. Desperate for his touch, she clung to him, gripping his broad shoulders as if they were the only thing holding her up.

A groan dredged up from deep in his chest, and he wedged himself tighter between her legs. His hands came up from her waist, one winding behind her back and the other cupping her breast. His thumb flicked over her stiff nipple, making it ache for more intimate contact.

She grew hotter, wetter, as his arousal swelled against her core. Heart pounding and breath coming as a searing blast in her throat, she dropped her hands between them, fumbling for his zipper—

"Sela?" Ulrika's voice accompanied a knock on the door, and Logan leaped back, face flushed, eyes glazed with lust that surely matched hers. "Dev is on line two. He wants to know if you've gotten the chupacabra photographed yet."

How did he even know she was at work? She was supposed to be on three days' leave. She sighed. "Tell him I'll get on it right now."

"Will do."

"Duty calls," Logan said, his voice sounding a little breathless.

"Guess so."

But she didn't remain out of his grasp for long. "Fuck getting back to work," he murmured, pulling her close again. "It's my turn to leave some impressions on your psychic memory."

SELA DIDN'T REALLY PROTEST—NOT ALL THAT HARD ANYWAY, and it was easily stifled with a kiss and a well-placed hand sliding back inside her shirt.

No, she wouldn't be doing anything right now—except him and only him. If Logan couldn't erase her mind of the other men she'd been with, he'd make damned sure he was the only one she saw.

He'd make sure he was the only one who could satisfy her. He'd already started to, judging by the way she moaned his name against his mouth while he worried a nipple with his fingers.

Her hands had long stopped pushing him away and were now yanking at him, pulling him closer. He obliged, ripping her shirt completely open without finesse, the tiny buttons popping and scattering along the floor, his mouth capturing a tight pink nipple.

And even as her hands worked to pull his shirt out of his pants and run her palms over his bare skin, he wondered if she wanted to know what he was thinking. As if she couldn't tell; but still, he knew what a relief it was for her to know she couldn't read his current thoughts unless he let her in. It was equally satisfactory to him that he *could* let her in if he chose to.

All that noise in her head—he couldn't imagine what it was like. But he did know what it was like to be different, to worry that everyone would find out your deep, dark secrets.

And he knew he could make her come so hard she'd forget all of it for a short while, and so he concentrated on giving her pleasure.

He sucked her stiff nipple harder. Her hands gripped his hair and then his shoulders as he made short work of her pants and thong. His free hand traveled between her legs to the heat of her center, a finger stroking her folds and making her shiver.

"Wet for me," he murmured against her breast.

Her response was to grip him even more tightly. Moaning in satisfaction, he lifed her onto the desk and trailed his tongue downward and buried his face in her sex.

God, he loved the way she tasted, would stay down here happily for a long time, swirling his tongue over the nub of her clit—until she nearly screamed, then caught herself with a hand over her mouth.

Good thing, because the last thing they needed was Logan's security escort barging in to check on Sela.

Hey, at least her back was to the door. Fuck security.

Her heels dug into his back as he continued to suckle and lave, to take her with his tongue and his fingers until she came in a shuddering rush against his mouth.

He was only vaguely aware that she was murmuring something—moaning a little—because the blood was pounding between his ears and his legs and he couldn't wait a second longer. Had to have her.

He stood.

"Sela . . ." It was all he could say. It was all he needed to.

When he entered her, she gasped and then wound her body

around his as though she'd never let go. He remained still while she adjusted to him, waited for her to begin moving against him, his face buried against her shoulder.

And then she did move. Slowly, exquisitely, she began to grind against him, a rhythm that threatened to drive him out of his mind as her tight pussy milked him slowly.

He needed faster. Harder. He grabbed her hips and pulled her into him, pistoning his cock into her in a way that made her bite his neck and hold him tighter.

He was close, but she was closer, and when her orgasm hit, she pulled him along for the ride, contracting around him until he came in hot spurts inside her, a loud groan drumming up from the back of his throat.

It might've been mere seconds, or minutes, or longer, when he felt her stir. But he didn't want to return from orgasm-land, didn't want to come back down from where his mind had floated.

Mostly he didn't want to let her go. Now. Ever. It was that simple—and for the past four years, nothing in his life had been that simple.

Damn, it felt good.

"Sela?" The voice on the intercom made them both jump. He pushed back and allowed her to get herself dressed again while he pulled his pants up.

Sela pushed a button on her desk. "Yes."

"Dev wants to speak with you ASAP about Chance. He said it's urgent to put the plans in motion."

"Tell him I'm on my way." She clicked the intercom off and looked at Logan.

They stood there, an awkward silence stretching between them. Logan cleared his throat. "Do you know where Chance is? No one has told me anything."

"He's at medical," she said, straightening her top, more for something to do with her hands than because it was disheveled.

Which it was. Half the buttons were missing—she'd have to wear a coat until she could get home to change. "They're working on a cure for him."

"What about Marlena?"

Sela blinked. "What about her?"

"Has she been to see him? Or was he just a job to her?"

Sela ground her teeth. "Are we back to that?"

"I get why I was a target," he said gruffly. "But Chance wasn't part of GWC."

"That's not what happened."

"No?"

She breathed out, resigning herself to answering his questions about this. He was a damned pit bull when he grabbed onto something. "You were there. You know he bonded with her without her consent. She'd had no intention of getting close to him."

"So what's going to happen with them?"

"I have no idea," she said honestly. "Why is this so important to you anyway?"

"He's in this mess because of my company. Then we treated him like shit. I have a lot of apologizing to do. I want to make sure he's treated well here and that Marlena isn't going to fuck with him."

God, he was such a good man, and it had taken her far too long to see it. "Trust me, he'll be treated very well. Haven't you been?"

"Yes," he hedged, "but your boss has been pretty vague about a few things."

Dev was vague about everything, but she wondered what Logan was talking about. "Like what?"

"Like what's going to happen to me and my dad."

"Oh." Sela wasn't sure what role Richard would play in the GWC/ACRO deal, but she knew what Dev had planned otherwise, and it must have shown on her face.

"Sela? What aren't you telling me?"

Panic squeezed her chest. Dev had asked her not to tell Logan anything about his plans for Caroline, either because Dev wanted to talk with Logan about it, or because he intended to go ahead with his plan and tell Logan afterward.

"Nothing," she said, turning to rearrange the papers on her desk.

"Bullshit." Logan brushed by her to tear open the door, but he paused, didn't look at her as he said, "I'm sick of secrets and lies, Sela. I can't live this way. So I'll let you make a decision. Tell me what you know . . . or don't."

A chill slid from her scalp to her feet. This was about Caroline. Well, it was, but it was about far more than that. It was about trust. Tell him what he wanted to know, and they started on new footing. Lie to him, or keep silent, and she'd be telling him that secrets and lies were okay . . . and he couldn't live with that. Any hope for a relationship with him would die.

And the truth was, he deserved to know. Dev had given her an order, but he didn't know Logan like she did. Her boss also owed her.

Which wouldn't keep him from royally chewing her ass out.

Taking a deep breath, she said, "Dev plans to have Caroline's memories wiped."

Logan's head snapped back. "He what?"

"Listen," she said, taking his hand, more to keep him from storming out of there than anything. Though it did feel good to be touching him again. "It's for her own good. She's been pretty traumatized—"

"She's strong. She can handle it. Your boss has no right to fuck with her head."

"Logan, trust me. The less she knows about ACRO and Itor, the safer she is. If she has all those memories in her head, she's fair game for them to grab her again."

Logan closed his eyes. "Fuck."

"She won't be harmed. I promise."

His eyes flew open, and he stared at her for a long moment. "I believe you," he said softly. He turned back to the door. "But I'm going to go make sure she's okay."

"And what about us? I know you can't trust me, but—"

"That's the thing," he broke in. "I do trust you. I know why you did what you did."

"But?"

"But I need to think about the rest. Your job, my job . . . it's all a jumble. Give me some time, distance. Can you do that?"

Yeah, she could do that. But she knew from experience that distance didn't always make things clearer. Sometimes, you got so far away from the situation, it all became a blur.

"YOU'RE IN SUCH FUCKING TROUBLE" HAD BEEN ENDER'S LONE words before he had escorted Gabe from the tarmac to his quarters. His only others had been "I heard you saved Annika. Nice job" as he slammed the door in Gabe's face, locking him in his room.

All Gabe could do was report to his bunk and wait there until Devlin called him in for a debriefing.

The jet ride home had been from hell. With Akbar's death, grief and loss permeated the air. Stryker looked both stricken and stoic as he sat across from Gabe for the long flight.

"You did good, kid. Devlin's still going to kill you, but I'll put in a good word," he'd promised Gabe.

It was more than Gabe could ask for. More than he deserved. And although he might've proven himself to Stryker—and maybe even slightly to Annika—there would still be hell to pay.

Would you have done anything differently, knowing what you know now?

He stared at the ceiling and realized he wouldn't have. Amazing how a single trip to the Amazon could make him grow up in a way nothing else in his life ever had.

He just wished it hadn't taken an agent's death to do so.

He rolled to his side and checked the clock. Hours had passed since he'd deplaned and walked past Devlin, who'd merely ordered Ender to take Gabe to his quarters and then walked away. It was well beyond midnight and even though Devlin worked late into the night, Gabe knew the daily debriefings were over. Now it was a matter of figuring out what punishment best fit Gabe's crimes. Maybe Devlin was even considering making him leave ACRO.

Ironic that that's all he'd wanted to do when he first arrived at ACRO. To leave. Now he couldn't imagine being anywhere else.

Devlin. He pictured the man's face—chiseled and perfect. Strong arms. Hands that had touched every part of Gabe, right down to his soul—and fuck, this hurt.

He wondered if Dev was even thinking of him. Maybe he was engrossed in Akbar's death—maybe his lover was in pain. Hurting, upset. All Gabe wanted to do was comfort him.

He called to Devlin in his mind, hoping his lover was using his CRV to look at Gabe, to see what he was doing.

Devlin, please, don't shut me out. I fucked up . . . but I've learned my lesson. I get it now. I get it.

Nothing. Except for the treadmill of his own thoughts, there was silence in Gabe's mind. Sighing, he opened his eyes—and froze.

He was no longer on his utilitarian bunk in his room on the ACRO compound.

No, instead, he was on a king-sized bed with the familiar rich chocolate-colored comforter, next to Devlin.

Next. To. Devlin. What the fuck?

The man looked as shocked to see him as Gabe was to be there. Devlin threw his papers down and cocked his head to the side. Stared.

"Gabriel, I'd have thought you understood the importance of not going where you're not invited."

"Dev, look, I didn't . . . I mean, I didn't come here. Not on purpose. I didn't do the invisibility thing."

Dev scowled. "What are you talking about?"

"I was thinking about you. Missing you. Worried that I'd fucked everything up. I tried to talk to you but you didn't answer. Then I ended up here."

Dev's mouth dropped open. "Are you saying you . . . transported here?"

"I guess. I don't know what to call it. One minute, I was in my room. The next, I was here." He ran a hand over his head. "Weird, huh?"

Dev shook his head. "Not so weird. But we've got a lot of work to do on this. More testing. Because if you can transport . . ." He trailed off and Gabe wondered if this would help with the big plans Devlin supposedly had for him, the plans Akbar had mentioned the other day in Dev's office.

Whatever the challenge, Gabe would be ready. "I'm so sorry about Akbar."

"You're going to need to see the ACRO psychologist," Dev said in response. "You saw the whole thing happen, according to Stryker. Ani said you saved her life." Dev's gaze hardened. "After you put her in danger in the first place."

Gabe didn't know what to say to that at first. And then, "I was such a fucking shit to all of them before this. They only wanted me to learn my job."

Dev sighed, and the angry light faded from his eyes. "You're learning, Gabriel. None of this is easy. It's not meant to be."

Never will be was the unspoken message. But when Devlin pulled Gabe into his arms, he knew that *some* things were meant to be.

CHAPTER *twenty-six*

Creed's motorcycle hummed along the highway leading to his newest job for ACRO, an overnight in a haunted restaurant thought to be inhabited by a demon.

He hadn't wanted to leave Ani alone so soon after they'd made up, hadn't wanted to leave her at all, especially without her powers. But Devlin had promised he would send someone to stick with her like glue.

Ani hated that arrangement, mainly because Devlin was sending Gabe. And so Creed promised he'd kick the demon's ass and be back by her side ASAP.

"Let me come with you," she'd cajoled right before he left, standing in front of the doorway holding a giant bag of M&M's that was half empty.

He'd already pulled his black leathers on and shouldered his bag. Normally, he'd have loved nothing more than to work with Ani. But even Kat, a vocal advocate for keeping the couple together as much as possible, didn't voice her approval over Ani's wish. "Ani, you stay here and rest. You know as well as I do that these things are unpredictable. If you get knocked off your feet—"

"Yeah, yeah, I know. Nine months, baby machine, take it easy, blah, blah, blah," she muttered. "You do know that, no matter what, this kid's going to be as tough as nails."

He'd kissed her on the forehead. "Of course I know that. Wouldn't have it any other way."

And as he cruised, he let himself think about his impending fatherhood. And marriage. And forever.

Maybe Ani was right and Oz had been fuzzy, or so caught up in the sacrifice he knew he'd have to make for Dev—trading his own life for the life of the man he loved—that he'd fucked up the prediction. Misinterpreted it.

Except Oz never really did fuck up. Even the time Ani had mentioned to reassure him, about the accident Oz saw Devlin getting into, Dev had only told Annika he'd helped victims of an accident. He hadn't wanted to upset her with the fact that he had indeed been the victim of a very serious car accident.

Think about the baby. Pure and good.

Oz, you're going to have to protect this baby—and Ani and me. The way you did when I was a baby.

He gave a quick glance up at the sky as he spoke to his brother and then continued down the highway with the wind at his back and his troubles hopefully behind him.

Caroline's mind-wipe had been exhausting for Logan, but it had been just what his sister needed.

He'd remained with her in the ACRO infirmary for a week—she needed to be strong and healed before they could work their magic. The doctors used some serums that accelerated her healing, because erasing the horror of her kidnapping wouldn't do much good if her face and body still bore the bruises of the beating she'd taken.

He'd apologized to her so many times, she'd finally told him to shut up. He took that as a good sign, although she continued to wear that same guarded look of fear. At the end of the week, he escorted her back to her school in Virginia, along with an ACRO psychic. Caroline needed to be in the place she was right before the kidnapping. And as she sat in the back of the van right across from the library path she'd been swiped from, Logan held her hand and watched the woman named Sam replace bad memories with good ones.

Within half an hour, he had Caroline back. She now believed she'd left school because Logan was in trouble—a minor car accident, which explained his insignificant cuts and bruises. She thought she'd spent time with him, and that Sam was a GWC colleague. And Caroline told Logan he needed to come see her more often.

Sometimes, ignorance really was bliss, he thought as he left her at her dorm, listening to her talking excitedly with her friends about the weekend of parties planned around campus.

He'd never be able to forget the way she looked when he'd found her in the jungle. Which was why working for ACRO was the best choice he and his father could make—they could still do a lot of good with GWC, and Devlin would make sure they wouldn't get into bed with the wrong players again.

The jet had taken him and Sam back to ACRO late that night. He'd hung around Caroline's campus for hours, just in case something went wrong with the mind-sweep, until Sam gently convinced him that she had an excellent success rate with non-specials. *Not that your sister's not special,* she'd said with a smile.

He'd been back at ACRO for less than fourteen hours and already he was restless as hell. He figured he'd meet with Devlin tomorrow, map out the changes for GWC. Figure shit out.

Dammit, he missed Sela.

A knock on the door roused him from his reverie, and he heard Sela call his name softly from the other side of the door.

He got up and opened it. She was leaning against the doorjamb, looking beautiful—strong and fragile at the same time. "Hey. I wanted to check to see how things went with your sister."

He stepped aside, motioned for her to come in. "It worked out really well. Caroline's happy now."

"What about us?" She shook her head. "Sorry. I'm impatient, I know. But it's been a long week without you."

He stuck his hands in the pockets of his BDUs. He'd missed the hell out of her, tossed and turned and paced the floors while he'd watched Caroline rest and recover and have her memories fixed on a trip to Virgina—and again since he'd gotten back here. "It's okay. I was going to come see you. Sela, I can accept your past...it's just, I don't think I could handle it—no, I know I couldn't handle it—if you continued working as a Seducer. I won't share you, Sela." His voice was fierce and his hand was on her waist, because he loved touching her. Loved being with her...loved *feeling*. "I don't know how or why you make me feel, how you've managed to get in where no other woman has."

"Maybe it's just the sex that makes you feel," she whispered, her eyes filled with pain.

But no, that wasn't it.

"It's more than that, Sela. I feel you here"—he pointed to his head and then his heart—"and here. And I don't want it to end."

"I haven't worked as a Seducer in years, Logan. I wasn't supposed to work as one on this mission either."

"Still, you tried to get information from me."

"I thought you were one of the bad guys—you can understand that. I work for the greater good, even if it goes against my own happiness."

"That's a hell of a sacrifice."

"It can be. But Devlin says that things happen for a reason. I used a skill I haven't used in years—and as it turns out, I can't read your immediate thoughts. You have no idea what a relief that is, how free I feel when I'm with you because of that. I can be normal with you. I can be in a relationship—and I really want to be. Because I love you."

He paused, feeling like the breath had been kicked out of him. And then, "Say it again."

She smiled shyly. "I love you, Logan. I want to be with you. I want you to stay here at ACRO and continue your work. I want you to go out on Crypto assignments with me. I like that you're possessive of me. That you want to protect me. I want our pasts not to stand in the way of our future, and I'm willing to fight to make sure that happens."

He lowered his head and kissed her, a soft kiss that turned bolder and hotter as she pressed against him, held him tight, as if she'd never let him go. He was more than happy to ensure that happened.

PHOEBE STORMED INTO ITOR'S OFFICE HEADQUARTERS, WHICH didn't look like a headquarters at all. Itor ran its operations from several locations all over the world, chiefly in populated areas, where activity was hard to monitor. But its main hub was in the middle of nowhere, disguised as a sheep ranch in the Australian outback. Most of the work took place underground, safely shielded from radiation, satellites and psychics.

The huge ranch house topside was staffed by Itor agents who actually ran the sheep operation—and ran it well, at a profit. About a dozen agents lived permanently in the house, and another dozen lived in the guest quarters behind it. All other Australian-based agents lived in the small town about twenty miles to the south, including Phoebe, though she also kept two smaller flats, near their Madrid and Kiev strongholds.

Her footsteps echoed with a metallic clang as she walked down the brightly lit, tubelike corridor. At the end of it, she submitted to a retina scan, and the titanium door whooshed open. On the other side, Dawn, Alek's hyperannoying assistant, sat at her desk, her fingers flying over a keyboard.

"He's waiting for you," she said, without even looking up. "You're late."

The head of Itor had absolutely no patience for tardiness, and even though Phoebe knew she got a little more slack than others, her stomach still knotted. She was in enough trouble as it was.

She entered his plush office, but the room was empty. He was either in the bathroom or the bedroom. Grateful for the extra time, she poured herself a brandy from the wet bar and settled into one of the overstuffed leather sofas.

She'd just taken her third sip when she felt Alek. Drawn to the dark power that emanated from him, she swung her head around to where he stood in the hallway, filling it more with his presence than with his size. He was tall, but lean, his muscular runner's body rippling with banked energy. Usually he wore slacks and a fitted shirt, but today he must have been handling ranching duties, and he looked as at home in jeans as he did in more formal attire.

But then, a man like Alek could wear anything he wanted and own it.

"So," he said tonelessly, "ACRO fucked things up again."

"There was no way we could have predicted—"

"Shut up."

She bristled, but shut her mouth. He was the only person on the planet who could do that to her. She wondered, though, if Devlin had the same commanding presence. She'd only seen pictures of Alek's son—he looked like a younger version of Alek, with the same piercing, knowing eyes, the same shade of brown hair. But she doubted Devlin's ruthlessness could compete with Alek's. Maybe his mother had contributed some weaker DNA. *Pussy genes,* as Alek liked to say.

"Did Melanie make an appearance?"

"Yes." Phoebe had no idea why he did shit like this: ask questions he already knew the answers to. The man could read her mind. Could read pretty much anyone's, even through shields.

Except Melanie's, which pissed him off to no end. It also made no sense, given that Melanie and Phoebe weren't split personalities. They were identical twins mashed into the same body. Then again, they possessed different abilities, thanks to the experimentation that had taken place while they were just embryos in a petri dish.

"When we're done here, I want to see her. You'll let her out."

Phoebe smiled. Melanie was in for a world of hurt. Alek didn't ask to see her very often, but when he did . . . well, Phoebe never knew exactly what he did to her, but when Phoebe got their body back, she was always bruised and sore. He never bothered to beat Phoebe; he'd learned a long time ago that she enjoyed pain too much to make the expending of energy worth it.

Which wasn't to say that he didn't punish her in other ways, and she sat nervously as he moved to the wet bar and poured himself a vodka on ice.

"You failed to procure the chupacabra, and you have probably lost us GWC as our primary weapons supplier." He didn't wait for an answer, because he wasn't expecting one. "On the other hand, you did arrange for the delivery of the Izapa crystal."

That had been a six-month-long endeavor. The crystal, covertly excavated from a Mayan temple, was part of the 2012 doomsday prophecy, which Itor fully intended to exploit. With the crystal, Alek planned to create a device that would harness the cosmic radiation scientists believed would be funneled toward earth on the day the winter solstice sun intersected with the Milky Way's dark rift. With that energy, Itor would be in possession of the greatest, most powerful weapon known to man.

And with that weapon, Alek intended for Itor to rule the world.

Phoebe planned to rule at his side, and she'd do anything to get there. But first, there was the small matter of getting ACRO out of the way. The bunch of meddling do-gooders.

"I didn't just arrange for the delivery," she said, with a trace of bitterness she hoped he didn't pick up on. "I supervised the excavation and made sure no one got in our way." Which meant that she'd killed a few government officials. "And I did it without alerting ACRO to our presence." She'd finished there just before she'd gone on the chupacabra operation that she'd botched.

He nodded. "No small feat," he admitted. And wasn't that the truth.

"Those bastards have been ruining more and more of our missions." Truly, it had been a miracle that Itor had been able to pull off something as huge as the crystal robbery without ACRO's interference. "It's time to go on the offensive with them. We need to take them out. Let me do it. Let me have Devlin."

"Why, Phoebe," Alek murmured into his glass, "you're talking about killing your own brother." He grinned. "Your ruthlessness makes me proud."

She stood, knowing she'd just gotten herself out of some horrendous punishment. Melanie wouldn't be so lucky. Smiling, she clinked glasses with him. "I learned from the best," she said, already savoring the taste of bloodlust on her tongue. "Like father, like daughter."

About the Author

SYDNEY CROFT is a pseudonym for two authors, who each also write under their own names. This is their fifth novel together. Visit their website at www.sydneycroft.com.

Unleashing the Storm

ACRO Series Book 2

Feel the heat. Hear the roar.

The fever has begun.

There's a storm rising. Electricity crackles in the air. For Kira Donovan, it's that time of year again: when the need floods her flesh, when almost any man—the bigger and the stronger the better—will do. For Kira, an animal psychic, the heat is a matter of life and death, and this year it has come at just the right time. Tom Knight, a natural-born predator, has arrived at her isolated Idaho farm—for reasons all his own.

At first Kira isn't interested in Knight's motives. She just needs him—his body, his hands, his scent. But soon, through a daze of desire and distrust, Kira discovers Knight's world—the world of a covert operative, one man among dozens of secret agents waging an astonishing global war. Knight's mission is to bring Kira—kicking and screaming if necessary—into the Agency for Covert Rare Operatives and harness her extraordinary gift. He never expected the powerful emotions she would ignite in him, or the fierce desire to keep her safe from harm. For as darkness gathers around them, Kira is feeling the heat once again, leading them both on a wild ride of delicious thrills . . . and terror beyond imagining.

"Red-hot romance and paranormal thrills from the first page to the last! Sydney Croft writes the kinds of books I love to read!"
—Lara Adrian, *New York Times* bestselling author

"Sydney Croft is a fabulous new talent."
—Cheyenne McCray, USA Today bestselling author
Seduced by the STORM
PLEASURE. POWER. FURY.
A SEDUCTION SO HOT...IT'S OFF THE RADAR.
SYDNEY CROFT
AUTHOR OF UNLEASHING THE STORM